TAELSTONE

TAELSTONE

BY

ROBYN PROKOP

Published by Toutouwai Publications 2019
Nelson, New Zealand

First published in New Zealand in 2019

Cover design and formatting by NOKNOK Studios

Softcover
ISBN 978 0 473 48509 2

TAELSTONE

BY

ROBYN PROKOP

Published by Toutouwai Publications 2019
Nelson, New Zealand

First published in New Zealand in 2019

Cover design and formatting by NOKNOK Studios

Softcover
ISBN 978 0 473 48509 2

— PART 1 —
EEROK

Chapter 1

THE CHOSEN ONE

L ord Lendri frowned, clasped his hands firmly behind his back and strode a couple of paces. 'Two slaves, you say?' The petitioner responded with an obsequious nod, although both knew it was nothing of the kind. Lendri blinked rapidly, paused. With an effort, he said, 'That seems perfectly agreeable.'

Lendri's embroidered collar felt chafed at his throat, accentuating the throbbing of his pulse. His armpits prickled with heat, and his mouth was dry. He glanced at the nervous clerk. Not in living memory had the Malshorne been seen in the courts of Mildaresh, nor even within the city circle. Up until now, the ancient arrangement had been dealt with discreetly and quietly, with trade being made through messengers sent in secret up the mountain path. Until today the stories they had related on their return had been deemed the mere babblings of witless slaves. Yet, here the Malshorne was.

Lendri took a measured breath. 'The slaves must be young, you say? And required every day from noon until the twilight bell?'

'Yes. They should come to … no harm.'

Lendri hesitated. He couldn't help thinking the Malshorne's twisted mouth indicated otherwise.

'And the same ... er, goods to be exchanged for their labour?'

'As you like.'

'That is agreeable.'

It wasn't.

'I will arrange for two of my own slaves to attend upon you.'

'No! The Eerok must be of my own choosing.'

The way the Malshorne's eyes glittered was more than enough to make Lendri waver. He paused for a long moment, but at last he bowed his head in agreement. He reached for a silver bell and rang it with as much composure as he could muster. On the entry of the guardian, he cleared his throat.

'Take our ... visitor ... to the Arion market. There will be children playing in the squares. Ensure that he finds two suitable, er ... Eerok, for his purposes. Only, take care not to draw two from the same House.' It felt strange to use the ancient name; no one called the slaves 'Eerok' anymore.

The guardian nodded, drew his hands together to form the sacred triangle and bowed his head to his fingertips. 'Yes, Mildari.'

The Malshorne smiled a thin smile. Then he bowed, turned and glided out of the chamber in one smooth, liquid motion.

Lendri sank behind his desk. The clerk of the court remained fixed to the spot. Their eyes met in brief recognition of the horror that had passed. Then Lendri drew himself up, smoothed his robes and straightened his papers. The petitioners kept coming, one after another. They wheedled and pleaded and left with varying degrees of satisfaction, until the line dwindled and finally dried up. At last, the great wooden doors were closed, but Lendri didn't move. The dying sun found him brooding at his desk, head in hands, worrying at the wisdom of his bargain.

❧

Across the city, in a broken courtyard, a game of pilat was underway. The courtyard wasn't ideal — it was small, and the withered tree in the centre limited the positioning of the triang. Still, it was out of the way of the bustling marketplaces, and the guardians usually turned a blind eye to pilat games. Two latecomers had joined the handful of youngsters loitering in the shade of a crumbling wall. Both wore the green tunics of the House of Aranti. The dark-haired girl whispered to her companion.

'Look, Pan! Ash is nearly there.'

The boy screwed up his thin, grubby face. 'I can see for myself, Kep. You needn't tell me everything.'

Kep raised an eyebrow, but turned her attention to the game. *Come on, Ash. This time ... this time.* It was a tense moment in the second phase. The three defenders were poised, eyes tight shut, straining every other sense to discover their opponents' whereabouts, weapons at the ready. Ash was sprawled flat, so close to the foot of a defender that he could have grabbed an ankle. His grey clothes blended into the dust. Just another stretch of his arm and he would be able to swap his white stone with the black one between the defender's feet. His face was pressed into the ground. Kep knew he'd be breathing gently to avoid stirring up dust. Her eyes darted to the face of the defending captain. If Braig signalled a view, Ash's position would be revealed. But for now he was cocking his head the other way.

The other two attackers circled, gesturing silently. The captain, Del, had made her swap and was running distraction. Kep watched Braig's expression carefully. 'Not yet. Not yet,' Kep whispered. She chewed at the top of her thumbnail as Del crouched and picked up a stone. 'Wait …,' she breathed.

But Del clicked her tongue twice and lofted the stone. Braig ignored the click, recognising the ruse, but when the stone thudded softly to his left he flung out his net. It landed fruitlessly, just as Ash was touching his fingertips to the black stone. Kep winced, counting heartbeats, guessing Braig couldn't bear to hold the blind. And she was right. Ash barely had time to jerk his arm back before Braig let out a whistle and called the view.

Opening their eyes, the defenders took in the fact that they had lost one stone and had been perilously close to losing another. They glared at one another, but only their captain was entitled to speak. Kep watched Braig assess his options. He'd be furious at falling for such a simple ploy. The question was: would he make a swap? Cairn held a sturdy stick, and had another strike, but he wasn't known for his ferocity. Even Ash could probably take a blow from Cairn without forfeiting the game. But the other defender was a different sort of boy entirely. He had bright blond hair and a thin, angular face. He was also armed with a swing-stone, which had the greater range.

Kep held her breath.

'Do you think he'll make the swap?' asked Pan.

Kep shook her head slowly. 'I don't know.'

Pan's eyes were worried. 'Is it true that Feld sharpens his stone?'

It was against the rules, and therefore against the gods, but Feld's stones did seem to cut deeper than anyone else's. Kep didn't want to admit her suspicions, it was too shocking. But Feld was a nasty one. She stared at his hard, eager face. 'I don't know.'

'I think he does. And I hate him,' stated Pan simply.

Kep frowned, raising both hands to shield her eyes from the slanting afternoon sun. She knew Braig wouldn't want to see Ash hurt badly, but she also doubted he would see past his need to win the game.

⁂

The guardian charged with escorting the Malshorne through the city was trying to locate a group of young slaves — and as quickly as humanly possible. They had certainly made swift progress through the crooked streets. Normally he would have had to push his way through the crowds, hollering 'Make way for the High Lord's business', but today the people fell back to let them through. A collective shudder seemed to sweep through the streets as they passed the fountains and food stalls. Everyone stopped to stare at the Malshorne's long hair and curious robes, but not even the children dared follow in their wake. Finally, after descending a winding staircase, they came out onto a high platform. Below, the result of a pilat game was hanging in the balance. The guardian made to rush down the steps to apprehend the slaves at once, but the Malshorne raised a hand.

'Wait. We will watch,' he commanded.

His escort stood to attention, paralysed. The Malshorne's voice was unpleasantly smooth and liquid. 'I do so love pilat. So ancient. So quaint. And, somehow, so appropriate, don't you think?'

The guardian had no idea what he meant. He just blinked his eyes, clenched his jaw, and waited.

In the square below, Braig called the swap. 'Feld for Cairn!'

Ash groaned, making the dust dance around his lips. As the two defenders traded places, Cairn shot him a look of sympathy. Feld was grinning, and adjusting his line. Ash tensed his body, preparing to launch himself out of the way. The urge to roll away before the clap was overwhelming, but there was no greater shame than forfeiting in pilat. The defenders closed their eyes, too, and raised their weapons, awaiting the restart. Ash clenched his teeth at the sound of the swing-stone humming above him. Not even Feld would dare commit the sacrilege of striking before the clap, but everyone knew how quick he was. Ash's heart raced as Del called on the gods to sanction the restart.

'By Telion, by Argess, by Narsis ...'

When Del smacked her hands together, Ash rolled to his left, but Feld was too quick. The swing-stone came hurtling down and Ash felt the side of his head explode in a hot rush of pain. He clutched at his ear, rocking himself into a ball. He didn't hear himself cry out, but the defenders' whoop of victory said everything. Ash had let his team down — again.

From above, the Malshorne watched with relish. He saw the sharp-faced boy strike; saw the triumph on his captain's face as he lifted the boy off his feet; and saw the rest of the slaves forming a concerned huddle around the fallen lad in Feyindi grey. He dragged his lips into a hard smile.

'Marvellous. I will go down now.' He glanced at the trembling guardian. 'You should stay here— We don't want you frightening the children.'

Ash just wanted to lie still. His head felt as if it would crack open. He knew he was moments away from vomiting, but that didn't bother him nearly so much as the tears that threatened. Overhead was a muddle of voices.

'Get him up.'

'No. He'll be better by the tree.'

'Hold his head.'

'It's all bloody! You hold it!'

'No way. I'll get whipped if I get blood on my tunic.'

'He's gonna spew.'

'He's fainted.'

'No. Stick his head between his knees.'

'Don't worry, Ash. You're fine. It's just a gash.'

Ash slowly became aware of something soft against his head, and a tree trunk hard against his back. He eased his eyes open. Kep was crouched beside him, her folded apron pressed against his face. Her bright blue eyes were disconcertingly close.

'I'm fine,' he croaked.

'Of course you are,' she replied too quickly. 'Ears always bleed a lot.'

Braig leaned in over her shoulder. 'Sorry, Ash.'

Ash forced himself to sound casual, despite an even stronger urge to vomit. 'No need. I wasn't quick enough.'

Braig looked a bit less guilty, until he caught the furious look Kep shot at him.

Ash lifted a hand to his throbbing ear. 'I can hold it myself.'

Kep released her hold on the apron and gave him space. Ash grimaced. He'd been so close to being the hero for once. In his shame, he wanted to hit out at them all — even Kep. Her expression of sympathy was much harder to bear than Feld's smirking face at the back of the group. Then all thoughts were erased as he registered a figure flapping towards them across the square. Ash cried out in alarm.

The others whirled around. Seeing the guardian standing on the platform above, tall and still in his black uniform, they tensed, ready to scatter. But the approaching figure was so unusual, so obviously not a guardian and so disarming with his gesture of wide-open arms that they hesitated, overruling the instinct to flee. As he neared, they saw his long hair was dressed unusually with silver braids at each temple. His garb was like nothing they had ever seen — he definitely wasn't a slave. His boots were high and polished, and he wore rich shades of reds and purples. But it was his proud bearing that most impressed them. As one, they made the sign of the triangle and bowed their heads in submission. Unable to rise, Ash just sank his head onto his chest.

The Malshorne paused for a moment, relishing the sight of the heads bowed before him. Then he broke the spell. 'Children,' he began silkily. 'Children, look up. You need not bow before me; I am not your master.' They lifted their heads and stared at him, transfixed. 'I have been observing your game. It gladdens my heart to see you play with such spirit — with such honour.' He paused. With the exception of Ash, who couldn't quite hear due to the buzzing in his head, the young slaves glowed with pride. The Malshorne shook his head slowly and thoughtfully. 'But I did not happen upon you by chance this day. No. I have been called here … on this day … in this place … at this time because I am looking for a young Eerok. A boy who will undertake a glorious quest. The noblest of quests.'

If he had intended to leave that last powerful sentence hanging in the air a little longer, it was not to be. Just at that moment there came an unpleasant gurgle from where Ash was propped against the tree: he had lost the battle with his stomach and was splashing yellow bile onto the tree roots. Kep shot him a look, a mixture of sympathy and disgust, but when she turned her attention back to the Malshorne she blinked, then frowned. Had that been a flash of anger in his eyes? Then, suddenly, as if taken by an impulse beyond his control, the Malshorne thrust his staff high into the air.

'Behold!' he boomed. The staff shook, seemingly with a life of its own. 'The Chosen One will be revealed!'

Mesmerised, they watched as the staff hovered over each of the boys' heads in turn: pausing for longer over some, moving swiftly over others. Finally it came to a rest above the head of 'The Chosen One'. The Malshorne grasped Braig by the chin. 'May you serve well, boy.' He nodded at the boy's overjoyed expression then bowed, moving stiffly.

'And now you must select a Second. One who will work with us to fulfil this great quest.'

The wide-eyed slaves fixed their attention on Braig, who answered promptly, 'Cairn. I choose Cairn.'

It was the expected choice; the two boys had lived and worked together since their bonding to Aranti as seven-year-olds, and were pretty much inseparable. But the Malshorne shook his head. 'No,' he frowned. 'That is not possible. The House of Aranti cannot be asked to relinquish two slaves. You must choose another boy.'

Braig paused, reconsidering. Then he gave an answer that surprised them all. 'Ash, then. I choose Ash.'

Pale-faced and startled, with bloodied hair sticking up comically on one side of his head and vomit on his chin, Ash was a most uninspiring sight. Surely, nobody had ever looked less capable of helping with a quest, let alone a glorious one? But it seemed the choice was made. The Malshorne smiled enigmatically as he raised his hands: 'So be it.'

Chapter 2

CONSEQUENCES

Ash swung his legs off the side of his narrow cot. It was well before dawn, and far too early for a boy who had barely slept. The air in the windowless cell was hot and stale. He kept his eyes closed, fighting against the churning in his gut and the prickling heat that swept his body. Pushing his feet flat onto the ground, he tried drawing calm from the cool, rough-hewn flagstones. The rasping of the old gardener's snoring was rising from the cot on the opposite wall, filling the small space with its cadence. Ash welcomed the sound as an old friend, and forced himself to breathe deliberately, in and out, in and out, until at last his heart stopped racing and the nausea began to pass.

Ash had shared the tiny cell with old Loth ever since being sworn to the House of Feyindi in his sixth winter. The ancient gardener was a man of few words. In fact, in all their time as roommates the two had barely spoken, happily making do with nods and grunts in passing, which suited Ash perfectly; he didn't mind one bit that the gardener was a rather more noisy companion when asleep.

He yawned and rubbed at his eyes. The ear that had caught the swingstone burned, hot and swollen. The side of his head was tender to the touch, too, but his body would heal; the other events of the previous day were far more frightening. Although he doubted an early start would make the Head of Kitchens any less angry, it couldn't make things worse. So, moving silently in the perpetual half-light of the slave quarters, Ash squirmed into his tunic, then retrieved a long grey apron from its hook on the wall and lashed it about his waist. As he slipped on his sandals, he couldn't help his mind returning to the most urgent on his list of worries: when would the messenger arrive?

A slave's life in the Feyindi kitchens wasn't as bad as some, and Ash had a talent for invisibility; he knew how to walk softly, work quietly, and get out of the way at the first inkling of trouble. He had certainly never come to the attention of the Lord and Lady, even though he waited silently on their table every evening. But that morning, as he stepped into the long, dim corridor, he knew everything was about to change.

The Feyindi kitchens were situated at the southern end of the villa, taking up the whole of the ground floor. They were separated from the sprawling slaves' quarters by a gated courtyard through which Ash passed quietly. He side-stepped the dozing guard and entered through a swinging service door.

The main kitchen boasted a massive hearth at one end, with a blackened chimney-piece. Sturdy workbenches were laid out in rows and hung with every manner of tools. Black pots, copper pans and utensils dangled from racks. Shaggy bunches of herbs hung down, too, their sweet, sharp aromas competing with the scent of plums, apples, onions and pork fat. Everything had been scrubbed impossibly clean, including the great stone flags on the floor, but the space was cluttered with evidence of the long, bountiful summer. Barrels and crates overflowed with fruit and vegetables, and sacks of grain were stacked in corners, awaiting a home in the over-stuffed storerooms.

Ash made a quick assessment and decided to deal first with the overflowing barrowload of onions. Drawing up a stool, he began weaving and twisting the dry tails into long, plump strings of onions. He worked steadily, ignoring the grumbling of his empty stomach, and by the time the baker was stoking the fires ready for loaves he had finished the barrow. He was tackling a pile of thorny artichokes when the Head of the Kitchens bustled in. A huge woman with a florid face, she blew her nose loudly, then gave the dawn bell a furious shake before noticing him. He couldn't tell if her shrewd eyes had taken in his good work, since she spoke as gruffly as ever:

'Finish that lot before you go to the dairy, boy.'

Ash ducked his head, swallowing his disappointment. He would have to wait longer to speak with Kep now. Picking up another artichoke, he glanced at the door. If only the messenger would come soon and put him out of his misery.

※

It was universally agreed that Mildaresh was most fortunately situated. The great Irian mountain range stood at her back, providing shelter from the harsh southerlies and enemies alike; the only break was the Felian Pass to the west, which was easily held by a single garrison. The city's honey-stone buildings basked in the sun on a large shelved plateau, just high enough above the rich valley soils to catch occasional summer breezes from the faraway coast. Three bright streams raced through the city, under bridges, splashing crystal waters into fountains, ponds and canals on their journey from the high woodlands to join the lazy waters of the river Rule.

The marauding Mildarens had done well to discover the place. In a suitably distant past, they had sailed their longboats up the river, meeting with scant resistance, coming as self-styled 'saviours' to the wretched and starving people whom they had found huddled in caves and broken towers. As one scholar put it: 'the remnant population was quickly subdued, since a life of prosperous slavery is infinitely preferable to starvation'. And so Mildaresh was born, grafted onto the bones of the old city. And, as time passed and her wealth grew, the origins of the city became overshadowed by much more glorious events. Those fragments of ancient texts which persisted in their references to the 'finders' of the city had passed into obscurity. These days it was much more fitting to speak of the 'founding' families — at least that was how Marlashetta Feyindi saw things.

The Feyindi family was one of the oldest in Mildaresh, and Marlashetta took her ancestry very seriously indeed. It was her constant companion, revealing itself in every thought and gesture; even in the upright way she held herself at breakfast. She had married a man as tall and thin as herself, who had nevertheless turned out to be somewhat disappointing, which was not altogether surprising, since Marlashetta found disappointment in most things.

That morning the pair sat opposite each other, taking breakfast in their private parlour. Marlashetta pushed the food about on her plate fretfully, before abandoning it altogether. She sipped warily at her tea instead, then, finding it passable, surveyed the morning through the parlour's expansive curved windows. The tall temples gave way to the stolid abbey walls, below which terracotta roofs tumbled down to the patched farmlands beyond. Here and there were tiny clusters of slaves in the golden meadows. She traced the line of the great canal along to where it met the river Rule, which was dotted with guard posts and slow-moving barges. On a clear day like this, it was possible to see across the river to the other side of Ereston Valley and the noikos fields. The distant smudge of purple brought her thoughts at once to business, and she turned abruptly to her husband, distracting him from his potatoes.

'How is the noikos harvest coming along, Analouie?'

'Hmm. Good, good,' he replied warily. Reading her expression, he carefully finished his mouthful before gathering his thoughts and continuing. 'Far beyond expectations. Indeed, I believe the overseer has set some of the slaves to processing already. Calkinon will receive its tribute early this year. The only foreseeable problem is a lack of labour, my dear. We might need to source some new slaves for the fields.'

It was pleasing news, but she did wish he wouldn't dab at his mouth in that manner.

She put down her teacup, and frowned at the cold venison sausage. 'Good. Then we must send some of the less satisfactory house slaves.'

When Analouie blinked and seemed to swallow a sigh, she pressed her lips into a sour line. Admittedly, house slaves were an expensive commodity. They were bred locally in the Holding and screened for aptitude. Most wealthy families bonded a few youngsters each year, typically favouring those who had seen out seven winters. As Marlashetta knew perfectly well, it took years to train each slave in the specialised skills of their calling, particularly if reading and writing were deemed advantageous, but that was hardly the point.

Her husband gave a weak cough, and to her mind an even weaker rebuttal. 'Possibly, my dear … But do consider the investment … There would have to be a very good reason this time.'

Marlashetta bristled, both at the cough and the reply. 'I would have thought poor service was a good enough reason for anyone.'

At that moment, a faint knocking halted further discussion and, at Analouie's somewhat eager command, the chief steward entered, bearing a silver platter. The message was stamped with the seal of the Mildari, proving it a most unpalatable addition to their meal indeed.

After reading its contents aloud for the second time, Lord Feyindi waved the paper indignantly at his dark-haired wife. 'What choice do we have but to yield to this unusual request? It is quite outrageous. Nay … offensive!'

Marlashetta pursed her lips and patted a napkin to her mouth before replying. 'Indeed, my dear. How is one to run a household with this type of meddling? And it doesn't specify for how long?'

'Indefinitely, it says. Indefinitely!'

Feyindi stabbed his finger at the offending word. 'Lendri is getting above himself this time. *Well* above himself. There's nothing for it, we simply must make a formal protest in the Senate.'

Marlashetta Feyindi rose to her feet and took the paper from her husband. 'Absolutely,' she murmured. It was far too trivial a matter for the Senate really, but political advantage often swung on trivial matters, and perhaps much could be made of it; besides, she agreed entirely with her husband's sentiment. 'It's just another example of Lendri power-mongering, my dear. Mark my words, when the name of Lendri was drawn from the sacred vessel I knew we'd be forced to endure a Mildari who takes liberties. As if the kitchen slaves aren't sluggish enough without being drafted elsewhere. It's shameful. Quite shameful.' Marlashetta put a rare consoling hand on her husband's shoulder. 'And how irksome to bow to the petty whims of a lesser man.' She read the words again. 'It is a rather unusual demand, though — even for Lendri.' She turned a steady scowl upon the steward. 'Who is this boy? This Ash? Is there something special about him?'

The man bowed deferentially. 'No, my lady. He's a thin, pale little chap, but he does what he's told from what I've heard. He's nothing special at all, my lady, unless you count his hair … That's unusual, I suppose. It's grey — matches his eyes. Shall I bring him up my lady?'

Analouie cut in petulantly, flapping a hand in dismissal: 'And what would be the point of that? He sounds wholly inconsequential.'

Marlashetta's mouth formed a taut line of disapproval, but he was right; there was little point. The boy was clearly unmemorable, precisely as slaves should be. Moreover, as galling as it was, they really had no choice but to yield to the Mildari's request.

She sniffed, drew herself to her full height and, with one eye on her husband, declared, 'Very well. Inform the Head of Kitchens, but let it be known: if there is any hint of trouble, he'll be sent directly to the noikos fields.'

❧

The Head of the Kitchens was overseeing the butchering of a hog when Ash was dragged before her. On discovering the peculiar new arrangement, she narrowed her eyes. Up until then she hadn't minded that he was scrawny; he followed orders silently, didn't drop things, and was pretty enough to serve at the table. Now she regarded him with suspicion. No one had ever heard of a slave getting the afternoons off to do something other than his master's bidding. Many of the slaves had Seconds, a younger apprenticed child who shadowed their tasks, but Ash hadn't yet been allocated a Second. His afternoon absences would ruin her system.

'You'll start early and finish late,' she growled, waving her blade at him. 'Be back at the twilight bell in time for service, or I'll find a juicier use for this beauty than skinning hogs.' He already looked suitably terrified, but she gave him a sharp cuff over the ear for good measure.

⁂

The lower skirts of the city were bustling with all the clamour and activity of the harvest. Wagons jostled each other for right-of-way. Their drivers cracked whips and shouted, hollering colourful obscenities. Some loads were toiling uphill to the city, while others lurched and trundled off down the Nocheir way, heading for the Felian Pass then south to the port of Idira. Slaves crowded the roads and choked the laneways, laden with sweet-smelling baskets, or shouldering scythes, rakes and hoes. Ash wove his way through the turmoil, dodging carts and animal manure until at last he reached the rich pastures of the Aranti estates.

There, he found Kep in the long, low milking shed, tucked beneath the velvety black udders of a gigantic kattlen beast. Most animals made Ash nervous, but he particularly disliked kattlen; it wasn't just their size and massive hooves, there was something unsettling about the expression in those deep, reflective eyes. He stood well back and waited, wrinkling his nose against the smell of dung, but enjoying the percussive rhythm of milk hitting the bucket. Then, all at once, the sound came to a stop.

'Oh no you don't!'

Horrified, Ash stepped back even further. The beast was shifting its bulk, trying to wheel sideways. At first Kep shoved back, spreading her hands wide and pushing her dark curly head against the massive flank. Then she surrendered. Kicking her stool backwards, she swung the bucket out of harm's way and stood up.

'Cantankerous old cow!' she laughed. 'All right. You win. Keep the rest for your calf!' She released the ribbon which secured the kattlen's long tail to its back leg, and was rewarded immediately with a swift swat across the shoulders. She just laughed again, giving the beast an affectionate slap on its neck. When she turned, her eyes were bright and her cheeks flushed. She gave Ash such a smile that his spirits lifted in spite of all his troubles.

'Hey! You're late!' She pointed at the milk pail. 'Is that full yet?' When Ash shook his head, she replied, 'Take the lid off then, we can both save some time.' She filled it to the top with warm, creamy milk. 'Perfect fit,' she added shaking the last drops from the bucket. Stretching, she looked about her. There were six other milkers in the shed and only a couple of beasts left in the holding pen. 'Good. I'm done here now,' she said, rubbing her neck. 'I need to get back to my bug-eyes. They're with Pan, just over that rise.' She wiped her face with her apron. 'You get that blessed while I put this old girl out. We can walk up together.'

The priest noted the colour of Ash's tunic, jotted some numbers in a ledger, then performed the rites, incorporating the long names of every living member of the Feyindi family into his incantation. Ash reclaimed his pail and quickly caught up to Kep, who had stopped to chase some birds out with a broom.

Kep glanced sideways at him as they passed through the gate. 'How's the ear?'

'Better,' he lied.

'That's good.' She didn't sound convinced. 'And your masters?'

He attempted a casual shrug, hoping she wouldn't sense just how pathetically scared he was. 'They've agreed.'

'That's good,' she repeated. She gave him a little smile. 'Braig says he'll meet you under the old archway, just before the mountain path.'

Ash groaned loudly. 'I don't know why he went and chose me. He hates me.'

There was rather too long a pause before Kep replied, 'He doesn't *hate* you, Ash.'

'Well, we're hardly the best of mates,' he retorted. 'He makes fun of me all the time.' It was true, Braig was always punching Ash on the arm, sticking his knuckle out to make a bruise, calling him 'Weed', or drawing everyone's attention to what a weakling he was. Ash couldn't imagine why Braig had chosen him. It just didn't make sense.

Kep was chewing her lip in that thoughtful way of hers. 'He doesn't hate you, Ash. It's just his way. He's always mucking around. He's just a bit boisterous, that's all.'

Boisterous! That was one name for it. Ash hated how Kep always defended

Braig. 'Well, if he thinks he's done me some sort of favour he's sure got that wrong!' he replied hotly.

Kep just sighed, and they walked in silence for a while. Then, as they climbed the rise she said, 'It might not be that bad, Ash. The Malshorne might not be as frightening as everyone says.' She must have sensed his dismay then, because she added quickly, 'I know there are stories, but he's probably just a bit odd, that's all. All that stuff about a glorious quest …' She tried to laugh. 'He probably just wants you to chop some firewood or something. Lots of people have been up the mountain to do chores over the years, and they've all come back.'

Ash swallowed. It was hardly reassuring. Just talking about the Malshorne was making him feel worse, so he was relieved when they reached the crest of the hill and caught sight of the little flock grazing in the dappled shade of the trees. The bug-eyes were such a skittish bunch; they all looked up in alarm, ready to bolt. Kep shook her head fondly at them.

'It won't be so bad, Ash. You'll see.' She gave him a smile that wasn't quite cheerful enough to be convincing.

He nodded his head. 'I'll see you tomorrow,' he muttered, turning back towards the path.

'Ash?' he heard her call. 'Look after Braig for me.'

He turned his head, but she was already walking away. *Seriously?*

Chapter 3

CREDÉ

Behind the city of Mildaresh, in the shadow of the mountain, was a small burial ground. It was filled with neglected mounds and terraced headstones, sad reminders of a forgotten time when the city's people had buried their dead. At the furthest end stood a crumbling archway, flanked by a pair of ancient trees. It seemed strangely placed, leading as it did to nowhere. Beyond the arch, a winding path ran faintly up the scrub-covered hillside and into the trees. Ash stood for a while, puzzling at the faded inscriptions along the top of the arch, then gave a deep sigh and slouched against the stonework. As he waited, he carved an angry rut into the dirt with the heel of his sandal. The longer he waited, the more he scowled and the deeper the rut became, until at last Braig's arrival was announced by the sound of tuneless whistling.

'Ready, Weed? They say it's about a half-hour climb. We'll do it in less, I bet!'

Ash didn't answer; he just gave Braig his best glare and ducked the hand that reached out to tousle his hair. *Why did he always have to do that?*

Braig grinned widely. 'Come on! Let's find out about this quest!' He took off at a rapid pace, still whistling away. He didn't seem worried about what might be in store for them; he probably thought anything was better than shovelling dung all afternoon. *Idiot!* Ash had imagined all sorts of possibilities, and none of them were good.

As the path wound steeply into the woodlands, it threatened to disappear, and they often had to scramble over roots and branches that blocked the way. The bushes were alive with singing insects and crawling things that rustled at their approach. Ash was soon sweating, and not just from exertion. More than once he wished himself back in the kitchens preparing vegetables. Then, just when he thought the path couldn't get any steeper, it began to level out and he was able to breathe without his chest burning. Through a gap in the trees he could see the city far below, so strange and distant — like a miniature clay model. It was unsettling to view it from so far away. He trudged on until a sudden turn brought him out into an unkempt clearing.

The Malshorne's hut brooded against the rock face, tucked under the wing of an overhang. It was unlike any building Ash had ever seen. Its five sides were made from grey shingles, with odd angles and parts that jutted out. The windows were small and shuttered. A thin column of smoke rose from the chimney, which somehow seemed an ominous sign.

Braig was swigging from a water pouch. He turned as Ash joined him. 'Do you think the rumours are true?'

'Probably,' Ash replied glumly. He had no idea what rumours Braig might have heard, and didn't want to know. He rubbed a sleeve over his hot face, trying to get his breath back.

'Right,' said Braig brightly, 'let's find out about this quest. Ready?'

Ash wasn't ready and never would be, but he followed the bigger boy to the door anyway. He noticed, with some satisfaction, that Braig hesitated just for a moment before lifting the curled, black door-knocker. It fell back with a sharp *thunk*.

They waited, straining their ears for any sound from within. Then, just as Braig went to knock again, the door swung open. The Malshorne wore a heavy, embossed tunic, which perhaps had once been blue. As it didn't quite reach the floor, they could see his bony ankles above a pair of thin slippers. He leaned heavily on a stick and blinked at them in the light. For a brief, hopeful moment Ash wondered whether there had been a mistake, but then the Malshorne drew himself up and nodded at Braig, pulling his lips into a gaunt smile. 'Ah, my Chosen One. Come in.'

Taking a deep breath, Ash followed Braig over the threshold and into the gloom of the hut. The first thing he noticed was the smell; it was most peculiar, like a combination of old mushrooms and aniseed. He looked around nervously, wishing his eyes would adjust more quickly to the change in light.

The hut was much larger inside than he expected, but even so it was filled with all sorts of clutter. The funnel-shaped fireplace occupying one corner was set with a small blaze, despite the summer heat. There, a high-backed chair with curved arms was drawn up almost up to the hearth, where a black kettle steamed gently on a tripod. Next to that was a low, round table, bare save for a glass goblet, half-filled with dark liquid. A narrow bed stretched against one wall, a rolled pillow at its head and folded blankets at its foot. Firewood was piled untidily against the wall opposite the fire.

The Malshorne adjusted a shutter to admit a little more light, which came in shafts across the floor. They saw then that every wall was lined with benches, nooks and shelves, even up and over the tops of the windows. All manner of curious objects cluttered the benches and hung from rafters.

'Pull up that stool,' the Malshorne commanded. 'There, near the fire.'

Ash moved to obey. 'Not you!' He froze in his tracks: there was no mistaking that tone of absolute contempt. The Malshorne glowered at him beneath fierce eyebrows, then favoured Braig with a cryptic smile and the slightest of bows. 'The *Chosen* One.'

Braig shot Ash a quick look before shuffling reluctantly towards the heat of the fire. At this point, Ash learned of his own part in the 'glorious quest'.

'*You* are here to scrub.' A crooked finger pointed at a bucket sitting alone in the middle of the room. 'You will scrub and you will polish, until it shines like glass.'

As he crept towards the bucket, Ash realised that the centre of the room was laid with some sort of hard, black matter in the shape of a large triangle. It seemed to suck in the light, and looked nothing at all like glass, more like hardened pitch or filthy, matted straw. Getting it to shine was clearly impossible, but he chose a spot as far from the fireplace as he could, and sank to his knees. Sick with fear, he began to scrub.

Meanwhile, the Malshorne joined Braig by the fire and lowered himself into his chair slowly, leaning heavily on its arms. Then he just sat there, all hunched up, eyes closed, with silver hair trailing across his face. In the silence, Ash became aware of a steady ticking noise, and soon he was scrubbing in time with the measured beat. Time stretched while the firelight flickered across the Malshorne's face. At long last, he lifted his head and fixed Braig with an intense gaze.

'I am Credé.' His voice was cracked, but proud. 'You will call me T'al Credé ... as a sign of respect for my age and wisdom. The paths of my life have been many, but ...' He paused and gasped a bit, clutching at his chest before continuing. 'But all *you* need know is that I am the Keeper of the Song.'

A sudden movement in the woodpile behind Ash caused him to jump. He scanned the pile anxiously, but, before he could train his ears on its source, the Malshorne began to cough. And he kept coughing, in horrible rasping rattles. When he reached for the glass goblet on the table beside him, Braig quickly leaned forward to guide it into his shaking hands. The Malshorne drew it at once to his lips, sucking at its dark contents, which left a black trace down one side of his mouth. After a few minutes, the dreadful spluttering began to ease, and Credé gestured again. 'The stone, boy. Pass me the stone!' He seemed to be pointing at a silver orb set on an elaborately carved plinth, which sat nearby on a bench. Ash completely understood Braig's perplexed expression: it looked nothing like a stone whatsoever.

'Don't touch the stone itself. Here! Bring it here!'

The contents of the orb swirled like liquid silver as Braig lifted the plinth. He carried it carefully, his eyes bright with curiosity.

Credé snatched the orb to his chest, and closed his eyes again. After long minutes of waiting, Braig began to shuffle on his stool. He kept stealing glances in Ash's direction, but Ash ignored him and kept scrubbing, terrified of what might happen if he stopped. Then, to Ash's absolute horror, Braig cleared his throat.

'Please, T'al Credé,' he spluttered. 'Please tell me about the quest. What is it that I am to do?'

Ash had to admire his nerve.

The Malshorne grimaced, but he opened his eyes and sat up a little. He took another sip of the black liquid and nodded slowly. 'The Song, boy. You must learn the Song.'

Ash sensed another movement in the woodpile. He jerked his head to look, and saw the shadows shifting. There! A pair of eyes glinting! Then, nothing. His heart thumped, but he didn't dare move nor stop the rhythm of his scrubbing.

'I am the Keeper of the Song. Long have I been its guardian.' Credé made a bitter face. 'But now ... Now, it is time. The Song must pass.'

They all jumped at the sudden crash. Several logs rolled from the pile. Ash leapt back, jolting water up from the bucket as a voice rang out. It was the clear voice of a woman, imperious, yet curiously muted as if it came from afar.

The Taelstaun must go to T'al Jazure!

The Malshorne turned his head, his eyes glittering. 'Be silent!'

But the voice repeated:

The Taelstaun must go to T'al Jazure!

'Enough!' With a strangled cry the Malshorne hurled his goblet at the woodpile. Glass shattered against logs, and the voice fell silent.

Ash exchanged a horrified look with Braig. The Malshorne's face twitched and twisted. 'You! Clean that up. You! Another goblet! There, in the cupboard.'

Ash jumped to obey, but Braig did not move. The peculiar orb was swirling madly now, erupting with light; glowing green then purple beneath the Malshorne's fingers. Braig stared as if hypnotised, then his eyes opened even more widely.

'That's it, isn't it?' he said breathlessly. 'I mean ... that orb ... That's the Taelstone ... isn't it?'

Alarmed, Ash held his breath, waiting for the Malshorne to explode, but Credé met Braig's eyes, paused for a long moment, then he inclined his head. 'Indeed.'

'And that's the quest? We have to take it to that nobleman? To T'al Jazure?'

Credé's lips parted. He raised a long, gnarled finger. 'You have a sharper mind than anticipated, my boy.'

Braig beamed, encouraged. He seemed about to ask another question, but the Malshorne cut him off. 'However, first you must learn the Song. Each day you will learn one verse. Then, if I am satisfied, we will move on.'

At that moment, the ring of a bell drew their attention. It came from a complicated-looking object on a stand in the corner, and Ash realised that was also where the ticking came from. The machine gave a second chime, then a third. The Malshorne blinked. 'Ah! It grows late and I am weary. We begin tomorrow.'

Ash finished cleaning up the broken glass and emptied the filthy water as directed. He was thankful the Malshorne didn't seem inclined to inspect his work — he had made no impression on the floor whatsoever.

Before dismissing them, Credé handed Braig a small package bearing a green seal and tied with red twine. 'You will deliver this to the courtrooms and hand it to Lord Lendri — in person.' Then he made an odd gesture with his fingers, passing them through the air in front of them as if tracing a symbol.

The Malshorne's final words were quiet but forceful: 'There is no need for either of you to discuss what happens here with anyone else.'

Chapter 4

THE SONG

There was nobody Ash wanted to see less the next morning than Braig, but there he was, waiting for him outside the gates of the Feyindi villa, showing off those huge tanned biceps and grinning that annoying grin. He seemed completely oblivious to the displeasure of the gateman who was sending him dark looks. No wonder! He looked so cocky in his Aranti green, leaning against that tree as if he owned it. Spotting Ash, he stopped flexing his muscles and, embarrassingly loudly, called out, 'Hi, Weed!' Ash grunted in reply and set off with his head down.

As they walked, Braig stretched his arms across his chest, grasping first one elbow then the other, trying to ease his aching shoulders. He had been picking, loading and unloading apples since before dawn. He was sick of the sight of apples; he bet he even smelt like one. As they passed through the Feyindi orchards he picked up a fallen pear instead, spat out a rotten bit, then munched away noisily, savouring its juicy, fibrous flesh.

He glanced at Ash from time to time, and made a couple of attempts at conversation, but Ash was sulking. In fact, he seemed in a real stew. Fair enough, he supposed. They made their way through the bustling squares of the Arion sector and crossed the Hartlin Bridge, then followed the cobbled streets towards the old city. The sun was high overhead as they moved through the crooked alleyways, so they kept to the cool shadows where possible. And still Ash didn't speak.

Braig blew out a long breath. It was against his nature to sulk, and he generally ignored it when others did. But he needed to talk, and he didn't know how to begin. 'Sorry' didn't really cut it somehow. Finally, as they neared the entrance to the burial ground, Braig cleared his throat loudly.

'So, did you tell anyone about what happened yesterday?'

'Nope,' came the curt reply.

Braig scratched his head and ran his hand through his fringe a couple of times. This wasn't going well. 'But ... Did you try to? I mean ... Did you want to say something ... but then you just ... sort of couldn't?'

Ash looked at him quickly at that, then he scowled and looked away.

'Not really. I didn't really want to talk about it.'

Braig searched his face. It didn't seem right. Braig had wanted very much to talk about it. He had tried to answer Kep's concerned questions, but there had been a strange blankness in his mind. All he had been able to come out with was 'it was all right'. He had intended telling her all about Credé and his strange moods and glittering eyes; about all the weird stuff in his hut, and the wonderful globe that the Malshorne had clutched to his breast as if his life depended on it; about the disgusting stench of that dark liquid … and the quest! But each time he had gone to speak, it was as if the words had been erased — and that didn't seem right at all. So, as they reached the ancient archway, he tried again.

'Well, I think maybe he's put some sort of spell on us. You know, a spell that stops us talking about anything that happens up there,' he tipped his head at the mountain. 'And, I was thinking that … um … if it was a spell or a curse or something, maybe it only applies to other people. I mean, do you think we can talk to each other about it?'

'Dunno.'

'Well, shouldn't we try?'

'All right.' Ash stopped in his tracks, and rounded on Braig.

'Let's see,' he began, his voice shaking. 'Oh, yes. My part in this *marvellous* quest is to scrub a creepy black triangle until it shines like glass. I don't have a choice about this, because, even though Credé is not my master, he *is* the scariest person I have ever met. I really have no idea what he'll do to me when I fail, but I'm sure it'll be something painful. He obviously despises me and I have no idea why. And I hate to think what he really has planned for you. I doubt there even is a quest. I suspect he's just insane. Oh — and one last thing — there's something black, with evil, shining eyes, hiding in the woodpile, right near where I'm working. And, this thing, *this thing*, sounds as if it's speaking from beyond the After.'

He spun on his heel and stalked off up the path.

Braig nearly laughed out loud. Since when did Ash speak more than three words in a row? But his grin quickly faded as he followed — there sure was a lot to think about.

❧

The Malshorne opened the door almost immediately at their knock. The bucket stood waiting, and Ash was shown a spring outside where he might fill it as required. Suspecting he would make little progress with cold water, he managed to stammer out a request to heat some over the fire. Then, encouraged by Credé's agreement, he produced an old pot-scraper that he had scrounged from one of the dish maids.

'Could I also use this? I don't think it will scratch,' he stuttered.

The Malshorne actually chuckled. The sound was so improbable that, rather than calming Ash, it set him even more on edge.

'Scratch it? No. There is no fear of that.'

Ash decided to try letting one area soak while he scraped at another patch. As he worked, he kept his body turned slightly so he could keep an eye on the woodpile. As before, Braig sat on his stool in front of the Malshorne's chair. A low table had been placed between them. Braig's hands were sandwiched between his knees, his shoulders low. Ash had never seen him cower like that. Perhaps scrubbing the floor wasn't quite so bad after all; he wouldn't swap places for anything.

'So. We begin!' The Malshorne waved a hand theatrically. 'The Song has many verses. You will learn one verse each day.'

Many verses? Braig's heart fell. If Credé had announced that they were to swim the torrents of great Caribis or fight the fanged beast of Unchor, he would have been less horrified. In fact, he would have quite cheerfully set out to attempt either of those things. But singing? Why couldn't they just start on the real quest and not worry about this song business. He gazed longingly at the Taelstone in its holder. It was swirling again: this time it seemed filled with grey smoke. He clenched his jaw and tried not to cringe as the Malshorne cleared his throat.

Ash was keeping his head down, just scrubbing and trying his best to be invisible. But when the first notes came, he felt as if he had been physically struck. He had to stop himself from crying out. It was as if the purest shaft of light had pierced the centre of his being. Could that be Credé's voice producing that astonishing effect? No. The Malshorne sang in a tenor, like one of the travelling minstrels, but his voice was cracked and weak, wavering on some notes. It was more as if there was some profound beauty in the Song itself, in the combination of notes and words. They rose and fell, creating strange images in the mind that dissolved as soon as they had formed, only to be replaced by others.

When the last note of the first verse died, Ash realised with a jolt that he had been staring, slack-jawed, and had completely forgotten to keep working. He snapped his mouth shut and resumed his scrubbing, praying that the Malshorne had been too intent on his pupil to notice.

The Song had a powerful effect on Braig, too, but it wasn't pleasant at all. A hard lump formed in his throat; his armpits prickled with sweat, and he felt his stomach was about to drop out onto the floor. He knew at once there was absolutely no way he was going to be able to repeat any of it. It was just a jumbled mess of meaningless sound and incomprehensible words.

But Credé seemed to sense his panic. 'Do not be alarmed. It is not necessary for you to understand the Song, merely to repeat it.' He leaned forward and picked up a small wooden box from the table. 'This will help.' Opening the box, he crumbled its contents into a shallow silver bowl. 'Just a little aid for your memory,' he murmured, 'and your nerves.' Then he held a long taper out to the fire and transferred the flame to the bowl. The crumbled material flared up energetically, but the flames were quickly exhausted, leaving a smouldering pile.

'Of course,' he continued, looking into Braig's eyes, 'as soon as you have learnt the Song, you can embark on the proper quest.'

Reassured, Braig nodded.

'Breathe,' the Malshorne commanded.

Surprisingly the smoke did not grab at Braig's throat as he had thought it might. In fact, although it looked like smoke, it was odourless, just purple air that wafted and spiralled about his face. He relaxed. Perhaps this would be all right after all.

Encouraged by Credé's apparently more gentle mood, Ash decided to try applying hot water to the section he had soaked.

'Yes, yes. Hurry!' the Malshorne muttered as Ash approached the fire.

Braig looked up with strangely glazed eyes, and Ash was relieved to return to his place, away from the spiralling purple haze. He carefully poured the hot water onto the soaked patch, and renewed his work. To his surprise, he found that he was now able to prise off black flakes, some as large as his thumbnail. Progress! But as quickly as the thought had entered his head it was gone again, driven out by a soft noise behind him. It was just the slightest hollow bump, the sort of sound a small log makes when it shifts in a pile, but it was enough to remind Ash that something was there.

Something lurking, watching.

'Again!'

The lesson by the fire continued. This time Ash knew what to expect. Bracing himself, he managed to keep scraping while Credé sang. He still felt his spirits soar as the beautiful images played through his mind, but he kept his head down and his mouth clamped shut. The Malshorne sang only one line this time, then he waited. Braig just gazed at him.

'Repeat,' Credé prompted with a wave of his hand.

Miraculously, what came out of Braig's mouth was a word-for-word, note-for-note copy of what Credé had sung. But to Ash it seemed like a weak reflection, completely devoid of the colour and emotion of its inspiration.

'Excellent!' cried Credé.

Braig blinked stupidly at the praise.

'So we advance! You! More wood for the fire.'

Ash jumped to obey. The pieces stacked along the top were too small and would quickly burn to nothing, so he reached into the pile for a larger log. But, just as he had got a partial grip with his fingertips, he felt a hard, sharp pain, as something stabbed deep into his flesh. He leapt back with a shout.

'Ouch! Aaargh!'

Ash clenched his teeth and wrung his hand vigorously, as if it were possible to flick off the searing pain. Several deep puncture marks had appeared on either side of the base of his thumb, and were flooding with blood. When he held his hand upright, the blood flowed down his arm, forming two rivers of red.

'Aha! You've met Tarlyn!' Credé laughed merrily as he rose from his chair. 'She does have rather a nasty bite.'

Ash had to fight the urge to pull away when Credé crossed the room and grasped his wrist to inspect the injury. Then, as the rivers of blood met up and dripped off the end of his elbow, Credé proceeded to mix up a soft paste, selecting ingredients from a variety of bottles and boxes. When he was satisfied with the concoction, he applied two thick smears to the puncture marks. The paste immediately formed a hard crust.

'Don't pick at it,' he commanded. 'It will fall off of its own accord when you have healed. It's quite all right to put it in the water,' he added, indicating that Ash should return to his bucket.

Ash inspected his hand in disbelief. The pain was completely gone. All that could be seen of his injury, apart from the bloodstains down his arm, were two bluish-green patches. After cautiously attending to the fire, he went back to his work, making sure to keep as far from the woodpile as he possibly could.

❧

When Credé released them, Braig bolted off so quickly that Ash had no chance of keeping up, so he settled into his own pace, thinking as he walked. After the excitement of meeting Tarlyn, which was apparently the name of the creature lurking in the woodpile, the events of the afternoon had settled into a bizarre rhythm. The Malshorne had sung; Braig had responded with those weird, empty echoes; and Ash had scrubbed. The Song had kept calling to Ash like a beautiful dream, then fading, only to call out again. The words had seemed to flow through him, creating strange visions of stony peaks and rushing rivers; tall men with clashing swords under threatening skies; and sun-drenched pastures with white flowering trees. Ash was so preoccupied with these images and melodies that he didn't notice Braig waiting for him in the trees near the end of the mountain path.

'I can't do it!'

Ash's heart jumped as he stopped in his tracks, startled from his thoughts.

'I can't do it.' Braig's face was flushed and contorted. 'I can't remember a single thing about that stupid, bloody song.'

Ash had never seen him like this — if it had been anyone else Ash would have sworn he had been crying. He hesitated before answering, 'What … nothing?'

'Nothing!'

It seemed incredible to Ash. 'But you were repeating it all right. And you sang the whole verse through at the end.'

'I know. But I was in a sort of dream with that purple stuff and everything. It's all gone now.' Braig flung out his arms in despair. 'I'm not joking. I can't do it.'

'Well,' Ash hesitated. 'I could help you … I suppose … if you like.' It felt like the strangest thing he had ever said. 'Umm. I'm pretty sure I can remember the whole thing,' he added tentatively.

Braig screwed up his face. 'You can?'

'Yeah. Well, it's a story, isn't it? There's a pattern. One bit sort of leads on to the next.'

'There is?' Braig regarded him doubtfully. 'It does?'

'Yeah.' There was an uncomfortable pause. 'Shall we go through it while we walk?' Ash suggested tentatively, and they fell into step.

'It all begins with a tree.'

'The aching tree? Yeah, I know. But that doesn't make any sense,' groaned Braig. 'How can trees ache?'

'Don't try to make sense of it. Just sort of picture it in your mind.'

When Braig screwed up his face in concentration, Ash had to hide a smile.

'Can you see it?' Braig made a different sort of grimace, so he went on. 'Right. Now what's beside the tree?'

'A river,' said Braig, hesitantly, 'a river ... of souls?' He groaned again.

'Right! See, you're remembering.'

Braig shook his head angrily. 'No, I'm not. And it's stupid.'

'Well ...' Ash swallowed. 'Try not to think of it as a song. It's more like a story,' he frowned, 'or a map.'

'A map?' Braig's face seemed to clear a little. 'Like the ones with little pictures and names and everything?' He tilted his head to one side. 'I like maps. Maps make sense, you can follow them places.'

Ash realised he'd hit on something. 'Yeah, it's just like a map. All you have to do is imagine a map inside your head and put each part of the Song onto that map.'

Braig nodded slowly, then grinned. 'Starting with that stupid tree, right?'

Ash couldn't help smiling back at him. 'Yes. Starting with the tree.'

Chapter 5

HERATI

Kep quite liked making butter. Of course she would much rather have been outside tending the flock, but there *was* something satisfying about butter-making. Already that morning she had made three stacks of golden bricks. As she finished scrubbing the big barrel churn once more, she wiped the sweat from her face and poked a couple of rebellious curls back under her cap. Set beneath a shady grove of trees, and with high, louvred vents, the dairy was usually cool until midday; but it was getting hot early, perhaps too hot to make good butter. She frowned at the remaining cream, wondering whether it would last another day. Probably not, she decided. She poured it into the barrel, clamped the lid on tight and started cranking the handle.

As she found her rhythm again, she tried to shake off the sense of uneasiness that had dogged her all morning. *A fretting mind will turn the cream*, the Dairy Master always said. But she couldn't help it; Braig and Ash were both behaving so oddly. Neither had told her anything at all about their afternoons with the Malshorne, and it felt wrong — very wrong. True, Ash never said much at the best of times, but he wasn't usually evasive. But Braig — she had known him since they were small children, since before the testing and their bonding to the House of Aranti — and he had never been able to keep a secret, or even keep quiet for long. He loved telling stories, the more colourful the better, but now all he could say was, 'Yeah. It's going well.' It felt horribly wrong. As she worked the heavy crank, she couldn't shake off the feeling that something awful was going to happen.

Kep was soon regretting that last batch of butter; it seemed to be taking forever, and her arms ached, forcing her to keep swapping sides. Then, at last, she heard the welcome sound of swishing buttermilk. She inspected the batch and was just starting to empty the churn when she was distracted by a commotion. A warning was rippling around the busy dairy: 'The cat! It's the cat!' The slaves were suddenly making themselves scarce. Some of the girls fluttered into the storage rooms, others flew out into the pastures. Kep suddenly found herself alone. Trapped! But there was nothing for it; the butter would be ruined if left to stand in this heat. Turning her head, she saw that it was too late anyway — Matapharni was there, at the door, ready to pounce.

The nickname fitted Aranti's stunningly exotic mistress perfectly: she was exactly like a prowling cat. Her long garments trailed from her shoulders and arms, accentuating her lithe movement. A predatory smile hovered at the corners of her mouth, as if the sudden evacuation amused her. Ignoring the Dairy Master, who had bustled in to see what all the fuss was about, she headed towards the only slave stubborn enough (or stupid enough) to remain at her post. The alluring scent of spicy musk wafted towards Kep as the woman approached. She stiffened, gripping her apron in tight bunches at her sides.

Matapharni was even more beautiful up close. It was easy to believe she could drive a man wild — even a man like Maliagne Aranti. They say she had been a slave in neighbouring Terastal, and Aranti, besotted by her beauty and talents, had brought her to Mildaresh, showering the dark-haired beauty with honours and power far above her station. Her skin glowed, lustrous and golden. Her eyes, the most extraordinary dazzling green, were set off by black paint and the darkest of lashes; Kep couldn't help blushing beneath the frankness of their gaze. The embellished sign of the herati adorned the woman's left cheekbone, stencilled in red ochre. The sight of it made Kep's stomach flutter horribly, but she held her chin high, determined not to cower.

Matapharni smiled and raised one perfect brow. 'The girl has spirit,' she observed in a low, sultry voice. 'And such eyes! So very, *very* blue!' She acknowledged the Dairy Master with a cursory glance. He was hovering and bobbing, wringing his hands in nervous circles.

'Take off your cap, my lovely,' she purred.

Kep dragged the cap off her head, releasing a tumble of black curls. Matapharni circled her once, nodding thoughtfully. Then she reached out and stroked the side of Kep's face with the back of a long fingernail. Kep felt a sharp thrill at the woman's expression: it was deeply intelligent, and suddenly oddly serious. Matapharni paused for a long moment, then lowered her lashes. 'Congratulations, child,' she murmured. 'You have been chosen to train as herati.'

They were the words Kep had been dreading. Her heart sank further as Matapharni tossed a casual command over her shoulder. 'She will be transferred to the house at once.'

The Dairy Master was a kindly little chap with dimpled cheeks, a round belly and one simple joy in life: making wonderful cheese. He treated his slaves well, and rarely found occasion to beat them. He was certainly no match for Matapharni. Indeed, the little cheese-maker was wringing his hands even more vigorously, and seemed completely flustered by the whole situation. But to Kep's great surprise, as Matapharni started to walk away he pushed out his chest and spluttered, 'Wait! Stop! You can't have her!'

Matapharni's expression when she turned made him wobble, and he turned an even brighter red, but he held his ground: 'I mean ... Take any of the others, but I need Kep. The beasts trust her, especially that mad bunch of bug-eyes. She has some sort of magical touch with them.'

This was clearly nothing to Matapharni. She made a dismissive gesture and continued walking. But, unbelievably, he tried again. 'Wait! Please ... wait ...' He cringed, as if frightened by his own audacity. 'Her flock simply can't be milked by another!'

Matapharni had reached the doorway.

'Well ... Just so you know, there'll be trouble if Lady Aranti can't have her chevrell!'

Kep caught her breath. It might just work! The bug-eyes were ridiculous creatures really, and so terribly nervous: the slightest fright made them leap and flail about — and they were frightened by just about everything. But their rich, creamy milk made the most delectable of cheeses: chevrell. The sweet, silky-soft rounds were highly prized, and — most importantly — were Capricia Aranti's absolute favourite. Everyone knew Capricia was a greedy, dim-witted woman with an insatiable appetite for sparkling trinkets and delicious treats. But her fortune was sizable, so her husband tended to indulge her every petty desire.

Aranti's beautiful mistress had halted, one hand on the doorknob. She turned and regarded the cheese-maker for an unbearable few seconds, no doubt imagining just how much fuss Capricia would make if deprived of the cheeses she adored. She pouted, seeming to hesitate, but then her reply snuffed out all hope.

'The girl will move to the house — immediately.' She held up a graceful hand, as if to fend off more protest: 'However, you may retain her services for the morning milking for one full turn of Eldar while she trains a Second.' She swept through the door then, and that was that; nothing could be done.

❧

It could certainly never be said that Maliagne Aranti was one to squander wealth on the comfort of his slaves. The women's quarters were surely the sparsest in Mildaresh. Kep had been shown to a space that was more tunnel than room. The six bunks lining the walls didn't ease the claustrophobic effect. Nor did the miserable window: it was round and dull, like a cataract — an insulting reminder of the sunshine outside.

Kep had been told to settle in before reporting to the Master of the Table directly after evening rations. Since that involved the simple tasks of making up the unoccupied bunk with its thin covers and placing her meagre belongings into the cubby-hole beside it, she had plenty of time — far too much time. She sat on the edge of the bunk and took a long, deep breath.

Kep wasn't used to stone floors and dark enclosures. She would miss sleeping outdoors — even rainy nights were preferable to being shut up inside stone, unable to breathe. She would miss watching the moons rise and the stars swing across the sky, and the way the flock gathered in close and warm, looking to her for protection. Sniffing and blinking, Kep squeezed back tears.

Standing up, she gave herself a firm shake. That was Pan's job now. Besides, this awful accommodation was only temporary, just until she had finished her milking duties; the herati had their own quarters in another part of the villa. She bit her lip, blinked and sniffed again. It could be a prestigious role, she reminded herself, and with considerable privileges. She would be taught to sing and dance and play a musical instrument, as well as the other pleasurable arts. She shivered then, but lifted her chin. It wasn't so bad. All noble households kept herati to provide entertainment and pleasure for guests. It was an honour really. It was silly to worry over the dark whispers about Aranti herati. Those missing girls had probably just fallen pregnant and been sent to the Holding to care for the babies. People did like to gossip, after all.

Kep laid out her new serving clothes, took a final dismal look about, then headed for the door with a sigh. Relieved that the washrooms were empty, she pumped cold water into a basin and washed thoroughly, making the most of the privacy while she could. Then she caught back her hair before approaching the altar. Kep always gave proper thanks to the gods. Her nurse at the Holding had been a firm believer; 'Never shun the gods my child,' she had murmured. 'The masters grant us the right to worship, and little else. The gods will guide you and protect you: they love slaves, just as much as they do free-folk.' Despite the fact that all evidence suggested that the gods actually cared very little for the fate of slaves, Kep didn't care. She would always remain true to the memory of the woman who had rocked her in large arms, whispering words of comfort into her small ears.

She knelt and formed the sign of the triangle: finger tips together at her brow with thumbs resting on each cheekbone. Breathing deeply, she bowed her head to Telion, Argess and Narsis, each in their turn, but it was to Narsis that she whispered her supplication: 'Mighty Narsis, please watch over Braig and Ash and keep them safe from harm.' She strewed a few red flower petals into the water. Then she muttered a short prayer for herself. As she rose, feeling calmer, she could hear voices. A group of kitchen slaves was entering, shedding their long green aprons and unfastening their caps. She slipped out quickly to avoid them.

The Aranti slaves ate their evening meals in a timber out-building with deep rafters, sawdust-covered floors and low, wooden tables. Kep received her ration at the hatch: a ladle of slops and a chunk of black-bread. Today, something which looked like meat was bobbing in her bowl. She eyed the glistening lump as she sat down, wondering whether or not to eat it. A few of the farm slaves had arrived, and were clustered together in their usual place.

She ate slowly, watching the door. Each time it opened, her heart skipped a little. Next time it would be him, she told herself. But when the door opened again it was only old Jed, who hobbled stiffly to the serving hatch. She wondered whether Jed had ever considered what life might have been like if he had been bonded to a different family. But then what if he had failed the Orlion trial altogether? He would have been sent to the noikos fields, doomed to a life picking the large purple pods, driven on by whips and his fierce desire for lamon berries. She shuddered at the thought.

Kep had seen the effects of lamon first-hand. Gangs of Blues were brought into Mildaresh when extra labour was required. The lamon made them incapable of performing any complex task, but they would toil all day under its influence — so long as they got berries to chew. If it wasn't for the grace of the gods, who had given her good looks and a sharp mind, that would have been her. It was a sobering thought. She sighed deeply. Yes, she would miss her flock and the outdoor life. But things were as they were. When Eldar next rose full in the night sky, she would begin training as herati, and there was no point fighting it — the gods knew their own minds best.

Kep turned her head once again as the door swung open, and felt her heart leap. There was Braig talking animatedly with Cairn. She could see Cairn's admiring expression and guessed at his one-word responses. 'Really? ... Really?' He was obviously impressed at whatever Braig was saying.

Braig was scanning the room. When he spotted her, he grinned; she felt her pulse quicken and her cheeks grow warm. He stopped to speak with a group of shepherds, and laughter erupted immediately. Tired slaves looked up from their food and smiled in spite of themselves. Kep smiled, too; it was hard not to — Braig had that effect on people. By the time the pair joined her bearing steaming bowls, her own was empty, except for a cold, gristly lump at the bottom.

Cairn spotted it immediately. 'Aren't you eating that?'

'No, you can have it,' she replied. He scooped it up instantly and ate it with relish.

Wrinkling her nose, she turned and gave Braig her full attention instead. She ran her eyes quickly over the familiar bulge of his chest and arm muscles, then down to rest on the soft, golden hair on his forearms. He had two little freckles on his left wrist, right where his pulse would be. She couldn't see them, but she knew they were there. She loved being this close to him. He always smelled so good, even after a full day's work: wholesome, like the earth itself. She realised she was starting to blush, so looked away, glad he was so absorbed in his meal.

'What were you two talking about when you came in?' she

asked quickly.

Cairn's eyes lit up instantly. 'Braig was telling me what he's been learning from the Malshorne.'

'Oh? Really?' She frowned faintly. *Had he really been talking to Cairn but not her?* 'So, how is it going?' she prompted, trying not to feel hurt.

Braig seemed suddenly interested in the back of his spoon, as if he had spotted some defect. 'Yeah. It's going really well.' He began breaking his bread into more pieces than seemed necessary.

'Going well?' Cairn spluttered between mouthfuls. 'Excellent more like!'

Kep studied his face, and put her head on one side. 'Oh? What makes you say that, Cairn?'

Cairn looked suddenly startled, almost certainly because he had been kicked under the table. He shot a look at Braig, then shovelled food into his mouth instead of answering.

Kep narrowed her eyes. Something was definitely up. 'Braig?'

'Look, Kep. I'm really hungry. We can talk about it later.'

She nodded, trying not to look upset. It was so unlike him; he was never brusque — not with her. While the boys ate, she watched in painful silence. While she had decided not to tell him about Matapharni just yet, and the fact that they would probably never see each other once she had started her training, she had wanted him to know she had moved to the house. His head was down, though, and he wouldn't even meet her eyes, so she hugged her bitter news to herself instead. It would keep.

'See you, then,' she said quietly as she rose.

'Yeah. See you.'

Chapter 6

TARLYN

A sh and Braig's afternoons had settled into a pattern. They would meet outside the Feyindi villa and walk together, so Braig could practise the verse he had learned the day before. Another strange lesson at the fireside would follow, to the accompaniment of Ash's scrubbing and scraping. Then, on return journeys, Ash would help Braig add new images to the map in his head. Slowly and painfully, verse by verse, Braig was learning the Song. Ash sometimes had to wrack his brain to come up with a way to make the new words stick, but it felt good when particularly tricky lines fell into place. Braig would sometimes dart him an appreciative glance as they walked — and he'd even stopped calling him 'Weed.'

On good days, Credé would greet them at the door. Occasionally he would clap Braig on the shoulder and say things like 'Not long now, eh?' or 'Well, my boy, we'll soon send you off on that quest.' His joviality always made Ash feel uncomfortable. It seemed so odd, and his moods were so unpredictable. Braig didn't seem to care, though; he always perked up at any mention of the quest. On bad days things were quite different. The Malshorne would clutch the Taelstone to his chest. His mind would wander, and he would mutter incomprehensible, strangely accented words to himself.

One day they arrived to find Credé in his bed, covered with blankets. A glass of the black liquid had been spilt by his bedside, and he gave no sign of recognising them. Braig sat near the bedside for a while, then gave up and offered to help Ash instead.

'You're making headway.'

Ash made a face, but it was true. He had managed to scrape most of the hardened grime from a large section to reveal a smooth surface that glinted in places.

'What *is* this stuff?' Braig squatted, and rubbed a finger over a shiny patch. 'I've never seen anything like it … Weird.'

They scrubbed, shoulder to shoulder, chatting quietly about pilat strategies and players they rated. As usual, Ash kept a close eye on the woodpile. Tarlyn had proved elusive since that first painful encounter. Once, a dark shape had materialised, and for a fraction of a moment he had glimpsed a lithe body and a long black tail, but the creature had shot out of sight so swiftly he had begun to doubt himself. He had definitely seen those shining eyes, though — several times. They would disappear, only to reappear in a different place. It was completely unnerving.

'Do you think he's going to die?' asked Braig conversationally.

Ash shrugged at first, then frowned and began to worry about what they would do if Credé did die.

'He doesn't look so good.' Braig peered at the figure on the bed. 'Do you think we should try giving him some of that black stuff? It smells awful, but it usually does the trick.'

Ash studied his face, wondering if he was serious. 'Well, you can try if you like, but I don't know how you'd get him to swallow any.'

'Yeah, you've got a point.' Braig returned to his scrubbing, but he looked up each time the Malshorne moaned or thrashed, then finally he stopped working and sat back on his haunches. 'Look. We've got to try something. I mean, we'd give something a go if one of the farm beasts was suffering, wouldn't we?'

Ash wasn't so sure.

'Surely we should do the same for a person? Don't you think?'

Ash wasn't even convinced the Malshorne was a person in the usual sense of the word, but Braig was persisting. 'You know, I got kicked by a kattlen once. She was trying to give birth, but the calf was stuck. Took seven of us to hold her down while we dragged the little 'un out. I caught a hoof right here on my thigh. It hurt like mad.'

Ash sloshed more water onto the floor, trying to avoid Braig's earnest brown eyes. 'He's not a kattlen, you know.'

'Yeah, I know. So it can't be that bad, right?' Braig set down his brush. 'You hand me that black muck while I hold his head still.'

Wishing he could think of some excuse not to help, Ash poured a fresh glass of black goo from the kettle and crept towards the bed. Every part of him warned against the plan, as Braig reached out to touch the pillow's edge. Immediately Credé's eyes snapped open. A thin hand shot out and grabbed Braig by the wrist. Ash let out a terrified curse and leapt backwards, but Braig was caught tight.

Credé dragged him closer with a dreadful grimace. 'Artus?' His eyes were wild as he cried, 'Artus! No! We can't — it's sacred!' Braig tried to wrench free, but the Malshorne held on. 'No! Not that! … Not that … Please!' He sobbed, clawing Braig's arm with his nails.

Braig writhed. 'Let go! I'm not Artus. It's me — Braig. It's Braig. I'm just here to learn the Song.'

The Malshorne fixed him with a crazed stare.

'You know.' Braig's voice cracked. 'The Song?'

Credé's eyes darted wildly as he shuddered. Then the breath wheezed out of him and his eyelids fluttered. 'The Song,' he croaked. 'Yes. The Song must pass. Must pass. Pass away.' He fell back, releasing Braig at last.

Braig threw himself backwards so forcefully that he tumbled over Ash. They scrambled in reverse, a mess of knees and skinned elbows, until they were hard up against the opposite wall. There, they sat in silence, not daring to move. Credé's crazed murmurings slowly subsided, until all they could hear was his breath rasping in and out.

'What by the dogs of Argess was that?' muttered Braig at last.

Ash shook his head. 'That's it: we're not trying that again. I mean it, Braig! That's it — we're never, ever, trying to help him again! Even if he does die.'

Braig nodded agreement. 'Who do you think Artus is? He must be one bloody scary guy if old Credé is frightened of him.'

They fell silent, trying to imagine anything that could scare the Malshorne.

'Do you think we should go?' asked Braig eventually.

Ash looked doubtfully at the bed. 'I don't think we should risk it. He's just as likely to wake up and carry on as if nothing has happened. We'd better wait until that clock machine rings.' If there was one thing they had learned about Credé, it was that he was wholly unpredictable.

There was nothing for it but to keep scrubbing until it was time to go.

❦

The boys worked solidly for a long while, until Ash gave Braig a sudden nudge. Holding a finger to his lips, he signalled with his eyes: a dark shadow was moving, deep in the woodpile. They held their breaths and watched. A pointed nose with whiskers appeared first, then a sleek head with ears laid flat. Tarlyn was the size of a small cat, except her body was lower, smooth and inky-black. A long black tail contributed to the impression of the creature moving in one fluid wave as she undulated over logs, stopping only once to blink at them with huge, shining eyes.

Reaching the end of the pile, she sprang to the nearest bench in a single liquid movement. Like a shadow, she prowled along the bench-tops, negotiating the clutter of caskets, bowls and books with precision, then she leapt to the top of a bookcase. The boys watched transfixed as she glided along the top of the bookcase, then crouched, quivering, at the far end. At the same time they saw that a fat wood-cricket was meandering up the wall. In a split second the creature had leapt and landed neatly back in the same spot. With a crunch the cricket lost its head, then its body and legs went the same way.

'So that's what she eats when she can't get thumbs,' Ash whispered.

As Braig chuckled softly, the strange creature turned her head and looked directly at them. Ash shivered. It was as if she had not only heard, but had understood.

Tarlyn finished her meal, and was returning along the bookcase when Credé gave a sudden shudder and cried out. Instantly, a large pair of ears flipped up from nowhere. A collar of quills sprang bristling about her face, and she bared impossibly sharp teeth. The boys gasped at the transformation, but what happened next was the greatest shock of all. The creature put her head to one side, half-closed those globe-like eyes, then spoke:

The Song is a harsh mistress.

They jumped. It wasn't the ethereal female voice they had heard previously; rather, the distinctive tones of an older man, speaking solemnly and sympathetically. As Credé stretched out his arms and gave a strangled croak, Ash thought he heard the words 'forgive me' among a string of otherwise foreign phrases that trailed off as the Malshorne slumped back on his bed.

The creature sat there, motionless, staring down at the delirious figure. Then she folded herself into her original sleek form, thrashed her tail noiselessly and resumed her journey. When she reached the woodpile, she poured herself into her hiding place and disappeared.

'That's it!' said Braig. 'Bell or no bell, we're getting out of here!'

As the boys hurried away, Ash kept imagining the Malshorne striding after them, his long cloak trailing and his eyes glittering. Only when they were deep into the trees, at the point where a tumbling stream crosses the path, did they stop.

'All thanks to Narsis!' gasped Braig, as he doused his face.

Ash drank straight from a rivulet pouring off a ledge to one side. The water pooled in his cheek and spilled down his front, wetting his feet, but he didn't care; he was so thirsty. When he had drunk his fill, he joined Braig, who had flung himself down on the mossy bank. Ash lay back, too, his hands behind his head, staring up at the canopy. There were birds overhead feasting on purple berries. Their breasts shone blue and green. He closed his eyes, appreciating their melodic calls.

'Ash?'

'Hmm.'

'Why do you think Credé's teaching me the Song?'

Ash rolled his head towards Braig, squinted painfully into the sun, then closed his eyes again. 'I don't know.'

He could feel Braig looking at him.

'That was really weird.'

Which bit in particular, Ash wondered, did Braig find weird?

'What that black ... thing said today.' He paused. 'What's its name?'

'Tarlyn.'

'What do you think she meant? That bit about the Song being a harsh mistress? Did you see Credé react? And what about that voice?'

Although Ash didn't answer, Braig kept talking: 'And, how come this ... Tarlyn, can speak with two different voices? What was Credé going on about with that whole "the Song must pass" stuff? And what's it got to do with me? What am I supposed to do with this Song anyway, once I've learned it? And — another thing — how come he couldn't have chosen someone who was a bit better at singing?' At last he paused. 'Ash?'

'I don't know.' Ash wasn't sure which question Braig wanted him to answer, but it didn't really matter, since that answer fitted them all anyway. Sitting up, he rested his elbows on his knees, then picked up a pebble and rolled it thoughtfully between his fingers. 'Maybe Credé was supposed to take the Taelstone to that lord ... to T'al Jazure. Maybe years ago. But he couldn't. I don't know why ... Maybe he got sick.'

'Yeah. That fits. Maybe it was *his* quest, but he was too sick to see it through! And that's why he needs me.' Braig sat up straight. 'Maybe he's too old now. How old is he?'

Ash shrugged.

'But the Song? How do you reckon that fits in?'

'I don't know … I think maybe it's the Song that's making him sick, though. Remember that first day? He said he'd been its guardian for too long? And then today, what Tarlyn said …' Ash trailed off, but Braig picked up the thread.

'Yeah, he did say that! And Tarlyn said "the Song is a harsh mistress" … But maybe you have to sing the Song before you start on the quest. It could be part of a quest ritual — you know, a hero's homage to the gods.'

Ash shook his head. It didn't feel right. The Song was too long to be a prayer. He tossed the pebble away and sighed. 'Well, we'll know soon enough — assuming Credé doesn't die. I reckon there can't be much Song left to learn.'

'Really? What makes you say that?'

Ash blinked. Why did he think that? 'I'm not sure. Just a feeling, I suppose. Like when someone is telling a story and you can feel that the end is coming up.'

Braig laughed. 'You're a strange one, Ash. Not in a bad way,' he added hastily, 'but strange nonetheless.'

With the conversation getting uncomfortable, Ash got to his feet and started brushing the broken leaves and moss from his clothes, leaving muddy smudges.

But Braig wasn't finished. 'Ash? Why can you remember the Song so easily when I can't?'

It was the most bewildering question of all. Ash had never told Braig about the uncanny effect the Song had on him. He wouldn't have known where to begin.

'I mean, have you ever sung before, or anything like that? You sure sound better than I do.'

'No, I've never sung before. But there was a woman who used to sing to me in the Holding—' He suddenly stopped himself short. He hadn't meant to tell Braig that. Feeling himself blush, he turned away. As a boy he had thought about her every night, before he went to sleep. But he couldn't remember her songs anymore. Now he wasn't sure he hadn't made her up. Or perhaps he had dreamt the whole thing. He shrugged as casually as he could, and cleared his throat. 'Anyway, we'd better get a move on or we won't make the twilight bell.'

᷍

As they reached the end of the mountain path, Ash felt faint. He made a mental note to filch an extra piece of bread from the kitchens in future. Fear was hungry work. Unfortunately, as they neared the crumbling archway he realised the day's nasty surprises were not over yet. A small gang of lads had invaded the peace of the burial ground. Three darted between the headstones, slashing at each other with sticks. One stood and watched, his hair glinting in the sun. With a sickening jolt Ash registered the orange tunics of the House of Moagli.

Braig tensed beside him. 'Stick close,' he muttered, as if Ash needed telling.

As they approached, the gang formed up in an untidy line across their path. Ash stiffened, his heart in his throat.

'Hey, Hob.' Braig nodded to a sandy-haired lad at the left of the group. The boy acknowledged him with an uncomfortable shuffle. The two boys to the right looked familiar to Ash; he didn't know them by name, but had seen them on the street crews hauling rubble. They were simple louts. Heavily-built, but not too much going on up top. And then there was Feld. Feld stood with one hand on his hip, like a young aristocrat posing for a portrait.

'Well, well. If it isn't the *Chosen* One and his apprentice,' he sneered, making a mock bow. His companions guffawed.

'Hey, Feld.' Braig grinned, ignoring the taunt. 'You guys been let off the leash?'

The vicious hierarchy among the Moagli Squad was well known. The younger boys had to yield to the will of the older ones, doing whatever mischief or dirty work they could dream up. They were the slaves of slaves, and you couldn't get much lower than that. Ash felt the blood pulsing in his temple. His fingers tingled as he fought down rising panic.

'We're scouting new training grounds, if you must know,' countered Feld. He glowered, perhaps realising that he had been forced onto defence. 'I see you and your little helper have been up the mountain.' Crossing his arms, he smiled nastily. 'Looks like he's soiled his pants.' His gang sniggered.

Ash gritted his teeth and tried not to look down at his muddy clothes.

'Yeah. We've been up the mountain. So?' Braig rolled his shoulders back and shook out his arms. He held up a fist, ever so casually, then flexed his fingers.

The Moagli boys bristled. Ash held his breath. It was coming.

'Oh, we just wondered how you were getting on,' smirked Feld. 'You know, what with helping out the scary old Malshorne. Creeeepy stuff.' He mimicked the sound of the wind howling, and earned himself another titter from his gang. 'What is it he has you doing up there anyway?'

Braig held his silence.

'I suppose you two are meeting his every need,' Feld pushed, smiling evilly. 'And, I mean, his *every* need.'

Ash glanced at Braig. Surely he'd bite — he wasn't exactly known for his restraint.

Braig smiled, shifting his weight so he was balanced equally on the balls of his feet. The Moagli boys shuffled, wondering who would catch it first.

'Yeah, it's been great,' Braig said coolly. 'We're undertaking warrior training.'

Ash struggled to keep the surprise from his face as he continued.

'Our quest is to visit the caves of Astran to collect the Chalice of Orion. That's why we need knife training.' He patted his pocket and the boys' eyes followed the movement. 'Those Gympin tribes can be pretty fierce, and we'll probably face a few of their warriors when we pass through the forest of Undor. Of course they're soft compared with the flyboys of Altrinium. That's where Ash comes in with his bow skills. His drawing arm is getting pretty strong with all the practice.' He jerked a thumb towards Ash. The boys stared at Ash's arms, which actually had thickened considerably with all the scrubbing. They swapped looks. Even Feld looked doubtful.

'He's got a great eye, too; one of the best the Malshorne has ever seen. Isn't that right, Ash?'

As Ash nodded, Braig pressed his advantage. 'We've only just begun the sword work. We'll need that in the caves when we take on the tough hides of the gnarkin beasts; you can't pierce one of them with just a knife.'

Two of the thugs nodded, as if everyone had heard of gnarkin beasts.

'Yeah,' Braig mused, 'there's a whole team of those brutes guarding the entrance. We've got some pretty good blades to choose from, though. Ornate, but heavy — you know the sort.' Feld's boys were blinking: it was a lot for their tiny brains to take in.

Then Braig dealt a final blow, 'Course, then there's the Astran militia.'

Even Feld looked dumbstruck by this point. 'Ash and I were just discussing our plans for dealing with them.'

Braig finished with a flourish of his hand. 'So, sorry boys. Would love to stay and chat,' he strode confidently at the line and the boys parted to let him through, 'but Ash and I have got to talk strategy. C'mon, Ash.'

And so they strode away, shoulder to shoulder, quickly but not too quickly, resisting the urge to look back. Then, as soon as they had entered the first alleyway and were out of sight, they began to run. They sprinted hard, just inside the old city wall, leaping broken foundations and dodging rubble, running and running, until at last they reached a broken watchtower. Much of the stone had been cleared away for newer works, but great piles remained. They clambered up over the fallen blocks, and entered the remains of the tower.

They climbed as far up the crumbling steps as was safe, then, heads together, peered out through a deep slit in the stone. From there they could see the burial ground off in the distance, and make out tiny figures standing in a group. They stared at each other for the briefest moment before Braig let out a great burst of laughter. And that was it. They just couldn't stop! They howled and hooted as the waves of mirth kept bubbling up.

'Did you see their faces?' Braig blurted.

'I know,' Ash snorted. 'But, but ...' he gasped, unable to get the words out. 'All those bits from the Song, and that other mad stuff!' he wheezed. 'Gnarkin beasts!'

Each time they sobered up, one of them would start up again, triggering a fresh bout of laughter. It took a long time before they were calm enough to climb down safely from the precarious perch. As they walked together they still kept sniggering, and they grinned madly the whole way back.

'You were truly inspired by Telion today,' Ash marvelled. 'You liar! You absolute liar! How did you come up with such a convincing story on the spot like that?'

Braig shrugged, somewhat shamefacedly. 'Well, I've sort of been practising on Cairn.'

Chapter 7

THE MALSHORNE'S FURY

'So? Do you think he's dead?'

Ash frowned faintly. 'I don't know.' Wishing someone dead was a serious offence to Argess, giver of life. But he had to admit, it would be wonderful to return to his predictable, invisible existence as a Feyindi kitchen boy.

'Well, I hope he isn't.'

Ash raised his brows, surprised by Braig's fervent tone.

'Think about it. If he's dead, we'll never know what it's all been about.' Braig tore another leaf from the frond he'd been stripping.

'I don't care what it's all been about,' Ash replied, 'I just want it to be over.' He instantly realised that wasn't true, though.

'Yeah, I know. I do, too, in a way.' Braig put the end of the bare frond between his teeth, then immediately took it out again. He spat several times and threw it away.

'It's just ... this is my one chance to do something important. You know? ... Something other than lifting sacks of corn and shovelling animal muck. I know you think we shouldn't trust Credé, but I get the feeling that this is important, really important.'

Ash let out a long sigh. 'Well, we'd better go in then, T'al Chosen One.' He made a slight bow to go with his pale attempt at humour. 'You can knock, though.'

Braig grinned. 'As if you ever would!'

⁂

The Malshorne was not dead. In fact, to Ash's dismay, he seemed entirely back to his usual terrifying self. Avoiding that intensely poisonous glare, Ash scurried for the bucket and renewed his attack on the strange triangle. Braig resigned himself to the peculiar routine of the past few weeks and sat by the fire. Soon his head was dropping, heavy from the effects of the purple fumes.

When Credé began to sing, Ash suddenly realised how much he had been yearning to hear those notes. At that moment, suspended in rapture, he felt that the Song was everything. There was nothing else, just the soaring notes and piercing images. Anything outside of the music faded to a dull insignificance. And when Credé stopped singing, Ash understood something he had only vaguely grasped up until that point. Braig was right. Somehow, this was important.

Unfortunately, the afternoon did not go well. Braig simply couldn't repeat the phrases correctly. He would either get the notes wrong or the words wrong, or both. Ash cringed at every mistake. Credé was becoming increasingly impatient as the afternoon wore on, until finally he rose with a curse. 'Kraacht! Imbecile!'

The Malshorne created more purple smoke, but it didn't help one bit. Braig just grinned manically, then fell off his stool with a crash.

Then, to make things worse, Tarlyn suddenly chose to speak again.

The Taelstaun must go to T'al Jazure.

The creature had actually crept out of her hiding place and was perched upon the woodpile. Credé gave a wild, incomprehensible cry. He leapt up, staggered to the woodpile, then struck. 'Insolence!'

The cane came down hard across the creature's haunches with a crack, and Tarlyn gave a high-pitched yelp. Seizing her by the scruff of the neck, Credé shook her violently. 'You dare! You dare to taunt me!' With a livid cry he hurled her hard against the wall. There was a soft smacking noise, then a thump as the creature fell in a crumpled heap.

Ash let out an involuntary cry of shock, and the Malshorne rounded at once, his eyes flashing a peculiar shade of purple. Ash could feel his hatred like a physical force. He cringed, anticipating the blow. But, fortunately, although Credé's anger was not spent, his energy was. He staggered, and leaned trembling on his cane. Pain had triumphed over fury.

'Help me, boy,' he wheezed at Braig, who had managed to struggle to his feet. With Braig's rather shaky help, Credé returned to his chair. Muttering oaths under his breath and clutching the Taelstone to his breast, he pulled the covers around him. 'The lesson is finished for today,' he announced acidly. 'I must rest.' Then he banged his cane on the floor. 'But it is *not* time — you *will* be of use! You will scrub! Both of you!'

So, while the Malshorne brooded bitterly beneath his blankets, both boys scrubbed on their knees. Since there was only one patch left to work on, their heads were almost touching. After a long time Ash plucked up the courage to steal a look in the Malshorne's direction. His eyes, which had been fixed on them in a relentless stare, were closed at last. His head had dropped almost onto his chest. Ash nudged Braig. He nodded, and they both relaxed slightly, but they didn't dare stop the scraping rhythm of their tedious work.

The fire was getting low when Ash sensed movement where Tarlyn had fallen. When her tail twitched again, he shuddered. The poor thing was still alive. After a few more minutes, miraculously, the creature started to drag herself along on her belly, her back legs trailing uselessly. Her progress was excruciating, but Ash was captivated. He couldn't look away. It was as if his own release from that dreadful place was somehow dependent on her reaching safety. He willed the creature on, even sending a silent prayer to Argess. When the tip of her tail finally disappeared into the woodpile, he felt a deep surge of pity. She probably wouldn't survive the night, and certainly wouldn't be able to hunt.

Whatever had made her speak? And why Credé had reacted so violently? Slowly, but surely, Ash felt an emotion awaken inside him that he had never felt before. He tried to push it down, recognising the danger, but he just got more agitated. He was angry. Really angry. He couldn't help thinking about the thwacking sound her small body had made against the wall. Then, with a thrill of horror, Ash knew he was about to do something.

Lifting the bucket carefully to stop it clanking, he crept to the door and lifted the latch. It was raining lightly outside, and he took a grateful gulp of fresh air. But there was no time to squander. After re-filling the bucket, he raced to a dead tree he had once investigated for firewood. The fallen trunk was badly weathered, its deep splits providing homes for tiny toadstools and bright green mosses. Ash wedged a stick into the most promising crack and pulled. The spongy deadwood gave way easily. The inside was loaded with juicy grey wood-grubs, each the size of his thumb; they curled in protest as he prised them from their refuge. In a matter of seconds he had a good number safely piled into the pocket of his tunic. So far so good.

The Malshorne stirred slightly when the draught from the door blew across his feet, but he slept on. Ash had a fair idea where Tarlyn was hiding, and a faint shuffle in the woodpile confirmed his guess. He scooped the wriggling grubs from his pocket and dropped them into a gap between the logs. In no time his pockets were empty, and he was back on his knees beside Braig, heart racing. To his joy, after only a few moments he heard the faint but distinct squelch of wood-grubs being devoured. Ash earned himself an approving nod from Braig, and grinned widely. It was a small victory, but a sweet one.

The two boys were scrubbing with renewed energy when Credé finally stirred. Determined effort in one spot had revealed a gleaming surface, hinting at a whole stratum of mysterious depths. In spite of their weary muscles and sore knees, the boys were fully absorbed in their task. In fact, they were so engrossed by the strange shadows that seemed to swirl below the dark surface that they didn't notice the Malshorne until he was looming over them.

'Good.'

Credé's eyes gleamed, every bit as enigmatic as the stone they were polishing.

'You — continue!' he commanded of Ash. But he held a hand out to Braig. 'Come.'

Braig hesitated, looking worried. Ash put his head down and kept scrubbing as the Malshorne ushered Braig out into the open air.

When they returned a few minutes later, Ash saw instantly that Braig's mood had altered. All of a sudden he looked every bit 'The Chosen One.' His shoulders were back and his eyes shone. What could possibly have brought about such a startling transformation? As Ash emptied the bucket and filled it with scrapers, rags and brushes, he heard the Malshorne directing Braig to retrieve a large glass jar from a high cupboard.

There was something most disquieting about the way Braig responded so eagerly to the request, and his deferential reply, 'Yes, T'al Credé.' Ash felt a shiver at the base of his neck when he saw Credé's reaction; those thin lips curling into an unnatural smile, the expression sitting oddly with his cold, unreadable eyes.

The huge square-edged jar had a thick cork that Braig had to prise out with his thumbs. The jar contained a fine crystalline power with a powerful odour, like pine needles. The Malshorne instructed Braig to sprinkle the contents evenly across the dark triangle. Then, when it was spread to his satisfaction, he released them from his service, giving another disturbing smile and patting Braig on the shoulder.

Ash frowned deeply at his friend's words.

'Thank you, T'al Credé.'

Whatever Braig's secret was, it fuelled an exuberant charge down the mountain path. Ash followed his hurtling progress as quickly as he dared, but was afraid of losing his footing on the steep muddy track. When he did manage to catch up, he grabbed at Braig's shirt.

'Braig! Stop!'

Braig whirled around, his brown eyes dancing with excitement.

'By Telion!' Ash gasped, and bent double, holding the stitch that stabbed in his side. When he could breathe, he studied his friend's beaming face. 'What was all that about? "Thank you, T'al Credé",' he mimicked. 'What have you got to thank him for? What's got into you?'

Braig reached out his arms and held Ash firmly by his shoulders. 'It's the quest, Ash! The quest,' he said solemnly.

'Right. I figured it might be.' Ash was struggling to keep the annoyance from his voice. 'Come on, then. Let me in on the big secret.'

Braig laughed. 'It is the best secret, Ash.' He flung out his arms. 'It's the slaves! The quest is to free the slaves!'

'Which slaves?' asked Ash stupidly.

'All of the slaves. You and me. And all of the others. And Kep!' Braig beamed. 'Don't you see? She'll be free — she won't be herati after all. We'll *all* be free!'

'But how?'

'I don't know. But that's why I have to find him — T'al Jazure.'

'But how's he going to free them?' repeated Ash dully.

'I don't know, but that's what Credé told me: T'al Jazure has the power to free the slaves! Those were his words.'

'Unbelievable,' said Ash, dazed.

There was no time to talk further. The twilight bell would soon ring out across the city, calling the slaves to evening service and the free-folk to their prayers and dressing rooms. The Feyindi kitchens would already be frantic with activity; if Ash was to avoid a beating, they would have to hurry.

They strode along, each absorbed by their thoughts.

Ash's mood alternated between one of disbelief and faltering joy. What if it were true? How could it be true?

Braig's expression had settled into one of calm determination. His earlier ecstasy seemed to have been absorbed into his body, and now revealed itself only in the way he held himself. He strode confidently with his head high and his eyes clear. He seemed to know his purpose now, and apparently that was enough.

On any other day, with their slaves' instinct for trouble, at least one of the boys would have seen the figure that skulked in a doorway and turned away on their approach. But they were preoccupied with doubts, and desires, and dreams of freedom. They didn't notice how the shape slipped from the shadows once they had passed and kept pace with them, always just a little behind. They stopped briefly at the point where their ways forked, but nothing was said. There was no time, and besides, it was too incredible for words. They just nodded and parted. Neither felt the stare of the one who was watching, and waiting.

Chapter 8

AMBUSH

The afternoon that would change everything began normally — or rather, no less strangely than any other. Ash hadn't been able to stop thinking about Tarlyn, and was anxious to see whether she had survived the night. Credé's violence towards the creature still sickened Ash. Why in the world would he keep a pet he so obviously hates?

'I wonder if Tarlyn eats butterflies,' he said out loud, watching one flit by.

'What? Oh. Yeah, probably.' Braig chuckled. 'Why? Did you catch one?'

'No. But there were giant weevils in the grain store, and I caught a nice fat cricket last night in the latrines.'

'How are you managing to keep that in your pocket? Did you squash it?'

'No, I wrapped it in a scrap of cotton.'

Braig grunted his approval as they walked on.

Ash still didn't know what to think about the quest. He wanted to believe what Braig had said, desperately, but … free the slaves? It seemed so unlikely. And there was something horribly unwholesome about the Malshorne. He just knew it. Every time he tried to picture Credé in his head, he failed. He couldn't remember the colour of his hair nor the shape of his face from one visit to the next. It was uncanny. He wondered whether Braig had noticed how the Malshorne's eyes changed colour. Probably not. But he knew one thing for certain after yesterday's violence: Credé despised him.

He glanced nervously at his friend, for a friend he now was. 'So … do you think it's going to be all right today?' he asked quietly.

Braig smiled a gently serious sort of smile, then put a hand on Ash's shoulder. 'It's going to be fine, Ash. Stop worrying. I know what I have to do now, and I'm going to do it. And then we'll never have to serve anyone again. None of us!'

Ash nodded and bit his tongue.

❦

To their relief, Credé was in better spirits. When Braig managed the first line of the Song without error, the Malshorne leaned back in his chair and aligned his fingertips. 'Excellent, my lad. Again!' Braig glowed under the praise, and so the lesson continued, echo by echo, line by painful line. Maybe it *was* going to be all right.

Ash relaxed a bit, and turned his attention back to the odd triangle. The powder had darkened overnight and seemed to have dissolved the remaining filth. He swept it clear, then began buffing. The more the surface shone, the deeper the reflections became, until he had the strangest sensation he was suspended above a glassy lake. The shadows below the surface seemed to move independently of the movements in the hut, as if there was a tantalising world in the depths, just out of reach — like a dream at the edge of consciousness.

'Wood! More wood!'

Ash jumped, startled from his reverie. This was his chance to relieve his pockets of several giant weevils and one large cricket. Under the guise of selecting suitable logs, he deposited the weevils into the same gap as before. Then he gave the pocket with the cricket in it a quick slap and sent the stunned insect the same way. He was rewarded almost immediately by the unmistakable sound of something stirring. He hid a smile, as he took the logs over to the fire, then returned to his work.

Ash was astounded when Braig managed to sing through an entire verse at the first attempt, but he was even more stunned by the transformation he himself had managed to work on the black triangle. It really did shine like glass. He was just giving the edge a final buff when the Malshorne hobbled over to inspect his progress. Credé moved slowly, wheezing and coughing. The lesson had clearly taxed his energies, but when he saw how the mirrored surface gleamed he stood up straighter and smiled. Ash shivered. He looked precisely as if he was he were about to bite the head off something innocent.

'Excellent.' The Malshorne gave Ash a cursory glance, then waved a hand in dismissal: 'You are no longer required.'

⁂

'I bet you're thrilled!' Braig puffed. 'No more creepy Credé for you! Not much of that song left either, I reckon. And I'll knock that off in no time.'

Braig was positively swaggering — any doubts he might once have had seemed to have vanished entirely.

'Yeah. Thrilled.' Ash felt strangely miserable. *No longer required.* They were precisely the words he had longed to hear, the words that freed him from the Malshorne's service. But now he would never hear the end of the Song, and something deep inside him ached at that realisation.

As they reached the graveyard, Braig fished a parcel from his tunic. 'Look. This one's bigger.' As usual it was tied with red twine and sealed with a large button of imprinted wax. 'What's in it, do you think?' he asked Ash for what seemed like the hundredth time.

'I don't know. What does it matter?' scowled Ash, scuffing his feet.

'Guess we'll never know.' Braig shrugged cheerfully. 'Reckon you can take a turn at delivery boy, though. I had to wait hours for ol' Lendri last time.' He tossed it high into the air and Ash stuck out his hand, but he missed. Braig gave a delighted hoot, then tousled Ash's hair as he leaned to pick it up.

'Get off!'

Braig just grinned. 'Cheer up, Ash.' He clapped him hard on the shoulder. 'If we hurry, we might catch a game of pilat.'

Ash scowled, but the thought of pilat was cheering. So when Braig shouted a challenge — 'Race you to the square!' — he put on a spurt.

He caught Braig as they rounded the corner, and together they hared through the cobbled alleyways.

At full pelt, the boys had no chance of spotting the tripwire. One moment they were running, the next they were sprawled, groaning on the ground. Ash clutched his knee and cried out, fearing he had broken something. But after a moment of agony, the pain subsided. It was badly skinned, but otherwise intact.

Braig sat rubbing his shoulder. 'What by the dogs of Argess was that?'

'That,' said a voice, 'was payback.'

Three figures appeared from behind a crumbling rampart. Feld tossed back his hair. Behind him were two of the Moagli thugs they had encountered before. The boy called Hob was missing.

'I've been asking around,' snarled Feld. 'Turns out there's no such thing as a gnarkin beast.'

Braig and Ash exchanged a quick look.

'Problem is: I don't like being made a fool of.' And before the boys could get to their feet, Feld gave his command: 'Get 'em!'

Battle erupted, the two larger boys launching themselves at Braig. One threw an arm around Braig's shoulders, trying to wrestle him off his feet, but Braig was too strong. Putting his head down, he thrust forward and upwards. The boy reeled and lost his balance, but the second thug was on Braig in a moment, fists flying.

Ash rolled away from the whirling scuffle, struggling to his feet and coming face-to-face with Feld.

'I've been looking forward to this, Weed.'

Feld lashed out with his fists, but Ash ducked, just in time. No time to think — he just reacted. His counterpunch whipped out, catching Feld's cheekbone. Just a glance. Enough to make his knuckles burn, nothing more. They circled. And circled some more. Then Feld feinted with his right, swiping with his left. Taking the blow hard on his jaw, Ash's head snapped back and he staggered. Before he could right himself, Feld was upon him, punching hard into his stomach in a vicious flurry. Ash gasped as the air was knocked out of him.

The world whirled, but Ash knew he must stay on his feet. In an act of pure desperation, he launched sideways, trying to spin out of Feld's reach. He was partially successful, and somehow, as they locked bodies in a fresh grapple, he managed to bring his elbow up sharply into the ribs of his attacker. Feld grunted and folded in pain. Pushing his advantage, Ash smashed his left hand upwards. It was not powerful, but it made good contact. He felt soft flesh yielding. Feld staggered back, blood streaming from his nose, mad fury in his eyes for a split second. Then something flashed. Gleaming steel arcing through the air. Ash froze.

'Surprised, Weed?'

Laughing and brandishing the knife, Feld's poise was restored. Ignoring his gushing nose, he advanced with small jabbing motions as Ash backed away.

'Let's see your fancy knife-work, then,' Feld snarled. 'What? No knife?' He feigned disbelief. The blade slashed the air. 'Well, there's a surprise.' Feld's face twisted into an ugly sneer. Ash knew his only hope was to disarm his assailant. He heard a crack and a sharp animal cry over to his left, but kept his eyes fixed on the swishing blade.

Suddenly Feld danced forward and jabbed. Ash leaned back, ducking the stroke, but the cobbles were loose; his arms flailed and his feet shot from beneath him. Sprawled flat on broken rubble, he was helpless. Almost immediately the knife was at his throat. Looking into Feld's eyes, he expected no mercy.

By now Braig was down to one opponent, and one arm. He had knocked the larger of the two Moagli thugs to the ground for the third time, and this time he didn't get up. But Braig had paid heavily. His left arm hung limp. His mouth bled freely. One eye was closing to a swollen slit. Fortunately, the boy coming at him was losing enthusiasm, and when his mate on the ground groaned and spat blood, he looked even more hesitant. Braig roared and attacked. Ducking his shoulder, he charged. The other boy swung and missed, his fist whistling over the top of Braig's head. When he turned, unbalanced, his face met with a large fist. His eyes rolled back and he collapsed. Braig spun around to see Feld crouching over Ash and sprang to his friend's aid.

Ash had just felt the knife nick his throat, when all at once a huge forearm swept in from nowhere. Under different circumstances Ash might have laughed out loud at the surprise in Feld's eyes when he was plucked backwards. But the torrent of relief was followed swiftly by a jolt of dread. He squeaked a warning.

'Braig! He's got a knife!' He stumbled to his feet. 'He's got a knife!'

The wrestling pair had tumbled against a low stone wall, Braig still hooking Feld's neck with his good arm. For a moment they continued to struggle, then Feld gave a sudden violent squirm. Braig's eyes flew wide with shock. His opponent dropped away. Ash froze, stupefied. The scene was so terrible he felt his eyes would never draw away from it. It was as if Telion, keeper of time, was holding a mighty breath, suspending the moment. Time ached. Then came a sudden release: Braig exhaled and slumped onto stone. As Ash leapt forward, Feld let out a strangled cry and fled.

Ash was only vaguely aware of the retreating Moagli boys — all of his focus was on Braig.

'He had a knife.' Braig's eyes flitted to and fro.

'I know. I tried to warn you.' Ash felt his voice crack. He stared at the hilt that rose and fell incongruously in his friend's chest. A dark stain was spreading rapidly, soaking Braig's tunic. Ash felt his own chest tighten.

'It'll be fine. You'll be fine.'

Braig gave a weak smile. 'No, Ash. It's bad.'

'You'll be all right.' Ash grasped his hand. The knuckles were raw and swollen. He felt hot tears rising. His stomach cramped in panic.

Braig's eyes closed, then flickered open again. 'Ash. You have to promise.' He had begun to shiver in a horrible, jittery way. Ash looked about, senselessly, hoping for something to keep his friend warm. It was futile. The alley was bare. Just ruined stonework.

'Ash?' Braig's face was so white. Even the afternoon sun couldn't lend it colour.

'I'm here.' Ash could barely speak through his contracting throat. He couldn't help the tears; they spilled down his face and ran into the corners of his mouth.

'Promise.'

'Anything,' he croaked.

'The quest, Ash.'

Ash bowed his head as Braig's fingers tightened on his hand.

'Please, Ash.' His breath rasped. 'You have to take it. Take the Taelstone to T'al Jazure so he can free the slaves. Promise? For me. For Kep.'

Ash lifted his head. Braig seemed to be staring through him.

'For Kep.' His words came weakly.

Through a blur of tears, Ash saw his friend's eyes dim and close.

'I promise!' he blurted. 'I promise.'

Braig didn't open his eyes again, but, with a final effort, he gave one last smile. It hovered feebly on his mouth, then died.

Ash didn't know how long he sat huddled next to Braig's body. It felt like a long time certainly. Who knows how much longer he would have stayed if he hadn't been disturbed. When he heard footsteps he knew he should run, but he just didn't have the heart. The cloaked shape was swiftly upon him. He caught a waft of musky perfume. It was a woman. She gave a quiet, startled cry, then crouched, taking in the wound and the weapon. Her voice was low and urgent.

'Guardians are coming. You must run!' She didn't lower her hood, but he caught a glimpse of dark lashes and the flash of her eyes.

'Run, fool!'

Shaken from his stupor, Ash heard the sound of heavy boots. At last, ignoring the pain in his body and in his heart, he stumbled blindly and ran.

Chapter 9

THE TABLE OF ARANTI

The dinner in honour of young Tindelfion Aranti was to be an occasion of high pomp and ceremony — an orchestrated expression of Aranti influence. The room was decorated especially. Great lengths of green fabric had been pinned to the rafters, creating shimmering cascades that fell into pools of silken opulence on the polished floors. Tall green candles in silver sheaths stood in clusters down the middle of the table, alternating with glass bowls of floating lilies. Portraits which usually sulked in dim corridors had been reinstated, so as to surround the guests with Aranti ancestry. The most recent, a huge gilt-framed affair, boasted a full-length depiction of Maliagne Aranti. The painter had captured the essence of the man admirably. Anyone who knew Aranti recognised the sharp light of ambition in those black eyes, and the thin, cruel quality that hovered about the mouth.

Kep hated the way his painted gaze seemed to follow her around the room. She was trying to give her full attention to the Master of the Table, a scurrying mouse of a man with sharp eyes and fluffy eyebrows. He was briefing them in the strictest terms. 'Nothing, but nothing, must mar the honour of Aranti tonight,' he squeaked. Kep nodded dutifully with the others, but her eyes kept straying to the runners' door. Surely Braig would have returned by now?

'Sauce! Sauce!'

Kep earned herself a glare of displeasure from Lady Aranti for her inattentiveness as she stepped forward and poured sauce. Almost immediately Capricia Aranti clapped her chubby hands and declared that 'the relish' (made by the hands of the hostess herself) would be passed, so Kep swapped her jug of sauce for a silver dish with startling red contents. She moved down the table, carefully doling out spoonfuls.

As she approached Mascellion Feyindi, she gritted her teeth. His ample girth was swathed in a flamboyant splendour of fine cloth, silken scarves and gold chains. A shining jewel trembled from one ear. He was mid-sentence and she saw her chance to slip past, but he looked up and, reaching for the dish, trapped her fingers beneath his. 'Utterly delectable, I'm sure.' His eyes bulged, bloodshot and leery from beneath their lids. Kep felt herself blushing, resisting the urge to pull away as he ran a greedy tongue over his fleshy lips. Instead, she set her jaw and fixed her eyes on one of the portraits. The framed woman with grey hair stared back disapprovingly — forever haughty, despite being long since dead.

Mascellion Feyindi had no particular love of relish, but, while Capricia Aranti might be a fool, her husband was a man to keep close — and by any means possible. Therefore, eat relish one must. He sighed. The slave girl was so much more to his taste. He let her escape, for now, then winked at his nephew across the table. 'Delicious.'

Analouie and his wife looked as if they had swallowed something unpleasant. Mascellion smiled rakishly — they did so provoke his taste for mischief.

'Analouie, my boy, tell me this. Wherever does Aranti find such gorgeous wenches? What luscious curves, eh?'

'I did not notice.'

'You know some of the slaves one encounters at the table are positively gruesome. And so flat-chested ...' Mascellion looked pointedly at Marlashetta's bony front. 'It's enough to put one off one's meal. Valentio Bardon has a girl with a great hairy wart on her face. How she ever got through the Orlion testing, I don't know. Still ... perhaps the wart came later.' He tasted the relish mid-sentence and grimaced. It was sour and thin, just like Marlashetta. 'Of course you avoid the problem by favouring boys, don't you? Such a pity.' He wiped a dribble from his chin. 'A real man needs lush, fresh young bodies to look at, you know. Keeps him virile.'

Marlashetta's downturned mouth was pursed tight, creating deep cuts at the corners, making her look even more like a fish than usual. Mascellion smiled triumphantly and lifted his glass.

Analouie was chewing his food as if it was gravel, poor boy.

'How was Idira as you left it, Uncle?'

At the mention of the name, the elegant woman opposite them abandoned her own conversation and leaned across. 'Idira! Do tell us, Mascellion. I would love news of Idira! Are the shipments in danger? Surely the rumours cannot be true?'

Mascellion shifted his corpulence, making the chair groan. 'Well, Anatha, my dear, rumours always run on ahead of the facts you know. Yet, in some part, the fears are well-founded.' He waved his fork dramatically, mostly to annoy Marlashetta. 'It's true, the Idirans have been hard-pushed to keep their northern border secure. Brigands of plains-men have been making incursions in greater numbers.' Mascellion paused as plates were replaced with huge platters of cheese and fruit.

'And the talk of pirates?'

He considered the question. It wouldn't do to frighten the ladies with ghastly tales, not at Aranti's table. Better stick to the facts. 'Alas, they, too, are more daring of late. Three ships boarded and sunk during the past turn of Eldar.'

'We live in violent and uncertain times.' Serenitia Moagli joined the conversation smoothly, her voice low and oily. 'Even in Mildaresh our guardians find it difficult to maintain order.'

'Nonsense, Serenitia,' snapped Marlashetta Feyindi immediately, 'Our guardians are fully in control.'

'Perhaps. But the citizens need further protection — in such troubled times.'

Lady Feyindi arched her brows, and replied acidly, 'If you're making hints about your so-called Cadet Squad again, you are sorely misguided. The Senate will never mandate private vigilante groups.'

'And since when did Marlashetta Feyindi become the voice of the Senate?' drawled Serenitia, her eyes dangerous.

It was a classic Feyindi–Moagli standoff, with every chance of becoming a full-blown scene. Mascellion toyed with the idea of letting it run; it could be fun. But he caught the desperation in his nephew's eye, and their host was inclining his head in their direction, too. 'Well, I'll tell you one piece of excellent news. If it's slaves you're after, then Idira is the very place. It's awash with slave flesh.'

Analouie seized the offering with a gratitude that bordered on the pathetic. 'Indeed, Uncle? Well, well! Now might be the time to invest in new labour, then. What do you think, Serenitia? Will you be re-stocking?'

Kep's duty during the cheese course was to serve tall goblets of warm mead. She didn't dare take her attention off the tray. As she moved down the table the conversation was buzzing with talk of slaves.

'Well, I simply don't care for slaves of conflict. Won't have them in the house.'

'Quite so. Our Eerok are much more trustworthy.'

'If I was to invest in a wild batch it'd be straight off to the noikos fields with them, no discussion.'

'Yes. That's one good thing about the Calkinon conflict — fresh slaves for the fields.'

'It's a sacred bond, you see. The Eerok know their place. I daresay many grow to love their owning families.'

Kep glanced at the speaker of this last comment — she obviously had no inkling what it was like to serve Capricia Aranti and her hard-mouthed husband. Then, at last, she caught the eye of the runner on his return from the kitchens. He just shrugged his shoulders: still no sign. Where was Braig? A cold knot of worry was starting to tighten in her stomach.

Kep had avoided Mascellion Feyindi as much as possible during the feast, but now she had no choice but to clear the platter in front of him. She held her breath and tried not to look at his bald, sweating head. Fortunately, as she reached for the dish, he was suddenly distracted.

'Now there's a slave for you,' he murmured salaciously. Every head turned as Matapharni entered the room. A slave Matapharni might be, but no one would ever guess that from her bearing, as she glided towards her master, drawing every eye.

Some guests gasped at the complete disregard of protocol; the herati never made an appearance until the last course had been cleared. Others gaped at Matapharni's stunning beauty, and strained to catch a glimpse of her bare feet, which, the gossips insisted, she only ever dressed in precious jewels. The guests whispered, taking in the emeralds at her throat, her plunging neckline and the sparkling green gown that clung to her curves and flared tail-like behind her. Had there ever been such loveliness; such elegance; such a disgraceful display?

Matapharni even dared to rest her hand on Aranti's shoulder as she murmured in his ear. Whatever her message, it caused her master to rise at once from the table and draw her aside. His guests exchanged looks. Tonight Aranti's son, Tindelfion, was to dedicate his tapestry to the gods and the city. He would be livid should anything disrupt the rites.

When their host returned to his place, an expectant hush fell.

'Continue your meals, I implore you.' Aranti held up his hands, palms outwards. 'It was merely a household matter. Wholly insignificant.'

He shot the Master of the Table a black look: 'I believe we are now to enjoy a cleansing broth. After which, my son Tindelfion will reveal his extraordinary work of history and scholarship.'

As he took his seat, Kep hastened to make room for soup bowls. This time there was no avoiding Mascellion Feyindi — he reached out and grasped her wrist. His wet mouth slobbered, 'Bring another a flagon, there's a good girl. Can't be expected to drink thin soup and listen to history without a little something to take the edge off.'

Tindelfion Aranti's defence of his tapestry would long be remembered. His presentation was long-winded, pompous and entirely unoriginal. Yet by the following morning Tindelfion's place in history was secure — he was known thereafter as the young man who managed to bore Mascellion Feyindi to death. Most of the guests had slipped into a state of stupor early during the speech, but everyone suddenly snapped to attention when Mascellion rose from his chair with a terrible groan. He clutched at the tablecloth, sending glasses flying and splashing the closest guests with wine. Locking eyes with the dumbstruck speaker, he seemed about to speak — then he fell. His soft bulk collapsed almost gracefully onto the floor, but there was nothing graceful about the sickening crack of his head smashing onto polished marble.

Those close enough to see the dead man's eyes threw back their chairs; many screamed involuntarily.

'Poison! He's been poisoned. Mark my words!' announced Serenitia Moagli loudly.

'Poison!' The word was repeated down the length of the table.

The guests clutched at their throats. Was it the soup? Or the wine? The collapse of two ladies into a faint did nothing to quash the general state of panic.

But Maliagne Aranti at once took command. 'Please, do not alarm yourselves! There is no danger.' He gestured to the guards who had leapt forward from their posts. 'My guards will make you comfortable in the adjoining room until the matter is investigated.'

The doors were swung wide and, rather unceremoniously, the shaken guests were herded out.

Lord Aranti glowered darkly. 'You! Guard! Go to the infirmary, find Matapharni and bring her here. And you,' — Aranti seized the Master of the Table by the collar and said through gritted teeth — 'send me the slave who served this wine!'

Kep trembled as her master poured from the suspect flagon. His black eyes seemed to bore into her as he passed her the glass. 'Drink!' he commanded.

Analouie Feyindi was watching on, his arms folded, mouth grim.

Knowing that hesitation would only confirm her guilt, Kep took a quick gulp. Then she gasped. The wine's burning acidity was so unexpected! It seared her windpipe, making her eyes stream. She choked and spluttered, clutching at her throat. Exchanging looks of horror, the two men leapt to the obvious conclusion.

'Guards!'

But, as the guards drew their swords, someone else spoke.

'Ignore the girl. It wasn't poison.'

The men whirled: 'What?'

Matapharni was crouched by the body. She had changed her dazzling gown for a white smock covered with a long apron.

'It was his heart.'

'Can you be certain?'

The woman rose. 'There is no doubt.'

To Kep's relief, Matapharni's authority seemed to be accepted without question, and attention shifted to the colourful mound that had been Feyindi's uncle. Kep hovered uncertainly for a while, then, since nobody seemed about to dismiss her, she crouched to collect splinters of broken glass.

Lord Aranti was speaking in that smooth, assured way of his. 'The House of Aranti offers sincere sympathy for your loss.' He gave a slight bow. 'Please, allow us to ... accommodate ... your uncle until ... Well, until appropriate arrangements can be made.' He coughed delicately. Everybody was thinking the same thing: a body of such a size would take some moving.

Feyindi replied somewhat tersely. 'I will inform my wife of your kindness.'

Aranti gave a knowing smile. 'I'm sure she will suffer greatly by the loss.'

'Indeed.' Feyindi bowed smartly, then turned on his heel and strode from the room.

Apparently forgotten, Kep stayed on her knees, piling the broken glass onto a tray as quietly as she could. Her throat was still stinging from the wine, and she felt sick with shock.

Maliagne Aranti turned to Matapharni. Although the pair kept their voices low, their conversation carried clearly across the room. 'So, my beauty. What shall we do with this mess?' Aranti seemed entirely calm about the situation; in fact, he actually yawned. He moved to a cabinet and plucked the stopper from a tall, square decanter. 'The celebration must go on, of course. Shall he be put in the infirmary?'

'No,' Matapharni demurred. 'There's a small storage room on this level. It will be easier to move him there.'

Aranti nodded. 'So be it, my lovely. Sage advice as always.' He selected a glass and poured golden brandy. 'It is most unfortunate that the old goat should die here, at my table. It reflects so poorly upon the glory of the House. And tonight of all nights. Poor Tindelfion.' He shook his head with a fond smile, then frowned. 'But what of the earlier matter? What of the young slave?'

Kep started at the words. Her stomach gave an ugly sort of flip. Matapharni paused for what seemed an eternity. Kep could hear the blood pounding in her ears. Then the woman answered coolly: 'He's dead. The blood loss was too great.'

Kep willed herself to breathe. It seemed as if the room had gone suddenly dim.

'A pity. And at harvest time, too.' Aranti raised his glass halfway to his lips. 'Still, with every loss comes opportunity,' he added thoughtfully. He took a deliberate sip and studied the swirling liquid in his glass. Then his lips parted. He held up a finger. 'Ah! … Yes, I have it. The slave will be presented to Lord Feyindi for burial with his uncle!' He chuckled quietly, 'And thus,' he announced with a flourish, 'thus shall the generosity of the House of Aranti be extended even into the After itself.' He raised his glass to the portrait of himself and smirked. 'Prepare the body as a gift to the House of Feyindi.'

Kep reeled at the woman's quiet reply. 'As you please, my lord.'

Chapter 10

FUNERAL PREPARATIONS

The Feyindi kitchens anticipated dawn in a frantic rush. The fires were stoked high and every clear-lamp was lit. The wooden benches were stacked high with vegetables that threatened to spill to the floor. Lids jittered on their pots. One table was dominated by a huge jumble of game, where a slave was removing the fine pelt from a hare. Her Second, a small girl not long out of the Holding, was tackling a row of gleaming trout, stuffing herbs into their bellies with tiny fingers, and rubbing sleepy eyes with her sleeve. In the fireplace, the heat-singed bristles of the roasting hog added an acrid stench to more pleasing aromas. A hot-faced woman gave her dough a final punch, hefted it into a large bowl and set it aside with a thump. The contents of other bowls were already swelling, like softly growing mushrooms.

The Head of the Kitchens rested floury hands on her great haunches as a battering at the service door announced yet another delivery. The tributes were piling up — literally — but all must be treated with the utmost respect and displayed on the high table. Somewhere among the confusion were ten brace of partridges from the House of Skagali, a great barrel of mead from the House of Moagli, and six crates of arkenpears from the Lendri orchards. And Lord Aranti's gift hadn't even arrived! No doubt it would be some ostentatious delicacy requiring special attention.

The Head of the Kitchens was inspecting the latest offer, a crate of snapping black lobsters, when she spied the gamekeeper attempting to sneak past the window. At once she charged out of the door bellowing: 'Pheasants! Where are my pheasants?'

Her Second scowled too, casting about: 'And where's that damn boy with the milk?'

⁂

Jem, the pastry maid who had been directly in the line of fire, found Ash in a back workroom, dozing over the half-plucked goose in his lap. At the sound of her alarm, he sprang to his feet, sending feathers whirling. Jem stood back, clicking her tongue at the mess.

'Ash! They're calling for the milk. Hurry and get brushed down.' She picked up two geese by their prickled necks. 'We'll take these for a start. You can finish the others when you've done the dairy run.' He swayed, uncertain on his feet. 'Ash! Stop acting like a Blue! Here, get that apron off.' She helped slap the feathers from his back, then led him to the kitchens.

Ash followed, silently accepting her help. He had collected the pails, and was trying to slip out unobtrusively when the Head of the Kitchens barged back through the door. The noisy kitchen suddenly fell completely silent at the expression on her face. Although it hardly seemed possible, she looked quite pale — it even seemed she might even be about to faint.

'Het? Whatever has happened?' the second cook clucked nervously. 'Here now,' she fussed. 'Sit yourself down. You look as if you might fall.' She put out a hand, but the huge woman brushed her off. 'It's that slave. The dead Aranti boy,' she said slowly. 'A sorry affair. Some sort of street fight.'

Puzzled looks were exchanged. It wasn't unusual; slaves often died from one mishap or another.

'Go on,' she was coaxed.

Her next words came unwillingly, and she had to stop to clear her throat, 'He ... he's to be Aranti's gift to Lord Feyindi, in honour of his uncle's passing.'

There was a terrible moment of silence before the little girl with the trout gave a terrified moan and burst into tears. She thought the boy was about to be cooked and served at the table with the other gifts. But that wasn't to be his fate — it was even more appalling.

The Head of the Kitchens nodded grimly at her horrified audience. 'He's to share Feyindi's fire of passing. There will be no bird to guide his soul to the After — he'll be bonded in servitude to Mascellion Feyindi for all eternity.'

✳

Don't think! Just don't think.

Ash burst through the gate, leaving the gatekeeper grumbling. Careering headlong towards the dairies, milk pails clattering, he raced across the knobbly bridge at Fell creek, *just don't think,* and tore along alleyways. By the time he reached the broad streets of the city centre, the sun was touching the tops of the buildings, just lightly, caressing her favourites. First to catch the light were the windows of the Skagali villa, glinting on the hill. Then the wide rows of the Foundation's windows winked back. *Don't think. Don't think.* By the time the fingers of light touched the towers of the priesthood, Ash was approaching the Great Centre. Finally, he dropped the pails and bent over, hands on his knees.

Over his own harsh panting he could hear the sharp crack of whips, and the rumble of wagons. He couldn't avoid the centre; there was no time to take the longer route via the slave markets. Retrieving the pails, he took a deep breath. He continued on with his eyes down, desperately trying to avoid looking towards the funeral pyre, but that nearly caused him to crash headfirst into a team of Blues. They halted in their tracks, eyes blank, stained mouths slack. Ash felt a bewildering surge of pity and revulsion.

'Sorry. Sorry.'

'Hey. Watch where you're going, lad!'

Cracking his whip, the Blues' herder broke through the dishevelled line. They staggered back into their places. 'These things aren't easy to drive, ya know!' He screwed up his bulbous face and gave Ash a wink before pushing them on.

Teams of carpenters were busy erecting the staged triangular platform. They moved with the intense purpose of their role. The slightest inaccuracy in its alignment with the three temples might hinder the flight of the souls into the After, or, worse, leave them stranded in the Midway. While Blues unloaded wagons of firewood, other less witless workers stacked the fuel beneath the growing structure. A priest flapped from a door in the temple of Argess, and joined his fellows at the edge of the works. It was fortunate Ash couldn't overhear their argument. The supervision of this particular pyre was proving a challenge. It was long years since a slave had been dedicated: it had been necessary to consult texts dating back to the founding of the city, and there was disagreement about the interpretation of the archaic diagrams. Just where should the body of the slave be placed?

Ash hurried through the quiet streets of the Salturne sector and took the uneven path to the dairy. Below, he could make out the slow forms of kattlen and hear their low, mournful calls. He looked for Kep's curly head, torn between his urgent desire to see her and his shame.

How could he look into Kep's eyes and confess that Braig fell defending a pathetic weakling who couldn't even stay on his feet in a fight? How could he tell her that the last word on Braig's lips was her name, and that he himself had made a ridiculous promise he had no chance of keeping?

At last he spotted the flock of bug-eyes under a low-spreading tree. His stomach lurched, and he swallowed hard as he approached. To his surprise it wasn't Kep milking them, but Pan, her Second. The boy looked up with a warning in his eyes.

'Crouch down,' he murmured. 'They're not used to me milking them without Kep. They could bolt.'

The jumpy creatures rolled their crazy eyes, but they had seen Ash most mornings and didn't think he was much to worry about. They soon returned to their grazing. They could talk, so long as they kept their voices low and calm.

Pan maintained a gentle rhythm, his cheek against the doe's flank. 'So, you've heard?'

Ash nodded weakly.

'It's sick. Imagine being enslaved in the After as well as this world.' Pan scowled. 'I hate Aranti.'

The doe rumbled a note of alarm, and Pan instantly stopped milking. He placed his hands gently against her sides and cooed, exactly as Kep would. Ash felt his heart wrench.

'I'd better go.'

Pan lifted his chin to signal agreement.

'Umm ... Where's Kep?'

'Last I saw her, she was chasing birds out of the creamery.' The boy's lip trembled. 'She's taking it badly ...'

Ash tried to swallow the lump in his own throat with no success.

'Yeah.'

❧

Back at the villa, Ash stared blankly at the half-plucked goose. Noon was drawing near, and his whole body rebelled at the thought. He was on his own; Braig wouldn't be waiting, grinning and joking. He slid to the floor and groaned, nursing his head in his hands. He had to make a decision, but his mind was whirling. *You are no longer required.* That's right, I'm no longer required. I've done my bit. The Malshorne isn't expecting me. He's expecting Braig. *Promise? Ash?* Yes … I made a promise, but it's no good. I'm not the Chosen One. I'm just a kitchen slave. *The Taelstaun must go to T'al Jazure.* How would I even find T'al Jazure? I can't even fight. *He's got a knife!* Braig's face was suspended in his memory, horribly pale and astonished. *Guardians are coming! You must run!* I can't do this. T'al Credé hates me. He's not going to send me on any quest. *You have to take the Taelstone to T'al Jazure so he can free the slaves.* He saw Braig's pale face again, remembered how his hands had trembled, how his lips had moved. *Bonded in servitude for all eternity.* He remembered the terrible knocking of the hammers at the funeral pyre. *She's taking it badly* … Then Braig's eyes, brown and earnest. *Promise. For me. For Kep.* At last Ash lifted his head. He took a deep breath. Noon was approaching, but the decision had been made.

Chapter 11

THE SONG PASSES

The curled black door-knocker fell with a thud.

The Malshorne wasn't dressed in his usual robes, but in a long, white tunic edged with gold trim. His silver hair flowed about his shoulders, and his eyes were unnaturally bright and expectant. His expression changed swiftly, however, when his eyes fell upon Ash.

'I told you,' he spat, 'you are not required.' He squinted down the sunlit path. 'Where is the other boy?'

Somehow Ash managed a reply. 'He is dead, T'al Credé.'

'Dead? How can the Chosen One be dead? Don't lie!'

'I'm not lying.' Ash wished with all his heart that he was. 'He is dead,' he repeated numbly. The Malshorne grasped Ash by the chin and looked full into his face. Then he released him. 'Then all is lost,' he uttered flatly. And that was all. Without another word, he turned and hobbled back inside.

It took Ash a long while to summon his courage, but he had sworn to fulfil his promise, at least until it was proven hopeless. He crept over the threshold and cleared his throat. Credé was crumpled against the nearest bookshelf, one hand cast over his eyes.

Ash couldn't think what to say, then at last he stammered: 'T'al Credé, I can sing the Song.'

The Malshorne waved him away. 'Be gone, boy. There is no time to teach you, even if I had the strength.'

Ash stood still, unsure what to do next. Then suddenly he knew there was only one thing he could do. He swallowed his apprehension and began to sing. The notes splashed like drops of light into the gloom of the hut. Credé lifted his head. Somehow Ash kept singing — only when the first verse was done did he stop. There was an excruciating silence until Credé spoke again.

'Can you sing the rest, boy?'

'Yes. Well, except the missing line.' When the Malshorne arched an eyebrow at him, he added, 'I've ... I've been sort of helping Braig.'

'And what makes you think there is a line missing?'

Ash stuttered. 'I don't know.' He honestly couldn't think why he had said that. He'd just panicked he supposed.

The expression on the Malshorne's face was unreadable. Ash couldn't tell whether he was alarmed, relieved or infuriated. Finally he lifted his chin and stabbed a finger at Ash. 'You, are not Eerok.' He looked as if he had swallowed something distasteful. 'I knew as much when I first laid eyes on you.'

Ash blinked, utterly mystified, but he didn't dare question the odd declaration.

Credé turned his back and brooded for what seemed like an age. When he turned back, his expression was as unfathomable as ever. 'We will try,' he announced.

The room was arranged according to precise instructions. The windows were shuttered; the only light came from the embers of the fire. The Taelstone was set upon the gleaming triangle, just inside one point. It glowed: a lustrous pearl floating on a black lake.

'Good. Only one thing remains.'

Credé took a crystalline box from one of the window sills. Of all the peculiar items Ash had seen in the Malshorne's hut, the thing in the cube had to be the oddest. It looked like a small spiky star with many points. It glistened as if wet.

'This is a dopple-star.' Credé tipped it from the box, examined its edges, then, with a sharp twist, split it into two. The stars flared brightly. He swiftly cast one into the air. Ash gasped as it disappeared through the roof. Credé shut the other star in the cube, where it glowed fiercely inside its crystal prison. 'Extraordinary things, dopple-stars. They do not obey the physical laws of this world. The one I threw will circle its twin indefinitely until such time as they are re-united, or die. The energy created by its orbit has created a shield around this place. We will not be disturbed.' He paused, then added coldly, 'Nothing can get in — and nothing can get out.'

The observation sent a shudder down Ash's spine.

'Take off your boots.'

It seemed an odd request, but Ash obeyed. The Malshorne's thin feet were already bare. He hobbled onto the triangle at the point nearest the fire and motioned for Ash to occupy the remaining point. Ash placed one foot on the triangle, then drew it back swiftly. The stone was warm!

'Do not be alarmed. The darkstone is a conductor. It intensifies your own energy, but will not harm you.' Something about the way Credé twisted his mouth made Ash even more reluctant, but he was waved on. 'Hurry, boy!'

Clenching his teeth, Ash took up his position, curling his toes against the disturbing impression that the darkstone was alive beneath his feet.

'Good. And so we begin. We sing together.' The Malshorne frowned. 'Do not resist the power of the Song. Be calm. If you don't relax, it may break you.'

The last thing Ash felt was relaxed. Nauseous, yes, and terrified, but definitely not relaxed.

'But ... I don't know the last line,' he said desperately.

'Be still.' The Malshorne lifted a crooked finger. 'All will be revealed. Wait for my signal.' He bowed his head.

Ash felt every fibre of his body straining with fear. He willed himself to relax, unclenching his fists and slackening his jaw. He took a deep breath and let it out slowly. But none of this helped. It was impossible; he was a mess of jangling nerves. He might as well have attempted to lift himself off the ground.

Ash felt a hot flush of panic. Credé was probably about to give the signal. How did the Song begin? Where notes and words had been, there was now a terrible blankness. Then, just as he was about to admit that it was no good, that he couldn't recall anything at all, the first image came back. The tree: that beautiful, aching tree. Gratefully, he locked onto the picture and gently, gradually, the melody returned. Breathing more normally, he watched for the signal.

Credé lifted his head almost immediately. He raised a solemn hand, let it fall and began to sing. Ash followed his cue. He'd never sung with anyone else before, and found the sensation quite strange, but after a slight quaver, his voice rose — a high, clear counterpart to the Malshorne's nasal tenor. As before, beautiful images flowed through his mind, but this time there was more. He sensed the darkstone resonating, echoing the melodies back. Then he realised they weren't mere echoes: they were harmonies, beautiful harmonies that grew in strength and complexity. The darkstone was awakening! Ash's eyes flew wide in shock, but he kept singing; he didn't think he could stop, even if he had wanted to. The music was so alluring;

he was captivated by its magic.

The first verse flowed into the second, the second into the third. Then something different began, like the subtlest of key changes. Noticing a tingling in his feet, Ash looked down to see thin threads of light flowing from beneath his soles; they spiralled away, fine gold traceries, inscribing the shining black surface. There were curious symbols and elaborate scrolls, fine flowing scripts and emblazoned motifs, all somehow interconnected with the notes he was singing. The same thing was happening at other points of the triangle. The entire surface of the darkstone was being ornamented with intricate patterns of flowing gold.

The tendrils of light wove and spiralled, reaching across the dark surface like fingers. Ash was fascinated by what would happen when the gold threads met up. Credé's eyes, too, were fixed on the centre of the darkstone, and Ash sensed his tension: it was as if he was steeling himself. He registered a quick stab of alarm, then everything happened at once as his voice soared and the melody swelled.

In his mind's eye, Ash saw great armies charging towards each other across the battlefield. It was so real! He could smell their bloodlust, hear their cries. Simultaneously, three bright lines of fire raced, then collided at the very centre of the darkstone. They burst upwards, spiralling into a tower of light and whirling gold, higher and higher. There was a pause, an intake of breath, then a tremendous crack. The spinning shaft ruptured into three dazzling lines of energy that hurtled down towards the points of the triangle. A great bolt hit Ash hard in his chest.

The surface of the darkstone has dissolved. They have fallen … into Song. Time is erased. Ash moves through a world of dark forests, silent lakes, and joyful dashing rivers, aware of Credé at his side. He sees people weeping over bodies laid in rows, pale and shrouded. He witnesses a mighty flood and a scathing winter of blue ice. He watches the birth of an island city, and sees it grow tall. Mighty ships sail in fleets, even though prophets scream their warnings. The Song flares and burns, scorching his heart. He sees vast plains with herds of shaggy beasts. And black-faced cliffs where people fly on silver wings. There are white-capped peaks, too, with towers of glass. Banners flutter as people acclaim their heroes. He witnesses the births and deaths of kings and queens. A small girl cries upon an ivory throne. There is fire, and revolution, and bitter, brooding peace. And still he sings. The verses fold into each other and the Song spirals to a new dimension. A hundred voices join them, a thousand. More. Countless stories unfold, all at the same time, but nothing is chaotic, everything flows. The harmonies cut his soul with their beauty. And all at once he sees the tree and he knows. The last line is the first line: the end is the beginning.

And thus Ash sang, until the last note fell and he sank into oblivion.

Chapter 12

YAGGLUTS

It was a painful awakening. Sensing cool stone against his face, Ash brought his hand to his cheekbone. It felt bruised and tender. His body ached. Who knows how long he had been sprawled there? As he struggled to his feet, he swayed, light-headed.

'Come. Sit near the fire.'

Credé gestured for him to sit on Braig's stool, and he obeyed, hugging his arms across his chest. Staring into the flames he tried half-heartedly to reckon the hour. Still daylight, he guessed; shafts of golden light peeped through the shutters, but for all he knew whole winters could have come and passed. His mind was too tired for thinking. He felt as if he had beheld all the joys and torments of the world.

After what seemed an age, Credé stirred and cleared his throat.

Although his face was haggard, Ash sensed some change, something subtle but far-reaching. His mouth looked less twisted maybe, or his eyes less haunted. Credé sighed deeply and nodded. 'Well, boy. I admit it. You have done me service. It makes what I am about to tell you more ... difficult.'

Puzzled, Ash followed Credé's gaze to the small table between them. The Taelstone was set there on its holder. Next to that was a twisted bottle, flanked by two crystal goblets, a flat silver case, and a small phial.

'You must understand: it is not my fault we find ourselves in this regrettable position,' Credé continued. 'I did not choose you as the Keeper of the Song. The other boy was much better suited. He was my Chosen One, do you see?' There was an odd note of apology in his tone. 'The other boy didn't understand the Song; he was an empty vessel into which it could be poured without harm to him, and without harm to history.' He frowned at Ash. 'The other boy could have lived.'

Ash felt a sudden surge of nausea. Blinking in confusion, he wondered whether he had understood.

'Yes,' the Malshorne nodded. 'The Song could have passed to the other

81

boy quite safely. He did not understand it. Not a note. He would have quickly forgotten what he was struggling to remember in the first place.'

Ash forced himself to speak. 'But ... the quest ...'

'Yes. There may have been disappointment there. But he would have soon got over that.' The Malshorne waved a dismissive hand. 'Young men always dream of glorious quests in faraway places. That's why he was perfect.'

'You lied to him,' said Ash weakly. 'You told him T'al Jazure had the power to free the slaves.'

Credé's eyes became slits. 'But it wasn't a lie. T'al Jazure does have the power to free the slaves. And much else besides.' He gave a bitter sort of smirk, then tilted his head, sensing movement. 'Nevertheless, contrary to what my remarkably resilient little friend insists, the Taelstaun must *never* go to T'al Jazure.'

Ash saw that Tarlyn had crept from the woodpile. The creature blinked huge eyes at them. She didn't come closer.

'I swore an oath, muttured Credé, holding a shaking fist to his breast, 'a long time ago.' He glared at Tarlyn from under his brows. 'And so shall it be ...' Turning his attention to the table, Credé picked up the bottle and flipped its silver stopper. Drawing a goblet towards himself, he poured a thin stream of deep, berry-red liquid. It shone through the crystal, glowing like a jewel. Then, with a great show of fastidiousness, he filled the second glass.

Ash found his voice. 'But what about the Song? If you never intended Braig to go on the quest, why did you teach him the Song?'

'The Song must pass before the Keeper dies, otherwise the Keeper becomes lost in the Midway,' replied Credé, flipping the stopper into place. 'And now the Song has passed. To you.' He returned the bottle to the table and picked up the silver case. 'Really, I am doing you a favour by freeing you from a lifetime of madness. Believe me, the Song is a harsh mistress.' His mouth twisted.

Although Credé didn't seem about to attack him on the spot, Ash was suddenly certain of his meaning. With a surge of panic he remembered the shield: nothing can get in, and nothing can get out. He forced himself to speak. 'So you mean to kill me?'

'Oh no. To kill the Keeper of the Song is to be stranded forever in the Midway.'

Ash relaxed slightly, until the Malshorne added, 'Yet ... die, you will.'

The boy got to his feet, knocking the stool over with a crash. His breath came fast and shallow.

Credé made a face. 'Oh, be still. There is no need to act so dramatically. After all, you cannot change your fate now.'

With that, he began prying open the lid of the case. It yielded, and several dried seeds, like small beans, bounced onto the table. 'Come closer. You must witness this, it is quite miraculous.'

Ash stayed where he was, his mind racing.

Credé shrugged. 'They are yaggluts. This is their dormant state.' He picked up the phial and unscrewed the stopper. Credé used the feather attached to the stopper to stroke fluid onto each of the seven seeds. 'Watch!' he whispered.

Almost immediately the husk-like shells of the yaggluts began to crack and peel back. From each emerged a wriggling maggot-like creature. They were translucent, except for a shining black tip at the end of their segmented bodies. When Ash shuddered, the Malshorne chuckled. 'I share your sentiments. As useful as they are, yaggluts are not attractive.'

While Ash was trying to imagine what possible use such revolting creatures could have, Credé rose from his chair, and, picking up the two goblets, held one out to Ash. Startled, Ash saw that his eyes, which had definitely been blue minutes earlier, were now an unnatural shade of green. It gave him a peculiarly crazed look — and his next words made Ash step backwards. 'It is poison of course.'

'No! I won't drink it!' Ash spluttered, gawping at the proffered glass.

'That is entirely your choice,' replied the Malshorne smoothly. 'It is my gift to you, for your service. I will leave it here, should you change your mind.' He set it aside on a bench. The yaggluts were now squirming towards the Taelstone but Credé plucked it up, out of their path. 'Not yet. Not yet,' he murmured.

When the creatures suddenly started vomiting white fluid, Credé chuckled appreciatively. 'It's acid,' he explained. 'The yaggluts use it to prepare their food. It converts any matter to a soft sponge.' It was true! The foul things were already devouring the table; Ash could see fragments passing through their insides. 'Aren't they wonderful?' cried Credé. 'They grow until their skins can't expand anymore, then they split open!' When the skin of a yagglut burst on cue, he let out a high-pitched giggle. 'Ha! You see?'

The creature fell to the floor, where it began chomping at the rush matting. Each yagglut was now the size of a mouse.

'They're terrible!' gasped Ash.

'Quite,' agreed the Malshorne. 'Just these seven could devour everything in the world.'

'No! We have to kill them!' Ash cast about for a weapon, anything with which to squash the horrid things.

'Stupid boy!' Credé's laugh was high and hysterical. 'Nothing from this dimension can kill a yagglut!'

His shoulders shook with mirth, then he pouted. 'Oh, don't be so alarmed, I'm not so bitter as to destroy the whole of T'al Agrion. The star-shield will contain them.' He tilted his head. 'It's charged by starlight, you know.' Ash was too stunned to respond. 'Yes. The shield will hold until the yaggluts have devoured everything: every book, every miraculous device, every secret ... A lifetime of secrets.' Credé spread his arms, nearly spilling the liquid in his glass. 'They will devour it all. Then, they will turn on each other. The survivor will starve of course. A pity really.' His eyes gleamed and slid sideways.

'You're insane,' whispered Ash.

'Perhaps.' Credé smiled. His eyelids flickered momentarily, then he gave a deep sigh. 'But no more,' he murmured. 'No more. The Song has passed.'

The Malshorne bowed slightly. Then he raised his glass and drained the contents, letting it crash to the floor. Jumping back, Ash watched on in horror as Credé crossed to the bed and lay himself down, grasping the Taelstone to his chest. The orb swirled beneath his fingertips, an eddying maelstrom of colours, then filled with a sudden blinding light as Credé gave a final cry: 'Leynore!'

When Ash managed to pluck up enough courage to creep towards the bed, he was confronted by a frightening sight. Credé's face was moving, changing before his eyes. The features contorted, then settled, then shifted again. Each visage lasted only fleetingly; as soon as one face was formed it began morphing into the next. The Taelstone captured each new image: faces trapped inside a bubble. When the transformations ceased, Ash found himself gaping: the man lying dead before him seemed a stranger — silver-haired with fine cheekbones and full, curved lips. The Taelstone was completely clear, just a perfect shining orb.

At a sudden crash, Ash spun about: the yaggluts were continuing their feast. The largest was now longer than his arm, and horribly engorged. Arching their bloated bodies, they were spraying acid in all directions, and shelves and cabinets came crashing down. Their terrible jaws were glistening and dripping.

Ash gave a low panicked cry. Acting completely on instinct, he hurled himself towards the door, bolting blindly for freedom. But he was immediately thrust backwards and landed heavily, stunned.

Dragging himself to his feet, he advanced again, slowly this time. Just past the threshold he could feel an invisible membrane pushing back against his shaking hands. Credé had spoken the truth: nothing could get in, and nothing could get out. Of course! If he could escape, then so could the yaggluts. He groaned and slumped to the floor.

In the frame of the doorway, the sun was dipping behind the highest trees. At the centre of Mildaresh the fires of passing would soon be lit, and Braig's soul would be chained forever to his new master. The full tragedy hit Ash like a punch. Braig had been so inspired by Credé's cruel lies, but it had all been for nothing. Ash buried his face in his arms and rocked himself into a ball.

Moments later the sharp crack of breaking glass forced him bolt upright. Credé's gift! To his relief, the goblet with its ruby contents was still where the Malshorne had set it. He got to his feet and walked towards its red, hypnotic glow. Picking it up, he cast his eyes again towards the bed. To his surprise, Tarlyn was perched there, near the pillow. He had completely forgotten her. The strange creature turned sorrowful eyes towards him and made a low burring noise. Was she mourning Credé's death?

Yet another object crashed off a shelf, making his stomach flip again. How long would it be before the yaggluts turned on him? He contemplated the fluted goblet. It winked back at him. He lifted it, to sniff the contents. Suddenly, in a flash of black, something struck his arm — hard. The goblet flew into the air. It hit the floor and exploded in a burst of crystal shards. Tarlyn was chattering excitedly, spinning in a circle at his feet.

Ash cried out in anguish. 'No!'

Chapter 13

THE FIRES OF PASSING

In the Great Centre of Mildaresh that afternoon, the sun was simply refusing to give ground. It was almost as if Telion wanted every detail illuminated so all could be witnessed. The funeral pyre seemed to glow prematurely, washed in orange light. Three red-faced seers had appeared at the apex of the triangular structure. Now they raised their arms towards their respective temples, fingers splayed. The murmuring crowd fell silent. Everyone waited as the sun sank — surely more slowly than usual — down into the pass of Felian. When the twilight bell tolled, the ceremony of fire would begin.

Karliana Lendri shivered. Dropping her eyes to the lower platform, she scanned the line of priests, but couldn't see Domberto anywhere. Her brow creased slightly. When had her childhood friend developed such a liking for doctrine? Her father said the priesthood was hopelessly corrupt, just a means towards political gain, and she agreed. Who would have thought her clear-eyed friend would become Aranti's pet priest?

As the sun hung on, Karliana found it increasingly hard not to fidget. The wooden benches set for the nobility were far from comfortable, and the stiff collar of her gown, insisted upon by the Lendri custodian, was making matters worse. Its gold ruffles scratched her jowl when she turned her head, and it kept getting snagged in the coiled hair at the back of her head. Goodness knows if she would make it through the ceremony with the elaborate affair intact, let alone the Feast of Passing. How ridiculous! As if a collar made any difference to family honour. She longed to shake herself free from all of the pins, clasps, combs and fasteners. She inhaled through her nose and let the air out silently. To sigh loudly during the ceremony of fire would be most inappropriate for a young lady of her standing.

If Karliana leaned forward slightly, she could see the profile of Maliagne Aranti. No doubt he was terribly pleased with himself. Always one for extravagant public bequests, he had certainly excelled this time. The gift of the soul of a slave! Trust Maliagne Aranti to come up with something so utterly repellent. Her father thought it set a dangerous precedent and meant to clarify the law in the next sitting of the Senate, and quite rightly.

Oh, that sun! Was it ever so tardy? She pursed her mouth at a sudden movement among the Aranti slaves. There must have been over sixty kneeling in the space between their master's feet and the funeral pyre. As she watched, one shuffled, standing out momentarily in the sea of backs. How dreadful to be born a slave. And how utterly dreadful to be that unfortunate slave doomed to spend eternity serving the vile Mascellion Feyindi.

At last a solemn tolling broke into Karliana's reflections. Finally! The sun had released its hold and dipped below the hills. As the last peal of the twilight bell died, her father, Torland Lendri, appeared on the high dais. With a mixture of pride and anxiety, Karliana watched him raise the staff of Mildaresh. The seers gave a long, wild call, then dropped their arms. The gods had given approval. Her father descended the steep ramps from his high position and took up his place at the head of his House. Karliana gave him a quick smile and received a small, sad one in return.

As the death drum began, one beat following another like footsteps advancing, a collective shiver went through the crowd. The seers began their shrill chant as they led the priests down into the temples. The air was charged with anticipation. The seer of Narsis was first to materialise at a tiny window halfway up the sheer tower. Then, when all three were in position, they sent up another terrible cry. The chants rose to a frenzy, and the pyre erupted with flame. Karliana wondered whether anyone had ever taken their eyes off the fires while the drums still beat. It was as if you had to watch, as if the freedom of the soul depended upon it.

There was only one thing left to witness. The seers would wait for the flames to die back before signalling the release of the birds. Karliana wondered what type of birds had been chosen for Mascellion Feyindi. Although one bird was sufficient, wealthy families often released several — sometimes as many as twelve. The flight of a soul bird was an omen of the spirit's journey to the After. The best omen was when a bird flew straight up and through the smoke to disappear into the darkening sky. Brightly coloured birds had become fashionable, although white sun-birds were traditional. Since Marlashetta Feyindi would have a firm grip on proceedings, it would probably be sun-birds this time.

Suddenly the drums began to roll. It was time. Karliana watched with the crowd, breathlessly awaiting the release, until an unexpected movement caught her eye. That slave in the Aranti pack was shuffling again! She frowned. He would have to watch it or the whips would be upon him. At that moment, the drums fell silent and the call rang out: 'We send up these birds for the spirit of Mascellion Feyindi, honourable son of Mildaresh. May they escort his soul to the After so he might dwell there in comfort and eternal peace.'

Twelve white sun-birds took to the skies. They circled, bewildered by the fire. As one dipped over the crowd Karliana watched in dread, hoping it wouldn't become confused and fly into the flames. It didn't, but then something even more dreadful happened. The slave who'd had trouble keeping still suddenly stood up! Karliana gasped. What was he doing? Then, in a flash, she realised it wasn't a boy at all. It was a girl, with black, curly hair. Whatever was she thinking?

Chapter 14

SOUL BIRD

'Tarlyn!' Ash's cry was hoarse and ugly. 'What have you done?' He dragged his fingers through his hair, gaping at the mess of shattered glass. He groaned. Although he wasn't sure whether he would have drunk the poison, now he didn't have the option. Tarlyn was whirling in circles at his feet, chattering and scolding.

'What have you done?' Ash yelled. 'We're both going to die anyway!'

The creature came to a stop and blinked her eyes. She raised the ruff on her neck, her ears unfolding like dark fans.

Nothing from this dimension can kill a yagglut.

Ash recoiled. It was enough of a shock to hear the creature speak again, but this time the voice was Credé's. He looked involuntarily at the bed then back again. It was definitely the creature who had spoken.

'What did you ... ?'

Tarlyn didn't answer. Instead, she thrashed her tail, folded her ears back and leapt onto a bench. She whipped through the clutter, then leapt again in one graceful arc to the very top of a teetering bookcase. Ash craned his neck, then jumped back when something clattered down in a shower of dust.

Tarlyn landed soundlessly beside him. *Nothing from this dimension can kill a yagglut,* Credé's voice repeated weirdly.

'Yes, I know!' Ash squirmed as another yagglut burst and wriggled from its skin. They were growing by the minute! 'I know,' he groaned.

Tarlyn had begun to run in circles again, this time around and around the item she had knocked down. Then she stopped. Her eyes shone, like black mirrors.

Ash crouched warily; he hadn't forgotten those teeth. He prodded the object, then picked it up. The outer casing crumbled in his hands, revealing the most curious knife he had ever seen. The blade was dark green; thin, but long. Ornate inscriptions flowed down its length.

Did the creature expect him to stab himself to death? Or slit his wrists before the yaggluts were upon him? It was a horrible thought, and the knife didn't look particularly sharp anyway.

He inspected it more closely. He had never seen green metal before; it was like something from another world. *Like something from another world?* Ash felt a flicker of hope as he ran a finger over the strange markings. Could it be?

'Nothing from this dimension can kill a yagglut,' he repeated slowly. The creature stared back at him, her flattened ears quivering. He hardly dared hope. 'This knife … ,' he quavered. 'It isn't from this dimension, is it?' Tarlyn gave a chirrup and spun in a circle. 'So I could use it to kill the yaggluts!' A series of excited chirrups seemed to confirm the conclusion.

Ash stood, gulping, but with new determination. He had a weapon! All he had to do was kill seven giant maggot-creatures.

He waved the knife in an experimental arc, took a breath and assessed the scene. The yaggluts had wreaked terrible destruction. The furniture around the hearth had disappeared completely, and the fireplace was badly damaged; the chimney could crash down anytime. Amid the sticky mess, four yaggluts were making steady progress towards the foot of the bed. Two more were demolishing the bookcases near the door. As he watched, part of the wall crumbled, letting in a flood of sunlight.

The nearest yagglut was almost at the edge of the darkstone. Its skin looked strained, ready to burst. He couldn't let these things get any bigger! Grasping the knife with both hands, and with a guttural roar that was really more of a frightened scream, he swiped. A sharp tingle shot up his arm as the knife made contact. Then the yagglut's head fell away. The bloated body jerked, flooding the floor with slime. Ash gave a shout of half-joy, half-disgust. He just had to keep going.

In a series of sweeping strokes, he whipped the heads off the yaggluts near the bed. They wriggled and oozed. He turned swiftly, only to stagger back in dismay. The two remaining yaggluts were rearing up, waving their terrible heads. They made ghastly, gurgling rattles as they swayed and acid dripped from their jaws— a spray could come his way at any moment. Ash cast about for something, anything, to use as a shield, and seized on a large wooden tray.

He knew he had to move fast. Holding the tray-shield over his head, he attacked the yagglut on the right, slashing wildly, screaming. The knife glowed bright green as it made contact. Its side split open, the creature lurched, blasting spray in his direction as it fell. Ash raised his shield and ducked, but everything was wet with slime. He skidded, and the knife slipped from his grasp, clattering out of reach. His shield disintegrated about him, like wet bark, leaving him completely defenseless against the remaining yagglut, which towered above. As it shook its awful head, a drip fell from its maw, searing the skin on his wrist. Ash screamed and cowered, expecting the strike any second. But it didn't come. Instead the yagglut began to sway violently back and forth.

Ash was confused for a split second, not knowing how to react, until he saw a blur of black fur, sharp quills and flashing teeth. Tarlyn! Without thinking, he rolled and, regaining the knife, leapt to his feet. With three swipes he hacked through the yagglut's trunk, then, as it crashed to the floor, he whipped off its head. Tarlyn chirruped beside him, whirling madly. The knife clattered to the floor. It was done! Trembling all over and covered in slime, Ash felt sick to his core, but he was alive!

Golden light was pouring through gaps in the walls now, warning of the late hour, but Ash hesitated as he approached the dopple-star. It was so bizarre, so otherworldly. He turned the cube in his hands, before cautiously opening the lid. Immediately there was a dart of hurtling light and the star was suddenly doubled, dazzling his eyes. Squinting, he shut its crystal prison once more and rushed to the door. Taking a deep breath, he stepped through and was free!

Bolting through the trees, Ash was vaguely aware of his hood dragging at his neck, but there was no time to lose; the fires might already be lit. Recklessly, he charged downhill, leaping over rocks and roots. By the time he reached the stone archway, his lungs were tearing. The light of the dying sun had emblazoned the script along the top of the arch; the sight tugged oddly at him, demanding attention, but he couldn't stop. He dashed past the broken graves and on into the old city.

When he reached the empty streets of the Arion Third it seemed he was the only person alive: everyone had gravitated to the ceremony of fire. To his dismay, as he grew closer he saw that the sky already glowed red. The Arion Aisle was blocked by onlookers, but thankfully there were no guardians. Ash wormed his way into the crowd. The flames were abating and the chants were rising; the birds would soon be released. He tried to work his way forward, but it was no use. The pack was too tight. He immediately realised his mistake. The Aranti block was swollen with free-folk seeking to align themselves with that House. It would be impossible to join the ranks of Feyindi slaves on the other side. There was just nothing for it but to stay put until the end of the ceremony.

As the fire slumped into itself, Ash swallowed hard. The death drum thumped in his breast like a second heartbeat. He felt tears stinging. This was a terrible end to a truly terrible day. When the drums fell silent and the call rang out, he recognised his master's voice. He watched the birds fly up in a cloud, white wings catching the rosy light.

One swooped low over the Aranti slaves where they knelt in a huddled mass. He saw it flutter, tumbling, circling in confusion. Then, with everyone else, he gasped. One of the slaves was rising! Awe gave way to dread. He couldn't mistake that stance, that dark crop of curls. It was Kep! Her voice sang out, clear and defiant: 'I release this bird for the spirit of Braig. May he be borne swiftly to the After and forever be free!' She threw up her hands and released a small grey bird. It beat its tiny wings and shot upwards. The crowd let out an astonished cry, as the bird burst through the smoke and vanished into the After.

For one terrible moment, nothing happened. Then Maliagne Aranti sprang to his feet. 'Seize her!'

The guards tried to obey, but Kep was at the centre of the Aranti group. While slaves scrambled to evade the bite of the whips, Kep just stood there, amidst the roiling mass, her head bowed, waiting. When at last she was seized and thrown before her master's feet, the crowd strained forward, silent, eager to catch his words.

'No one humiliates the House of Aranti! Pray now that death takes you swiftly, for soon you will have neither strength to pray, nor a tongue to pray with!'

Maliagne Aranti raised his hand as if to strike. Then the crowd gasped again. The Mildari had risen to his feet! He was holding the rod of office over his head in a silent command. Aranti's face twisted into a furious mask of disbelief, but he dropped his hand.

Torland Lendri's voice carried clearly, calm and measured: 'Hold! This slave's crime is against the city of Mildaresh. She will be taken to the courtrooms to be tried, in accordance with our laws.'

The crowd whimpered, a great chained beast subdued only by protocol. Then, as soon as the seers had sung their final call to the sky, the people erupted. The solemn procession from the courtyard was completely abandoned as tongues wagged and opinions flew. Rumour flew through the city on the swift wings of scandal. Some heard in astonishment that a slave had released a bird for the soul of that boy, then thrown himself into the flames. In another version the girl had slapped Maliagne Aranti across the face before vanishing into thin air! Those who were able to discover the truth found it no less shocking and utterly compelling. Undoubtedly, there was widespread glee that for once Maliagne Aranti had not got things his own way.

Chapter 15

THE FEAST OF PASSING

Back at the Feyindi villa, the Head of the Kitchens seemed already to know everything there was to know.

'And what does any of this have to do with the two hundred guests we must feed tonight?' she rapped. 'Get to work!'

Of course everyone jumped to obey, but something was undeniably different that evening. Slaves shared secret smiles and precious fragments of knowledge about the courageous, dark-haired girl who had taken on the arrogance of Lord Aranti, all of the priests, and all of the masters, to free the soul of that poor boy.

The Head of the Kitchens raised her eyebrows at the sorry state of the boy before her. 'I suppose that Malshorne beat you, did he?'

Ash nodded miserably; it was true, up to a point.

'Well, I'm sure you deserved it.' Normally she would have called him a useless, shirking, good-for-nothing, dolt of a boy, punctuating each point with a cuff, but today she just folded her arms and regarded him with bemusement. 'Whatever is that on your tunic, lad? Did he wipe his nose on you as well?'

Ash just shuffled his feet and made no reply.

'That's a fine purple bruise you've got on that eye,' she chuckled. The other slaves stole nervous glances; nobody, as far as they could remember, had ever heard her laugh before. 'Well boy, you'll be of no worth at Table tonight,' she growled. 'Get yourself cleaned up. You'll do for dish duties.'

As Ash struggled to take in this wholly unexpected reprieve, the Head of the Kitchens declared the fire-boy too spotty and gormless, he would drop plates and spill the wine, but the butcher boy had barely had any teeth and his breath reeked. Neither would do. 'Jem, you'll serve at Table tonight! Off you go, girl. You don't have to look so terrified — if that little girl can stand up to Lord Aranti and all those priests, then surely you can pour a bit of wine, eh?' She gave an uncharacteristic toss of her head. 'Don't you worry, I'll answer to the masters if there's a problem.'

Ash still hadn't moved.

'Don't stand gawping boy! Get on, before I blacken your other eye to make a matching pair!'

Ash hurried to his quarters, not knowing how long the Head of the Kitchen's oddly benevolent mood would hold. The tiny dorm-cell was empty; even poor old Loth had been found extra duties for the night. Ash looked longingly at the narrow bunk with its lumpy mattress. When had it ever seemed so inviting?

As he eased his filthy tunic over his head, he suddenly became aware that the hood seemed heavier than usual. He frowned at a lump in it, then gave the garment a shake. Out rolled a tight black ball, not much larger than his fist. It hit the mattress and uncoiled with a rapid whirling of black fur — and there sat Tarlyn, right in the middle of his bed. Ash clamped a hand to his mouth, flabbergasted.

'Tarlyn! You can't be here!' he croaked, hoarse with panic. The creature simply blinked her eyes and gave a chirrup. 'No, no, no,' he groaned. 'This is not good. You have to hide!'

The creature regarded him for a moment, then began washing her paws.

Not knowing what to do, Ash hauled a basket of clothes from under the bed. 'Here! Get in here!' When Tarlyn ignored him, he winced. He couldn't risk getting bitten. 'Right. Well. Just ... keep out of sight.' Tarlyn paid him no attention and kept washing. It was impossible to tell if she understood.

He groaned as he hurried out. The last thing he needed was a demonic-looking creature hiding under his bed.

As Ash left the dormitories, he nearly collided with Jem. She had changed her clothes and brushed her hair. She looked very pale under the clear-lamps.

He realised she had probably never even set foot in the Long Hall, so he tried to reassure her as they scurried along. 'Don't worry, they'll be so busy talking about ... well ... what happened today, they might not notice you're a girl.' She shot him a terrified look. 'Just keep quiet and copy the others. And stay clear of the Mistress if you can.'

She nodded. 'What happened to you anyways?'

When Ash didn't answer, she frowned. 'You look terrible, Ash. Were you at the Fires of Passing?'

He made no answer as they passed into the main house. Soon they would part ways.

'Well, I think what that girl did was the bravest thing.' She bit her lip. 'Makes a person feel ashamed.' As they reached the end of the hall, she added, 'Don't think I could be that brave. Could you?'

'No.' Forgetting to wish her luck, Ash charged at the door and made his escape.

The Long Hall of the House of Feyindi was one of the oldest and most dignified in Mildaresh. While the current mistress favoured austerity, that only allowed the refined architectural features to stand out more impressively. The mighty vaulted ceiling was held up by pillars of greystone, which rose like columns of twisted silk. The floor was shining white marble, inlaid with coloured tiles depicting victories on the battlefield and honours in the Senate. A series of tall, arched doorways opened onto a huge garden at the heart of the villa, with swathes of drapery caught back to admit the scented evening air and the music of fountains playing.

The banquet was laid out at the northern end. Succulent meats and all manner of fruits, cheeses, pastries and delicacies were displayed in huge mounds. Marlashetta Feyindi's firm belief that pedigree was of far greater value than wealth was reflected in the seating arrangements. Indeed, Lady Feyindi's opinion, that you couldn't go past the Orlion ranking when it came to assessing a family's worth, had seen many a powerful family usurped from the higher tables by those with a longer lineage. Tonight, everyone could see how Maliagne Aranti's eyes glittered to be seated at a table in the second flight. Nor did anyone miss the arched brows of Serenitia Moagli, deeply insulted by her place halfway down the hall. 'Virtually out on the street' was what mischievous tongues would report the following day.

As daughter of the Mildari, Karliana Lendri sat near the top table; not that her father's current office made any difference — the Lendri family was one of the oldest in Mildaresh. Karliana had fixed a smile to her face, the stupid ruffle now firmly entangled in the back of her hair. She clenched her hands in her lap as someone commented, yet again, on the delightful regard for ancestry and tradition.

'So much more important than the sordid scramble for riches,' the Dowager of Wendsor concurred, the infamous rubies of Wendsor glinting, blood-red, against her scrawny bosom. It was the same all the way around the table: haughty aristocrats with their impossibly long names, fraught with nasty secrets and thwarted ambition.

As Karliana smothered a sigh, a sudden image of the brave slave girl came unbidden to her mind, and she found herself marvelling again at the swift little bird and the pure, clear voice. What a rash act of courage! Wherever had she found such defiance, such bravery?

As the evening wore on, Karliana couldn't shake the dark-haired girl from her thoughts. She endured the long speeches with growing irritation. Who was this man of whom the eulogists spoke? They practically dripped compliments. What a statesman he had been! How cultured! They all drew the line at 'virtuous', but apparently he had been both generous and intelligent — a true loss to the city. By Telion, they would claim he was skinny next! How wonderful it would be to jump up and shout the truth: *Actually, he was a greedy, lecherous old toad!* She frightened herself by imagining she might just do it … Then the danger was over, the last speech had finished and Karliana was clapping politely with everyone else. Where had it come from, that girl's courage?

'You look rather pensive, my dear.' Guardulian Skagali peered across the table, looking even more reptilian than usual. He made her skin crawl at the best of times, but tonight he seemed the epitome of everything she hated.

'What could be on the mind of such a beauty, eh?'

Karliana blushed irrationally — it wasn't as if he could read her mutinous thoughts.

'Aha! Have I stumbled upon the impure thoughts of youth?' The old man winked a heavily lidded eye and sniggered.

Madalinelle Skagali was instantly alert. 'Whatever are you saying, Father?' Her eyes flicked to the Mildari as she honeyed her voice. 'Karliana, my dear, pray excuse my poor father, he is getting on in years and sometimes quite loses track of propriety.'

Karliana didn't know which of them repulsed her most. She lifted her chin, ignoring the drag of that ridiculous collar. 'I was merely thinking about that slave girl and her actions at the Fires of Passing.' There! It was said! Her heart pounded.

'Oh, my dear!' Madalinelle Skagali's eyes flew wide. Several people seated nearby stopped eating, their forks suspended. 'What a quaint thing to say, Karliana, dear!'

Karliana went to speak again, but faltered when she caught her father's eye. Nobody had dared broach the subject, given the sensitivity of the time and place, but now everyone murmured to their neighbours.

'It's an outrage. That slave should be put to death — why bother with a trial?'

'Certainly. The sacred traditions of our city mustn't be flouted!'

'Aranti is positively fuming, and quite rightly: he should have been free to punish the girl himself.'

'No, no. It's a civic matter. The slave's sin was against the gods.'

'Well, she'll be off to the noikos fields on the first barge, mark my words.'

'That won't do. The priests are baying for public execution. A clear message must be sent.'

Karliana suddenly felt quite nauseous. She hadn't considered what might happen to the girl. Since a few of the guests had already begun to drift into the gardens, she excused herself and went in search of fresh air.

Avoiding the clusters of people on the upmost terrace, Karliana headed down a broad flight of steps. Tears sprang into her eyes as she fled along the mosaic pathways, before taking refuge in a nook with a little fountain, which was tucked behind the hedging. She ran a finger under each eye to smooth the moisture away, and breathed deeply, trying to focus on the water. It tumbled into a wide, shallow vessel from a lip set high on the wall; there, it was infused with moonlight before cascading over the edge into a series of lower bowls. It didn't seem right that anything should be so beautiful on such a dreadful night.

Soon she became aware of someone approaching, so she clasped her hands and turned with a brittle smile. The man was silhouetted against the clear-lights, but she couldn't fail to recognise him from the cut of his attire. Her smile faded as the tall young priest approached — the last person she wanted to speak to was Domberto Hamalton. They exchanged awkward bows.

'It's a beautiful evening.'

'Yes,' she answered coldly. It wasn't. It was a horrible, terrible evening. Plucking a flower from a vine against the stonework, she put it to her nose and inhaled. It smelt over-sweet. She glared at it. Domberto just stood there quietly, watching the water; the side of his neck looking soft in the moonlight. She sniffed. 'I'd have thought you would be entertaining Lord Aranti.' She tore a sticky petal from the flower.

'Lord Aranti left early.'

She hated him for his calm manner. 'Good. I hope he's pleased with the suffering he's caused.'

The young priest didn't reply.

'They say the priests will demand a public execution for that poor girl.'

'Possibly.'

He was trying not to upset her. How infuriating! 'And what of the gods?'

'The gods?' He tilted his head.

'Yes, the gods. *Our* gods. Those gods *you* serve. What do they think about a soul doomed to eternal slavery?' She ripped a few more petals off the unfortunate flower, then crushed the remains between her finger and thumb.

He sighed. 'What the gods think is irrelevant. It's what the people think that will dictate that girl's fate.'

'Well someone should do something!' Karliana hated the way her voice sounded, like a petulant child's. She nearly stamped her foot, but caught herself just in time, instead throwing the ruined bloom into the pool with a scowl.

Domberto caught her hand as it swung back, and he clasped it between his. Even in this light, his eyes were a bright, piercing blue. His skin felt so warm.

'Karliana, nothing can be done.'

She knew it in her heart already — he didn't need to say it out loud. With a toss of her head, she snatched her hand away and left him there.

As her feet flew along the path she had the strongest urge to glance back, but she resisted. If she had, she would have seen how he stood there for a long time in contemplation, until at last he reached out and scooped the broken flower from the water.

❧

'Well, I'll say it again: someone ought to do something.'

The kitchen underlings were chewing over the matter as they tackled the last of the greasy plates and overflowing bins.

'I told you. There ain't no point hoping at that. Nobody can do a dot to help that child, and that's a fact.' The sweet-maker hung the last of his tools on hooks.

'Seems a shame no one knows her name, though.'

Ash emptied another kettle of water into the tub. *Kep — her name is Kep.* All evening it had been the same. All those questions, each with the power to twist his gut. How did she catch that bird? How did she keep it quiet all that time? Was she in love with the boy? Did the gods sanction her actions? Wasn't she afraid?

Now, someone asked the worst question of all.

'So, what do you think will happen to her?'

'Don't know. But it won't be nothing good that's for sure.' The third cook dumped more stripped carcasses into a huge pan. 'We've stock enough for weeks,' he commented, shaking his head.

'Hey! Here's Jem back! She'll know the latest!'

Jem met the clatter of questions good-naturedly. Unfortunately, she had been so terrified of coming to the mistress's attention that she had missed a lot of the goings-on. Nevertheless, she did her best to satisfy her audience.

Finally, the sour-faced sweet-maker cut to the chase: 'What of the girl? Was anything said of her fate?' His question put an end to all of her merry gossip.

Jem's face dropped at once. 'Trial's in morning. They say it might go on past noon, with so many wanting to speak. Most are calling for execution—' A great crash of pots stopped her short.

'Hey there, boy!' The third cook rounded angrily on the source of the commotion.

Jem assessed Ash's white face in a second. 'The lad's spent, that's all,' she laughed. 'I'll take over. I've had an easy night of it, and I don't mind a bit a gossip.' The others shrugged. 'Probably do a better job anyways,' she added, surveying the mess.

When the others had gone back to their tasks, she spoke sharply under her breath: 'You've made a poor day of it, Ash, and that's for sure. Get away to bed.' She retrieved a skillet from the floor and gave him a gentle push towards the door.

Not stopping to change his clothes or even remove his sodden sandals, Ash crawled into bed. He closed his eyes, wishing for darkness, craving unconsciousness, without light, without memory. But all he could see was Kep, her cheek against the side of a doe as she milked, her laughing eyes, her smile. He tried not to imagine her lovely head upon the executioner's block, or picture her toiling in the noikos fields, her mouth stained blue by lamon berries.

He stared fiercely at a crack in the ceiling instead, as if it was a talisman to ward off the unthinkable. But there was no magic to protect against such pain. Tears spilled hot from the corners of his eyes, and there was no holding back the wracking shudders of grief. Wave followed uncontrollable wave, until body and mind could cope no more. Finally, succumbing to the balm of tears, he slept.

⁂

Ash stirred long before the dawn bell. There was something ... something ... but he couldn't quite pinpoint what. He hovered between sleep and being awake — grasping at bright images. Was it a dream, or had he fallen into the Song? The melody was fading. The more he stretched out his mind, the more it drifted away. And there was something ... something else demanding his attention. He wavered, made a choice, and the Song was gone.

Suddenly Ash understood what had woken him: there was something on his bed, something warm. He put out his hand, and sure enough his fingertips made contact with soft fur. Tarlyn! The creature was curled in the crook between his stomach and his thighs; he could feel her breathing. He wanted to touch her silky fur again, but he didn't dare. She might wake. So he lay still, even though his body ached to change position.

When an early rooster crowed, he shuddered. If only time would stop, he thought, here and now. But time wasn't about to stop, and every minute brought Kep's fate closer. His neck was so stiff. He pushed his hand under the thin pillow to bunch it higher. When his fingers touched an unfamiliar edge, he remembered Credé's package with its special seal. He would have to take it to the courtrooms later—

And there it was! Not hope, not quite, just the stirring of a possibility, the first inkling of a vague idea.

But by the time the dawn bell jangled, Ash was wide-eyed with thinking. It was dangerous, but he had to try. The first thing to do was find Pan.

Chapter 16

THE WATERS OF JUSTICE

The robes of the Mildari weighed heavily on Lord Lendri that day. He suspected that, rather than being the epitome of stateliness, his ceremonial garb was perilously close to being absurd. Along with a sumptuous fur-edged cloak, destined never to see the light of day let alone bad weather, there were three embroidered tunics, all in the colour of justice: blood red. The clasps, chains, buttons and tassels all had to be positioned precisely, lest they diminish the power of the Mildari: first citizen of Mildaresh, caretaker of the law and dispenser of justice. His clerk was still fussing with the black sash of Narsis, which had to cross the breast at an exact angle. Lendri suppressed a sigh. If only there were some correlation between wisdom and layers of clothing.

'Thank you, Pelor. I can manage now.'

'Very good, my lord.'

Pelor removed himself stiffly. It was impossible to tell if he was affronted, as his facial expressions for dignity and hostility were identical.

Lord Lendri closed his eyes and sighed.

May justice be done were the words inscribed over the entrance to the courtrooms. But the world was not just, and especially not for slaves. His only prayer was that his daughter might forgive his part in what must come.

When the ancient horn of the Mildaren blared thrice, the crowded courtroom was immediately hushed. All eyes fell on the first citizen as he made his way into the room. Many nodded as he entered: he made a fine figure in his robes, tall and majestic, but not too proud. No one liked a Mildari who swaggered. He passed between the crowded tiers of free-folk and crossed the lacquered floor towards the statue of Narsis. Rising nearly to the ceiling, the divinity towered over proceedings: the very embodiment of grace and strength. Sculptured robes fell to the floor in deep, carved pleats, stone curls tumbled to the shoulders, and a simple wreath of candrel leaves, beloved herb of healing, graced the mighty forehead.

As always, Lendri found himself looking up into the face, as if he might glimpse some expression on that featureless oval. Today, he couldn't help feeling, Narsis must be displeased.

The altar of Narsis took the form of a simple but elegant trough, cut from white stone and filled with clear water. Set above it were the twelve glass cylinders containing the judgment waters, each with a silver tap at the base.

As Lendri approached, a beam of light from a high window caught the liquid, making it dazzle. He knelt, casting petals and spices into the water, then lifted his hands in supplication. A priest, chanting sonorously, placed the sacred triang over the Mildari's head. She repeated the ancient entreaty — may justice be served — and Lendri mounted the steps to the high bench. The court officials were already in place one platform below. As soon as he was settled, the crowd's gaze turned like a re-directed beam to the door through which the accused would emerge. It opened almost immediately to admit the slave, who was escorted by a single guardian.

The girl's tunic was crumpled from a night in the cells. Her hair fell in ratty pieces, and her face was smudged with filth. She had been crying, one would imagine; yet the tilt of her head seemed to deny this. Lendri felt a stab of grief to see how she, too, gazed into the face of Narsis; her expression was so serene, as if she were truly placing her fate in the hands of the gods. What a tiny bundle she made, kneeling there at the altar. When she took her place on the simple wooden chair, her chin high, he was reminded sharply of Karliana. He sighed inaudibly. If only his daughter had listened to his plea and stayed away.

Seated among the ranks of nobility, Karliana was finding it almost impossible to take her eyes off the slave girl — she made such a small and tragic figure, yet so resolute in her bearing! It sent a thrill down one's spine. She had to drag her attention away to the speakers. Today there were twelve: one for each of the vessels of judgment. They sat in a long line, with their backs to her. Maliagne Aranti was there at the end, hunched up like a bird of prey. Next to him was the tall figure of Marlashetta Feyindi, then old Fabrinet, wearing the cylindrical headdress of the priesthood. No guesses for what his stance would be: any sniff of novelty usually sent him into a long ramble on the sanctity of doctrine — thank goodness a strict time limit was imposed.

Karliana frowned doubtfully at the backs of the other speakers. Perhaps she recognised the wide shoulders and black hair of Rutholine Moagli, or was that his brother Castronon? They looked so awfully alike. The shining bald pate belonged to the High Protector, and there was another priest, right at the end. That was interesting. Two priests? But there was no time to puzzle it out, the preliminary rituals were complete.

The Clerk of the Courts examined the tattoo on the slave's wrist and announced that the prisoner was Kep of the House of Aranti. The Slaves Decree was far too long and complicated to be read in full, so the clerk simply recited the most important section: *No slave may undertake any action that in anyway causes hurt of any kind to any noble or free-person.* Slave trials were rarely about ascertaining guilt or innocence, but rather about compensation for those offended.

Once more, Karliana could not take her eyes off Kep. She was wondering what the dead boy had meant to her — surely she had been in love with him? — when the Clerk of the Courts gave a blast on a thin silver whistle. 'The court calls Maliagne Aranti!'

Lord Aranti swept to his feet, as only he could.

'Declare your right to speak!' the clerk commanded.

'I claim my right as master of this slave.' He bowed with a flourish.

The Keeper of the Waters, a thin, grey stick of a man, was signalled to turn on the tap of the first judgment vessel, and the water began to trickle out.

Aranti flicked his short cloak over his shoulder and began: 'It is with some reluctance that I speak today …' He raised one finger in the air. 'For — to quote one of the esteemed founders of our city — if a man is not master of his slaves, then how can he be called a man? However, those with higher authority, if not wisdom, than mine have decreed that this slave be dealt with here under the auspices of Narsis. And who am I, a simple man of Mildaresh, to argue with that?'

At this, the faintest murmur rippled through the crowd. The Clerk of the Courts put her whistle to her mouth, but silence resumed of its own accord.

'Be that as it may …' He closed his eyes as if in pain. 'This slave has wronged me indeed, and has cost me sorely. Her worth alone is set at ten thousand gold felans.'

Karliana sniffed. A slave so young? What an exaggeration! She watched the girl's face. How could she sit there so calmly?

'Chosen to train as herati, she would have been greatly honoured in my house, had her spirit not been so foully corrupt, had her nature not harboured such impertinence!' He shook his head. 'Nevertheless, my call for justice rests not on financial loss, but upon loss of honour — a thing that the *truly* noble value more than wealth.' He paused there, and looked pointedly at Marlashetta Feyindi. 'This wretched slave sabotaged the gift made in honour of my friend, dear Mascellion Feyindi. A gift made in the spirit of generosity. A gift that was *shamelessly* negated by this slave, without thought for the indignity it would bring upon her masters. I ask you: When in Mildaresh has any slave thwarted gracious nobility in such a manner? ... *Never!*' He spat the word with such force that the people in the front seats shrank back involuntarily. 'My recommendation, in lieu of being allowed to punish this wretch myself, is that she be put to death in the Great Centre before this day is out!'

Although Karliana was prepared for his words, they made her shudder. But the slave girl didn't even flinch. How extraordinary. What courage!

Predictably, the next few speakers all called for public execution. Each claimed to defend either the honour of the dead, or the spirit of the city, or the sanctity of religion, or everything Mildarens hold dear.

When the High Protector rose, Karliana sighed. The poor girl's fate seemed sealed. Carlton Enegi certainly didn't look much like the head of the city guardians. His short, stocky build, combined with a smoothly-shaved head and dark, fluffy eyebrows made him look somewhat comical. He looked more suited to inn-keeping than peace-keeping.

'May it please Narsis, I object strongly to the public execution of this slave,' he began.

Karliana leaned forward in her seat.

'Such an action would be most unwise. It seems the actions of this girl have sparked a spirit of rebellion in some quarters of our city. I am afraid she has been embraced as some sort of heroine, not just by the slaves but by the free-folk as well. "Kep the Valiant", "Courageous Kep" and "Kep the Defiant" — these are just a few of the names that have been reported to me.'

Karliana felt a surge of joy, and had to suppress a smile. Goodness lived yet in Mildaresh!

Carlton Enegi continued: 'Now may be a pertinent time to remind you all that, even in the city alone, we are heavily outnumbered by our slaves. For every Mildaren there are five slaves, without counting those multitudes in the noikos fields. We simply cannot risk an uprising. If this girl is executed it could spark a revolt, something which has not happened since the time of the kings.' He paused to let the point sink in. 'My recommendation, therefore, as High Protector, is to avoid execution. She should be sent to the fields.' A ripple ran through the crowd as the waters ran out. He had certainly given them something to think about.

Castronon Moagli pounced gleefully upon the argument. 'Our High Protector is right! This slave's actions have revealed a dreadful truth,' he warned: 'the Orlion Testing no longer ensures our Eerok are passive and manageable!' He wagged a finger. 'Mark my words, here is a danger that lies dormant behind our very walls, an enemy who sleeps only lightly!' He stared at the prisoner as if she were about to leap up and throttle him on the spot.

Idiot, thought Karliana. But he painted a vivid scenario — the city in flames, women ravished, tiny babies butchered in their beds — then called for immediate powers to be granted to the Moagli Cadet Squad, to bolster the strength of the guardians. His request of course was wholly irrelevant, but was referred to the Senate, which was no doubt precisely his objective. He smirked at his mother as he made his way back to his seat. *How transparent!*

'And will you be favouring us with a recommendation, young man?' demanded the clerk.

Castronon gave the crowd a winning smile. 'Oh, yes. Public execution of course. We mustn't allow such sacrilege!'

Karliana fumed through the next few speeches. Only one other speaker recommended the noikos fields, and that on financial grounds: Aranti should at least gain compensation from the slave's lifelong labour. Then at last it was time for the last speaker, the second priest. Her father had been right; she shouldn't have come. She sighed as the Clerk of the Courts blew her whistle for the final call.

'On behalf of Narsis, the court calls Domberto Hamalton.'

Karliana sat up in her seat, horrified. Domberto had never been one for public speaking. Whatever was he thinking?

'May it please Narsis ... I apologise if I lack the eloquence of those who have spoken before me,' Domberto began. 'Indeed I stand here in some trepidation.' He smiled faintly. 'Yet I fear the consequences of not speaking more than I do your disdain at my poor performance.'

He was certainly the most humble speaker of the day — and the most endearing. Many people nodded benevolently as the handsome young priest struggled to gather his thoughts.

'I believe … I mean, I fear … our city is in grave danger.' The nobles rustled in their seats. 'I fear we are poised to make a decision today that could imperil the prosperity and grace of our beautiful city. We have heard that this slave should be put to death because her crime was one against tradition, but my greatest fear is that her action was the very opposite.'

Karliana blinked, perplexed. Speaking definitely wasn't one of Domberto's talents; she hoped he wasn't about to make a complete fool of himself. Then he stared up at the face of Narsis with that expression Karliana knew so well: the one where he seemed to gaze into the very nature of things. He seemed truly anguished by whatever it was he saw. She caught her breath. If he was acting, then it was a very good performance — the crowd was entranced. Then the moment passed, and he regained himself and carried on.

'It has been many centuries since a slave's soul has been gifted to another. Lord Aranti, of course, thought only to honour the spirit of Mascellion Feyindi. Yet, while he acted within the law, his gift can no longer be seen as traditional.' Domberto was avoiding looking towards Aranti, which was just as well — his courage surely would have quailed at the black fury in those eyes. 'Although Lord Aranti acted honourably, he may have been misguided.' Karliana pressed her hand to her mouth, willing her friend to stop. Maliagne Aranti was not a man to cross!

But Domberto continued. 'Look at this girl. She's so young, just a simple milkmaid. Surely she was aided by Telion in obtaining a bird, keeping it secret and releasing it at the precise time? And this bird, as many of us witnessed, did not flutter in confusion but flew straight through the smoke. Does that not suggest the gods were smiling upon her?' The silence was absolute. 'My faith tells me it would be unwise to risk the displeasure of the gods. If they did sponsor this girl's rebellion against a break with our sacred values, then imagine their anger at her execution. My recommendation is that she lives out her days in the noikos fields.'

The vessel of judgment wasn't quite empty, but its remaining waters were allowed to run out in silence. The young priest had spoken so ardently and with such honesty in his eyes. Many people stared up at the face of Narsis. Some bowed their heads and made the sign of the triangle. Inevitably there were mutterings and shuffling, but the Clerk of the Courts blew several piercing notes on her whistle, then pounced upon a woman who was whispering to a neighbour. Both parties were ejected from the court forthwith, with the effect of settling the room completely: no one wanted to miss the sentence.

But the Mildari did not yet rise to his feet. Instead, he gestured for the clerk to approach. Those acquainted with court procedures realised at once that something unconventional was happening. The officials bristled. There was a tense whispered debate, then, finally, Lord Lendri stood.

'I thank you all for your patience,' he began quietly. 'After listening to the speakers, I find it of vital importance that we understand this slave's extraordinary actions. Although it is not customary for a slave to speak during trial, I believe this case calls for unusual measures. Therefore, taking full responsibility for the break in precedent, and in the name of Narsis, I call upon Kep of the House of Aranti.'

Scowling with displeasure, the Clerk of the Courts motioned for the prisoner to stand. 'Well, slave? Can you explain your actions?'

Kep's face was pale, but she lifted her chin and answered without hesitation. 'I prayed the gods would help me to do what was right, and they did. That's all I can say.'

Chapter 17

THE SENTENCE

The waiting was over. All eyes were on Torland Lendri — Mildari, dispenser of justice. Karliana barely recognised the man who rose from his chair. His face looked so grey and anguished. She cringed as the rod of Mildaresh came down with a boom. Then his judgment rang out: 'Kep of the House of Aranti, by the power vested in me, I hereby sentence you to a lifetime of servitude in the noikos fields. There you will repay your debt to your master and do penance for dishonouring the customs of our city.'

Karliana sucked in a sharp, shocked breath. The speakers had recommended nine over three that the girl be executed! Her father had not only gone against court tradition in letting a slave speak, he had set himself above the nobility!

The courtroom was in an uproar. Had mild-mannered Torland Lendri really seen fit to ignore the advice of eight of the city's most prominent nobles *and* her most learned priest? What a scandal! Some of the nobles struggled to hide their elation at this unlooked-for turn of events; here perhaps was hope for their own high ambitions.

The clerk blasted on her whistle with all her might, but it was some time before the excitement subsided enough for it to be heard. She glowered, but there were no reprisals — she could hardly evict the entire courtroom. With a contemptuous sniff, she called the tracker: 'The court of Narsis calls Gooel.'

Karliana shuddered to hear the name. Gooel was notorious. Of all the snouts, he was considered the most skilled, and the most cold-blooded. He seemed to prowl towards the bench like an animal on the hunt. He wore close-fitting garments in shades of green, and was typical of his type: short, wiry and bandy-legged. Karliana estimated he wouldn't even come up to her shoulder, and she was not considered tall. His face was dominated by a huge flat nose, and his ears and eyes were over-large, too; it was said that snouts could see in the dark and hear someone hiding at a hundred paces.

Still, it was also said they could change the colour of their skin and outpace a fall-deer, both of which seemed rather unlikely.

The clerk addressed the court: 'Know all: Kep of the House of Aranti is exiled to servitude beyond the city. By the power of Narsis, I hereby assign this tracker to her person. He has full authority to hunt and kill in the event of escape.' She motioned Gooel forward, and he circled Kep several times, snuffing in her scent. Then he stood back and nodded.

To Karliana's amazement the girl didn't flinch once during the ordeal. As she was led down through the crowded aisles towards the cells, her back was straight and her head high. Karliana dropped her eyes at last; she couldn't bear to watch.

⚘

Lord Lendri swept through his rooms, collecting his stiff-faced clerk in his wake. He shed the heavy cloak with relief, but nothing could relieve the sorrow of sending that girl to the fields. Pelor's usually impassive face twitched as he packed the sash of Narsis into its velvet case. Was that tenderness in his eyes as he looked up?

'A sorry business, my lord.'

Did he mean the sentence? Or Lendri's blatant disregard of court procedures and vetoing of the speakers' recommendations? It was hard to tell. Perhaps both.

'Yes. A sorry business indeed, Pelor.' Lendri rubbed his furrowed brow. 'The girl must be sent to the fields on this evening's barge.'

The clerk's lips twitched ever so slightly as he unbuckled the scabbard. 'And the procession through the Great Centre, my lord?'

'No procession. She must be moved quietly. Ask the High Protector to send his two best guardians. I want you to deal with this personally and discreetly, Pelor. Direct them to take her through the Salturne Third, along the Nocheir way.' Lendri lifted his arms so his clerk could unlace the layered tunics. 'We don't want them attracting attention. There are those who would take their own actions in relation to this prisoner. Tell them to dress her in a hooded jerkin or similar, not her Aranti tunic.'

'Very good, my lord.'

At last most of the ceremonial items had been packed away. The rest Lendri could manage himself. But still the clerk hovered.

'Is there something else, Pelor?'

'Yes, my lord. A slave has been waiting — he bears a package and insisted on handing it to you in person.'

'Very well, where is he?'

'In the reception area, my lord. We passed him on our way through.'

Lendri nodded wearily. 'I will see him now.'

The slave wasn't the one he had expected. This boy was small and thin and strangely grey — no wonder he hadn't noticed him earlier. He had one bruised eye and a pinched, frightened face. He must have leapt from his seat when the door opened. He looked both guilty and terrified, as if he expected a beating.

'What is your name, boy?' Lendri asked gently.

'Ash, your lordship. Mildari ... I mean.'

'There's no need to be frightened, Ash. ... I believe you have a delivery?'

The boy handed over the package with shaking hands, and Lendri examined it carefully. The seal was intact; however, it was larger than usual. He frowned.

'Was there any message from, er, from the Malshorne?'

'No, no message, my lord.' The boy was clearly petrified. Lendri looked quizzically at his swollen face and wondered briefly whether to question him further, but the day had already been fraught with serious and exhausting matters. The Malshorne could wait.

'Very well. You may go.'

⁂

As expected, messengers came in the late afternoon, confirming the intention of three Houses to challenge Lendri's actions in the Senate. Such a storm was wholly predictable, but when a soft knock disturbed Lendri yet again, he sighed deeply.

Pelor crept in. 'My lord, there are men here whom you may wish to interview.'

Lendri frowned, rubbing his eyes. He just wanted to be left in peace, but he had to admit, the man had impeccable judgment.

'Who is it, Pelor?'

'It's the guardians ... those sent to take the girl to the barge.'

Lendri sat upright. 'What do they want?'

'Perhaps it's best they tell you themselves, my lord,' answered the clerk, his face as impassive as ever.

Two heavily-built guardians were ushered in at once. Their uniforms were stretched tautly across their bulging stomachs; if they had ever fitted properly, they certainly didn't anymore. They looked like brothers, with the same brown eyes and sandy hair. Or was it just their shape and earnestly stupid expressions that made them so alike? As they bowed and shuffled their feet, Lendri made a mental note to review the guardians — supposing that he managed to retain office. If these were the two of the best, what must the others be like?

'Well, what is it?'

'My lord, we regret to inform you that the girl has escaped.'

'Escaped?' repeated Lendri sharply. Was there ever to be an end to the trials of this day?

The taller one, apparently the more senior of the two, began to relate the tale, his eyes wide and imploring.

'It was goats, your lordship.'

'Sheep,' the second corrected.

'No, they was definitely goats. Those little, bug-eyed ones. You know the ones?'

Lendri waved impatiently. 'Yes, yes. I think I know the creatures.'

'Oh.' The guardian looked impressed. 'And are they goats, my lord?'

'I really don't know. And I suspect it may be irrelevant. Pray continue.'

'Yes. Of course, you are right. Sorry, your lordship.' The guardian scowled at his partner before resuming. 'We was taking the back route as directed, my lord, proceeding along the Nocheir way, and the girl was giving us no trouble.'

'No trouble at all,' his companion confirmed.

'Nobody pays us any attention. Then, we reach the little common, just past the potteries. There was a flock grazing, but we didn't think twice about that; slaves often graze their animals there. It was all very pretty and quiet.'

'Very peaceful,' his partner chipped in.

'Then, all of a sudden, these goats look up and see us. And what do they do? They charge right at us, all a-bleating and jumping on all fours. You've never seen such excited beasts, my lord! The two shepherd boys did their best to control them, they were a-flapping their arms and shouting, but the daft things had just gone crazy!'

'Crazy,' confirmed his partner.

'Before we knew it, they was falling about us, jumping at the girl and rolling their bug-eyes. Some fainted, then got back up and fainted again. We'd never seen the like of it, had we, Mevlin?'

'Never.'

'Then in the middle of it all, the girl leaps up onto a water barrel. Somehow she's got her hands free! Up she jumps onto the roof, and off she goes! She was a-leaping and a-springing across those rooftops as fast as a wild thing.'

'That she was.'

'Now I can guess what you might be thinking — and you'd be right, my lord — we should have given chase. But there was no going after her! Mevlin and I are quick when need asks, but we're not made for leaping over rooftops.'

Lendri suppressed a smile. 'No, indeed,' he murmured.

'Then one of the shepherds he ups and offers to help. "I'll get her," says he. And off he goes, as quick as he can scamper. He might have caught her and all, but we don't know about that. We lost sight of the pair of 'em.'

'Oh, they were that quick,' his partner shook his head dolefully.

'So,' the storyteller cleared his throat, 'we regret to inform you that we have failed in our duties, your lordship. We are deeply sorry and will shoulder our punishment cheerfully as befits our standing as guardians of the city.'

It was obviously rehearsed; the other chimed in with the last few words, and they stood to attention, thrusting out chests and bellies.

Lendri's mouth quivered slightly as he nodded. 'I will deal with the matter and speak to the High Protector regarding your discipline. Should you tell anyone else of this, you will be dismissed,' he added sternly. 'Is that clear?'

The pair nodded and bowed. 'Thank you, your lordship,' they mumbled as they backed clumsily out of the door.

Pelor crept closer. 'Shall I send for Gooel, my lord?'

'No,' Lendri shook his head. 'I think not Pelor. Take a couple of my guards and search the streets of the Salturne sector — discreetly. If she's still not found by morning, then Gooel can pick up the scent.'

'Very good, my lord.'

For the first time that day Lendri felt his spirits lift. Kep the Valiant, indeed! The gods were surely with this child. It was unlikely the guards would find her among the rambling sprawl of the Salturne Third. He smiled sadly. At least she would have one last night of freedom.

Chapter 18

SMOKED KARLIMON PIE

When Ash vaulted onto the crooked rooftops of the Salturne sector, Kep was a long way ahead already, running along the ridge of a shambling building. She would be making for 'the hide' on the other side of the city. He slipped off his sandals. Barefoot was safest: broken tiles and uneven shingles made the going treacherous, but there was no time for hesitation. He leapt a void, almost falling short. Wheeling his arms, he gripped the edge with his toes, heart hammering. A fall would be fatal.

They kept running, helter-skelter, until the tiles underfoot became the reddish variety, faded and scorched by long years. The crooked landscape started to look more familiar, with the arches of the ancient law courts lying just ahead. Creeping behind the stone façade, they leapt the gap and landed on the sloping roof of the Weavers' Guild. They had to slow down then, picking their way over fragile tiles, the discoloured ones softened by moss and time. Filthy windows allowed glimpses of the weavers far below, bent over their clattering looms.

Kep was already at the edge of the roof, adjusting a plank between the buildings, then, arms wide and head straight, she walked across. The precarious plank was an old enemy, rocking and wobbling.

Don't stop. Don't look down. Ash warded off a hot rush of panic, then, sick with relief, gained the other side. Reaching the entrance to the creep, he cast a swift look around, before following Kep inside. There was no turning back now.

He crawled on in the dark, worming into the hidden structures of the buildings. The tunnel bent and turned, unbearably tightly, until at last he heard a scraping noise ahead. The faintest glimmer lit his way, then the floor opened. Working himself into the gap, he dropped into the hide.

The hide was a strange space, accessed only by the secret tunnel. It was roughly square, with a tiny window that stared at a blank wall. Who knew how it had come to be built? Perhaps it had been designed as a hiding place all along, or perhaps the building plans had gone awry, leaving the little room stranded. Braig had discovered it quite by accident, and Ash had always thought that it had been such a stupid thing to do, crawling down a dusty tunnel into the dark, with no idea where it led. Now he blessed Braig's foolhardiness with all his heart. It was the most secret of places. He scanned the room, and was relieved to see that it was just as he had left it that morning. Good. Then he saw the expression on Kep's face.

'Ash! Why did you follow!' She had her fists clenched at her sides. Her dark brows were twisted, her eyes flashing. 'You have to go! Now!'

Ash blinked. He had expected tears, or shock, but not this angry outburst.

'Don't you realise what you've done?'

'I've rescued you,' he replied stupidly.

'Yes, and that was clever of you. And very brave. But also very stupid! I've got a tracker, Ash! You can't be here. Go! Now! While there's time.' She waved her hands, as if to shoo him away. 'Go! I made my choice. You shouldn't have put yourself in danger. It was stupid. Stupid!' She lashed out and hit him with the flat of her hand. Then to his horror she burst into tears. 'Please, Ash,' she sobbed. 'I can't bear it if you end up in the fields because of me.'

'But I had no choice,' Ash stammered in his defence. 'I made a promise!' He hadn't meant to shout, but it was true. He hadn't asked for this; he'd had no choice about any of it.

'A promise?' she spluttered. She put both hands to her head. 'For the sake of Telion, Ash! What could you possibly have promised to make you act so rashly!'

'I promised Braig I'd free you!' he blurted. There — it was said. He swallowed hard. Something in his throat hurt when he thought about those awful last moments.

'Braig?' Her expression transformed. 'You promised Braig? When?'

'Just before he died.'

'You were with Braig when he died?' Her mouth quivered.

He nodded wretchedly.

'And you made a promise to him that you'd free me?' she asked in disbelief.

'Yes ... And all the slaves.' It sounded so utterly foolish that he blushed.

'But I wasn't sure the quest was real, then,' he added miserably.

'Oh, right. The quest.' Kep's blue eyes flashed dangerously. 'Of course!' She threw up her hands. 'Braig's big secret quest! The one he wouldn't tell me anything about. The one he lied to Cairn about. The one that obviously got him killed!'

Ash was bewildered. 'How do you know Braig lied to Cairn?' he ventured, when the silence grew too loud.

'How could all that rubbish not be a lie? Flyboys and gnarkin beasts? Honestly, Ash… Don't you lie to me, too.' She turned away, but her anguish filled the room. Ash rubbed his head. Somehow he had to make her understand. But he didn't even understand himself; all he knew was that he had made a frightening decision and had no idea what to do next.

'I'm leaving Mildaresh,' he blurted at last. Saying the words aloud twisted his stomach with fear, but he pushed on. 'The quest, well … It might be real. And I promised to see it through. At least, I promised to try … And I want you to come with me.' His voice broke as he added, 'I can't do it on my own.'

Kep turned to face him. Wiping her tears away, she took in her friend's appearance. He had a nasty cloud of purplish-yellow blotches around one eye, with an inky smudge underneath. Instead of his grey tunic he wore a dark green jerkin with a deep hood and brown leggings. It was odd; she had never seen him in anything but grey. Whatever had happened? She could tell he had a story to tell, but surely he must realise that what he had just come out with was complete lunacy?

She spoke clearly and slowly: 'Slaves don't go on quests, Ash. And they don't leave Mildaresh. If they do, they get hunted down and killed. No one escapes the snouts. No one.'

Ash frowned. This was going to be much harder than he had thought. Somehow he had to make her listen. But how could he convince her to embark on a quest that he hadn't even believed in himself until Credé had tried to kill him?

'Thanks for rescuing me,' she was saying, more gently. 'Really, Ash. You can't imagine how happy I was to see my dear bug-eyes.' Her eyes filled with tears again. 'And you, too,' she added. 'But don't you see how crazy you sound? You've won me one last breath of freedom, and for that I'm grateful. I really am, but I'll turn myself in tomorrow. And you must forget this quest nonsense. Go back to the House of Feyindi now. Please? Before it's too late.'

Ash ran his hands through his hair, but he couldn't think how to make her listen, so he just stood there in confused silence. Then something happened that had more impact than anything he could have said. There was a movement from deep inside his hood, and Tarlyn clambered up to perch on his shoulder.

Kep jumped back at once with a cry.

The creature shivered and her ruff went up: *The Taelstaun must go to T'al Jazure.*

Kep froze and turned pale.

'It's all right,' he said quickly. 'This is Tarlyn.'

'Tarlyn?' Kep squeaked.

'Yeah. Credé's pet.' Tarlyn's low growl made him reconsider. 'Well, sort of … I don't know really.'

'Credé?'

'That's the Malshorne's name.'

'It— It spoke!' Kep's eyes were wide and frightened.

'Yeah, I know. But don't worry, it doesn't happen very often.' Ash grinned a small grin. 'It's a bit creepy, isn't it?'

With Kep apparently speechless, Ash seized his opportunity and spoke all in a rush. 'Please listen, Kep. If you listen you'll understand. I can tell you all about Credé, about the Taelstone, about Braig and the Song and everything. Then, when you've heard the full story you'll see why we have to go. Please, will you listen?'

Kep didn't take her eyes off Tarlyn, but she nodded her head slowly. She was very pale, and looked as though she might faint.

'Here. Let's sit down and have something to eat.' Ash uncovered a bundle in the corner, revealing a number of parcels, all wrapped in grey paper and stamped with the Feyindi crest. He picked one up and folded the covering back. 'I think this one's smoked karlimon pie.'

'Smoked karlimon?' Kep looked from the tiny pie being offered, to Tarlyn, and back again in a daze. 'Wherever did you get it?'

'It was easy,' said Ash shyly, unwrapping cold meats, cheeses and pastries. 'They put me on alms duty this morning to distribute the banquet leftovers to the poor and needy. And I couldn't think of anyone needier.' He caught her eye, and added, 'Don't worry, there was plenty for the poor families, too.'

Kep didn't know which was more unbelievable: the sight of all those leftover delicacies; Tarlyn, who had left Ash's shoulder to explore the room; or the transformation of her timid friend into an accomplished thief and rescuer.

They stuffed the delicacies into their mouths with their fingers, marvelling at the flavours. Then, falteringly, Ash began his story. It made a pretty peculiar tale. He didn't think he would have believed it. Kep listened intently and only spoke once. 'Feld!' she exclaimed. Her blue eyes shone bright with anger. Apart from that, she remained silent.

The twilight bell was tolling just as he was describing the trouble of keeping the bug-eyes calm until the right moment. They laughed together, remembering the surprised looks on the guardians' sweating faces, and their pathetically grateful acceptance of Ash's offer to 'apprehend the prisoner'. Their laughter echoed weirdly in the small room.

All of a sudden it felt very odd being there together, alone.

'And ... well ... that's it. You know the rest,' Ash ended lamely.

Kep folded her arms. 'And where is this Taelstaun? Still in Credé's hut?'

'Taelstone,' he corrected. 'Yes.'

'But Tarlyn said "Taelstaun".'

'I know. I've wondered about that, but I don't think Tarlyn really speaks. I mean, she just repeats the words of others. So maybe it's a different accent or something.' Tarlyn blinked at him.

'Hmm.' Kep looked doubtful.

'Oh, I nearly forgot.' Ash rummaged in a haversack and produced a jar of assorted weevils and bugs. Placing it in the opposite corner of the room, he removed the lid. The creature immediately pounced upon a sleepy moth and munched it with relish.

'Sorry,' he said when Kep pulled a face. 'I think she only eats insects.'

They watched on as Tarlyn dispatched the remaining bugs. Kep seemed so deep in thought that Ash was reluctant to speak. Finally, he could bear it no longer.

'So, what do you think?'

'About what?'

'About the quest,' he said, as patiently as he could.

'Oh! Yes. Of course we have to try.'

He blinked in surprise.

'Well, Credé said T'al Jazure had the power to free the slaves and he had no reason to lie, because he thought you were about to die. So that must be true. He obviously didn't want anyone taking the Taelstone to T'al Jazure, so ...' she held out her hands, 'that's exactly what we should do.'

Ash stared in amazement. In minutes she had come to the same conclusion he had agonised over for hours. She smiled a little at his confusion, then said soberly, 'The hard bit isn't working out the right thing to do, Ash. It's working out how to do it without getting ourselves killed.'

Chapter 19

CREDÉ'S LEGACY

The shadows are moving again: forming pictures. New shapes rise from the music. The figure of a child wavers then becomes clear. The boy gestures at the wall before him. He has been painting. Someone has brought him materials. He has painted mountains and turrets and shining towers. His home? The boy shakes his head. It's a secret. Nobody must know. He holds out his hands to reveal two crescent moons, one etched on each palm. The melody changes again and the vision fades.

The Song was still haunting the edges of Ash's mind. Now he pushed it away more firmly: he needed all of his attention on the task at hand. In the weak light of dawn, the Malshorne's hut looked even more dishevelled than usual. The door hung crookedly on its frame, the chimney had fallen sideways, and the roof sagged like a broken hem-line. The clearing was unnervingly quiet. If there were birds in the trees, none had the heart for singing.

Tarlyn gave a low growl in Ash's ear, but the warmth of her tail around his neck was reassuring.

The plan was to get in, grab the Taelstone and anything else that might be useful, and get out. Then they would head back to lie low in the scrublands on the old road to Idira, where they would risk jumping one of the loaded wagons. Idira was full of traders and travellers, so it seemed as good a place as any to inquire after T'al Jazure. Judging by his title, he was a man of some importance. Perhaps someone would have heard of him? Maybe he even lived in Idira. Ash knew that this was unlikely, and that their plan was pretty weak, but it was the best they had come up with. Kep seemed optimistic, though, convinced that the gods were on their side. Ash wasn't so sure.

He took a deep breath. Gods or no gods, they had to get this dreadful step over with first. He swallowed his forebodings and edged around the broken door.

A powerful smell of decomposing matter assaulted them at once, and it was difficult to see in the gloom.

'Is there a light?'

'I don't know.' Ash was acutely aware of the figure lying prone on the bed. He tried hard not to look, afraid of what he might see. 'I suppose there must be.' Fighting down panic, he remembered a sconce on the wall above the woodpile. The darkstone shone like a black void beneath his feet as he crossed the room. He shivered, glad to step off the other side. 'I think this might be one.' He lifted the object from its holder, frowning. It was elliptical in shape; one of the tapered ends felt cold and seemed to be made of polished metal. The middle section certainly seemed to be a light chamber of some sort, but Ash couldn't see where the elpha fuel would go. The whole thing was completely smooth. Kep had crept to his side. They both peered at the strange item. Perhaps it was just an ornament after all?

'Try turning it upside down,' suggested Kep.

Ash couldn't see what good that would do. 'Here, you take it. I'll keep looking.' He passed the object to Kep, who promptly inverted it. Instantaneously the chamber filled with golden light.

'That's neat,' said Kep. Holding up the curious lamp, she clamped a hand over her mouth. Her eyes darted from the ghastly forms of the yaggluts to the awful sight of the body on the bed. 'Let's hurry,' she quavered.

Ash couldn't agree more. He knew what he wanted: his boots, the knife and the Taelstone — preferably in that order. He certainly wasn't going anywhere near that bed until the very last moment.

'See if you can find a flint over on that bench,' he suggested. Sadly, only one boot had survived the yaggluts, but he spotted the knife, and stepped around rotting corpses to retrieve it. As he fed it carefully into an old scabbard he had scavenged from the kitchens, Kep spoke quietly.

'Ash, what's this?'

She was staring at the time-piece.

'Just a machine — it keeps the time.' He wished she would concentrate on looking for a flint, but she seemed mesmerised.

'What happens when it reaches this red line?'

'What red line?' he snapped.

Moving to her side, he suddenly realised the machine was making quite a different sound to its usual ticking. It sounded louder — more deliberate. He cocked his head, frowning. Had there been that many cogs and wires before? He was almost certain the big dial was new, and its hand *was* moving steadily, towards a bright red line. With a sudden jolt he realised the Malshorne's tricks were not yet exhausted. 'Get out!' he shouted. 'Now!'

Kep needed no encouragement. She was through the door in a split second, Tarlyn at her heels.

Ash made a lunge for the bed. He was neither cautious nor reverent, this new fear blocking out everything else as he wrested the Taelstone unceremoniously from Credé's dead grip. As he launched himself through the door the time machine gave a final emphatic click. One minute Ash was running, the next he was spat up into the air. The hillside came down around him in a sliding lurch.

Ash coughed and spluttered, rolling free from the debris. The hut was totally buried. Credé had certainly been serious about hiding his secrets! As he pulled himself upright, Tarlyn leapt onto his lap chattering. The Taelstone was burning in his hand like a bright, indestructible bubble, as if some energy had brought it to life. He rubbed his eyes, making them smart.

'By Argess, that was close,' gasped Kep.

For a stunned moment, they gaped at the pile of rocks and broken trees, then shared a terrified look of realisation. That boom couldn't have gone unnoticed, and there was only one path down the mountain — their escape route would be cut off!

'Come on!' Kep yelled, pulling Ash to his feet and flying off down the path. Like a dark ribbon, Tarlyn flashed ahead, then all of a sudden she stopped dead. The ruff on her neck went up, her quills quivering a warning. They skidded to a halt.

'What is it? What's she doing?'

'Shush!' Ash held his finger to his lips. The blood pulsed at his temples. At first they heard nothing, then came the unmistakable sound of dogs baying. Guardians!

They turned and pelted back up the track, racing across the devastated clearing in a blind panic, then scrambling up and over the huge mound of debris. With wide, terrified eyes, they crouched there, peeping through the branches of a broken tree.

'What do we do now?' Ash panted through gasping breaths.

Kep shook her head, dizzy with fear. What could they do?

Then, to their horror, a figure emerged from the trees. There was no mistaking that wiry build and prominent snout. Kep stifled a scream. The tracker was sniffing the air.

The snouts used long, thin pipes to spit poisoned darts, and Gooel unslung just such a weapon from across his back and started to climb the rubble, moving directly towards them.

With sudden conviction Kep knew she should give herself up. She took a deep breath, steeling herself, trying to find the courage to move. But Ash was tugging at her sleeve, speaking quietly but urgently. 'The steps behind the temple!' It made no sense, but he kept dragging her by the arm, so she scrambled blindly after him. *What temple?*

Plunging into a deep bank of ferns, they began to climb. The ground was dark and scented, and slipped away underfoot. After minutes of frantic scrambling, Ash cried out: 'Hurry! Up here!'

Kep followed, pushing hard with her feet and hauling herself upwards. At last, to her great surprise she pulled herself up onto a giant stone step. Above, a mossy stairway wound brokenly up the hill, hampered in its progress by plants groping from every crack.

'Hurry!'

Ash was climbing already. There was no time to stop and marvel. Heart pounding, Kep followed. The steps were so wide and high that she had to push her burning leg muscles to conquer each one. Then, finally, there were no more steps, just a long, wide path — and suddenly that ended, too, blocked by a sheer wall of rock.

Kep spun around, just in time to see the canopy of ferns shaking wildly and Gooel appearing on the stairway. Immediately he started bounding towards them, taking the stairs with ease. Kep's heart sank. It was over.

Ash was standing, calmly gazing at the rock face. Then he suddenly did something completely unexpected: he pushed his hands flat against the rock face, fingers splayed. With a groaning shudder the rock folded back into itself, and Ash stepped forward without hesitation into the yawning darkness.

Kep gasped and stumbled backwards — Gooel was only a few paces away, but he had stopped dead. The last thing Kep saw before the mountain swallowed her was the snout's strange flat face, twisted into an expression of utter disbelief.

— END OF PART 1 —

— PART 2 —
FLIGHT

Chapter 20

DARK

Darkness. Dense, debilitating darkness. Kep wasn't afraid of the dark, she had spent many nights alone under pitch-black skies, but this was different. She held her breath to listen. Nothing. Just total, utter silence. A cold jolt of panic hit. 'Ash?' Her voice seemed muted. No answer. 'Ash!' It wasn't quite a scream, but it wasn't far off.

'I'm here.'

Ash's voice sounded distant and muffled.

She swept her arms through the air, stretching out her fingers blindly. 'Where are you?'

Silence.

She edged forwards. 'Keep talking so I can find you.'

'Here ... I'm here.'

He sounded strangely distant. Kep shuffled forward, feeling her way. Were they in some sort of cave? If only she could see. Of course! The light! What had she done with it? She wriggled the bag off her back, lifted its canvas flap and rummaged. After impatient moments, her fingers discovered something smooth. She pulled out the lamp and tipped it upright.

In its dazzling light, she saw that Ash was nearby, huddled on the floor with Tarlyn beside him. She quickly went over and knelt beside him. 'Are you all right?'

'I think so,' he muttered.

It wasn't convincing, but she was too distracted by their surroundings to argue.

They were in a perfectly round room, which had been hewn from the stone of the mountain itself. All trace of their entry had disappeared. The walls rose straight and sheer, and supported a domed ceiling that had been carved to resemble an inverted flower. Holding the light up higher, Kep gasped at the intricate lines that swept out from the centrepiece. Rubbing the dusty floor with her foot, she realised it was inlaid with mosaic tiles, which radiated outwards in a geometrical pattern. This was no cave.

'Where are we?' she murmured.

'We're in the vestibule.'

Kep turned sharply. 'The vestibule?'

'The threshold to the realm of Eeroktan.' Ash's eyes were glazed. He gestured with one hand: 'The faithful are bearing the Tall One to his final rest.'

Tarlyn gave a mournful murmur and thrashed her tail.

'Oh.' Kep blinked. 'Right. Well ... that's good to know.' Ash must have bumped his head, she reasoned. She touched his shoulder lightly. 'Let's not talk for now. Come on. We'll sit against the wall here and have something to eat.'

They had decided to eat the perishable food first, keeping back the nuts, bread and dried fruit, since those would keep longest. As she took a slightly squashed parcel from the front pocket of her bag, Kep's brow furrowed. How long would the food last if they were stuck in here?

The remaining tarts were filled with a luscious custard that flooded their mouths with creamy sweetness. The light, buttery pastry broke into soft flakes and melted on their tongues. Ash instantly thought of Jem as he bit into the crust. He had watched her rolling out these little tarts so many times; he could never have imagined that he would end up eating one. The memory of her deft, floury hands helped bring him back to himself. He smiled wanly at Kep, who gave him a relieved smile in return.

When the last morsel was finished and washed down with a mouthful of water, she looked at him expectantly.

'Well, are you feeling better?'

He nodded, although his head was aching as if it would split.

'Good. So would you mind explaining what just happened? How did you know about that stairway, and the door?'

He swallowed, avoiding her eyes. 'I don't know. I just saw it in my mind.'

'Like a vision, you mean?'

He shrugged uncomfortably. 'I suppose.' He hesitated before adding, 'I think I could open it again ... but if I did, we'd be caught.'

Kep frowned at the place where the door should be, and shook her head. 'Not necessarily. We could wait until it's safe.'

Ash returned his eyes to hers unwillingly. 'But there's another door,' he faltered. 'I think it leads through the mountain.' He winced, not daring to tell Kep about the solemn procession that he had watched passing through the vestibule: the cloaked men with the grave faces of priests; the keening women; the soldiers weeping as they walked, carrying the body of their young king on a bier strewn with flowers. She would think he was losing his mind. He probably was. He could still hear music, faintly. Nevertheless, he was wary. It might get stronger at any moment and sweep him from himself once more.

When Tarlyn leapt onto his lap, he stroked her head uncertainly. She was so alien with those huge, mirrored eyes, but he had the strangest feeling she knew exactly what was going on. What had she said? *The Song is a harsh mistress.* He shivered at the thought.

Kep narrowed her eyes as she watched her two companions, the one so dark and the other so pale. The creature certainly seemed to have attached itself to Ash, and Kep wasn't at all sure that this was a good thing. She folded her arms.

'Right,' she began firmly, 'I said I'd help you, Ash, and I will, but you have to be honest with me. I know there's something wrong, and you'd better tell me what it is before we go any further.' She was perfectly aware that they might not actually be able to go any further anyway, but that wasn't the point. She waited, tapping one finger on her arm.

Ash rubbed at his head, then sighed. 'I think it's the Song,' he confessed. 'Ever since I sang with Credé there's been music in my head and running through my dreams. I think it has something to do with these visions.'

Kep nodded thoughtfully. Ash hadn't actually described the passing of the Song in any great detail, so she had little clue what he was talking about, but it was a start. 'So it's the same song then?' she asked. 'The same one you sang on the darkstone?'

Ash didn't answer. How could he even begin to describe the complexity of the Song and all its strange layers and intricacies? He frowned at his feet.

'Well, you know what I think?' said Kep after a pause. 'I think these visions have been sent by Telion to guide us. The gods often send visions to people in need.' She gave him a look that dared him to disagree. 'Besides, we can't stay here,' she added, brushing the pastry flakes from her clothes. 'Let's start by finding out if there really is another door.'

As they approached the opposite wall, Ash caught his breath. A woman wrapped in a blue-hooded cloak had suddenly appeared and was walking right towards them. When the image dissolved, like fog in the sunlight, he gasped involuntarily.

'What is it?'

'Nothing. Just a headache, that's all.' Forcing himself to breathe normally, he stepped forward, stretching his hands out to the wall, and closing his eyes. He couldn't help feeling ridiculous. What if nothing happened?

But as soon as his fingers made contact, Ash somehow knew exactly what would happen. A shudder ran through his entire body, and, opening his eyes, he saw that the darkest of tunnels had materialised, framed by an elaborate arch.

Kep's eyes flew wide open and she held the lamp higher. Its light barely pierced the darkness — beyond was a deep, yawning emptiness. The archway itself was exquisite, rich blue and impossibly smooth. With one finger she traced the pearly-white inlay that ran along the inside edge. She shook her head slowly.

What strange power was at work here?

'Well,' she said thoughtfully, 'what do we do now?'

⁂

'It smells fresh at least,' Kep remarked, as she stepped into the tunnel. 'And there's water somewhere, too. I can smell it. Come on.'

Ash followed with a sense of dread. He was finding his friend's cheerfulness both impressive and annoying in equal measure. Once she made up her mind to do something, she seemed able to put all apprehensions to one side and just get on with it. He wished he could master his fears as easily. Even though they had decided to risk the mountain path, he was still horribly uncertain. They only had enough food for two days, three if they were careful, and they would have to ration their water strictly, too.

How long did it take to walk through a mountain? They had decided to give it a day, then turn back if things didn't look promising. As Kep had pointed out, it did seem better than sitting in the vestibule hoping for a miracle, but now Ash wished he had kept his mouth shut. The thought of surrender to Gooel and the guardians suddenly seemed appealing in comparison to the nightmares that might lie in wait, deep in the mountain's heart. It took all his courage to follow the wavering light into the void. While the ground underfoot was quite smooth, the walls were rough-hewn, and there were no features to mark their progress, just the tramping of their feet and the beating of their hearts. The tunnel took a gentle turn every now and then, but otherwise ran straight. Before long, reality shrank until it consisted entirely of the shining glow of their lamp and the looming darkness beyond. They soon realised that their plan to walk for a day was flawed: how long *was* a day in an underworld? Indeed, they quickly lost all sense of time; minutes gave way to hours, and hours to timeless dreams and memory.

Kep had been pushing thoughts of Braig to the back of her mind, but now it was impossible to keep them at bay: Braig's delight at his own silly pranks; the concentration on his face during pilat; his whoops of joy at winning; that strong, tanned neck with the soft hollow at the base of his throat ... Tears coursed silently down her face as she remembered his cheerful grin at dinner and how he always made everyone laugh. The knowledge of Feld's betrayal, too, had been sitting in her stomach like a tiny ember, starved of attention. Now it flared and caught. Her pace became a march as her thoughts took shape, her hatred a welcome counterbalance to grief. She saw Feld in her mind's eye, standing over Braig's poor body. She guessed at how he might have boasted afterwards. With every step her anger grew, and with it a terrible oath to Narsis. She would never, *never* let herself forget. As she swore to herself that she would deliver vengeance upon Feld one day, or die trying, she strode ever more resolutely, holding the lamp high and feeling the darkness yielding before her.

Following behind, Ash felt more as if the darkness was pursuing them; it seemed to lap at his heels like an evil presence. He kept his gaze firmly on Kep's shoulders and tried to count their steps, but the thousands quickly defeated him, further fuelling his anxiety. The Song was a constant presence now, hovering at the edge of his mind. He tried replaying pilat games in his head — anything to block out the melody. When that failed, he forced himself to imagine every detail of the Feyindi kitchen, but nothing could stop the notes that seeped into his consciousness — then, all at once, he found himself in a courtyard full of light.

The breeze blows cool against his face. He watches the banners of gold and blue rippling atop the mighty watchtowers; the insignia of bird and leaf flies proudly against the sky. The voices of children intermingle with melody as they race each other across the square. They skip and shout in celebration. Tiny tots are swooped into the arms of doting uncles and wave their little fists in protest. Women flutter in knots of delighted chatter. The young girls are all ribbons and curls and swaying skirts. Everything is familiar, yet so unfamiliar. The buildings seem freshly cut. The abundance of water puzzles him, too: it gurgles from faucets, dazzling and dancing in fountains, and splashing in shallow pools. He realises he's thirsty. A little girl drinks from a spout, standing on tippy-toes on the pedestal. He wants to put his hand out to touch her glinting hair as he waits his turn. The melody is racing now, the notes tumble over themselves in their exuberance. He leans forward to drink. Then the smell of blood hits him full in the face. 'No! Nas elart en!'

The scream Ash let out was so anguished and so strange that Kep screamed herself. She whirled around just in time to see him crumple forward.

'What is it? What is it?'

'Blood! Blood!' he gasped. He staggered, staring at his hands.

She grasped his wrists. 'Ash, it's all right. You're all right. There's no blood.' She felt sick with shock. What was wrong with him? His whole body was trembling. He was staring wildly into her face.

'It's blood! The fountains are running with blood!' He turned away and retched.

⁂

'Sorry.'

'It's not your fault.'

'No. I should have helped you,' Kep answered firmly. 'I forgot about your visions, about the Song.' She patted his hand. 'I forgot you were ... struggling ...' Her sentence trailed off. 'Anyway ... Sorry.'

They were sitting close together against the wall, knees pulled up to their chests, their shoulders almost touching. Ash could feel the warm space that her body carved from the darkness. His heart sank. 'No, Kep. I'm sorry. I shouldn't have asked you to come.' He groaned. 'We can't do this. We can't just keep walking into the dark like this. It's madness.'

'I know. It's very strange.' Kep sniffed and rubbed at her face with her sleeve. 'The dark messes with your mind until you hardly know what you are thinking.'

He wondered at the sudden bitterness in her tone.

'But we can't go back yet, Ash. We haven't done what we agreed. We haven't walked for a day. I'm not hungry enough for it to be twilight yet. It could be noon, though. She nodded firmly. 'Let's agree that it's noon now, have a bite to eat, then carry on until we're really hungry again.'

Ash remained silent. He wasn't sure he could face another march into the darkness.

'And look,' Kep continued, 'the tunnel is wider now, so we can walk side by side. And we'll talk as we go, to stop us thinking, or dreaming ...' She trailed off again.

'I don't think it was a dream,' he said quietly.

'No? Well, perhaps not: it did sound more like a nightmare.'

He frowned and went to speak, but she cut him off.

'Let's not talk about it. Let's wait until we are out in the sunshine on the other side of the mountain.' She unwrapped a soft, round cheese. 'Tell you what: I'll teach you how to make cheese!'

❧

They set off again, this time walking shoulder to shoulder. Kep was true to her word in keeping the conversation going; in fact, Ash was tempted to tell her to shut up. He did learn how to make cheese, though, or at least the main principles. Then they competed for the best gossip from their masters' tables. Even though Kep had been waiting at table for such a short time, she won convincingly; the House of Aranti had no rival when it came to gossip and political intrigue.

Despite aching feet and a growing hunger they kept walking, and talking, until all of a sudden the air changed and the tunnel flared out. At their feet lay a wide staircase, disappearing into the gloom.

'Well, that looks promising,' Kep remarked.

Ash wondered if she was being sarcastic; it was hard to tell.

Ash couldn't help feeling even more anxious as they descended: every step down was one more to climb back up. The staircase sank swiftly, taking them deeper underground. When it finally came to an end, the wall to their left ended suddenly. The ground on that side fell away in a bank of shale and rocks.

'Where are we?' Kep whispered.

Ash didn't answer. He held the light as high as he could, but it couldn't penetrate far into what seemed a massive cavern. While the path curved down before them, they could no longer see a roof above; the wall on their right went straight up, sheer and glistening.

'Listen! Something dripped,' Kep whispered.

They both listened intently until they heard another echoing drip, somewhere far below.

'Water!' They grinned at each other, their teeth shining weirdly in the light.

'Let's drink before we go on,' Kep suggested.

Ash nodded. His mouth was parched. Reaching for his water pouch, he was just about to remark that they didn't really need to whisper when the hairs on his neck prickled. Suddenly, for no reason, he felt sick with fear. One urgent thought leapt into his mind: something was coming, coming swiftly through the dark — something they should avoid.

He felt Tarlyn whirl and dive into his hood, and that decided it. 'Hide! We have to hide!'

Ignoring Kep's protests, he pulled her off the path, the loose material skating underneath them, making them lose their footing. For a moment it seemed they might just keep sliding, then a sizeable rock slowed the avalanche and halted their progress. Ash hauled Kep behind it and extinguished the light. 'Be quiet!' he ordered.

Kep couldn't help feeling indignant at such rough handling. She had scraped her knee, and the palm of one hand was stinging. Frowning, she raised it to her mouth and sucked it silently. Ash was trembling beside her. What if he *was* losing his mind? There in the darkness it was all too easy to get dragged into his fear, and as they sat in silence, their backs against the hard rock, her own heart started pounding, too.

She told herself not to be so silly. Then, all of a sudden her mouth went dry and her scalp crawled. Craning her neck, she looked towards where the path must be. Something *was* there. A blacker piece of darkness was moving swiftly along the narrow walkway! Her spine suddenly felt as if it had been shot full of black ice. Her heartbeat surged. It was upon them: a terrible vortex of snaking tails. Her throat constricted. She was suffocating, falling, whirling into darkness.

Chapter 21

ARANTI'S VISITOR

As the Aranti household slumbered, a lone watchman scratched the stubble on his chin and frowned. Although the night was still, and full of the song of crickets, somehow it weighed oddly upon the soul. For thirty-eight years he had paced this courtyard, and every sound, every shadow was familiar. Yet on a night like this anything could put your nerves on edge. It was nothing tangible, just a feeling — something you couldn't put your finger on.

When leaves rustled, he found himself swinging about, half-drawing his sword. Scanning the trees, he jumped, momentarily shocked by the round face staring back. Just a barn-owl. Nothing more. He released his grip on the sword and scolded himself. He was far too old to be spooked by shadows and be jumping at owls. But as the long hours wore on he couldn't throw off his feeling of dread, and when the clatter of carriage wheels came to his ears it was a true blessing. He honestly couldn't remember when he had felt such enthusiasm at his master's return.

Maliagne Aranti dismounted from the carriage and brushed past the gateman with customary impatience. He entered the villa, and swept off his cloak, surrendering it to his secretary who had materised on cue. 'Were there developments in my absence, Kartor?'

'No, my lord. However the Calkinon ambassador seeks audience with you tomorrow.'

'Indeed,' Maliagne nodded. It was not unexpected. Never missing a whisper, the ambassador would be seeking assurances of political stability in Mildaresh; an upheaval in the Senate could disrupt the noikos supply, and the demand for elpha fuel was stronger than ever now with the Skavian war intensifying. Calkinon's envoy would require very careful treatment indeed.

A tray of sweetmeats had been set in the library with a decanter of sweet wine. Maliagne eased his travel-weary body into an armchair and drew the glass towards him.

'No visitors?'

'None but Fenic, my lord.'

Maliagne looked up sharply. 'Does he wait?'

'Yes, my lord. Shall I send him through?'

He nodded with a frown. It was late, but he knew how his mind would only niggle after the man's news. Best to see him before retiring.

Maliagne leaned back and laced his fingers together. The day had been long but fruitful, and most of the pieces were in place. The Feyindi had been easily won over. Admittedly, it had been galling to swallow Marlashetta's insult from the Feast of Passing, but such was the game. He was willing to defer his revenge: it would be all the more potent for a longer brewing. Serenitia Moagli hadn't batted an eyelid at his overtures, she had told him to stop being coy and had proposed her own deal: the legitimisation of the Moagli Cadet Squad in turn for unqualified support in the Senate. He was wary of her motives, but it was an acceptable arrangement.

He yawned, continuing his tally, counting off each alliance on his fingers. As expected, the priesthood hadn't resisted; they were howling for blood. Only one man was more damned than Lendri as far as the priests were concerned — Domberto Hamalton. Maliagne lifted a displeased eyebrow. He had believed the young priest satisfactorily bound to his service. Taking a sip of wine, he made a sour face in spite of its sweetness. How extraordinary that Domberto should ruin a promising career for the sake of one moral outburst. As he puzzled over the young man's peculiarity, there came a soft knock at the door.

Fenic had the perfect face for his profession, utterly unmemorable — the sort of face no one would look at twice. He bowed, too slightly for Maliagne's liking. 'Report,' he commanded.

'I followed the woman as requested.'

'And?'

'More of the same my lord. She spends her time in the poor quarters, visiting the sick. Some try to thank her with gifts, but she always refuses.'

'Yes, yes. The hands of a healer and all that.' Maliagne picked up a stuffed fig and bit into it. How did she always manage to make him feel like a spoilt child? But that was the deal, after all: her mornings were her own to spend as she pleased, and he was well compensated by her attentions in the evenings. He scowled. The fig had been a mistake: its sticky sweetness stuck between his teeth. Damn the woman. Damn her gorgeous body and green eyes. And damn Fenic for that insolent smirk!

He struggled to keep his tone cool. 'So … Nothing unusual?' It had been the same story for months. Perhaps he should leave off fretting and trust his beautiful mistress after all. He toyed with his glass, running his thumbs over the rim.

'Same as usual my lord. At least … until this morning.'

He knew it! The blasted man was playing with him. 'Tell me,' he snapped.

Fenic smirked slightly, but not enough to attract censure. 'I followed the woman to the courtrooms, my lord. There I saw a snout coming out. Short fellow, bandy legs and big ears — ugly chap. Gooel is his name. Now here's the funny thing. She pulled him to one side, and kept looking about as if she didn't want to be observed. They spoke for a while, then he went on his way.'

Maliagne frowned. What would she want with such a repulsive creature? 'What did they say?'

The man shook his head. 'I was too far away to hear.'

Maliagne narrowed his eyes. He agreed it was odd, but it wasn't particularly disturbing. Why did the man look so smug, then? 'And then?'

'I followed her to a side entrance. She didn't enter, just waited. But after a while a man came out and they walked together.'

'A man?' Maliagne crushed his napkin in his hand. 'What man?'

'I couldn't see at first. He was heavily cloaked and hooded. But I followed. I didn't dare get close, but I did see him give her something.'

'What? What sort of something?'

'I don't know, my lord.'

'And you didn't see his face?'

'Well, here's the thing, my lord.' Fenic licked his lips. 'I invested a small coin and paid an urchin to bump into the pair.'

'And?'

'I'll be reimbursed?'

'Of course.' He knew the man was goading him intentionally, holding back his prize until the last moment. He ground his teeth. 'And? You saw his face?'

'He did look my way, my lord.' The man paused again, relishing his moment. 'It was Torland Lendri.'

Maliagne stood alone on his balcony glaring into the darkness. He could barely think for fury. No longer suave politician, canny diplomat or arch manipulator — all of these aspects of his personality had fled. Now there was just rage and fierce, burning jealousy. *Matapharni!* He wanted to scream her name. How could a woman be so beautiful and yet so treacherous? Damn that woman!

He tortured himself by imagining the meeting, her face, those eyes dancing the way they did. Did they laugh together? Was she laughing at him now, cheating and revelling in his despair?

An owl hooted nearby. Holding out his hands, Maliagne saw they were trembling. He had to get a grip on himself. He straightened his back and sucked the night air into his lungs.

But something felt wrong. His scalp prickled with a sudden instinct. Gripping the balustrade, he scanned the gardens. Had something moved below? He squinted. Yes, there! That patch of darkness was blacker than the rest. There! It swayed across the lawns and hovered near the fountain. Maliagne watched, enthralled, trying to make out its shape. Taller than a man, it wavered.

His gut crawled as fascination changed to dread. He opened his mouth to call the guards, then stopped himself short. It had vanished!

Striding up and down the rail, he cast his eyes back and forth, trying to penetrate the gloom. He would have doubted himself but for the icy tingling in his spine. He strained his eyes until they watered. Then he reeled. There it was!

He turned in horror as a stream of dark shapes poured over the balcony wall, writhing and squirming, liquid black, like eels. As he staggered backwards, the mass swept upwards into a black swirling tower.

'Guards! Alarm! Alarm!' It was too late. The darkness swarmed at Maliagne, rushing down his throat in a swift black surge, stifling his agonised shriek.

Chapter 22

SHADES

'Ash? What was that?' Kep couldn't stop trembling.

'I don't know,' he answered weakly. Whatever it was, it had gone. The normal darkness felt strangely comforting. Ash activated the lamp, cupping it with shaking hands to dim the glow.

'Do you really think it's all right to use the light?' Kep's face looked drawn and frightened.

He wasn't sure, but he nodded anyway. 'Let's rest here for a while. The ground's quite soft really.'

It wasn't at all. He unfastened a coverlet from the top of his pack and unrolled it. 'Here, tuck this about you.' It was hard to keep his voice from wobbling. 'You sleep. I'll wake you in a few hours.'

Kep didn't argue. Dragging the cover over her shoulders, she curled herself up.

'We can investigate that dripping when you wake,' he suggested. 'Do you suppose there'll be enough to fill our pouches?'

Kep didn't answer. She was already asleep.

Ash tucked the lamp into the front of his bag and propped himself upright against the hard rock, forcing his eyes to remain open in the pitch black. He wondered where Tarlyn had got to. She had given a low growl and vanished into the darkness. Perhaps she was hunting. But what could she hunt in such a place?

He trained his ears but couldn't hear anything, only the sound of the drips, which seemed even louder now. Some made a resonant plop, as if falling into deep water, others a lighter plash. It was soothing, hypnotic, and it wasn't long before he was drawn unavoidably into the watery music.

A flute is playing; the notes call to him. He climbs, sunlight warm upon his back.

'Look, Papa. My craft's the best. It has real cloth sails. Not just leaves and sticks!' The child's high voice drifts down to him.

A smaller boy pipes up: 'My boat's better!' His boat is tucked safely in a sling around his neck. 'Mama says leaf sails are just as good.'

One of the elders answers kindly, 'Oh, they are, lad. Some leaf-sailed boats have been known to cross the lake!'

'Do you think mine will cross the lake, Tenalt?'

'It may well, lad. It may well.'

The boy's eyes shine. 'It's my first journey,' he puffs, 'to the Source, you know … I'm doing very well to keep up.'

There is gentle laughter. 'That you are, lad, that you are.'

The flautist stands at the threshold; her notes are pure and hollow, amplified by the space behind her. Passing into the cave's mouth, they feel the cool soil-breath of the mountain. The dark journey is made quietly, in groups. Then, at the Source, globes are sent up to light the cavern. There is a great shout of joy. Darkness has been lifted! They raise their voices in worship and set their little crafts upon the lake. They jostle and hang together in fleets upon the dark, shining water. Their tiny candles shine like clouds of fire-flies. The people join hands and sing. They are the blessed.

Ash was still smiling as he woke, grasping at snatches of the dream. Then he came to and groaned. Lifting his hand to his cheek, he brushed away pieces of sharp gravel. Beside him Kep stirred, but didn't wake. He pulled himself up, rubbing his neck. Something felt different. He strained his eyes. It was still pitch black, but something was definitely different. Puzzled, he stared about, then finally looked up.

There, above his head, were two roughly oval shapes, fuzzily grey. He blinked and squinted. As he watched, they seemed to be getting closer. No, it wasn't that — they were getting brighter.

At that moment Tarlyn materialised, a piece of the darkness suddenly become solid. She gave a soft chirrup.

'Where have you been?' he murmured. 'Did you find anything to eat?'

She ignored him, so he turned his attention back to the unexplained shapes. Could they be windows to the outside world? Holes that were letting in the light? He held his breath and watched. When his excitement became too great, he shook Kep's shoulder gently. 'Kep! Kep wake up! I think it might be morning!'

Kep lifted her head. 'Telion's light!' she whispered in awe. The apertures were so high it barely changed what they could see, but the precious reminder of the outside world instantly renewed their hope. Neither mentioned the terror that had passed — that could wait. It was time to move.

They stretched their stiff bodies, and ate as much food as they dared. There was still half a loaf of bread, a squashed cheese, some nuts and two handfuls of dried fruit. The urgent problem was water.

'Right,' said Kep determinedly, 'let's find those drips.'

It was quite a scramble back up to the path, with the shale slipping and sliding. When they reached the top, they were already tired and panting. From there, the path took them downwards in a gentle curve, still hugging the sheer wall on their right. Ash held the lamp higher at intervals, but nothing was revealed. Occasionally they came across brackets bolted to the stone at eye-level. They must have once held torches to light the way. But for whom?

As the path dropped more sharply, the drips sounded closer and closer. Kep let out a startled cry, as a cold drop splashed onto her forehead.

Now they could see shadowy rock formations, like cones growing from the ground. When they finally reached the bottom, they gasped: stretching out as far as they could see was a vast lake, shining green in the dark.

'More than enough to fill our pouches!' Kep laughed. Ash nodded soberly, overawed. The water was icy cold, but deliciously fresh. Having satisfied their thirst, they sat for a while, just marvelling.

Ash frowned. Why did he feel as if he had always known there was a lake here at the heart of the mountain?

'I'm going to wash and give thanks to Narsis,' said Kep.

And there it was again! The brush of memory —soft, like the wings of a moth.

After anxiously skirting the edge of the water, they finally picked up the path again. It was wet, steep and treacherous, and their fingers soon ached from clinging onto the slippery rocks as they climbed. Then, just as the path levelled out, they rounded a corner and were confronted by two tunnel mouths, side by side. Tarlyn made no pause; she went straight to the left.

'By Argess! What next?' Kep panted. 'Well? Is she right? Is it that one?' She just wanted the horrible trek to be over. It felt as if they had been underground forever. Ash didn't respond. In fact, he seemed paralysed by panic.

Kep let her bag fall. 'Well, I'm just going to sit down here while you decide.' She swallowed small sips from her water bottle, forcing herself to breathe more calmly.

Ash stared blankly into each entrance in turn. He rubbed his eyes and pushed his thumbs into his temples. Tarlyn was staring out expectantly from the left-hand tunnel, so he was tempted to go that way, but was she right? Suddenly he felt overwhelmingly afraid. They should have turned back at the lake.

After a long wait, Kep broke the silence. 'It's all right, Ash,' she said shakily. 'The gods will guide us. We're not meant to die in this place.'

He swallowed, not trusting himself to answer. After another tense silence, she suggested they eat something. It wasn't a good idea, as they had so little food left. He nodded anyway. But then, as he was feeling in his bag for the last package of food, his fingers touched something smooth and warm. He drew it out.

He hadn't given the Taelstone any thought whatsoever since shoving it in his bag for safe-keeping. He weighed it in the palm of his hand. Then, peering at it closely, he noticed a tiny blue flame at its very centre. As he watched, the flame grew, opening out like a flickering flower.

Kep gasped and leaned toward him, reaching out tentative fingers. But before her fingers could touch the orb, she recoiled. 'Ouch! Ash, be careful! It ... it *bit* me!'

Ash didn't answer. The Taelstone held him in its thrall. Cupping the Taelstone in both hands, he gazed into its heart. The flames were eddying and swirling in a hypnotic dance. He felt so much calmer all of a sudden. He let himself drift. 'It's all right, Kep,' he said dreamily. 'I can hear the flute. It will lead us out.'

Kep wasn't at all happy, but she followed Ash into the left-hand tunnel. Although he was totally confident all of a sudden, his eyes seemed glazed and oddly-coloured, as if they had taken up some of the ball's weird light. The enigmatic smile on his lips was completely at odds with the boy she knew, and Tarlyn rode high upon his shoulder like some sort of black demon. She shuddered. The sooner they could hand that creepy orb over to T'al Jazure, the happier she'd be — but first they had to get out of this awful mountain.

They walked without resting, climbing gently all the while. For Ash the time rolled by swiftly. He was no longer afraid of the figures who walked beside him, then dissolved into nothing. He didn't know what they were — figments, shades, memories maybe? — but he was no longer worried that they were the souls of the dead. He understood that their journey was one of peace and togetherness. The notes of the flute rose and fell, easing his mind and blocking out his fears. He didn't have to worry anymore, he just followed the melody and was content.

Pain jarred down Kep's arms as she hit the heels of her hands against the wall. But she hit it again anyway. *Stupid. Stupid. Stupid!* And Ash was just standing there swaying and smiling! He didn't seem to have registered the wall of stone at all. A dead end! And now they were dreadfully deep inside the mountain. She was certain they would never make it back.

Still Ash didn't move. He just stood there with that stupid, dreamy smile on his face. Rage bubbled up inside her, and she slapped him. She was so angry, and so horribly, terribly frightened. Then she pushed him — hard. 'I hate you! I hate you, Ash!' He staggered back. 'I hate this mountain — and I hate *you*!' she shouted.

At last her wild sobbing seemed to penetrate his trance, because he shook his head and blinked.

'What is it?' he asked, bewildered.

'*Seriously?*' Kep raised her hands in disbelief. 'It's a dead end,' she answered, exasperated.

'No.' Ash spoke slowly. 'It can't be.'

Kep just sank to the floor, overcome at last by fear and exhaustion. *How could you argue with a wall of stone?*

Ash frowned, perplexed. Kep's terror had made him waver momentarily, but the notes of the flute had not quite faded. He stepped forward, reaching out his hands until his fingertips touched the rock. Then, flattening his palms, he let out a slow breath.

For a split moment there was resistance, then a quiver. He felt for the note. As it rumbled through him, the stone resonated and began to change. Kep sprang to her feet. She cried out when the archway revealed itself, unfurling across the rock face. Its dark blue frame shone, embellished with pearl inlay. Then, with a crack, the rock parted! They staggered in the blinding light, dazzled by the glory of a pink and orange sunset.

Chapter 23

LIGHT

The beauty of the hills and trees and pink-flamed clouds was almost unbearable after the long darkness. It was as if someone had switched the world back on and they didn't quite know what to do with it. So they just sat there in silence, in the mouth of the cave, trying to take in the remarkable fact that they were free.

Ash turned the Taelstone over in his hands. It was cold now, a solid silver ball lying heavy in his hand. He gazed at it longingly. Somehow he felt sure it was the key to understanding everything: the quest, their freedom, the Song — everything.

At last a small voice broke into his thoughts.

'Ash. I don't hate you ... I'm sorry I said that.' Kep paused. 'I don't hate you. I was scared ...' She was watching him intently. 'And I'm still scared.'

Ash didn't know what to say. He gave an awkward nod and kept his eyes on the horizon. He was scared, too. In fact, he was terrified. The hills were falling quickly into shadow. They could shelter in the cave for the night, but they had no food, little water and no idea where they were going. Perhaps being a slave hadn't been so bad after all. You might get beaten, but at least you got food and shelter.

A sudden scuffle caught his attention, and he looked over to see that Tarlyn had pounced on a tiny, flecked gecko that had ventured out from its hiding place. Ash shivered, reminded of Gooel. The tracker was out there, hunting them, and sooner or later he would catch up with them.

Ash stared at the Taelstone. Free the slaves? It was all very well being free, but what if that just meant free to die?

Kep sniffed beside him. He swallowed and tried to sound reassuring. 'I'm scared, too. But we'll be all right, Kep. There must be food and water of some sort down there.'

To his surprise, Kep snorted derisively and waved her hand.

'Of course there's food! Those are ramon bushes. There'll be nuts this time of year. And a stream runs along that gorge, judging by that line of kellor trees.' She narrowed her eyes, searching his face. 'I'm not scared of starving — I'm scared of *you*, Ash.' Then she bit her tongue because he looked so hurt and bewildered. 'Well ... No, not *you* ... I mean, *that thing*.' She pointed to the orb in his hand.

She would have included Tarlyn as well, but the creature was staring at her with part of a gecko dangling from her mouth. It was creepy how she seemed to understand them. 'We don't know what the Taelstone is, Ash. All we know is it belonged to Credé, and that isn't exactly reassuring. And you ... well you're not yourself, and that thing definitely isn't helping.'

Ash didn't reply. He turned the Taelstone over in his hands. How did it manage to look transparent at some times and solid at others? True, they didn't know anything about it, but holding it made him feel calmer, more in control. How could that be a bad thing?

'If you want to know what I think,' said Kep — as if he had a choice — 'I think you should just hide it safely in the bottom of your bag, and *don't* keep touching it.'

He took a breath and let it out slowly.

'Ash? Promise?'

'Maybe,' he answered casually. It was time to change the subject. 'We'll see. Besides, I've got something else to show you.'

To his relief, Kep was instantly distracted by the dopple-star. She pushed against the invisible shield in disbelief. 'It's like being inside a bubble! Can we be seen from the outside?'

After a quick experiment they found out the answer. 'It's incredible! I know you're there, I just can't see you.' Kep shook her head in wonder. 'Well, that'll certainly make it easier to sleep.'

Ash grinned. He couldn't help feeling a little bit pleased with himself.

❦

'Ouch!' Ash stopped in his tracks. The plant had attacked his legs with a ferocious volley of tiny spears. He swore violently.

'Oh, Ash,' Kep scolded. 'Not again. Didn't you see them?'

'Obviously not,' he snarled. He sat down to begin the painful process of removing the barbs one by one, knowing they would only fester if he didn't. The wilderness was an absolute torment. As well as attacking plants, there were stinging insects that buzzed in his face. He hated being startled by birds in the daytime, and by furtive rustlings at night. But most of all he hated his own ignorance.

He couldn't master Kep's habit of scanning for food as she walked along; he was always stumbling over something. And it didn't help that she was constantly checking on how he was feeling. It was none of her business if he heard strains of music from time to time. He hadn't mentioned the nightmares— it was much better if Kep believed he was recovering from whatever madness had possessed him. And perhaps he was, he told himself.

'Well it's good to have an excuse for a rest,' said Kep, stretching out in the shade. 'You sure you don't want help?'

'I'm sure,' Ash replied through gritted teeth.

Kep shrugged. Since dawn they had been working their way down a ridge in search of a lake they had spotted the previous night. She checked the angle of the sun: still early afternoon. With the gods' help they might make it by nightfall.

She frowned uneasily as a flock of birds took to the sky in a flurry. Gooel was constantly in her thoughts now. But could he have travelled through the pass of Felian and across the wilderness already? She doubted it, but she could no longer ignore the creeping feeling in her gut.

'Ash, do you think the star-shield would work tonight?'

The star-shield had failed after the first night; the dopple-stars had just lain inert on Ash's palm like two spiky lumps. Their star-fuelled energy was exhausted so quickly that Ash and Kep had decided to use the shield in emergencies only.

He nodded. 'We've had enough clear nights. But why?'

'Oh, it's just a feeling — it's probably nothing.'

THE TANGLEWOOD

*T*he great banner of Eeroktan flies proudly against the sky, a blue bird
fluttering against rippling gold. Again he watches the children playing.
*Again? Yes, he recognises the scene. He knows the toddlers will be swept into
loving arms, just as he knows how the women will laugh and chatter, and
exactly the manner in which the young girls will shake out their skirts. It is
happening again.*

*Again the unfamiliarity confuses him: the fresh, clean buildings; the
watchtowers tall and proud; and all that water dancing and sparkling about
the children's feet. When the small girl with golden hair stands on her toes to
drink, the music begins to race as he knows it will.*

*He wills himself to wake. If he could just cry out he might save himself from
the images that will come. He tries, but is struck mute. The water gushes red.
He tries to shield himself from the child's fate. All his fault. Don't look. Don't
see. The bodies float so softly; the water animating their tiny limbs as if they live
still, but their faces ... their soft cheeks. The eyes, unseeing in the bloodied water
... He screams a scream of such horror it threatens to rip out his soul.*

Ash sat up, reeling. His tunic was sticking to his back with sweat, his heart
racing wildly.

Kep sprang into a crouch, scanning the surrounding scrub.

'What is it? What is it?'

'It's all right. Sorry. Just a dream.'

He watched her hand go out to check the star-shield. Her relief was
audible as she breathed out. 'You scared me half to death, Ash!'

'Sorry.' His heart was still pounding, his body drenched with some
powerful emotion. Was it grief? Guilt? Maybe. Whatever it was, it was
strong enough to make him feel sick.

Rubbing her eyes, Kep tried to reckon the time, probably a few hours
from dawn. 'Are you sure you're all right?'

He nodded. 'Just a bad dream.'

Something in his tone made her anxious. He was breathing too quickly. She put a hand on his arm. 'Ash, you're shaking. Tell me what's going on. You know I'm going to keep bothering you if you don't,' she added firmly.

He sighed, but after a pause he answered: 'Do you remember what I said to you when we first went into the mountain?'

'Yes.' She settled down near him again, hugging her legs, with her chin resting on her knees. 'You said we were in the vestibule of the realm of Eeroktan.'

He nodded. 'Well, this dream, it was in Eeroktan. Don't ask me how I know, but I've had the same dream lots of times now, only ... it gets worse every time.'

Kep searched his face. 'It could help to talk about it,' she urged.

Ash didn't think it would help, but, lying back down, he tried to describe the scene as accurately as he could. He faltered when he came to the end, though — it was too horrible for words.

When Tarlyn crept like an inky shadow to lie on his stomach, he ran his hands over her fur, drawing comfort from her silky warmth.

'And it ends with blood in the water?'

It was worse — much worse — but it made him sick to think about it. 'And then I wake up,' he said evasively.

Kep was silent for a long while. An owl hooted sadly nearby. 'It's just a dream, Ash.'

'But ... That's the thing. I'm not sure it is a dream. It feels more ... like ... like a memory. The place is so familiar. The courtyard, the towers ...'

'But you can't have been there, Ash. The only city you know is Mildaresh.'

It took a moment for her words to register. Then, like a puzzle, the images came together. 'That's it! He sat up, spilling Tarlyn from his chest. 'I *have* been there. It's the old city! I didn't recognise it, because it looked so new ... The watchtowers, the arches of the ancient law courts! There must have been fountains once! But something happened — something terrible.'

'So you're saying Mildaresh used to be Eeroktan?' Kep was looking at him doubtfully.

His thoughts were racing. 'Eeroktan — the home of the Eerok. Why not?'

'Perhaps,' Kep frowned. 'But that doesn't explain how you could possibly be dreaming about it.'

Ash realised that. But somehow it didn't matter. It was a start. At last, one tiny thing had started to make more sense.

There was no getting back to sleep, so they watched the dawn creep closer until it was light enough to shell more ramon nuts. They ate in silence, chewing determinedly. The nuts were certainly better than nothing, but their flesh was bland-tasting and fibrous.

Kep took a gulp of water to wash the last bits down, then stood up. 'We should find that lake today. It must be near: just look at all these midges.' She slapped her arm and squashed two at once.

Privately, she was worried that they had missed the lake entirely, as the undergrowth hadn't allowed them to travel in the right direction. The main problem was a stout species of bush with rambling, tangled branches. Any effort to push through was met with springy resistance. Their only option had been to continue along the edge of the thicket in the hope of finding a less dense patch.

Tarlyn, at least, was undeterred by the tangled terrain. The bushes were home to all kinds of crawling, leaping and flying prey. Ash was thoroughly captivated by her antics. She seemed able to change her shape and size to negotiate even the most difficult snarls, and was exceptionally fast, striking her prey with elegant precision. He'd discovered that she did indeed eat butterflies. He couldn't help feeling sorry for the luminescent creatures, but that didn't diminish his growing affection for his curious companion. He loved her soft weight on his shoulder and the way she nuzzled his neck. Sometimes when she blinked her solemn eyes at him, he felt she entirely understood him. It was disconcerting and comforting all at once.

'Ash?'

Kep broke into his thoughts. She had stopped dead, and was frowning and sniffing, tilting her head on one side, then the other. 'Can you smell that?'

He dutifully sniffed and, catching the acrid scent, matched Kep's frown with one of his own. 'Smoke!'

She nodded grimly. 'Could be a campfire. We'd better keep moving.'

※

It was mid-morning before they found a less tangled area. Motivated by the smoke, they decided to try forcing their way through. They were soon frustrated, and when Ash caught yet another lash across his face, he let out an angry shout, 'By Argess! Just let us through!'

'Shhh!' Kep warned.

He scowled. As if anyone could hear anything above the deafening wail of those crickets. He stared crossly at the weave of branches. If anything, this area was worse. The thin branches criss-crossed all around them like some sort of nightmarish cage. 'This is pointless,' he grumbled.

Kep wiped her forehead with a sleeve. 'It can't go on forever. But it would help if we had an axe.'

'An axe?' he snorted. 'Perhaps we should have brought a couple of kattlen to trample it down for us? Shame we didn't think of that!'

She rolled her eyes at him. 'What about that knife of yours?'

'It's too short, and it wouldn't cut through these anyway,' he kicked at a branch, and cursed when it whipped back at him.

'Oh, for the love of the gods!' snapped Kep. 'You could at least try. Give it here!'

He handed over the knife with a scowl, knowing already that it wouldn't work: he had tried using it to cut all sorts of things with little success. Its sole purpose seemed to be slaying yaggluts, an activity he fervently hoped to avoid in the future.

Kep hefted the blade in her hand. She marvelled again at the strange designs. Surely this was a blade that could cut through anything! When she grasped it more tightly, she felt a weird tingle run up her arm. Holding her breath, she slashed experimentally at the tangled barrier. The knife sliced through the branches so easily she nearly lost her balance. Laughing out loud, she aimed another stroke. Again the blade swished through smoothly. She beamed triumphantly at Ash, who spluttered back in disbelief.

⁂

With Kep in the lead wielding the knife, they made much better progress until, finally, she gave a shout: 'Look! It's there!'

Then, a little further on, they caught the sweet sound of running water.

Kep swung the knife wildly to and fro, and they trampled their way forward with renewed purpose, neither paying any heed to the noise they were making. At last, they crashed out of the bushes onto a shingly river bank and charged whooping towards the water. The gravelly sand sank in pits beneath their feet, and Kep's shoes filled quickly with tiny stones. She paused to drag them off.

Ash was already wading in, plunging his hands into the water to scoop it over his hot face. He bowed his head in supplication and thanked Narsis with all his heart. Trailing from his neck, his water-pouch floated emptily on the surface. Then, just as he was lifting his hands to form the sacred triangle, the water surged. In a split second the water-pouch disappeared, his neck snapped forward and he was being dragged under.

'Ash!' Kep screamed, and ploughed into the shallows. 'No!' Grappling for a hold, she dragged at his legs as hard as she could. For a terrible moment something pulled back, then there was a sudden release. Ash popped up, spluttering and choking.

As they fell backwards, the water surged again. A turquoise tail thrashed, then a thorny, green head broke the surface and was hoisted high upon a scaly neck. Two sets of gills flapped as the creature surveyed them with monstrous eyes. When it spread its splayed fingers, they screamed in unison.

It opened its jaws wide, revealing rows of sharp teeth, then it arched its terrible neck and let out an awful hiss. It was about to strike!

But suddenly there came a new sound: a swift whining, followed by a thud. The creature jerked violently, an arrow sprouting from its neck. A second arrow dived through the water and struck. As the creature thrashed, the arrows were followed swiftly by a man.

Ash saw a mane of red hair and the quick flash of a curved blade — then there was blood. It gushed, staining the water red. Blood. Blood and water.

His senses reeled. He felt himself falling — the last thing he saw as he lost consciousness was the expression in the dying creature's eyes.

Chapter 25

HOT TEA

It took all Ash's effort to find himself again, the dream's hold was so strong. Only slowly did he become aware of someone speaking beyond its turbulent waters. He held onto Kep's voice, willing her to speak again.

'Ash? … Ash? … Ash, wake up and have some tea.'

His eyes fluttered open. At first he could see only fuzzy green shapes, until his focus sharpened, revealing them to be leaves. They hung down nearly to his face, in long trailing ribbons. Kep was beside him sipping from a battered mug.

'Thank the gods,' she smiled sleepily.

He pulled himself up on his elbows. They were on a grassy knoll set back from the river's edge, under a huge willow. Nearby, a campfire flickered and smoked. Someone was crouched there. Ash put his hand to his head. 'How did I get here?' he asked groggily.

'Rufen carried you,' Kep answered dreamily. 'He saved us, Ash.'

'Rufen?' He stared at the brown figure. The man looked in their direction and stood up. The man's mighty frame was topped by a great shaggy head with red hair that shook on his shoulders as he walked. Although his beard was greying, his eyebrows were a startling red and stuck out in untidy tufts. He came over to them and crouched down, and Ash found himself looking into a pair of intense brown eyes.

'Rufen Karendon at yer service,' said the giant. 'Most people call me Karendon. Ya can call me Rufen if ya like.' He grinned. 'Would ya like some tea?'

Ash accepted the mug and took a tentative sip. Contrary to its scent, the tea wasn't sweet, but it was wonderfully refreshing. He drank slowly, watching their unlikely host fussing at the fire.

Kep smiled happily. 'He's making us stew. Real stew with meat in it.'

Ash nodded. Every now and then he caught a whiff that made his mouth water. He felt the tea's calming warmth flow through his body. 'What happened?' he asked at last.

Kep drained her own mug and settled back. 'There's not much to tell really. Rufen heard us screaming when the marmon attacked.'

'The marmon?'

'The creature that tried to kill you. Rufen says marmon are really vicious. If he hadn't heard us screaming …' She half-closed her eyes, squinting up at the trailing leaves. 'Well … He brought us here, then went back to deal with the body.'

'Deal with the body?' Ash realised he was repeating everything, but he was finding it hard to concentrate.

'Hmm? Oh, I suppose he buried it.' Kep had closed her eyes.

Ash blinked stupidly, looking around.

Where was Tarlyn? He tried to remember when he had last seen her. Before they had broken free of the tanglewood? He rubbed his eyes. She'd be fine. She could look after herself. He buried his nose in his tea and inhaled the sweet, steamy fragrance.

⁂

Much later, Ash awoke with a sickening start. He blinked about him in confusion, trying to gather himself. Kep was fast asleep beside him. There was no sign of Rufen, although his gear was still stacked in various piles about the campsite. The sunlight was slanting low through the trees. Hauling himself to his feet, Ash stretched, then wandered into some nearby bushes to relieve himself; his piss smelt oddly strong and grassy. Making his way to the water's edge, he felt as if every move was an effort. He let the water wash over his bare feet. What had he done with his sandals?

As Ash splashed his face and head, Rufen Karendon suddenly emerged from the trees, carrying a huge pile of firewood under one arm, and several metal contraptions in the other. A long cloth bag was strung about his neck.

'Ahoy there!' he called. 'Good to see ya on ya feet, boy. Come — the stew must be ready!' The man grinned through his beard, and raised his scruffy eyebrows. 'Ya must be hungry. Had quite a scare.'

Kep took a long time to wake up, then sat blinking and yawning, leaves and twigs tangled in her curls.

'Here, take this. Sure looks like ya need it. Scrawny little things, the pair of ya.' Rufen passed bowls of steaming stew. 'My Nellie would take one look and make plans to fatten ya up. An' that's the truth.'

Ash spluttered his thanks.

'Now, don't go overdoing it. Just mind the bones, that's all,' growled their host.

The stew was thick, and rich with meat and root vegetables. Ash couldn't think when he had ever had food as wholesome. Rufen watched them eat with satisfaction, then, furnishing himself with a pipe, he settled his bulk on a blanket. Soon he was blowing smoke out of his mouth in long, thin streams.

Ash had been determined to keep quiet, but the fire was warm and he felt heavily content, and suddenly he found himself asking whether Rufen lived nearby.

'Hmm? Here? No. My lodge is on the lower lake. I come up to set traps once in a turn of Eldar — until winter that is, and he's drawing closer day by day.' He waved his pipe at the top of the trees as if to gesture at some sort of evidence.

As darkness fell, Rufen rose to feed the fire. They accepted more mugs of tea, and he poured something for himself from a bottle. They drank and watched the hypnotic dance of flames in companionable silence until at last Rufen spoke again. 'So are ya heading downstream? If so, like as not our paths will tend the same way. I'd be happy of some company.'

Ash found himself answering — it seemed ungrateful to evade the questions of the man who had saved their lives. 'Yes, we're heading downs dream.' He frowned. It was oddly difficult to form the words.

Kep nodded agreement. 'We're looking for the nearest settlement.'

Rufen grunted, seeming more interested in refilling his pipe.

'We lost our party,' Kep went on. Her words sounded blurry, too. 'We were attacked by wolves and scattered. We've been hoping to find a village to ask after the others. We're of the ... Skagali household. If we can't find them, we'll just have to go on alone ...'

Ash blinked. She'd trailed off lamely, but it was a pretty good story, and a good idea to associate themselves with a noble family — they didn't want anyone guessing they were slaves.

Rufen took a series of short puffs on his pipe. 'House of Skagali, eh? Sounds Mildaren. You two from Mildaresh, then?'

Ash nodded. There seemed little point denying it.

'A fine city, Mildaresh. Never been there myself, though.' He coughed.

'An' where did ya say yer family was headed to?'

'We're not sure exactly,' Kep replied. 'We do know the name of the man we were travelling to meet, though.' She glanced at Ash. 'His name is T'al Jazure. It's a noble title, so we expect people will have heard of him.'

Rufen Karendon took a sip of his drink. 'T'al Jazure. Hmm. Now just let me think.' The man scratched his huge beard and muttered. 'T'al Jazure. Now, maybe that does sound familiar. T'al Jazure.' He watched the fire, sucking on his pipe. 'Hmm. Do ya know, I think I have met a man by that name.' He nodded, making his beard waggle. 'If it's the same man I'm thinking of, then he's from Skarfell. On the coast. You know it?'

They didn't of course, but they exchanged quick glances. Had he really met T'al Jazure? Ash felt giddy at the prospect. 'Do you think you could tell uz how to get ther?' He wondered vaguely why his words kept slurring.

'I'll do better than that, by the gods!' Rufen Karendon slapped his thigh. 'It's high time I made a trading trip to Skarfell. Marvellous town for silk. I'll take ya there myself!' he beamed.

They grinned back happily. For once Ash had to agree with Kep: the gods were smiling on them indeed.

SARIN

How long had they been journeying with Rufen Karendon? Two days? Four even? Time had become strangely blurred since the marmon's attack. Rufen was leading them downstream to his campsite at the tip of the lower lake where he had left a longboat. They had been travelling in short bursts, with Ash and Kep resting along the way while their guide set his traps.

Ash couldn't remember what Rufen was hunting. He had the distinct feeling he had asked and had forgotten the answer. It seemed he couldn't train his mind on anything for long, and it didn't help that he kept falling asleep. Kep was the same; he would wake to find her snoring gently beside him. It was odd: he had never noticed her snoring before.

Rufen had laughed merrily, saying that the plants in these parts gave off scents that made travellers drowsy. 'Just as well ya've got old Karendon to watch over ya,' he'd chuckled. And so they stumbled along, one leaden foot following the other, through a hazy world of sunlit leaves, until one afternoon Rufen's booming voice announced their arrival at the campsite. 'Here we are then!'

However, Ash's leafy dream state was instantly dispelled by the sight of a huge wolvern. It bounded at them, all wild eyes and slavering jaws, until jerked to a halt by a chain around its neck.

'Halstar!'

At Rufen's shout, the snarling brute cowered and sank to the ground, its ears back.

'Don't mind him. He's protecting the goods, that's all. He'll not harm ya.'

Ash wasn't so sure. He felt sick with shock. Why would anyone keep such a beast?

The campsite was well situated. There was clean, level ground with a large stone fireplace, and a semi-circle of bushes provided cover from the fitful breeze. Beyond that, the surface of the lake shone through the trees. Rufen's long, narrow boat, which had been hauled right up onto the pebbly beach, was loaded with sacks and crates. Another stack of equipment stood under the trees. Rufen swept the cover from a large square cage, making the inhabitants flutter and chirp loudly.

'What are they?' asked Ash, peering at the small black birds.

'Swifts,' answered Rufen, adding grain to the feeder.

Ash looked at the birds with new interest. He knew they carried messages far and wide, but he had never seen one. Rufen retrieved a huge side of meat from somewhere and flung it to the wolvern. Ash watched in horror for a few moments as the beast ravaged flesh from the bone, then joined Kep who had settled herself beneath a tree.

When a shadow moved in the undergrowth, Ash was suddenly reminded of Tarlyn. He decided to look for her, but involuntarily nodded off again; when he awoke, the side of his cheek was wet where he'd been drooling.

Dinner took the form of meat threaded onto sticks and roasted. There was also a bowl of sweet gruel to which a leafy vegetable had been added, plus the inevitable mugs of tea. Ash drank thirstily. The fragrant liquid seemed more enjoyable with every mug.

As they ate, a flock of black-and-white birds settled in the canopy; their sweet evening melodies tugging at something in the back of his mind, but he just blinked sleepily at them, his thoughts too dull to respond.

With bellies full to bursting, they were settling into their nightly contemplation of the fire when Kep suddenly shattered the peace with a cry.

'There's someone there! By that tree!'

Rufen reacted swiftly. He leapt to his feet, drawing a blade from nowhere. Sure enough, a dark figure hovered just outside the circle of the firelight.

'Show yourself!' Rufen snarled, gathering up an axe for good measure.

Ash felt a swift appreciation of their protector, followed by a stab of fear when the figure by the tree moved. Then a voice spoke. 'So you'd hurl an axe at an unarmed man would you, Karendon?'

A young man stepped into the light, holding his palms open in front of him. 'That's not terribly friendly, you know.' He clicked his tongue. 'And after I've found what you wanted and all.' He gave the slightest bow, without taking his eyes off Rufen's face.

'Sarin! I might have known,' the big man growled. 'Young fool! What're ya playing at, creeping up on folk like that?'

The young man gave a twisted smile. 'What am I playing at Karendon? I might ask the same of you. I was looking for you, of course. I must say, it wasn't hard — just followed the trail of blood.'

The newcomer's eyes flickered over Kep and settled on Ash. His long, black hair was tied back at the nape of his neck, and his cheekbones were high and slanted. Although he had called himself a man, Ash guessed he was only a couple of winters older than he and Kep. He met Ash's gaze and raised his eyebrows inquiringly.

'Who's this? Don't tell me you've found someone to put up with your bad breath and wicked ways, you fat old goat. It's a wonder you could squeeze through the cut — your gut looks as bloated as ever.'

Rufen folded his huge arms across his chest. 'And your tongue is as impudent!'

'Thank you!' The boy waved a hand in a flourish.

'These are friends of mine, if you must know,' Rufen growled.

'Friends?' The stranger laughed.

Rufen frowned. 'I'm guessing you've something to trade; if so, we can settle in the morning.' He coughed. 'Yer welcome to share our fire,' he offered. 'And have some tea if you will.

The unexpected guest raised just one eyebrow this time. It was his turn to fold his arms. He tilted his head to one side. 'How kind. I'll be glad of the fire. But ...,' he paused, 'I don't want any tea.'

'Suit yourself,' Rufen shrugged.

Sarin stared at Ash and Kep for a moment longer, then seemed to dismiss them and set about making his meal. Rufen returned to his place and lit his pipe. He soon managed to swathe himself in a cloud of smoke and apparently paid no more attention to the newcomer.

Ash stared from one to the other. He commanded himself to stay alert — and stay awake. There was something strange about this dark-haired young man and the offensive way he spoke to their friend. Sarin was moving with the graceful air of one who had completed the same tasks many times. He set a billycan on the fire, then produced a parcel of some sort, which he placed into the embers. Ash couldn't guess what it was. It smelt like hot nuts or toasted corn. When his food was done, he didn't join them. Instead he withdrew to sit against the tree where he had first appeared. When he had finished eating he just sat there, eyes glinting in the firelight.

Kep nudged Ash. 'Is he going to sit staring at us like that all night?'

Rufen stirred at her words and answered, 'He could well do so, missy.

He's a Farling. They're an odd bunch. They don't have proper homes like decent folk — they roam far and wide, leaving trouble behind them. Thieves, murderers and liars they are. And this one's the worst of all. He's got the eyes of a devil he has.' He spat into the bushes. 'It's wise to have no dealings with 'em. And if ya do, ya can't never trust 'em. Not ever.'

Ash stared hard at Sarin, trying to make out his features in the dark. If he had heard this disparaging account of himself he made no sign.

'Well, I don't want anything to do with him,' announced Kep.

Rufen nodded. 'You two just stay well clear of him. Don't you worry, missy. He won't try anything with me here. We'll see the back of him come morning.' With that Rufen knocked his pipe out against a log and heaved himself to his feet. 'It's time for old bones to get themselves off to bed. And young uns, too, mind you.' He shook a finger at them, gave them a kindly wink and trudged off to fetch more firewood.

Kep tipped her mug upside down. 'Is there any more of that tea?'

Ash stared at his own dregs.

'Mmm… I'll get it.' He approached the fire and set the mugs upon a flat rock. As he picked up the pot he jumped at the hand on his sleeve. Sarin had moved incredibly quickly.

'Don't drink the tea, you fool!'

The boy's eyes were the strangest colour; they seemed to reflect the orange of the firelight. Before Ash could protest, a water-pouch was thrust into his hands. Sarin held a finger against his lips, cocked his head in Rufen's direction, then retreated to the shadows just as quickly. Ash stood there, frowning stupidly at the water-pouch, then, for some reason, thrust it under his shirt. Just at that moment Rufen turned in their direction. He dropped the armful of wood. 'Now what're ya up to there, lad?' he yelled.

'Just getting more tea,' Ash called back. He knew he sounded guilty. He felt guilty. 'I hope that's all right?'

Rufen lumbered over. 'I'll deal with that! Ya don't want to go scalding yerself. Just sit back down there an' I'll bring it over.' Ash wondered at the way his eyes darted to where Sarin was sitting. Whatever was the story between those two?

Ash watched Rufen smooth out his bedroll, take off his giant boots and lie himself down. He watched Kep finish her tea and slump beneath one of Rufen's coverlets. He watched the moons rising. He watched Sarin, too, motionless in the shadows of his tree. And all the time he was watching, he fought against the impulse to drink the tea that grew cooler between his hands.

His mouth was parched. He had to drink something. But what? Tea or water? Rufen had saved their lives, hadn't he? He had fed and protected them. He had proved he was their friend. But Ash couldn't stop the words running through his head: *Don't drink the tea!* And the one thing he really, *really* wanted to do was drink the tea. The more he thought about it, the thirstier he became. He couldn't stand it much longer. Could he trust water given to him by a stranger? Thieves, murderers and liars, that's what Rufen had said. He gazed at Sarin, wondering which of those things he was — and Sarin gazed back. It was as if some magic had bound the two of them in a bizarre staring competition.

Then all at once, something moved. Ash's heart thudded. The wolvern was on its feet. It shook itself. He shrank, sure that it was heading straight for him. But the beast slunk past and skirted around its master's sleeping form. Ash held his breath as it approached the stranger. He heard a soft whine and a murmur above the rhythm of snoring. Unbelievably, the wolvern bowed its head and settled its bulk at Sarin's side, blending into the shadows.

Ash sat and thought for long minutes. Then, slowly and deliberately, he poured the tea out onto the ground beside him. It was hard to be sure, but he thought he saw a smile flicker across Sarin's face.

Chapter 27

UNFINISHED BUSINESS

Feeling more awake than he had for days, Ash woke to the sound of voices. He was desperately thirsty, but didn't dare move: Rufen and Sarin were talking nearby, their voices low and intense. Ash adjusted his arm slightly, so he could watch them unobserved. Rufen was running a silky white tail through his fingers.

'And you've three of these. All the same quality?'

Sarin nodded. The young man looked even more remarkable in the daylight. His hair was jet-black, darker even than Kep's, but dead straight. While his olive skin reminded Ash of the merchants who visited Lord Feyindi, his eyes were the most unusual Ash had ever seen: they were yellow — gold even — and constantly moving, like those of a predator.

Rufen had the look of a man trying to appear indifferent, but his tongue ran along his lips: He was clearly struck by the beauty of the tails. 'Good. I'll give ya two silks for the three. I think that's a fair offer.'

Sarin made a pained face. 'And *I think* we'll stick to our bargain. One skein for each tail.'

Although Rufen scowled, his desire to possess the soft tails must have been strong. 'Choose yer colours,' he snapped.

'The peacock blue, and the gold,' said the boy, 'and I'll take a magenta.'

'Magenta?' Rufen puffed noisily through his lips. 'No. Not the magenta.'

'Suit yourself,' the boy shrugged. 'Out-of-season termil tails fetch a pretty price up in Kardesh.' Sarin moved as if to reclaim the silken tail, but Rufen snatched back his hand.

'Now, don't be hasty. Since I'm in a good mood, ya can have the magenta and the gold.'

'And the peacock.'

Although Sarin seemed completely relaxed, Ash noticed that the fingers of his left hand just brushed the hilt of a hunting knife strapped to his thigh.

Ash held his breath, then, all at once, Kep stirred beside him. Frowning, she tried to wet her lips, and went back to sleep.

Rufen darted a look in her direction, then back again.

'All right, all right. Ya drive a harsh bargain, boy,' he muttered. 'And mark me, one day yer cleverness will catch up with ya. Someone'll stick a hole in yer belly or, better still, cut out yer insolent tongue.'

'Perhaps.' The young man with the golden eyes smiled as he packed his new silks into his jerkin.

'Yer'll be going now,' stated Rufen gruffly turning away.

'Don't worry, I'm going. I'll leave you to your other business.' Sarin looked so pointedly in Ash's direction that Ash felt his heart jump. Had he guessed he was awake all along? Just before turning into the woods, the young man paused and tossed some last words over his shoulder: 'Oh, and Karendon, you might want to keep to the shallows. The marmon are mourning one of their daughters.'

Ash kept very still. He had a lot to think about, not least the expression that had crossed Rufen's face at Sarin's parting shot. What was it? Anger? Fear? A mixture of both? For the first time, Ash started to wonder about the man's character. The conversation with Sarin had revealed a very different side to the friendly giant. Sarin's mention of his 'other business' worried Ash, and when a blue-black bird shot by his head, he was completely startled. A swift! Why would Rufen be releasing a swift? Was he sending a message? If so, to whom? Ash sighed and added that to his list of things to worry about.

By the time breakfast was ready, Kep was starting to stir. She sat up and rubbed her eyes.

Reuben waved a spoon in greeting. 'Morning, missy!'

She waved back. 'Isn't he kind, Ash?'

Ash was painfully aware of how vacant and unfocused her eyes were. He smiled weakly and nodded. 'Yes, very.'

As they ate a hot breakfast of gruel with dried fruit, Rufen stowed his gear in the boat. There seemed to be an increased urgency in his movements that morning.

'Let's be going then, young uns. Drink up! There's a stop to make, but we should cross the lake before evening. Might well get rain. No sense spending another night out of doors if we don't have to, eh?'

Ash nodded dumbly. The thick feeling in his head had developed into a painful thumping. He waited until the man was occupied in putting out the fire, then quickly poured his tea away and refilled his mug from the water pouch. He gulped it down. It did little to quench his scraping thirst.

He got shakily to his feet, wondering if he would be needed to help launch the boat. But Rufen had no need of any help. He grasped the bow in a mighty embrace and shoved the hull back down the beach, carving a great gash in the sand. Then he climbed aboard and began fiddling with something at the stern. When Ash saw him filling a reservoir with elpha fuel he realised the boat had an engine. He suddenly thought of Tarlyn. If she had been following she would be left behind for certain!

'Rufen, I need to ...' He gestured vaguely at the bushes.

The man frowned, but handed him a small spade. 'Make it quick, boy.' Ash nodded and walked slowly to the edge of the trees.

He peered into hollow logs and scanned the treetops, but there was no trace of Tarlyn. He did find something else, though. A spring! He gave thanks to Narsis and gulped his fill. After replenishing the pouch, he continued his search. Nothing. Maybe Tarlyn hadn't followed at all. Maybe she had stayed in the Tanglewood. Dejected, he made his way back.

Kep was already tucked into the bow, wedged between crates and sacks. He clambered into the mid-section, amidst a pile of cages and traps. The large covered cage of swifts shielded him from Rufen's eyes at the stern, but he was rather too close to the wolvern for his liking. The canine smell of wet fur and meat-breath made Ash nauseous, but, fortunately, the beast just cowered unhappily in the bottom of the boat and showed no interest in him whatsoever.

Ash shared its misery. He had never been in a boat before, unless you counted his childhood journey on the slow barge from the Holding to Mildaresh. As they shoved off with a loud scrunch, he felt his stomach turn. The water looked murky, full of weeds and mystery. He concentrated instead on the throbbing beat of the elpha-engine, and trying to work out what to do next.

⁂

Ash had plenty of time to think as the boat worked along the edge of the lake. And the more he turned things over in his mind, the more he worried. What exactly was Rufen hunting? Why had he sent that swift?

But, most of all, why had he drugged them with sleep-inducing tea? None of it made sense.

But if they didn't trust Rufen, what then? He said he knew T'al Jazure, and would take them to meet him. What if that were true? Could they throw away such a chance?

Perhaps they could try to make their own way to Skarfell. He looked doubtfully at Kep. Her head was lolling as she dozed. Somehow he had to stop her drinking any more of that tea.

It must have been midday when the southern shore came into view. The lake was narrowing and Ash could just make out a line of dusky brown trees, with the merest suggestion of faded hills behind. At last the elpha-motor dropped its pitch. The front of the boat veered sharply, and moments later the boat crunched onto a skinny beach lined with scraggly trees.

'Here we are. Chance to stretch our legs and there's traps to check. You two have a nice rest under the trees. Then it's off home for tea and a hot bath.' Rufen grinned and winked.

Ash waited until he was certain the man was out of sight, then he leapt to his feet. He sprinted to the boat, taking care to follow in the footsteps they had already made. Fortunately, Telion was with him. In no time he had located several large flagons of water. He emptied tea from Kep's bottle, rinsed it and refilled it with water. After doing the same with his own, he replaced the flagons exactly as he had found them. So far, so good.

Waking up Kep was much harder than he had thought. He shook her gently by the shoulder, then more roughly. At last he tried patting cold water onto her face with his fingertips. When she opened her eyes, he quickly held the water bottle to her mouth.

'Here! It's water. Drink some.'

As soon as the drops wet her tongue she clutched at the bottle and drank eagerly.

'I've switched the tea with water. Don't say anything to Rufen.'

Kep looked confused.

'Just don't say anything, okay?'

She nodded groggily. Satisfied, he let her go back to sleep and shut his own eyes against the throbbing in his head.

❧

By the time Rufen returned, the sky had darkened. There wasn't a breath of air. The sounds they made as they prepared to set forth seemed stifled: it was as if the gods had cast a grey blanket over the world to muffle it. The lake's surface was eerily calm; a flat slate under sullen skies. Rufen scratched his beard and muttered. He loaded a last bundle into the boat, then lifted Kep over the side. Ash settled himself into the same spot as before, but was surprised when a large paddle was thrust into his hands. Why didn't Rufen want to use the motor?

'It's best if we cross quietly. No sense disturbing the peace,' was the strange explanation. 'You just paddle as best you can, lad. I'll keep us straight.'

Ash nodded and looked out over the lake. It was quiet, but it didn't exactly feel peaceful — menacing more like. Halstar clearly thought so, too. The wolvern was quivering and whimpering on the shoreline like a frightened, oversized pup. Rufen yelled and picked up a stick, but the animal just shied and cringed, avoiding the giant man's furious passes. Finally, Rufen let out a great growl and flung the stick away. 'Stay here then, ya stupid mongrel!'

Halstar hovered on the beach whining as they took to the water, then turned tail and slunk back in among the trees.

The behaviour of the wolvern was unnerving, but Ash had something new to worry about. The paddle was large and cumbersome, and in no time his arms and shoulders were aching, and he kept bashing the side of the boat. He had finally found some kind of rhythm, when he noticed the mist. Ash was hardly an expert, but even he could tell it was no ordinary mist. It rose off the water in eerie drifts, and spun into spirals. The oddest thing was the way it hung about the boat. Rufen was staring at the wispy tendrils, too, and had stopped paddling. He pulled his mighty crossbow within reach.

Turning his head, Ash found himself looking into Kep's frightened eyes.

'What is it? What's happening?' she whispered.

'Shhh!' Rufen scowled. 'Keep paddling, boy. Let's just get to the other side.'

Ash obeyed, and they paddled on into the deepening mist. They must have been about halfway across the lake when they sighted a great ripple, spreading towards them. Something had disturbed the water. The boat glided forward soundlessly as they strained their eyes into the depths. Ash thought he glimpsed a shadow, then, to his horror, the water churned and a glistening head broke the surface. He didn't need to see the rest of the creature to know what it was: a huge pair of deep green eyes stared into his — the eyes of a marmon.

Terrified, he gave a shout to raise the alarm, but the creature wasn't alone. The surface of the water erupted and the boat was surrounded. There must have been eight or nine of them, all staring with that same terrible gaze. Rufen raised his crossbow, then before he could take aim the creatures let out a piercing, shrieking wail. Rufen bellowed in agony, his weapon clattering into the bottom of the boat. 'Cover your ears!'

Kep and Ash were already clutching at their heads, desperately trying to block the excruciating screech. The terrible note grew louder and more intense as the marmon rose higher in the water. Then, like a circle of dancers, they arched their bodies backwards, their tails slapping hard against the water, and disappeared.

Anxiously, they scanned the waters, and for one precious moment there was no sign of the creatures. Then the water rippled with dark shapes, and began to swirl. The marmon were circling their craft, faster and faster, creating a whirling frenzy. The boat rocked and swung, sucked stern-first into the whirlpool.

Ash saw Kep screaming, and knew he was screaming, too, but the noise was drowned out by the marmon's wail. He clamped his hands to his skull, trying to dull the awful siren. Then all at once the note splintered into many, a painful agony of song. With a sudden shock Ash realised the creatures were not just wailing: they were singing! The first terrible harmony was so powerful that it knocked the breath from him. The marmon's song and the whirlpool had become one, a whirling turmoil of water and wrath — and Ash suddenly knew he was compelled to listen. Dropping his hands, he screamed in agony, letting their song penetrate his heart. Their anguish for their lost daughter coursed through him, resonating with his own grief. All at once he understood.

In minutes the boat would disintegrate and cast them into the water. In that moment of comprehension he accepted his fate utterly. They were justified, wholly justified in their rage. And he knew what he must do before the end. He lifted his head, held out his hands and began to sing.

Chapter 28

KARENDON LODGE

'It was a bloody miracle, that's what it was, Nellie. I tell ya, I ain't never seen nothing like it. We was all about to be tossed into the water and drowned when that boy, he starts up singing.'

'Singing?' Nellie Karendon re-filled her husband's tankard with ale.

'Well, singing of sorts, but not like any music you'll ever hear, I can tell ya.' He drank deeply, leaving a frothy trace about his beard.

His wife was wide-eyed. 'And what happened then?'

'It was the damnedest thing, Nellie. The boy, he just sits there, all weird and pale-looking, singing if ya please! With tears streaming down his face like rivers, and ya know what?'

She shook her head, spellbound.

'The marmon, they calm down. They keep up their own awful wailing, but they stop circling, see?' He scratched his beard. 'It was unnatural the effect that boy had, unnatural. But the whirlpool slowed then, and the boat righted itself. Good boat, that one. Then ...' he spread his fingers, making a pass through the air, 'it all went quiet.'

Nellie Karendon barely breathed while her husband took another draught of ale. 'It all went quiet,' she repeated.

'Aye. And the marmon, they stick their ugly heads up again. And ya know what they do?'

She didn't, and she said so, breathlessly.

'They stare. That's all.' He opened his eyes wide to demonstrate. 'They just stare. Like that.'

Nellie's own eyes were round with dread.

'They were staring at the boy, see? Imagine it! Nine of 'em, with nine tails. Just think of all them beautiful scales!' He shook his head sorrowfully.

'And the boy, what did he do?'

'Nothing. He just sat there, all still and trancelike. Unnatural it was.'

'Unnatural,' echoed his wife. 'Can't say I like the look of him.'

'Then, when the marmon were done with their staring, they sank beneath the surface and vanished. I didn't hang about in that creepy mist, I tell ya. I got the motor started quick smart and headed home. I can't never remember a stranger day.'

'Well!' Nellie Karendon folded her arms across her ample breast. 'You've had an adventure, Rufen Karendon! You're lucky to be alive, and that's a fact.' Sweeping away empty plates, she set out his smoking things and took up her sewing. 'Still, you've not done badly for us.'

'Aye.' He filled the pipe and lit it. 'Not badly at all,' he wheezed through the smoke.

Nellie squinted at the button that needed securing. 'And they're both marked, you say?'

'Aye. Look like Mildaren marks.'

Stabbing her needle through cloth and button, she raised her brows. 'They've made it a fair way, then. Are they being tracked?'

He grunted. 'Could be. I sent their marks to the registry. We'll know soon enough if there's a claim.' He blew out a long, deliberate stream of smoke. 'If so, we can expect compensation. The Mildarens pay well enough.'

His wife flashed her needle in and out, yanking the last stitches tight. Then, satisfied the button would never again work its way free, she cut the thread with her teeth. 'Be a pity,' she mused. 'That girl would clean up nicely.'

'Aye. She's a beauty, and strong, too, I'd wager. The lad's thin, though, and so pale.'

Nellie nodded, frowning, then she had a sudden thought.

'Here! We could always tell the buyers he can sing!'

She earned herself a great guffaw from her husband.

'Well, just pray he don't start up tonight, I'm eager for bed and that's a fact.'

Putting her hand on his shoulder, she gave him a knowing wink.

'Don't you worry about them young uns, my love. They'll sleep all night and happen much of the morrow.'

'Winking at me, are ya now, Nellie Karendon? What sort of wife winks at her husband?' Rufen shook his head in feigned astonishment, and pushed his chair back with a scrape. 'Come here to me, ya cheeky wench!'

Letting out a giggle completely at odds with her size and nature, Nellie Karendon pushed her sewing to one side.

Kep scowled at the laughter coming from the lodge. Her head was splitting, and she'd had quite enough of 'the missus'. On first sight Nellie had shrieked: 'Where in the wild worlds did you find those two, Rufen Karendon?' A loud commentary had accompanied her bustling activity. Having escorted them across a yard to the old barn, she had scurried back and forth bringing bedclothes, bread, cheese, soup and 'a nice big pot of tea'. Not once had she left off her chattering:

'It's not fancy, mind, but it's clean and dry and it'll do you for now, 'specially given the state of you both. My guess is you've slept in worse! May hap we can move you up the big house when you're scrubbed. There's a lovely pot of tea there, but if you fancy cordial there's a jug of that there, too. Now I've set some things out for a wash if you care, but don't you be worrying too much 'bout that tonight.'

On she'd prattled, ranging from her own boys' grubbiness, to the state of their footwear, and her intention to take matters in hand in the morning: it was a blessed relief when she finally ceased her clucking and left them in peace.

Sitting on the bed, Kep held her pounding head in her hands, and tried to gather her thoughts. She was awfully thirsty, but the pain in her head was making it hard to move. She winced, forcing herself to concentrate. How had she ended up in a barn and under the care of 'the missus'?

She wasn't at all clear about recent events. It was hard to put things in order, and some bits didn't seem real at all. Their time with Rufen seemed like a dream — all jumbled and confused. 'Telion help me,' she muttered. She remembered birds, black-and-white, singing in the trees. And eating meat on a stick. She definitely remembered a wolvern charging at them, all teeth and lather. And there was that boy, the rude boy by the fire. After that, things were very hazy.

There was a boat. She remembered the sound of a motor pulsing. No. Paddles splashing. She opened her eyes wide. The marmon! The marmon had attacked. And that terrible whirling water! Or had that been a nightmare? No, it was real, she was sure it was real. She remembered their screams and — and Ash singing. No, that must have been a dream, surely?

Ash was curled in the middle of his bed, his face turned away, but she didn't think he was asleep.

'Ash? Are you all right?

'I'm fine.'

He didn't sound fine. He sounded all choked, as if he was crying. 'Ash? How did we get here? Were you singing? ... I thought ... I dreamt you were singing.' She moaned. Her head really felt as if it was splitting.

Silence.

'We'll talk tomorrow then.'

He grunted, sat up slightly and, without turning, swung a pouch at her. It fell to the floor. 'Don't drink the tea,' he muttered. Then he curled himself up again.

'No, I won't,' she promised.

Kep dragged her attention back to their surroundings. The barn was packed to the rafters with winter stores. There was a stack of folded chairs and a ladder leading to a loft. The air was stuffy with the smell of hay; it made the back of her throat itch. She spied a shuttered window on the opposite wall and rose gingerly. Keeping her head as still as possible, she crossed the floor. The heavy shutters swung inwards, revealing thick bars. She breathed in and the musty smell of ripe fruit and farm animals brought a memory flooding back: Braig leading out the workhorses, clicking his tongue and grinning as he passed. She gulped, stared fiercely at the stars, then turned away.

Their supper things were set on a small table. Kep put her hands around the sides of the teapot. It was still warm and she had the strongest urge to pour herself a cup, but her headache was making the room spin. Better stick to water. She eased her way back to the bed, glancing at Ash as she passed. His knees were drawn up, the Taelstone clasped to his breast. She frowned in disapproval, but it hurt to frown. She needed to lie down and close her eyes. With the gods' help they'd soon be rid of the cursed thing anyway.

As she manoeuvred herself onto the bed, the lamp began to gutter, sending shadows dancing along the rafters. She swallowed. They were safe, she reminded herself. Then there was a noise. Something had moved! She stared into the darkest corners, one by one. Nothing there, just farm equipment casting sinister shadows, and the rickety ladder flickering weirdly in the dying light. *Nothing. It's nothing.* But something *was* shuffling. Kep stared at the edge of the loft. Mice? Her eyes ached, but the more she stared, the less she seemed able to see. When the lamp gave one last flicker and went out, her heart thumped. 'Ash?'

No answer. *It's just mice. Relax.* Then a scraping noise set off every nerve in her body. Thanks to a faint glow of moonlight, she could just make out the edge of the rafters. A black shape was moving along the central beam. A pair of eyes gleamed. Then a crash shattered her nerves completely. Kep squealed as something ran down the ladder, pursued by the darkest of shadows. There was a great commotion in the hay, the most piteous squeaking, then a crunch.

'Ash! Ash!'

He was already sitting bolt upright. 'What was that?'

Kep had scrambled backwards and was hard up against the bedhead. 'I don't know, I don't know,' she garbled.

'Is it a rat?'

'No. No — it's too big for a rat!'

'Did you see it?'

'Yes! I saw its eyes. It's horrible! Where's the lamp? Hurry, Ash! It's moving!' She pointed futilely in the dark. 'There! I'm going to shout for Rufen.'

'No! I have the lamp.'

Ash fumbled. The lamp shook in his hand as he held it up. They dreaded seeing what new terror lay in wait. And there it was.

Ash let out a cry of pure delight: 'Tarlyn!'

Chapter 29

QUESTIONS AND ANSWERS

They were woken early by the sound of buckets clattering. Someone shouted and a gate banged. Kep swung her legs off the bed. Her throat was so dry it hurt to swallow. Tarlyn was curled at Ash's feet. The creature lifted her head and fixed Kep with a disdainful stare, before arching her back in a stretch. Then she crept along the bed to nuzzle Ash's chin. It was good to see him smile and open his eyes; perhaps Tarlyn's return wasn't entirely a bad thing. The thought didn't improve Kep's temper at all.

Ash reached out to reclaim the water. 'How's your head?' He was clearly avoiding eye contact.

'Painful.'

'It'll wear off. Mine's not anywhere near as bad now.'

Ash looked terribly pale. She wondered if he had slept. 'Why do you think—' she began, but he raised his hand. Kep had heard it, too: the sound of footsteps approaching.

Tarlyn disappeared like magic.

'Act confused! We'll talk later,' muttered Ash, as the door rattled and swung open.

Act confused? Well that wouldn't be hard! Kep winced as Nellie Karendon sailed in.

'My, my! Just look at you both. Awake! Fancy you being awake so early.' Hands on hips, she surveyed the untouched food. Then she weighed the teapot in her hands and narrowed her eyes.

Kep got shakily to her feet, but staggered a little, her head swimming.

'Never mind,' beamed their hostess. 'Happen it's a good thing. You can sleep later, for as long as you like. It'll take some work to get you cleaned up, I can tell you that! We probably won't be through till noon! You just lean on me, missy. That's right, Nellie'll take care of you.' She turned her attention only briefly to Ash. 'I'm guessing you'd rather manage yourself.' She gave him a wink. 'There's hot water and soap and towels in the bathhouse just across the way there, see? I've set clean clothes for you.

You'll find all you need. I'll leave the food here, too, in case you feel like a bite. I can't be feeding you a proper breakfast. Right now it's this little missy who needs my attention. Just look at those tangles! You've picked up half the wood I'll warrant!' She tucked Kep under her wing and ushered her out of the barn.

❧

Ash was greatly relieved to be left alone. He breathed in deeply, trying to control his shaking. After a few minutes he drew the Taelstone from his pocket. It was heavy in his hand, but completely clear — just a glass ball. Tarlyn crept from her hiding place and sat beside him. As he began to feel calmer, he looked from the Taelstone into her huge eyes. 'I wish I knew what it was, Tarlyn.'

She just thrashed her tail. He sighed. Presumably T'al Jazure would know what to do with it. How would he feel, though, when it was time to hand the Taelstone over? It fascinated him and made him feel calmer, all at the same time. Perhaps Kep was right. Perhaps he should be careful. He wrapped it carefully and stashed it again before seeking out the bathhouse.

❧

True to her word, Nellie Karendon wasn't finished with Kep until nearly noon. Ash had wiled his morning away with worrying. When at last he heard a door bang, he leapt up to see them coming across the yard. The 'missus' had a huge basket over one arm. He barely recognised the lovely girl at her side. Kep was clad in a dazzling white dress. Her hair was a wondrous affair of glistening braids and cascading curls. Ash hardly knew where to look. Nellie Karendon was ecstatic about the 'marvelling' changes she'd managed from such poor beginnings, and she said so — several times. Then, fortunately, she remembered her wifely duties and ceased her torrent. 'I'll leave you now, my lovelies, and see to my dear Rufen's victuals. A good man should be rewarded with a good table I always say.' With that she left them to rest, pulling the doors firmly behind her, 'just so the hens don't get in, see?'

'You look ...' "Beautiful" was the word Ash really wanted, but for some reason he changed his mind at the last moment. 'Really clean.'

Kep scowled. 'Well I ought to be. I've been soaked and primped and plucked and buffed. It's ridiculous! That foolish woman even coloured my toenails. Look!' She held out a sandalled foot. 'I wanted to slap her fat face. And just look at this dress! "Everyone's wearing them in Skarfell" according to ol' Nellie.'

Ash smiled. She'd captured the woman's inflection perfectly. Something must have been done to accentuate her eyes; they looked impossibly blue.

'As if I care! If they're all dressed like this it must be the silliest place ever. Look how flimsy it is.' She held out the skirt. Ash felt himself blush, but fortunately Kep was too fired up to notice. 'And these sandals! As if I could walk anywhere in these, let alone Skarfell. The straps are so thin, I swear they'll break if I walk more than ten steps.' Ash realised he was staring, and hurriedly turned away on the pretext of investigating the food. Kep stopped her raving at once. 'Sorry. I was going on a bit. You look better, too.' She paused. 'Funny how she gave you grey clothes.'

Ash nodded, not confessing that there had been a selection to choose from.

The food looked good: there was a game pie, bread, slabs of smoked meat, cheese and pickles, and some oblong fruit they didn't recognise. The pie was steaming hot, so they helped themselves first to bread and a tangy cheese.

'So, what do you think?' asked Kep between mouthfuls.

'About what?'

'About when Rufen will take us to Skarfell. Nellie hinted it might be in the next couple of days. That's good, isn't it?'

Ash swallowed a chunk of bread, then shook his head. 'I don't know. I'm not so sure I trust him.'

'But Rufen's been so kind. He saved us from the marmon, and I know she's dreadful,' Kep pulled a face, 'but I think she means well.'

He scratched his head. It just didn't feel right somehow. 'But, what about the tea?'

She shrugged. 'Maybe he thought it would be good for us. And we've got water this time … I drew it myself.'

Ash had so many doubts, now he'd had time to think clearly. 'It's not just the tea. Doesn't it seem a little unlikely that Rufen would know the very man we're seeking? And he sets traps, but never seems to catch anything. Doesn't that strike you as odd? I mean, what exactly does Rufen hunt?'

'Ah! Now there's a question!'

They both jumped, jerking the table. Ash's beaker hit the floor and bounced away. They looked up at the loft and their hearts leapt into their throats to see someone sitting there leaning against an upright, his leg dangling over the edge. They recognised him immediately.

'Perhaps you're not so stupid after all.'

'You!' Kep cried.

Sarin got to his feet. 'Apparently.' He stepped onto the ladder, gave a little hop, then slid all the way down, not troubling himself with the rungs. Landing neatly, he tilted his head and addressed himself to Ash. 'To answer your excellent question, Rufen Karendon hunts anything he can make a profit from. Caralots mainly, if there's nothing of greater value on offer.'

They gaped.

'Did you know caralots have a special gland in their necks?'

'How long have you been up there?' Kep spluttered.

He ignored her. 'No? Well, these glands contain a rare essence. Makes a perfume that lasts for days … The ladies of Calkinon are crazy about it. It's much more valuable than the pelts, and so much easier to transport. Your friend, dear ol' Karendon, has made it a bit of a speciality. He traps the caralots, cuts out their glands, leaves them to die and re-sets his traps. Easy. So long as you choose a new spot; even caralots are unnerved by the sight of bloodied carcasses. His mouth slid into a twisted smile.

Kep was beside herself. 'How dare you! How dare you spy on us! It's, it's rude — it's despicable!'

Sarin calmly ignored her. 'Of course he has other prey, too.' He lifted an eyebrow. 'How's your head by the way?'

'Better,' Ash mumbled.

'What would you know about it?' Kep snarled. 'Ignore him, Ash. Don't talk to him. We can't trust anything he says.' She glared at the intruder. 'We don't want you here! Just go away!' The laughter in his eyes was infuriating. She turned to Ash. He looked oddly embarrassed. Then to her complete confusion, he unlaced the top of his tunic, drew out a water-pouch and held it out to the stranger. 'Thanks for the water, and um … the advice. You'll want this back.'

'Ash!' Kep was aghast.

Sarin waved the pouch away with an air of benevolence. 'That's all right, you keep it — it's one of Karendon's.'

Kep snorted. 'See, Ash? He's a thief, and no doubt a liar, too — and who knows what else!'

Sarin held his head on one side. 'A murderer perhaps?' His eyes laughed.

Ash intervened quickly. 'I think we can trust him, Kep. He warned me about the tea.' He made an apologetic face. 'Sorry I didn't tell you, I just didn't get a chance.'

Kep redirected her glare to Sarin, who was suddenly looking at her with rather more interest.

'That your name? Kep?'

'Yes, that's my name,' she snapped, 'not that it's any of your business.'

He narrowed his strange eyes. 'You're sticking with your slave names, then?'

Ash and Kep froze.

'Just seems a bit reckless, that's all.' He gestured at the table. 'Do you mind?'

Ash and Kep exchanged looks.

'No. There's more than we could ever eat,' answered Ash weakly. 'Help yourself.'

Kep wasn't giving in that easily. 'What makes you think we're slaves?'

'Got it written all over you,' he replied cheerfully. He sniffed a slice of meat before taking a bite. 'Oh, yeah, and it's written on you too. Did you forget? Rufen's probably sent your numbers to the registry.' He munched appreciatively. 'Mmm this is good. One thing you can say about the Karendons, they do feed their captives well.'

Kep felt her legs wobble. She looked at Ash and saw her own dismay reflected back. Then she lifted her chin. 'I don't believe you.' She made a move towards the door.

Sarin shook his head in the most patronising manner. 'Go ahead. Try the door. You didn't really think smelly Nellie shut it to keep the hens out, did you?' He rolled his eyes. 'What about the bars on the windows? Are they for keeping hens out, too? Ha! Pretty determined hens she has there!'

Kep turned her back on him. She knew in her heart that the horrible young man was telling the truth, but that didn't mean she had to watch him gloat. She wanted to throw herself on the bed and cry, but she refused to give him the satisfaction. She felt sick.

Returning to his chair, Ash watched dully while Sarin investigated the pie. He ran a knife around the lid and lifted it. Then he smelt it and made a face. 'Smells great. Wouldn't eat it, though. Smells too much like tea.' He cut two large portions and put them on plates, saying, 'I'd ditch those.' He helped himself to a wedge of cheese instead. 'Of course it's up to you,' he added, skewering a spiced onion on the end of the knife. His eyes constantly flicked to the window and its view of the yard. 'You got a tracker?' he asked conversationally.

Ash couldn't think of a reason not to answer. 'Kep does. A snout.'

Sarin gave a low whistle. 'And you've stuck by her?' He seemed taken aback. 'More crazy than stupid, then.'

Ash folded his arms and tried to change the subject. 'How did you get in? And why all these questions?'

'Just interested. Came through the door when you were busy making yourself pretty.' He grinned. 'I sometimes sleep here if I'm passing. Don't usually have company, though.'

Ash frowned. It felt like there was something the young man wasn't saying.

'Don't get your hopes up,' Sarin added. 'I'm not about to rescue you or anything like that. Why would I get myself involved with you two idiots? You'd just get me killed.' He sniffed the water, then poured some into a mug.

As he was sipping it, Tarlyn emerged from the bedclothes and shook herself. She ignored the newcomer entirely. Sarin's eyes flickered with interest when she leapt onto Ash's shoulder and sat there with her tail curled around his neck.

Ash frowned. 'You knew the marmon would attack us,' he said quietly.

'Not really. Thought they might, though. Maybe Karendon deserved to die.'

'And us?'

Sarin shrugged. 'How much of their daughter's death was your fault?'

Ash faltered under his steady gaze.

'Oh, for goodness sake, Ash!' cried Kep. 'Stop looking so pale and guilty. It wasn't your fault. None of it. That creature did attack Ash, you know.'

Sarin twisted his mouth. 'Marmons don't attack humans. Only a few people have ever seen one. They're shy, noble creatures; an ancient breed.'

Ash read his bitter expression. The young man had dropped his careless air entirely. This was something he cared about.

'To slay a marmon is sacrilege; it's a sin against the gods.'

Kep had seemed ready to argue, but his words silenced her. After a pause, she said, 'But it wasn't our fault. We thought … It reared up! It was …' She fell silent again, trying to remember.

Sarin spoke coldly. 'There's no excuse for killing a marmon. They live alone in secluded places, but they share one consciousness. Do you know what that means? Every one of them would have felt her pain, shared her suffering. Tell me. Was she dead when he gouged out the beautiful scales on her tail? When he dragged her body out of the water so her kin would never find it? It was a revolting thing to do, even by Karendon's standards.'

Ash reeled. All the pain of the marmon's song came flooding back. Then suddenly, something fell into place. 'You found her,' he whispered. He caught a flicker of surprise in those golden eyes and knew he was right. 'You found her and returned her to the water so her people might claim her. Didn't you?' Sarin didn't say anything, he simply nodded.

Kep looked from one to the other, trying to understand. The pain in her head wasn't helping. She pressed the heels of her hands to her forehead. 'So, you were tracking us?'

Sarin sighed. 'No. I was tracking Karendon. He was tracking you. It's what he does. He takes his opportunities where he finds them, and what a wonderful opportunity you two turned out to be. Well done.' He clapped slowly three times.

Ignoring his derision, Kep turned to Ash. 'It was Rufen's campfire we smelt, then. He must have been following us. And he killed the marmon, and drugged us. And lied to us! About — everything.' The full horror of the deception was hitting home.

Ash nodded miserably.

'So!' Sarin stood up. 'There you have it. All of the answers to all of your questions. Thanks for the victuals. Someone will soon be here to collect the leftovers, and make sure you are sleeping soundly no doubt. I'd get rid of that pie if I were you. Wouldn't want to disappoint them. I'll make myself scarce.' He made for the ladder, but then he paused and turned back. 'Just one thing puzzles me. Why would you two be so keen to get to Skarfell, the biggest slave port on the entire coast? Even Karendon's tea doesn't produce stupidity on that scale.'

Ash ran his hands through his hair. Sarin was right. They had been incredibly stupid — just a couple of stupid slaves. The first person they had met had completely taken them in. 'It was another of Rufen's lies,' he answered quietly. 'One we desperately wanted to believe.' He saw how Sarin rolled his eyes, but he went on anyway. He wanted to explain, to show him they weren't complete fools. 'We are searching for a man. His name is T'al Jazure. Rufen told us he lives in Skarfell and that he'd take us there to meet him. Of course, we realise now that's not true ...' His voice trailed off.

A sudden transformation had come over Sarin. There was something new in his expression, some emotion he couldn't control. It made Ash's heart skip a beat. He saw that Kep had seen it, too. There was an enthralling pause, then at last Sarin responded.

'It's not true, because it's impossible.'

For a split second Ash thought he was mocking them again, but there was no laughter in the young man's eyes. His expression was utterly sombre.

'T'al Jazure isn't a man,' he said. 'It's a place.'

Chapter 30

STRANGE MAGIC

'Not a man? A place. Are you sure?' Kep's hands were on her hips, her eyes hostile. She seemed convinced the strange boy was lying.

'Of course. But it's not just any place. T'al Jazure was the city of the Azuri.' When they didn't react, Sarin arched his brows in disbelief. 'Seriously? You've never heard tales of the Azuri? All of the stories about their inventions and their tragic fate?' He seemed genuinely astonished. 'Don't you have storytellers where you're from?'

Kep scowled darkly. 'Of course we have storytellers.'

'Do you think you could take us there, to T'al Jazure?' asked Ash quickly. 'Is it far?' He ignored Kep's fierce glare and kept his eyes fixed on the stranger.

It was impossible to tell what he was thinking, and there was a long pause before Sarin replied, 'Maybe.' Then his eyes flicked to the window. 'But right now you've got a rather more urgent problem.' In seconds he had scaled the ladder and disappeared into the hay.

There was barely time to act: Rufen and Nellie Karendon were coming across the yard. Ash grabbed the water pouch. After looking wildly about, Kep dumped the portions of pie under a pile of rags. She shoved the plates back on the table and leapt to her bed just as the barn door began to rattle.

Ash was already imitating deep slumber. Kep knew she had to let her body go limp, but every muscle was tense. She forced herself to breathe slowly and deeply. It was hopeless. She had never been any good at pretending. She hid her face in her elbow and prayed silently as the door opened with a scrape.

Nellie Karendon beamed broadly at the empty plates. 'Looks like my game pie went down a treat,' she commented, as she clattered things into her basket.

'Aye, we'll not have any trouble from these two. They're sleeping like babes.' Her husband towered at the foot of Kep's bed, rubbing his chin. 'Shame it's the girl who's under claim. Ya did a fine job fixing her up, Nellie.'

His wife nodded and moved to his side. 'Never mind, my love. We'll get our compensation tomorrow. And you can sell the boy on at Skarfell. Still, I won't deny it's a disappointment.' She gave a little sigh of regret, then made a mental note to reclaim the dress in the morning; no need for that to go to waste. 'Will we search their bags now?'

'No. Leave it till morning, my love. No point disturbing things until after the tracker arrives. Don't get your hopes up, though: they won't have anything of value. These slaves never do.'

'Just their sweet young bodies,' she murmured.

'Aye. It's a shame.'

They left, congratulating themselves again as they went.

❧

'So you'll help us?'

'Maybe.'

Although he was the very picture of nonchalance, with boots propped up on a box and arms folded across his chest, Sarin had the air of someone turning a problem over in his mind. Something in his attitude had definitely changed, Ash was certain of it.

Kep seemed to have decided that the best way to deal with the unwelcome visitor was to pretend he didn't exist. She was busy pulling at her hair, dragging out the braids and fastenings and tugging at a comb that had become entangled at the back.

'Here, don't rip it. I'll help.' Ash worked gently, trying to unpick the mess she had created in her fury.

Sarin's eyes slid sideways, watching. 'You're not lovers, are you?'

'No!' they retorted in unison.

Ash dropped the comb as if it had stung him, and stepped away. He felt his face flush.

'All right! Don't get all hot and bothered.' Sarin seemed amused. 'Just want to know what I'm dealing with, that's all. Lovers are unpredictable, makes them dangerous associates.'

Associates? That sounded promising. Pouring himself a mug of water, Ash perched on a bench. He eyed Sarin's boots as he sipped. They were made of soft leather, with deep cuffs at the tops. The sides were laced for a perfect fit. Although they bore the marks of long journeys, they were obviously of the highest quality. They would fetch a pretty sum in the markets of Mildaresh. He studied Sarin's face. However could he afford such boots?

Sarin caught his eye and swung his feet down. Then he stood up and stretched. 'I'd need compensating of course.'

Kep rolled her eyes. She was sure she had never met such an offensive person. She didn't like him and she didn't trust him — quite frankly, she wanted nothing to do with him.

'A deal isn't a deal without some sort of consideration.'

'All right.' Ash frowned. 'But we don't have any coin.'

'What about your pet?'

Tarlyn had reappeared and was stalking a spider. She gave Sarin a scornful look, and raised the ruff on her neck slightly.

'Tarlyn? She's not a pet. She's ... well, a companion. Sort of.'

Kep arched her eyebrows.

'Pity.' Sarin watched admiringly until the spider was caught and dispatched. Then he grinned and turned his attention back to Ash. 'Well, what else do you have?'

'I've got a knife.'

It was a shrewd guess that Sarin would be interested in the knife. He examined it closely, running his fingers along the script. 'Where's it from?'

'Er, I don't know exactly. It's a good one, though. We used it to cut our way through the Tanglewood.' At this Kep blew a loud stream of air between her lips.

Sarin raised an eyebrow as he thumbed the dull blade, but he seemed satisfied. 'It's a deal. I can't think how you came by such a thing, but that's not my concern. In exchange for the knife I'll get you out of this mess and take you to meet someone who knows about T'al Jazure.'

'You don't *actually* know where it is, then?' Kep threw up her hands.

Sarin shook his head. 'It's complicated.'

Of course it was disappointing, but still much better than nothing. Ash clasped Sarin's proffered arm to seal the bond. 'Do you want the knife now, or later?'

Sarin laughed. 'You really are new to this kind of thing, aren't you?' He shook his head. 'Later. Mine will do me for now.' He pulled a broad hunting knife from the sheath strapped to his thigh. Kep rolled her eyes, but Sarin didn't notice; he was busy walking about the barn as if searching for something. Picking up several long pieces of broken wood, he examined each carefully and discarded all but one. Then he sat on one of the low benches and began to whittle.

Kep arched her eyebrows and seemed about to speak when Ash shot her a warning look. She pulled a face at him, and continued the battle with her hair instead. Ash hovered uncomfortably, then sat opposite Sarin, watching as the shavings curled and bounced to the floor. Quite a pile had formed before the young man spoke again.

'We don't have much time. From what Karendon said, it's a fair guess the tracker will arrive early in the morning. That means we have to move quickly. Karendon's a good bushman, but not as clever as he thinks. And he's greedy. I think we can outwit him with a bit of luck. The snout's our biggest problem. Does he have kill orders?'

'Yes.' Kep just managed to keep her voice steady.

'Right. We can't let him get close, then. He'll take his shot if he gets in range.'

Ash frowned. 'Mmm. That's what I'd have thought, too, but …'

Sarin looked up, his hands suddenly still. 'But?'

Ash hesitated. 'Well, he's been within easy range twice and he didn't even raise his weapon.'

'That's true, Ash!' Kep's eyes widened. 'He got really close, especially the second time. He could easily have shot me!'

Sarin frowned and began whittling again. 'That is strange.' The length of wood was getting thinner by the minute. 'So we have a curiously incompetent snout. But he's still likely to shoot on sight. We can't outrun him and we can't evade him for very long in the wild, even with my superior knowledge of these lands.' He ignored the derisive snort that came from Kep's direction. 'We'll need the Karendons to hold him up a bit.' After a pause he looked doubtfully at Ash, then at Kep. 'How good are you at hiding?'

They smiled at each other. 'Pretty good, actually.'

To Sarin's amazement, Ash pulled the dopple-star from his bag and gave a quick demonstration.

'Ha! And you palmed me off with that old green knife! I should have made you turn out your pockets.' Sarin laughed. 'I might have underestimated you, grey boy.'

Ash couldn't help feeling stupidly pleased at the compliment. He hid a smile, though, as he watched Sarin carving a notch into the top of the stick.

'That should do it. What do you think?' He held it up.

Ash blinked. 'What is it?'

Sarin grinned. 'Here. Hold that.' In a few minutes he had found a length of old wire. He measured it against the door, then wiggled it back and forth until it broke in two. Wrapping one end of the longer piece around the notch at the top of the stick, he bent the other end up and used the short piece to add two extra points.

When he held the stick out, the wire dangled with the pointed hook at the bottom. 'Right. Let's go fishing.'

Ash and Kep watched in disbelief as Sarin selected a large knot in the door and tapped it sharply with the hilt of his knife. It fell out with little resistance. He threaded his contraption through the hole, squeezing the wires together to ease them through. Then, his strange eyes half-closed in concentration, with his cheek against the wood, he jiggled the stick up and down. After only a few minutes he grinned. 'Gotcha,' he said softly. As he pulled the end of the stick slowly and smoothly towards the floor, they heard a heavy scrape. With a push the door was open.

Even Kep couldn't help looking impressed, but her scowl returned immediately when Sarin gave her a wink.

He swivelled the catch around, pulled the door to and tucked a wedge of wood underneath to hold it in place. 'Right,' he said, rubbing his hands together, 'here's the plan.'

⁂

'He's been gone for ages,' Kep whispered. 'Perhaps we should make a run for it.'

It was awfully tempting. It was unbearable waiting in the dark, knowing the door was open and that dawn was creeping closer, bringing Gooel with it. But, they had agreed to do what Sarin said. Besides, how far would they get on their own without decent shoes or food? They would just have to trust him and wait for the signal.

After a few minutes, Kep whispered again. 'Is the dopple-star ready?'

'Yes.' Ash squeezed his fingers around it. 'We just have to wait.'

'Well, I'm not very good—'

195

They both jumped. Even though the howl was precisely the signal they had been waiting for, it was utterly chilling, as if a real wolvern was right outside the door. They sprang to their feet.

A second howl rang out and, frighteningly, was joined by another on the opposite side of the barn.

'There are two! How's he doing that?'

'I don't know.' Ash couldn't help fumbling with the dopple-star, but then the shield was set. He put out his hand and felt its reassuring resistance. At that moment the howling became a loud yelping that slowly faded into the distance.

Almost instantly, the yard was assaulted with other noises. Doors slamming. Swearing and shouting. The Karendons were awake.

'It's wolvern, my love! I tell you it is. A pack of 'em, I warrant!'

'Just let me catch a sight of one and I'll stick an arrow in it. Where are those damned dogs? Jaws! Ripper! Where are ya, by the gods?'

'Rufen — the barn! It's open!'

There were footsteps, great hurried footsteps, and panting. 'The slaves have escaped!'

'What strange magic is this?' Nellie Karendon's face was red and wondering in the lamplight.

Her husband growled. 'Magic! Nonsense. Those wolvern probably rocked the bar loose and the young 'uns saw their chance and legged it. That's all. You search here while I have a look around.'

Nellie Karendon picked up a pitchfork, and began stabbing its long prongs into the hay. 'If you're in here, you'll be sorry!'

Ash and Kep cringed as she worked her way towards them, thrusting and jabbing. They could see her boots, dirty under the hem of her nightgown, when her skirt brushed the shield.

'I'll show you, you good-for-nothing little ...' She made another futile thrust at the hay. 'Spurn our hospitality, would you? We'll see about that!'

Having satisfied herself that there was no one hiding on the ground level, she looked uncertainly at the rickety ladder.

'Don't bother, Nellie!' her husband thundered. 'I've picked up their tracks: they've headed for the back woods. They can't have got far.' He hoisted his crossbow across his shoulder. 'Don't you worry, my love. You get back to bed. Ol' Rufen'll have those pretty things back for ya in no time.'

Ash and Kep waited for a long while. First, they had to be sure Nellie was safely back in bed, but truth was they were also shaking too much to move. Finally everything was still.

'Ready?'

'Ready.' Kep rearranged her burden so it hung over her shoulder. It rustled as she tucked the coverlet around it more securely.

'Are you sure you can manage that?'

'Of course. It hardly weighs anything. Let's just get out of here.'

They crept across the yard and through a small gate into the fields. There, they found a sketchy track. As Sarin said it would, it took them along the fence, towards the lake's edge then down to the jetty. The longboat was moored at the end, along with a smaller dinghy. In minutes they were settled and Ash had reset the shield. They resigned themselves to wait once more.

There was no point going back to bed, so Nellie Karendon swapped her boots for slippers, put the kettle on the range and took up her knitting. Soon her needles were clicking in time to her thoughts. When her hens made a sudden commotion, she lifted her head. Then, before she had time to rise, they settled again. It was a strange night, she thought to herself. A strange night indeed.

'Ash? Are you all right?'

He was staring oddly into the water, but he snapped that he was fine, so Kep chewed on a thumbnail and let the silence deepen.

At long last they saw Sarin sprinting down the jetty, a dark shape bounding behind him. *Halstar?*

Sarin reached the end of the jetty, stopped and stared.

'Nice trick,' he said softly when the boat reappeared.

He caressed the wolvern's head, and for a brief, horrible moment they thought he was bringing it aboard. Then, at his quiet command, the beast slinked off.

In a few moments Sarin had the elpha-motor going and had set the longboat on its course across the lake. The boat rocked alarmingly as he took his seat, before righting itself.

They were far from shore, when he suddenly grinned and held out his closed fists. 'Guess what I've got?' Before they could answer he opened his hands. Lying on each palm was a gorgeous luminescent disk.

'What are they?' Kep gasped in wonder.

'Marmon scales.' He gave a twisted sort of smile. 'Worth a small fortune.' Then he did something utterly unexpected. He leaned over the side and dropped them into the water — first one, then the other. The shining scales tumbled into the depths.

'Precious!' Sarin locked his hands behind his head and leaned back contentedly. 'What a wonderful night.'

⁂

Nellie was nodding over her knitting by the time she heard her husband's footsteps. She smiled and yawned. But then the door slammed open, quivering on its hinges. Her husband's face shone angrily over his red beard. 'They're not on foot! We spotted the longboat from the top of Krassen Hill and could see the girl — in that damned white dress! We're taking the small boat—'

When his son burst in, yelling that the small boat was missing, too, he slammed his fists on the table. 'Who'd have thought they'd have it in 'em? Just slaves. Just dumb slaves!'

'Better wait for the snout, my love,' Nellie murmured. 'He'll find 'em.'

'And lose our compensation? No! Garyn's got a boat. And he owes me. They're not getting away that easy!'

'But the snout's due at dawn, my love!' Nellie exclaimed.

'Stall him, woman. Feed him! By Argess, bed him if ya have to! Just keep him here till we get back!'

⁂

'We're nearly there. That's Senna. See the lights?'

Kep peered ahead anxiously. From what Sarin had told them, Senna was a tough town, full of crooked men and unscrupulous women. She hoped he knew what he was doing. She was worried about Ash, too. He had been strangely quiet.

As they edged towards the darkened wharves she heard him catch his breath and she leaned forward to touch his sleeve.

His eyes were shining oddly. 'There are bodies. Floating in the water.'

Not now, Ash. Please, not now. She squeezed his arm. 'It's all right,' she whispered. 'There's nothing there. No bodies.'

She could feel Sarin's interested gaze on them. Then they all heard it: the sound of an elpha-engine. Their hearts pounded. A boat was coming up behind them, fast.

Nellie Karendon had never felt so ill at ease. The snout didn't speak; he just stared at the wall with those huge blank eyes. She had offered him food and drink; he had refused both. She could tell there was little point offering him her bed. She took refuge in her knitting, and when her husband appeared at the door, she couldn't think when she had been more relieved — until she saw the look on his face. Whatever has happened?

'Straw!' he spluttered. 'Stuffed with straw! No one in the damned boat. Beached on the other side of the lake. Empty. Except for this!'

He shoved the white dress at her; tell-tale pieces of straw were caught in the lace.

The snout stood. His voice rasped: 'Girl. Not here.'

Rufen growled as if he would take him by the throat. 'No. Girl is not here. And I'm done with her, damned witch!'

Gooel nodded and left the kitchen without a word. Not there. But had been there. He sniffed the air and crossed to the barn. The door was hanging open. He entered and stood quietly, eyes closed. Not there, but the place was full of her presence. But where now? He let the world shift and sent his mind out. Searching. He had lost her several times. It was curious. She was different. The last and different. It was fitting. He let the sounds of the morning come and go. There was a fresh outburst from the house. 'The little thieves!' He let it go. Where now? A rooster crowed. He let it go. Where now? A town. His mind flitted, then settled. A grubby, dirty town. He knew it. He opened his eyes. Senna. She was in Senna.

Chapter 31

SENNA

The sound of the elpha-motor got louder as the boat approached. 'Ash, can we use the shield?' asked Sarin. 'Ash?'

Ash was gazing into the water; it was as if he hadn't heard at all, so Kep answered for him, 'We can't use it while we're moving, and I think they've seen us anyway.'

She was right: the sound of men shouting carried clearly across the water.

Sarin cursed. 'Probably poachers — just what we don't need. Keep quiet and leave the talking to me.'

As the craft veered towards them, he sat up and gave a wave. 'Ho, there!'

In a few swift moments, it came alongside. At first all they could make out were three burly figures. Then a lantern revealed three of the ugliest faces they had ever seen. Nobody in Mildaresh had such faces; they looked as if they had been stitched together from rough leather, and inexpertly at that. Each face suggested its wearer would happily reach across and throttle them given half a chance. But Sarin seemed completely unperturbed by the men's evil countenances; you'd think he had bumped into three of his dearest acquaintances.

'Ho, friends! Has Narsis blessed you this night?'

The men clearly weren't used to being addressed in such a cheerful manner, and certainly not in the dead of night. The man in the centre snarled out of the side of his mouth: 'What be it to you?'

The others muttered and glared. 'Aye, what be it to you?'

'Oh, we was just sayin' we 'oped you'd 'ad more luck than us, that's all. Narsis has sure forsaken us, we ain't caught a thing.'

Kep couldn't help stealing a look sideways: Sarin sounded so different.

She had thrown a blanket over her head to hide her face, and now shrank back into it, but fortunately the leering men seemed more interested in the bottom of their boat. The one holding the lantern scowled. 'And what did ya think ya were gonna catch? Ya ain't got no gear.'

Another growled: 'Oi! You young uns ain't been pulling up pots, 'ave ya?

It'll go badly for ya if you 'ave.'

They all bristled. They obviously thought if anyone was going to rob pots it would be them, not a bunch of thieving young rascals.

Sarin laughed. 'Course not. We ain't pulled up no pots, 'ave we?' Kep and Ash shook their heads.

'We don't need no pots.' Sarin dropped his voice conspiratorially. 'We was tryin' for nightsarks.'

Kep and Ash nodded, as if they knew what a nightsark was.

'Nightsarks? This ain't the season for nightsarks,' growled the man with the lantern. 'Anyhows, where's your bait? Where's your poles?'

'Ah, that's the thing.' Sarin looked up at the skies, then spoke in a hushed voice, as if letting them in on a secret. 'Don't need no gear for nightsarks under these moons. Ya just swing a lantern and they leap outta the water 'an throw 'emselves right in the boat!'

There was the slightest pause before all three men burst into howls of laughter, revealing just how few teeth they had between them. They guffawed and wheezed and puffed before putting the young fool straight. 'Who told ya that, ya soft lads?'

'That's just a tale, that is. Ya must be silly in the head to believe such nonsense!'

'No one's never caught a nightsark that way.'

Sarin's face was a picture of hurt and embarrassment. 'You mean we been tricked outta our coin, for nothin'?'

The poachers erupted in a new wave of hilarity, smacking their hands on their thighs. It seemed this was the best joke of all.

'Well, I'll swing for that, Tomus Hardling,' spluttered Sarin, 'you just see if I don't!'

The men wheezed and nodded. 'You do that, laddo. You do that. You been sold a crock you 'ave, and that's a fact.'

Sarin turned to Ash and Kep. 'C'mon, lads. Don't just sit there. We gunna get even with that filthy, lying little—' he let out a string of curses and foul language.

The poachers chuckled appreciatively.

'Good on ya, boy. Give 'em what for. No one likes looking a fool.'

Sarin waited for the sound of their boat to fade before letting out a low whistle. Then he spoke in his normal voice: 'Let's get ashore before anyone else comes along. Here, put these on.' He flung a jerkin and some leggings across to Kep. 'Even Senna folk would raise their eyebrows at a girl dressed in a sack. The boots might be too big, but they'll do.'

A pair of boots spun towards Kep, tied together by the laces. She frowned. The clothes smelt fresh, as if they had just been laundered. 'You stole these from the lodge, didn't you?'

Sarin put his head on one side. 'Stealing's a harsh word, especially where the Karendons are concerned. Remember them? The ones who planned to sell you as slaves? It's not so much stealing as redistributing goods to more deserving people.'

'It's stealing,' said Kep hotly. 'See Ash? He *is* a thief, and, I might add, a pretty good liar, too.'

Sarin just responded 'Why, thank you', and laughed.

Ash didn't say anything. He was staring at the water.

❧

At last the little boat nudged up against a crooked wharf. Sarin grasped a huge wooden strut to steady them while Kep scrambled up. The rungs on the ladder were slimy and crusted by time. Once up, she realised Ash hadn't moved at all.

'Ash, you next,' Sarin urged. He nudged the boy's shoulder when he didn't respond. 'Ash?'

Ash flinched at the touch, then recovered himself. 'Right. Sorry.'

Kep put out her hand, but he managed to haul himself up unassisted. In seconds Sarin was beside them. 'Let's get out of sight. Keep low and watch your step.'

The jetty was treacherous. Black, shining water could be seen through splits in the slippery planks. They made such slow progress that Kep began to wonder if it would be better to crawl on all fours. When they finally reached a line of broken boat sheds, she wrinkled her nose. The stench of fish guts, old oil and rotting wood was revolting. 'This place stinks.'

'Yeah. Welcome to Senna,' replied Sarin with a grim smile.

❧

Everything in Senna was dank and filthy and unloved. The alleys wound about in crooked confusion, as if reluctant to draw closer to the heart of

203

the town. Black brick buildings with mean little windows crowded the laneways, their walls glistening under the dispirited glow of an occasional elpha-lamp. Although she would never admit it to Sarin, Kep was glad of her stolen boots; they were dirty and cumbersome, but did protect her feet from the rubbish and broken glass.

The streets of Senna were far from empty despite the late hour. More than one ale house remained open to accommodate the desires of the sleepless. Groups of ruffians spilled from the entrances, and they had to change course several times to avoid fighting men and staggering drunks. Finally they entered a filthy alleyway overhung by dingy garrets. The stink that hung in the air probably had something to do with the yellow slime that spewed from a broken spout onto the cobbles, pooled, then slid into the gutter.

Sarin led them to the end of the alley. 'This is the place.'

A sign hanging crookedly above the battered door featured a woman with abundant chestnut hair and an equally generous bosom. It read *Rosie's Heart*.

'Are you sure?' Ash said doubtfully, trying to peer through the filthy glass of a window. 'It looks ... well, it looks pretty dangerous.'

'The whole town looks dangerous,' Kep muttered. She didn't care much for the way Sarin's eyes seemed to glint in the dark either.

He smiled. 'Anywhere's too dangerous for the likes of you. Which reminds me, we need to hide your wrists.' He reached inside a pocket. 'Kep, you wear this. Ash, you take mine.' He unfastened the leather cuffs around his own wrists.

Kep struggled with the fastener on the leather bracelet. 'I suppose this is stolen, too?'

Sarin shrugged, 'If you say so.' Then he frowned, 'You're far too clean, but we can't fix that now. Just keep your heads down and don't make eye contact.'

Rosie's Heart was not nearly as bad on the inside, so long as you discounted the clientele. The people at the bar all looked like close relations of the poachers they had met earlier. Others lurked in various nooks and booths; the whole place seemed designed specifically for shady dealings. A barmaid with a broad face and huge arms leaned on the bar. As they entered, faces turned in hostile curiosity. But thankfully, by the time they had reached the anonymous gloom of a back corner the other patrons had mostly returned to their ale and conversation.

'Good.' Sarin shrugged off his gear and pushed it under the table. 'I need to buy some drinks. I'll send something over. You two just keep quiet here, out of the way.' He looked meaningfully at Kep: 'Try not to do anything reckless.'

'What did he mean by that?' demanded Kep.

'Don't know.' Ash ducked his head, pretending to rearrange the bags at his feet. Tarlyn was deep inside his hood, and he murmured for her to stay there.

They heard Sarin call out as he sauntered to the bar. 'You must be, Rosie!'

Kep rolled her eyes.

'I'll take some ale and a bottle of fireshot, please, Rosie.' Sarin tossed a pouch onto the counter and the barmaid laughed merrily, probably at the loud jingling of coins. Patting her hair, she protested in a voice matching her low-cut dress. 'Ooh, you cheeky young thing! Fireshot it is.'

Within minutes a surly waitress approached Ash and Kep, bearing a tray. She plonked down two tankards and a plate of coarse bread.

Kep looked at the ale uncertainly. 'Is it strong?'

The girl shrugged, she obviously had better things to do than waste words on them. The ale was pleasant enough, bitter and tasting faintly of honey. They sipped it slowly between mouthfuls of bread.

A bottle of fireshot had appeared next to Sarin's elbow, and each time they got a view of it through the group at the bar it looked emptier.

'What's he doing?' demanded Kep. 'Is he getting drunk?'

There was too much hilarity from the bar for them to hear the conversation. The only thing they could hear clearly was the barmaid's braying laughter. It seemed she had never met anyone as charming as the young man who insisted on calling her Rosie and kept urging everyone to raise glasses to her health.

'Ash, I don't like this. What's he up to? Surely it's dangerous to be drinking with those types.'

Ash rubbed his eyes and yawned. 'I suppose he's trying to find that friend of his. We don't have a choice, Kep. We just have to trust him.'

'Trust him? We already know he's a thief and a liar. I wouldn't put it past him to do his own deal with the slavers.'

Ash was taking another sip of beer when Kep grabbed his arm. 'Ash! They're looking over here!'

It was true. The conversation had suddenly got quieter. Most of the people around Sarin were staring in their direction. 'He's talking about us,' Kep muttered. 'I knew we shouldn't trust him. What if he wants the bounty for himself?'

Ash didn't have time to respond. The serving girl was heading towards them. Her manners were so changed that it was hard to believe she was the same girl. She made a reverent little bob, then placed a bowlful of something that looked like thick gruel in front of Kep. 'Some slosh to have with your bread. On the house, miss.' She nodded at Ash: 'And you can have some, too.' Then with a shy smile she bobbed again before scurrying back to the bar. They stared at each other, baffled.

'What was that about?'

'I don't know. What's slosh?'

The slosh turned out to be delicious. After testing some on their fingers, they tried dipping the bread. Soon they were scooping it up eagerly. They were scraping the bowl clean when the front door was suddenly flung open. Their hearts plunged into their stomachs. A bandy-legged figure stood on the threshold casting huge, solemn eyes around the room.

Instantly the place erupted as everyone began fighting and pushing and wrestling on the floor. Furniture flew through the air. Glasses were smashed. A great tumult of bodies suddenly blocked the space between them and Gooel.

Sarin burst from the midst of the mêlée. 'Back door! Left corner. Run!'

Catching up their things, they fled the chaos. As they spilled into a rubbish-strewn courtyard, Kep demanded: 'What was that? What did you do?'

'Just told them your name,' answered Sarin with a swift grin. 'They did the rest. Now follow me!'

With that he vaulted neatly over a low wall. There was no time to stand about looking shocked; they followed as quickly as they could. He led them on a long chase through twisting alleys, until at last he swung around a bend and held up a hand. Gasping and wheezing, they tried to catch their breaths. The walled area must once have been a garden, but now the beds and tubs held nothing but the skeletal remains of dead plants. The pale morning light made the scene even uglier.

'Found out where he is ...' Sarin panted. 'Barnham ... *Dawn Star* ... Down there ... near the flock.'

They looked in the direction of his pointing finger. The hillside beyond the garden gate fell away steeply. Below was a cascade of dirty roofs, and beyond that flat ground rimmed by forest. They could just make out a cluster of shapes sitting on the plain. From the distance they looked like stranded boats. A giant ball sat in the middle of each.

'What are they?' Ash asked, squinting.

'They're elpha-birds. And one of them belongs to Barnham. All we need to do is collect him from the tavern and he'll fly us out of here. Easy!'

Kep raised her eyebrows. *'Fly us out of here?' Just like that?* Why did she have the distinct impression it wasn't going to be easy at all?

Kep's fears were soon confirmed. Sarin was unslinging his bow. He strung it and repositioned his quiver. 'Ash, get your knife out.'

'What is it? What's wrong?' Kep pushed her hair back from her eyes.

'Nothing. Just have to be ready for cessrats. Ash, your knife.'

Ash drew his knife and looked at it uncertainly. Then he handed it to Kep. 'You take it. It works better for you.'

She nodded, ignoring Sarin's raised brows. 'What's a cessrat?'

Frowning, Sarin drew a thin blade from a sheath on his quiver and handed it to Ash. 'Take this, then; you need some sort of weapon. They're not really rats. They're bigger and deadlier. They live in the sewers, hunting in packs. Dawn's not the ideal time to be in this part of Senna.'

'Great.'

'Keep on the move and, whatever you do, don't let them near you. The slightest scratch will have you raving in a few hours and dead soon after.'

Kep gripped the knife tightly. 'So we head for this tavern?'

Sarin shook his head. 'Not you two. The *Dawn Star's* too rough. You and Ash head for the elpha-birds. Barnham's will stand out. It's unusual: small and blue with a pearl-coloured elpha-ball. Don't go near the red ones, they're Calkinon ships. Barnham will have avoided docking anywhere near them. Find the bird and use the shield to hide. I'll be as quick as I can.' The garden gate screamed in protest when he pushed it back. 'Let's go.'

Although the light was growing brighter by the minute, the same couldn't be said for Ash's spirits. This whole place seemed steeped in misery. Ever since they had arrived he had been trying desperately to ignore the laments singing in his head, but the melodies were so insistent that they stole into his thoughts. The further they went down the winding path, the more urgent the Song became, then, all at once, time dissolved and he was lost.

Smoke catches in his throat. He sinks to his knees, choking, clutching the wound in his belly. The defences are failing. Falling stone. Clashing swords. They're coming! The battle screams of horses shatter the sky. People scream, too, in cruelty or agony. We can't hold them! The lower levels are burning. Smoke rises, blocking his vision, but nothing blocks the shrieks of death. To the citadel! To the citadel! All is lost. All is pain. The Manohans have broken the lines. Retreat! Retreat!

The others were halfway down the hill before Kep realised Ash was no longer behind her. 'Sarin, wait!' She raced back and there he was, just off the path, huddled near a broken pillar.

Kneeling in the dirt, she grasped his shoulder. His eyes were unfocused. He was moaning and dragging at his clothes, babbling something about fire and smoke, then he kept repeating: 'The citadel's on fire.'

The madness in his eyes filled her with dismay. 'There isn't a citadel, Ash. It's just a town. A disgusting, filthy town.' Suddenly distracted, she looked around, certain that something had moved — there, behind the broken stone. 'Ash, please! Just get up!' She shook him roughly. 'There is no fire!'

She didn't realise Sarin was at her side until he spoke.

'There is for him. Best not to argue.'

'And what would you know about it?' she snapped.

He didn't answer. He just put his hand on Ash's shoulder. 'C'mon, Ash.'

Ash stared through him. 'The Manohans have broken the defences.'

'I know. We need to get out of the city — now!' Sarin put his hand under his elbow.

'Sarin ...' Kep was watching the bushes. 'Sarin!

Sarin rose, turned and loosed his arrow in one smooth movement. There was a whine and a thud. The cessrat spun into the air, then lay twitching. Sarin fitted another arrow. 'Careful, there'll be others.' When three of the foul creatures appeared on cue, he swore under his breath.

The creatures had bristly hides and high, hunched shoulders. They must have been named for their pointed faces, and red, rat-like eyes.

Sarin let another arrow fly. It whizzed and bit. The middle cessrat thrashed and squealed, but the other two flew at him, snarling. Crouching, he hurled his knife. It plunged into the nearest creature's breast and sent it tumbling. But the surviving cessrat was just paces from his face!

Almost without thinking, Kep ran forward with a cry, sweeping the knife in a wide arc. The blade sliced through bone and muscle as if it was soft cheese. Sarin blinked in surprise at the beheaded corpse, then flashed Kep a smile. 'Thanks.'

Kep wanted to vomit. But a rattling snarl took her mind off her quivering stomach: another cessrat was creeping out from behind the rocks towards Ash. Sarin lifted his bow, but then he hesitated. He didn't dare take the shot — there was too strong a chance that he would hit Ash.

Then something moved in a dark blur. The cessrat was there one moment, poised and ready to spring, the next it was rolling and snarling, fighting off the blackest of shadows — a shadow with teeth as sharp as its own. There was a squeal, then the two creatures separated. Kep gasped.

Tarlyn was barely recognisable; she seemed twice her usual size. The ruff of spines around her neck stood out quivering, and her ears had opened out like fans. Her bared teeth looked demonic. She stood her ground in front of Ash and gave a low growl. The cessrat let out a rattle, signalling its intention to attack. It never got the chance. An arrow thudded into its throat and flipped it backwards.

Sarin's eyes flashed. 'Let's go.'

⁂

'Just as well he's so skinny,' Sarin panted as he lowered Ash to the ground.

It had taken all their effort to get him down the hill and into a small hanger at the edge of the airfield. They had been lucky; it was windy, and none of the crews seemed to be stirring. Ash didn't respond to their attempts to rouse him.

'Does he have a talisman? Something that calms him?'

'No.' Kep frowned. Sarin seemed to know an awful lot about this sort of thing. Then she remembered the Taelstone. 'Well, maybe.'

'Give it to him.' He cocked his head at the stacks of supplies. 'This place is too dangerous to stay long. Someone's bound to want this stuff. If Ash comes around, try to get him nearer the elpha-bird and set up the shield. It's not far. I spotted it from the hill.'

Kep nodded. She had seen it, too.

As Sarin turned to leave, he caught sight of Tarlyn. She was lying by Ash's side, her body limp and her eyes closed. His quick fingers found a gash on her front leg and he shook his head.

'That's not good.'

Kep stared in dismay; the gods knew she had no great love for Tarlyn, but Ash would be devastated if she died. They had become inseparable.

Sarin took something from a pocket on his shoulder. 'Here. Candrel leaves. Wash the wound, then bind three or four straight onto it. It might do some good. I've treated other creatures like that, but cessrats ...' Their eyes met briefly. 'Good luck,' he said, and he was gone.

It was the oddest feeling sitting there on the open airfield waiting for Sarin's return. They had tucked themselves under one wing of the blue elpha-bird and the star-shield was in place, but they felt utterly exposed. The worst scare came when a pair of guardians walked straight towards them. Their collars were red, signifying they were from Calkinon itself. Kep was sure they had noticed something suspicious, but they just stopped and pointed up at the designs painted on the sides of Barnham's ship. When the guardians laughed in admiration and moved on, Kep let out her breath. Her nails had dug deep crescents into her clenched hands. She hoped Sarin wouldn't be much longer. The shield might not hold, and Ash was hardly in any state to make a run for it.

He looked dreadful, like someone woken from the dead. Still, at least he was conscious. She had to admit that the Taelstone did have some strange restorative power. He sat quietly with his eyes closed, nursing Tarlyn's limp body in his lap.

They heard Sarin coming before they saw him; or rather they heard his companion singing. The man had one arm slung around Sarin's neck in an affectionate strangle-hold. He wore a floppy blue cap with a broken feather in it. From his other hand swung a bottle. Although Sarin was doing his best to steady him, they swayed and staggered. Barnham, as Kep rightly supposed him to be, was dressed in a mishmash of badly fitting garments, some brightly coloured, the others shabby and faded. His face shone ruddily through two or three days' growth. Blond hair straggled from under his cap.

'Ther she iz! Therz my georgeouz girl.' He grinned blearily up at the ship. 'Izn't she georgeouz?' he slurred.

'She's a beauty, Barnham. Best bird in the flock.' Sarin was scanning the area.

'Sarin! Tell yer what! Yer can do the honours, kin!'

Barnham grasped at something about his neck, then lost his balance entirely, causing the pair of them to stagger sideways and tumble in a heap. Sarin disentangled himself, scowling, but Barnham just chortled and lay sprawled flat. 'Good ta be 'ome,' he breathed.

'Oh, no! No you don't! You can't sleep here!'

Lifting a whistle from his companion's throat, Sarin blew a high-pitched note. It was answered by a loud click inside the breast of the elpha-bird.

As a flight of steps floated down, Sarin shook the man roughly. 'Wake up! Barnham! Wake up!' All he got in response was a loud snore.

Sarin threw up his hands. 'Now would be a good time for you two to show yourselves if you're here!'

⁂

It took quite an effort to get Barnham onto the lower deck. When finally he was safely deposited, Kep stood over him, her arms crossed. He smelt strongly of fireshot and stale sweat. 'Fly us out of here, will he? Not likely!'

Sarin ignored her. 'Find something to tie him up with Ash.'

'Tie him up? I thought he was a friend!'

'Family. Different thing entirely.'

Sarin leapt up the steps, two at a time, and Kep chased after him, leaving Ash to deal with Barnham.

The upper deck was dominated by the elpha-ball. It ballooned out, like a giant pearl caught in a net of silver mesh. The ship's wings were pleated against her hull, and her prow swept forward proudly, like the neck of a bird. The raised platform of the flight deck had a curved seat, which was surrounded by levers, wheels, dials and whirling gadgets. Sarin leapt into the seat and studied the array of switches. He muttered to himself, then flicked one. The ship shuddered and the giant ball began to glow. 'Good. That's fired up the elpha-core. Now ....' He frowned in concentration.

Kep scowled. 'You can't fly this thing, can you?'

'Not really,' he admitted. 'But I think I can get it off the ground. And unless you want *them* to catch us, you might try helping.'

He nodded calmly towards the group racing towards the ship. One was smaller and dressed in green. He ran low to the ground, quickly outpacing the others.

Kep gulped. 'What can I do?'

'We have to release the mooring cables. Can you see a switch? Or a lever?' Sarin experimented with a red button, and the wings unfolded with a sudden whoosh, reminding Kep of silver bats' wings. Sarin cursed. Then he smacked a palm against his forehead. 'Of course! Silver levers! Front and back.' He leapt from the seat, nearly colliding with Ash, who had arrived on deck looking dazed.

Sarin found the lever he was looking for and pulled it down hard. There was a sharp ping, then a whirring sound as the cable retracted into the hull. The deck shifted underfoot. The wings fluttered madly. He winced.

'There's three more. One on the other side and two near the tail. Hurry! I'll try to keep her stable.'

As Sarin regained the controls, Kep ran for the other side of the ship while Ash headed for the tail.

The elpha-core hummed urgently as the bird dragged at her restraints. Kep quickly found a lever and pulled it down. Immediately, the ship pulled sharply upward. Losing her footing, she slid helplessly along the slanting deck until she hit the stern with a bump.

The wings were straining and flapping now — the bird would surely be torn apart! She had to reach that other lever. Hauling herself up, she pushed with her feet, gripping the ribbed sides of the hull with her fingers. But, just as the lever was almost within reach, the bird lurched again. Ash had reached his lever first! The ship whirled sideways. Kep's fingers scrabbled and lost their grip, as she was flipped up and over the side!

The only thing saving Kep from plummeting to the ground was the rigging, where she swung like a fish in a net, completely helpless. The elpha-bird screamed and strained. The remaining cable was just below her, and perilously close to the wing. She hated to think what would happen if the wind blew harder.

There was nothing for it. She said a prayer and drew the knife. Clenching the handle between her teeth, she hooked her feet into the rigging, then lowered herself until she was dangling upside down. She fixed her eyes on the last mooring cable, trying to ignore the spiralling ground below. Rocking her body, she swung out, once, twice, then grabbed the cable. Her heart was pounding with fear and exertion as she started sawing, but, one strand at a time, the cable yielded then snapped. The bird broke free with a drunken lurch and began to rise.

Flung back against the hull, it took Kep a while to register that Ash was shouting her name. 'I'm here! Here!' she yelled back. A moment later his worried face appeared over the edge.

It took a lot of disentangling and all of their combined strength, but finally she hauled herself back onto the deck. The elpha-bird was rising quickly, but they could still see Gooel far below. Unbelievably, he hadn't moved — not once. He hadn't raised his weapon. He had just stood there watching.

Chapter 32

FLIGHT

'Sarin! I'll bloody kill you, Sarin!'

Kep's eyelids fluttered. She would probably have stayed asleep for hours if the shouting from below hadn't woken her. Squinting at the sun, she guessed it must be early afternoon. When Barnham yelled again, she swung her legs cautiously to one side. At least getting out of the hammock proved easier than getting in had been. She unhooked one end, twisted it into a thick rope and let it retract into the siding. *Clever.* Ash was still fast asleep, despite the racket from below deck. She resisted the urge to touch his face to check he was alive.

Sarin was where she had left him, at the controls of the elpha-bird. The ship was shuddering and vibrating, but he did seem rather more in control. He half-turned, but didn't speak, and he didn't react when the man below hollered again: 'Sarin! I'll knock your head off when I get hold of you!'

'Well?' she said, folding her arms. 'Are you going down there?'

He shrugged. 'Probably not. He sounds pretty angry to me.'

Kep snorted. 'Well he has a right to be, don't you think? I mean you did practically kidnap him and take over his ship.'

'*We* did,' Sarin corrected.

When Barnham cursed and bawled again, threatening all sorts of bodily harm, Sarin nodded sagely. 'He's angry. I'm definitely not going down there. Don't let me stop you, though,' he added tilting his head. 'In fact, that's a good idea. Take him water and some of that bread. Just don't untie him, whatever you do.'

Kep let out an exasperated sigh before snatching up the water-pouch and a chunk of the bread. 'Well, we can't just leave him there hollering!'

Sarin gave a half-smile and turned back to the controls.

'About bloody time! By the gods, I'll—' Barnham stopped mid-sentence as Kep reached the bottom step. His furious expression melted at once into bewilderment. 'Who by the flaming devils are you?'

Kep made an apologetic face. She held out the water, then realised both of his hands were tied behind him to a railing. 'Oh! Sorry ... sorry.' Fumbling with the pouch, she held it awkwardly to his mouth. To her relief Barnham kept his eyes closed while he drank.

Only when he had quenched his thirst did he open them again; she flinched under the curious gaze of warm brown eyes. He had lost his blue cap and his sandy-blond hair fell in a mess about his face. He wasn't as old as she had first thought, perhaps only four or five winters older than Sarin. She wondered how they could possibly be related — they seemed so totally different.

'Thank you,' he smiled. She nodded, embarrassed. Barnham ran his tongue around his mouth and frowned. 'I suppose it was you who rubbed the candrel essence on my gums?'

'No.' She shook her head. 'That was Ash. Sarin told him to.'

He made a face. 'Hmm. Tastes horrible. Expect it's done me good, though. Ash, eh? So exactly how many stowaways have I got? Assuming you are stowaways — and not pirates?'

'Just Ash and Sarin ... and me,' she stammered. 'No, we're not pirates. We didn't ... I mean ... I'm sorry we took your ship,' she winced, 'and tied you up. It's just we were in desperate need.'

'In desperate need, eh?' He grunted. 'Doesn't usually entitle you to a man's ship. No matter how blue your eyes are.'

She dropped her lashes. 'No.'

'Hmm. I had a bottle here somewhere.' He looked around at the floor. 'Don't suppose you happen to know where it went?' When she shook her head, he shrugged, 'Ah, well. Probably just as well. Might find it later.' He coughed. 'Well, you'd better tell me your name. It's always good to know the name of your captors.'

'Sorry ... Kep. I'm Kep.'

Barnham's whole face seemed to go up in an arch. 'Kep?' His eyes flicked to her wrist. 'Not the Kep everyone's talking about?'

She remembered the strange behaviour of the people in Senna. 'I don't know ... Maybe ...'

'Ha! Well, I'll be. Desperate need, indeed.' Barnham shook his head wonderingly. 'Well, well. So tell me: are you Kep the Valiant or T'al Kep?'

She frowned. Was he mocking her? He looked quite serious.

'Hmm ... Perhaps you don't know ... Well, Kep the Valiant is the girl who stood up to the nobility of Mildaresh and sparked a series of uprisings across the lands. She's the one with the pure heart and a love so strong she risked her life for the soul of another. A symbol of hope, of course, but still human.' He was watching her carefully, no doubt noticing that her cheeks were burning. 'Whereas T'al Kep, she's something else entirely. Some say she actually threw herself into the flames in defiance of her masters, but was resurrected by the gods to wreak vengeance upon oppressors everywhere. T'al Kep has the power of invisibility. Well, not everybody believes that bit, but she has the mandate of the gods and the ability to strike down her enemies.' He cocked his head to one side. 'So, which one are you? Kep of the people, or Kep of the gods?'

Kep tried to swallow. 'Neither. I'm just Kep,' she said in a small voice.

He smiled. 'Good answer. I'm just Barnham — not that anyone's ever accused me of being valiant or divine. I am hungry, though. Is that bread you've got there?'

Kep stared dumbly at the bread in her hand. 'Yes. But ... you might not want it. It's stolen.'

Barnham assumed a shocked expression. 'Oh? And who did you steal it from?'

'I didn't steal it. Sarin did, from a man called Rufen Karendon — well, from his wife, really.'

He laughed. 'That's all right, then. It's only stealing if you take from poor or good people, and from what I've heard the Karendons are neither.'

Kep frowned at him doubtfully. Did all of Sarin's people hold such strange notions?

He was eyeing the bread. 'Are you going to untie me, then? ... I suppose Sarin told you not to.' He made a face and rolled his eyes.

That was enough. He couldn't eat by himself, and Kep didn't fancy feeding him by hand. Besides, he didn't seem that dangerous — and it was his ship after all. If he did run straight upstairs to 'knock Sarin's head' off or 'bloody kill him', then it would serve Sarin right.

Ash had created a mess of weirdly intricate knots, but in a few moments Barnham's hands were free. To Kep's slight disappointment he didn't show any signs of seeking immediate revenge on Sarin; he just smiled his thanks and accepted the loaf.

Barnham spoke between mouthfuls. 'So, "Just Kep", it seems I know the beginning of your story, or at least a version of it — what I can't imagine is how you happen to be aboard my ship, with Sarin of all people.'

Kep was no longer afraid; he had an honest face and gentle eyes, and he deserved an explanation. She sat beside him and related briefly how they had met Karendon, how they had ended up at his lodge and how they had escaped.

'So Sarin rescued you?' Barnham looked incredulous. 'He doesn't usually make a habit of rescuing people. He is awfully crafty, though. Could probably rescue someone from the Calkinon dungeons if he put his mind to it, but he's not really your noble type, if you understand me.'

Kep nodded. She understood entirely.

He glanced at the bracelet on her wrist. 'You two aren't ... ?'

'No! Definitely not!' She scowled at the insinuation. 'He just promised to help us with something ... We've got a sort of deal.' She knew it must all sound very weak and mysterious.

'A deal, eh? Well that sounds more like Sarin.' Barnham rubbed his chin. 'So where are we heading? Assuming my poor ship will make it anywhere with such rough handling — just listen to her complaining!'

'Sarin's taking us to a place called Pendle Ring. There is someone we need to speak with—'

She stopped in surprise when Barnham let out a groan and put his hands over his face.

'Oh no. No, no, no,' he moaned, shaking his head.

'What is it?' asked Kep in dismay. Was Sarin taking them to another den of criminals?

His reply was pained. 'Pendle Ring is where the clans of the Haelrum meet at the crossing of the moons.'

'The Haelrum? I thought your people were called Farlings.'

'No!' Barnham's eyes went hard. 'Don't ever use that term. That's what ignorant people call us on account of our wandering. They think it's clever.'

'I'm sorry,' Kep blushed. 'I didn't know.'

'Five clans make up the Haelrum; ours is the Aurum. The clans meet at Mooncross to negotiate kinship lines and share stories.' He shook his head sadly, then fell silent.

The pause grew too long for comfort, but Kep wasn't sure what to say. 'Are they so frightening, then, your people?' she faltered.

'Frightening?' He blinked. 'What? No. Well, only a few of them. They're a secretive bunch and they don't take kindly to strangers — "outlings" they call them — but they're not exactly frightening.' He scratched his head then sniffed. 'No, the problem's me. I can't go back, I've been ousted you see.'

'Ousted?'

He nodded. 'Every member of the clan votes at the beginning of spring. Anyone with more than a tenth of the vote has to leave and not return until autumn.' He rubbed his forehead. 'It's a way of keeping the peace.'

Kep stared at him with wide eyes. What an odd idea. She had a sudden thought. 'Has Sarin been ousted, too?'

'Hmm? Well, yes, but it's a bit more complicated in Sarin's case.'

She might have known it would be. She was about to ask how, when the ship gave a loud, creaking moan.

Barnham reacted immediately, leaping to his feet. 'The wind's getting up! She won't handle that with Sarin at the helm.'

'By Telion! What are you doing to my poor bird?' Barnham thundered.

Sarin lifted his hands in a show of surrender, then stepped back. At once the ship banked sharply.

Barnham aimed a cuff at him before seizing the controls. 'You bloody rogue!' With a grimace he righted the bird's trajectory and started adjusting levers and winding wheels. Within seconds the wracking vibrations had ceased. Then, with a satisfied grunt, he cut the motor.

The sudden absence of noise was wonderful — truly wonderful. They drifted for a while, just like a bubble on the breeze, then Barnham tipped the wings and the elpha-bird began to soar, riding the unseen currents of Telion's breath. Kep felt her heart leap with joy. She smiled happily at Barnham and received a grin and a wink in return.

Sarin leaned back against a strut and folded his arms. 'Show-off,' he murmured, just loud enough for Barnham to hear.

Barnham glared at him. 'You stole my bird!'

Sarin gave a crafty smile. 'Stole? Now that's a strong word, kin — you seemed happy to give me a lift. And I believe the coin I offered was quite attractive, too.'

Barnham growled. 'You knew damn well I'd never agree to go to the Gathering! Don't remember you mentioning that little detail.'

'No?' Sarin feigned surprise. 'Guess it must have slipped my mind.'

'Well, we can't go. Wouldn't make it to Pendle Ring. Haven't got enough fuel.'

'There's plenty of fuel: look at the gauge. Besides, the way you fly this bird we could reach the Ring on just a spoonful of elpha.'

Barnham scowled. 'Well, if there is fuel left that's no thanks to you,' he grumbled.

Kep watched him closely. She could tell he wasn't nearly as angry as he acted. But his jaw did have a stubborn shape to it. She doubted anyone could convince him to do something he didn't want to, not even Sarin.

'Can't go even if I wanted to,' announced Barnham loudly. 'I've been ousted.'

Sarin laughed. 'And how long ago was that? You could have returned the following autumn and they'd have welcomed you back with garlands and feasts — you know they would.'

'Well, they won't now. A proper outling I am. And that's the way I like it.'

'Nonsense. You're just scared of Nalina.'

Barnham busied himself with checking dials.

'Who's Nalina?' Kep asked.

'The chieftain. Barnham's terrified of her.'

'No, I'm not. I just know when I'm not wanted, that's all. Nothing's getting me near the clan again, and that's that.'

Kep noticed how Sarin's eyes kept flicking towards Ash, who was stirring in his hammock.

'Hmm. That's a shame. I can think of a few pretty girls who'd be glad to braid your hair.'

'Humph!' Barnham stuck out his chin. 'I know lots of girls, and they're a lot less complicated to woo than clan girls — assuming I want to woo anyone!'

Sarin nodded sagely. 'Ah, well. I see you know your mind. And it's entirely your decision of course.'

Barnham looked slightly surprised. 'Yes, I know my mind, and it's set. That's final.'

Sarin's eyes slid sideways. His mouth curved when Ash emerged sleepily from his hammock. What did it mean, that glint in his strange eyes? Kep felt sure he was up to something.

'By the way,' added Sarin casually, 'this is Ash.'

Barnham hardened his jaw, probably intending to blast the boy who'd had the nerve to tie him to the railing of his own elpha-bird, but as soon as he set eyes on Ash his mouth dropped open in shock. Ash blinked his grey eyes at him, obviously confused by the reaction. His hair was all ruffled up like the feathers of an owl, his face pale.

Barnham kept looking him up and down, then he turned to Sarin. 'Is it … ? Really? …'

Sarin raised his shoulders and eyebrows, that secretive smile playing on his lips. Kep looked from one to the other, then to Ash. What in the world was going on? Their behaviour was too strange for words.

Barnham shook his head again, his eyes full of awe. 'Well, I never. So you're taking him to see her? Well, I never,' he repeated. He kept gaping, then suddenly checked himself. 'Sorry … er … Ash. Just never thought I'd see the day … Well, never really believed you existed, to tell the truth.'

Kep put her hands on her hips. 'Right, that's enough. Someone explain what's going on!' She glared at Sarin. 'What's the big secret?'

Sarin shrugged, then leapt lightly up onto the gunwale. He sat there, with one leg dangling and his arm hooked through the rigging. 'You tell them, Barnham. You're the story-man.'

Barnham shot him a look, then sighed. 'All right, then. But you two sit down. Can't tell a story properly with people hovering.'

When Ash and Kep had settled themselves on the curved benches fitted to either side of the prow, Barnham began, 'Sarin has a younger sister. Her name is Rilka. She's … well … she's a lovely girl, but let's just say she's always been different. She has visions, you see.' He seemed to be choosing his words carefully. 'She falls into trances, and sometimes the things she sees come true. Not always, but often enough to scare people.'

Kep couldn't control the disbelief in her voice. 'So, she sees things … and then they come true?'

Sarin's reply was flinty. 'Yes. She sees things. I'd have thought you two would understand that.' He shot her a look.

Barnham made a soothing motion with his hands.

'Anyway, Rilka sometimes upsets people with her visions, and her behaviour can be disturbing. She has rages and nightmares. She often screams at night. That's why her name comes up so frequently at the ousting ceremony.'

Kep suddenly thought she understood. 'So she was ousted, like you,

Barnham? But,' she frowned, 'you said she was younger — surely children don't get ousted?'

'Haelrum are eligible for ousting after their tenth winter,' he replied sadly. 'But, no, Rilka has never been ousted: Sarin has always taken her place; it's the family's right if a stronger sibling is willing.'

Kep bit her lip.

Ash was completely confused. None of it made sense. 'What's all this got to do with me?' he asked quietly.

Barnham paused, as if reaching for the right words. But it was Sarin who answered. His golden eyes gleamed: 'Because you are the Grey Boy.' He swung about, then dropped noiselessly to the deck. 'When my sister was small, she used to pester everyone about the Grey Boy, whether they'd seen him in their travels; whether they knew where he was. It was one of her peculiarities. It was the first thing she'd ask any stranger: had they seen a boy dressed in grey with grey eyes and grey hair? Sometimes some well-meaning person would try to tell her that boys don't have grey hair, and she'd fly into a terrible rage. Then, the first time I was ousted, she stopped bothering strangers. She seemed convinced that I would be the one to find him and bring him back. Every time I return from my travels, it's the first thing she asks. It's become a longstanding joke with the clan.' He grimaced and fell silent.

'And you think it's me?' said Ash. 'You think I'm the boy in her visions. This Grey Boy?'

They all stared at him. Kep couldn't help thinking that if anyone deserved the title of 'Grey Boy', it was Ash. It wasn't just his clothes and the odd colour of his hair; it was something in his soft grey eyes that went beyond colour.

'Honestly?' Sarin frowned thoughtfully. 'I don't know.'

'So you tricked us?' said Ash dully. You told us you could help us find T'al Jazure for the sake of your sister?'

Kep gasped. The liar!

'No.' Sarin shook his head. 'It was only when you mentioned T'al Jazure that I put my doubts aside.' He folded his arms. 'The one person who can help you find T'al Jazure is Nalina, my grandmother.'

Kep didn't trust him. 'Well that seems awfully convenient,' she pointed out.

Barnham was scratching his chin thoughtfully. 'Actually, there's a good chance Nalina may know something. There was an outling, a wanderer. He lived with the Aurum for a time, years ago. They don't usually accept outlings, but they did in his case. Perhaps he had something special to offer. I remember him, even though I was a very small boy. It was the stories he told: wondrous stories of great deeds — and T'al Jazure.' Barnham's eyes were shining at the memory.

Ash and Kep spoke at the same time.

'Where is he now?'

Barnham shook his head. 'Eventually he moved on. Sarin's right, though. If anyone knows anything, it'll be Nalina — assuming you can convince her to tell you. She's a stubborn old witch.'

Sarin raised his eyebrows in a question. 'So, Ash? Do we still have a deal?'

Ash could sense Kep's disapproval, but he answered steadily: 'A promise is a promise. Take us to see Nalina, your grandmother.' He swallowed. 'I just hope your sister won't be disappointed.'

'I guess we'll see.' Sarin turned to include Barnham in his smile.

'Oh, no! No, you don't!' Barnham held up his hand. 'I know what you're thinking, Sarin. You think I'm going to change my mind and take you to the Gathering.' He waggled his finger. 'Well, I'm not. Not even for Rilka.'

Sarin shrugged. 'What about Kep, then? She'd stand a much better chance of evading her tracker if she had the protection of the Haelrum, and you know it.'

Barnham scowled. He wiped at a pressure gauge with his filthy sleeve. 'You think they'd grant protection to an outling in these times?'

'I think they'd grant this outling protection. She is Kep the Valiant, after all.'

Kep frowned. Being called an 'outling' was definitely unpleasant, but 'Kep the Valiant' was even worse, especially when it fell from Sarin's lips. She interjected: 'It's all right, Barnham. You don't have to do anything he says. I'll be fine. Honestly. We've made it this far.' She glared at Sarin. 'Don't let him manipulate you,' she added hotly.

Barnham stared at Kep for a brief moment, then he screwed up his face, hit himself on the forehead and threw his arms in the air. 'Damn it, he's right. I hate it when he's right!' He shook his head. 'All right, I give in. I'll take you to Nalina.'

Kep chewed her lip. 'Are you sure? You don't have to, you know.'

Barnham smiled ruefully. 'Yes, I do. Couldn't live with myself if I didn't.'

Then he shot a fierce look at Sarin. 'But I'm damned if I'm going to the Gathering. We'll have to catch up with the clan before then.'

'Fair enough,' answered Sarin smoothly.

He was smiling so smugly that Kep had a nasty feeling he had planned the whole thing, right from the moment he had sent her down with the bread and water.

⁂

'We can intercept the Aurum at the Glade, but we'll have to stop at Ginba for provisions.'

'No. No towns. It's too dangerous. And besides, I don't want to have to haul you out of another ale house.'

'We'll need to put down somewhere. There's hardly any water, and only parch-cake to eat.'

'The Cranok?'

'Those clouds are building, but, yes, we could probably make it by nightfall.'

'Good. There'll be plenty of game. And you can bathe in the waterhole — you smell like a cessrat's backside.'

'You cheeky little—!'

Ash left the pair to their bickering. His head was spinning with new worries, and he needed a quiet place to think. But first he had to check on Tarlyn. He had left her to rest on some some soft rags in a crate underneath his hammock. Reproaching himself for not checking on her earlier, he mouthed a silent prayer to Argess as he pulled the crate toward him. When he saw that it was empty, his heart sank. He checked the whole area for hiding places. Nothing. Had she crawled off somewhere to die? Feeling sick at the thought, he made his way to the lower deck.

As soon as he stepped off the bottom step, Ash became aware of a presence. Something stirred in the gloom. 'Tarlyn?' he whispered. 'Tarlyn, is that you?'

'It's me.'

Ash blinked. The only light came from the pinkish glow of the elpha-ball, which he realised wasn't actually a ball at all. More like a giant tear-drop, it tapered at the bottom and disappeared into the depths of the hull. Kep was sitting on the rim of the lower housing, silhouetted against the light.

'I was looking for Tarlyn.'

She nodded, sniffing, and wiped her sleeve across her face. 'I thought you might be. I was just about to come and get you.' She sniffed again. 'Look,' she pointed.

Above her two giant moths were flapping helplessly against the elpha-ball, caught in a fatal dance with the light. And there, balancing on one of the casing bands, was Tarlyn! She greeted him with a chirrup, and in a flash was on his shoulder, nudging his face and winding her tail around his neck.

'She's all right!' The words came out in a funny squeaking sob, but Ash didn't care.

'Perfectly all right, by the look of her,' agreed Kep quietly.

Perching beside her, Ash lifted Tarlyn down to his lap and ran his hands over her shoulders and down each front leg: there was no trace of the injury. What had Credé called her? Remarkably resilient? Well she was certainly that.

'Who'd have thought those candrel leaves would work so well?' remarked Kep. Her voice sounded funny, as if she was trying to keep it steady.

Only then did Ash realise that she had been crying. He released Tarlyn, who prowled back to watch the moths. 'Are you all right?' he asked quietly.

Kep stood up at once. 'I thought that question was banned.' She wiped an eye that was refusing to co-operate. 'I'm fine. It's just … I suppose it's really sunk in now. Gooel's not going to give up the chase. And there's no getting away from him, not even with the protection of the Haelrum. Unless I kill him, of course.'

Ash studied her face, shocked by the bitterness in her voice.

She rubbed her eyes. 'It's stupid, but I just want my old life back. The life where I'm not hunted by snouts or given ridiculous names by people who don't know me.'

Ash wanted to point out that 'Kep the Valiant' was considerably better than 'the Grey Boy', but he wisely held his tongue.

She sighed. 'It feels like we've fallen into the middle of someone else's story. It was bad enough before, but why does Sarin have to be involved, and his crazy sister? How did we end up here? I mean, why us?'

Ash couldn't think of an answer.

They both jumped when the silence was broken by a woman's voice. *The Taelstaun must go to T'al Jazure.*

Kep winced. 'I hate it when she does that.'

'Me, too,' Ash confessed, earning himself a faint smile.

Chapter 33

THE CRANOK

By the time Kep re-emerged on the top deck, the sun had dropped towards the horizon. She would rather have stayed below, but the desire for fresh air and light had won over her need for sanctuary. Barnham's eyes looked tired and his shoulders sagged, but he smiled and gestured for her to sit beside him.

'Where's Sarin?' she asked, trying to keep her voice neutral.

'Sleeping.' He nodded towards the tail. 'Make the most of it. He doesn't do it often and never for long. Just a few hours.'

Kep added this information to the growing list of Sarin's oddities. Being high in the sky was the strangest sensation. The wilderness seemed to flow on endlessly below them. Green tussocky hills rolled away to her left, punctuated by bulbous outcrops of stone. Ahead were sharp ranges, dark with forests; their valleys were made deeper and shadier by the sun's afternoon rays. When she saw a dark shape chasing across the landscape she was momentarily startled, until she realised it was just the shadow of the elpha-bird. Fascinated, she watched the shadow bird fly over the creases and folds of the blanket world below. It all seemed so unreal.

Barnham met her eyes and smiled. 'There are parch-cakes if you're hungry. Wouldn't recommend them, though. They're not nice to start with, and these are pretty old. Better if you can wait until we put down at the Cranok. Shouldn't be long.' He frowned at the bank of clouds rolling in from the west. 'But that doesn't look too good.' He scratched his chin. 'In fact, you'd better get Ash and strap yourselves in. Things might get a bit rough.'

※

Things got more than a bit rough. When the front caught them, they completely lost sight of land. The clouds swirled like living things, threatening to destroy the strange bird that was invading their space.

Kep was praying under her breath when a sudden drop made her stomach

227

sink. She stifled a scream. Their little craft was shaking and shuddering, plucked this way and that. She exchanged a terrified look with Ash. Could those thin wings survive such a thrashing?

On they flew, into the wild, blinding mist. Then suddenly a jagged face of rock materialised straight ahead. Kep screamed as they swooped, barely missing the peak.

Barnham tipped the wings, sending the bird into a deep plunge. Kep felt as if her insides were spinning. Then the bird spiralled into a sharp turn and levelled out.

It was remarkable: everything had suddenly changed. It was as if Telion had turned off the wind.

A grim-faced Barnham made a few checks, then pulled a square-handled lever. The wings folded away with a swoosh and they began to drift, down towards the ground.

The clouds still swirled overhead, wild at losing their prey, but the Cranok was calm and sheltered. There were trees with lush green foliage, huge tree ferns, and a waterfall, cascading down in a long, thin stream.

'Why's it called the Cranok?' asked Ash, unclipping his harness.

'Because it's shaped like one.' When Barnham explained that a cranok was a cooking pot with a wide, flared spout, they nodded; it felt exactly like being inside a pot.

The ground was covered in moss and ferns, with patches of soft bracken. Barnham settled the bird with a gentle bump. 'Right, that's my bit done. Sarin, you can set the mooring cables, or what's left of them.' He eased himself from his seat with a groan, rubbed his bleary eyes and stretched. 'Wake me up when dinner's ready.' With that he disappeared below deck.

❧

Ash sucked the last morsel of duck from the bone, then tossed the bone into the fire. He leaned back with a sigh. He liked the Cranok. It was a peaceful place, filled with the gentle rhythms and melodies of Nature.

Dinner had been delicious. Sarin had raised his eyebrows at Ash's offer to prepare the water-fowl, but he'd handed them over. Of course Ash had dressed fowl more times than he could remember, but he couldn't think when he had enjoyed the job so much. His fingers had moved quickly, his blade accurate as it sought out joints and severed tendons. In no time at all he had plucked, gutted and jointed both birds, and set them to brown in a pan. Kep had found herbs and creamy root vegetables to make the meal complete. Ash didn't know which he had treasured more, the look of surprise on Sarin's face or the appreciation on Kep's.

There was still light left in the sky when they had finished their meal. Kep muttered something about washing, and headed for the waterhole. As she disappeared into the ferns, Barnham gave Sarin a knowing grin. 'She's a beautiful girl, Sarin.'

Sarin returned his own eyes to the fire. Ash ducked his head, busying himself with re-tying the bindings that kept his sandals together.

A smile played at the corner of Barnham's mouth as he prodded the fire with a long stick. 'Now, c'mon, cuz. There's something special about her, don't you think? I mean, what she did for that boy.' He stirred the embers, making them glow. 'Remarkable.' His eyes studied Sarin's face. 'And valiant, you have to admit that.'

'Reckless more like. That's just the sort of thing that gets people killed.'

Barnham grinned. 'Still, imagine being loved by someone that much. That'd be something, wouldn't it, Sarin?'

Ash looked up sharply. Kep would have done the same for any of her friends — wouldn't she?

Sarin was scowling. 'I really wouldn't know, Barnham,' he answered deliberately.

Barnham let out a delighted laugh that echoed back off the cliff. 'I'm only teasing.' He broke the stick in two and cast the pieces on the fire. 'Interesting reaction, though,' he chuckled. 'Very interesting.'

Ash blinked rapidly. Was it?

❧

As darkness closed in, Ash found himself alone at the fireside with Sarin. Sarin had his head bent over an object he had taken from his pack. 'It's a gift,' he explained. 'For Rilka.'

Ash marvelled at the exquisite piece of embroidery. The bird was beautifully proportioned, with long tail feathers and a proud, arched neck. The stitches were so tiny it looked as if it had been painted. It was nearly finished except for a bare patch on its breast.

'It's beautiful.'

Sarin shrugged. 'The Aurum people have many crafts. This is one of mine. I trade pelts for silks and make patches to sell — crests and things like that. Rilka loves birds, so I always try to bring her one back. This one's a rainbird. It took me ages to get the magenta for its breast.'

Ash nodded, remembering the negotiation with Karendon.

'I'd hoped to finish it tonight, but the light is fading too quickly.'

Ash rummaged in his pack. 'Here, use this.'

Sarin inspected the curious lamp for several minutes, flipping it in his hands, watching its light go on and off. 'It's incredible. I can't even begin to think how it works.' He shook his head. 'You're full of surprises, Grey Boy.'

Ash frowned uncomfortably at the name, but there was something else he wanted to say, before Kep and Barnham returned. 'Sarin,' he said quietly, 'I see visions, too … like Rilka.'

Sarin looked up. 'I know. Only you see the past, don't you?'

Ash nodded, surprised. 'How did you know?'

'You mentioned the Manohans at Senna. There was a great city there once called Caladin — long ago, before the time of the Azuri even. They say its white tower was the most beautiful in all the lands. Well, the Manohans destroyed the tower and slaughtered every last Caladine. Is that what you saw?'

Ash didn't answer. He felt suddenly sick: the melody was there again, at the edge of his mind.

Sarin looked at him curiously. 'Do you see good things, too? Or just bad?'

Ash frowned. It was time to change the subject and the others were approaching. 'Tell me about the Azuri.'

'Now, Ash, you don't want to go asking Sarin about the Azuri. He'll tell you nothing but good.' Barnham chuckled as he placed a billycan onto the coals. 'He's always been fascinated by them. Nearly lost him once when he was just a tot. All packed up, he was. Off to find T'al Jazure, with a handmade bow and a bundle of bits.' He gave Sarin an affectionate pat on the head.

Sarin made a face. 'You tell the story, then, story-man.'

'Please do, Barnham,' pleaded Kep. She settled herself beside Ash. 'It's about time we learned more about T'al Jazure.'

He nodded. 'All right, then. Is everyone comfortable?'

Strangely enough, they were. The clouds were parting above to reveal patches of starry sky. The fire was crackling and their stomachs were full of warm food. It was the most comfortable they had been in ages. They lay back to watch the sky and waited for Barnham to begin.

'Hmm. How to begin? There are so many ways to start a story, especially this one. It all happened so long ago, and storytellers are such dishonourable souls. They don't mean to be, but they can't help filling the gaps with their own desires, stroking brighter light onto things that stir their imagination, painting out details that ruin the shape of their narrative.' He shook his head. 'Dangerous things, stories. That's why it's wise to start with a prayer.' He put two fingers to his forehead. 'May Telion guide my tale and give it wings of peace.'

Barnham's voice seemed to become deeper and richer as he adopted the persona of the story-man. 'To understand the real mystery of the Azuri we have to go back to the days before they appeared, when the moons were some two thousand years younger. T'al Agrion was caught in a conflict that had raged for hundreds of years. Three empires had grown up, each as noble, each as evil, as the others. At first they were separated by mountains and seas and forests, then by their growing hatred and mistrust of one another.

'One of these great peoples was the Wimsari, the sea folk. Their city on the Isle of Baktah had towers the colour of seashells, and shaped like flutes so that they crooned different notes according to the sea breezes. The Wimsari bowed down to one god, Narsis, goddess of the seas. I see in your eyes that this shocks you, but you must be patient. Hold the thought softly.

'The second great power was the Eeroki Empire. The centre of their realm, Eeroktan, was away beyond the mountains to the north. Their lands were rich and fertile, blessed by the flow of rivers and the fall of soft rain. They bred fine kattlen beasts, magnificent steeds for riding and grew crops of all kinds. The god they worshiped was Argess, because he gave them the soft earth to till. I see your dismay, Kep: I only ask you to bear it gently for now.

'The last great realm was the largest and the most unstable. It was made up of many tribes united by the strength of one man, Dengar the Bold. The Dengari included warrior tribes from the roughlands, cliff dwellers, and desert peoples. Dengari lands were rich in ore, their people clever miners and metal-workers. Telion was their dearest god, for those who toil in the dark will ever worship the light.

'So, our world was torn by the struggles between these three empires. Each believed their god most high, their cause most righteous, their claims most just. Bloodshed led to bloodshed, atrocities to revenge, revenge to atrocities. All were exhausted by war, but peace was impossible; that is, until the coming of the Azuri.

'They appeared as if by magic, and walked amongst the people in cloaks of blue, teaching and healing. They listened to all, and spoke softly of peace. Some say they used magical powers to bring the warring parties together, some say it was by virtue of the beauty of their words. But one thing is certain: the Azuri brought peace and were beloved by all. The age that followed was a golden age of tolerance. T'al Jazure, their city, was a centre of learning and shared wisdom. The Eerok, the Dengari and the Wimsari all sent scholars and artists to learn and share ideas. The Azuri gave the peoples elpha-fuel, irrigation, the common tongue, medicines, new building techniques, and many other wondrous inventions, not to mention the game of pilat. Which brings me to the most important point: the Azuri also changed the gods forever.'

At this Kep couldn't contain herself any longer. 'How can you change the gods?' she blurted.

Barnham held up gentle hands. 'You are right of course, Kep, that's impossible. Rather, they helped people to see the gods in different, more harmonious ways. I am not a priest or a philosopher, but I'll try to explain. You see, the Azuri taught that divinities could never be male or female, nor split into entities to worship separately, because each divinity always embraced its opposite. So Argess was the divinity of life and death, Narsis reigned over war and peace, Telion over darkness and light, and so on.'

'Well, I'd have thought that was obvious,' Kep muttered.

Barnham smiled. 'The Azuri proposed that the gods could never be at war with each other, but were bound in a relationship of harmony; it was they who gave us the sacred triang. Of course individuals probably favoured one divinity over another, just as we do today, but all three realms adopted the new "understanding", each after their own fashion. And it worked. Finally there was peace, and it lasted for nearly a thousand years.'

Barnham accepted a drink from Sarin, and sipped on it reflectively.

It was Ash who broke the silence. 'So what happened?'

'No one really knows. But somehow the Azuri fell from grace. Some say they began to favour some peoples over others, creating fierce new rivalries. Others say there were powerful secrets they refused to share. There was surely jealousy over the fabled beauty of T'al Jazure and the wonders that so few were allowed to see; and people distrust things they cannot see. Or perhaps they were betrayed by one of their own. Whatever the case, a new darkness came into the world. People started to behave like monsters again, only it was worse, much worse. Conflict spread like a disease. Ancient grudges were revived, and the world was swept into a maelstrom of destruction.' Barnham put his cup down and sighed. 'Peace is a fragile thing, you see; it's easily crushed, especially by fear.'

He paused for a long minute. 'There's one thing the stories all agree on: the Azuri met a terrible end. For some reason they left the safety of their city, trusting perhaps in their peaceful intentions, or perhaps in their allies. Whatever their thinking, it was foolish. The rival factions were intent on discovering the whereabouts of T'al Jazure and seizing its treasures, and the Azuri were hunted down, captured and tortured. The city was never found, but they all died — every last one.

'Why didn't they go into hiding?' Kep asked, horrified.

'That's the most tragic thing. Even if they did find people who were brave enough to hide them, the Azuri could not hide their identity for long; they were marked, you see. They all bore the symbol of T'al Jazure: two crescent moons, one etched on the palm of each hand.'

Ash had been watching the flames. He looked up sharply. 'What happened to Eeroktan?'

Barnham shook his head. 'I do not know the story of Eeroktan, only that it fell. In their lust for war, all three empires had left their homelands vulnerable. Perhaps some power had set itself against them. Whatever the case, their cities were destroyed, the citadels razed. The people were scattered or enslaved. War raged for many, many years, until at last the world was made new. The powers we know now struggled forth from a time of darkness and mud and hunger. Much that was good and beautiful was lost forever. Now, all that survives of those ancient times are scraps of songs, a few names and the shattered fragments of long-forgotten stories.'

Ash took the Taelstone from his pocket and cupped it between his hands. If he parted his thumbs, he could see stars winking deep within it, mirroring the sky. He bowed his head and closed his eyes, struggling against the Song which haunted the edges of his mind.

'So,' Kep sighed heavily, 'we're looking for a city that's been hidden for centuries — longer, even. How do you even hide a city anyway? And how by the gods are we supposed to find it when nobody else has been able to?'

She wasn't speaking to anyone in particular, but it was Sarin who answered. 'We don't know that nobody's ever found it.'

'Right.' Kep rolled her eyes. 'Well, thank you for pointing that out. But it's not terribly helpful, is it? Here's hoping your grandmother will be of more use. Though, I have to say, it seems pretty unlikely.'

Barnham looked closely at Sarin. 'What makes you so sure Nalina knows something, cuz?' he asked.

Sarin stretched his arms, 'Because she told me she did.'

'She told you?' Barnham's eyebrows flew up in surprise.

Sarin nodded. 'I ran away more than once. I didn't give up. The last time I managed to get a whole day ahead of the defenders before they found me and brought me back. Nalina had only just been made chieftain. She was furious. Precious hunting time had been lost, all because of me. She said she knew I'd never stop seeking, but that the time was not right. And we did a deal. I promised never to run away again; she promised that one day, when it was time, she'd tell me how to find T'al Jazure.' He rose and picked up his bow. 'Nalina is a hard woman, but she doesn't make hollow bargains.' His eyes flickered dangerously in Kep's direction, then he turned away. 'Going hunting,' he threw back over his shoulder.

'Good idea,' answered Barnham, a little too cheerfully. 'Just be ready to leave at first light.'

Sarin raised a hand in acknowledgement and melted into the darkness.

Chapter 34

THE AURUM

The air was crisp when they took to the skies, and the few stars that hung on were soon banished by the light. 'The wind is with us, Kep,' Barnham remarked as he set the wings. 'Should be there before nightfall, easily.' His face was clean-shaven, and he wore fresh clothes to match his newly brushed cap. The odour at the helm was greatly improved. Kep just wished he would stop drumming his fingers and sighing.

Sarin was below deck helping Ash weave a holder for the dopple-star. Those two were getting on so well that it was making her uneasy.

She hung over the side of the elpha-bird, surveying the changing landscape. The plains became grasslands dotted with small hills and round boulders: much better grazing land, decided Kep. She wondered for a moment if Pan was finding enough feed for the flock, then pushed the thought away; it just made her feel more lost and out of place.

The others joined them as Barnham was pointing out a line of mountains. 'See that triangular smudge? That's where the forest of Ustaar meets the plain. The Glade's right at the tip. The clan should be there ... if we haven't missed them.'

⁂

The forest of Ustaar spilled onto the plain in a dark, shadowy mass. Barnham's bird dipped low, then, tucking in her wings, drifted down towards its edge. Hauling at the mooring lines, they pulled her under the shelter of the mighty canopy.

'Never hurts to be out of sight,' Barnham remarked. He gave a deep sigh. 'Are they here, then?'

Sarin nodded. 'They're here.'

The figures coming through the trees blended so well with the foliage that they seemed to appear by magic. Barnham groaned.

'You two stay near the bird,' Sarin advised. 'And try to look meek. Some of the defenders are a bit jumpy. We don't want you getting shot before I've had a chance to plead your case.'

The lead group advanced quickly, and Kep and Ash were soon surrounded by bristling weapons and hostile eyes. They had no problem looking meek — they hardly dared breathe. Then the crowd parted and a tall woman strode forward. A tiny woman followed in her wake, dressed all in black.

'That's Nalina,' Barnham muttered in explanation, 'and Henna, the sage.'

The pair halted, and the defenders waved Sarin and Barnham forward. The tiny sage held up her palm in challenge. 'Who approaches the clan of the Aurum?' Her voice carried clearly, although it quavered with age.

'Sarin of Aurum, returned from exile.'

'Barnham of Aurum, returned from exile.'

They answered in turn, bowing their heads.

Nalina stood straight and imperious. Her hair was long and silver, caught by a band across her brow. Black feathers adorned the shoulders of her long green cloak.

She placed her hands upon Sarin's shoulders first. He lifted his head.

'Hear this! Sarin of Aurum is returned; all grievances are hereby forgiven and banished from memory.' The woman in black clapped her hands thrice.

'Sarin of Aurum, we welcome your return,' the crowd chanted.

Next the chieftain turned to Barnham. She held his head between her hands, fixing him with a fierce gaze. 'Barnham of Aurum is returned; all grievances are hereby forgiven and banished from memory.'

Again, three claps were sounded, and the crowd echoed the call: 'Barnham of Aurum, we welcome your return.'

When the chieftain grasped the hands of the returned ones and raised them high, the tension broke. The people cheered and shouted greetings. Sarin managed to extricate himself efficiently, but Barnham was swamped. The children danced about him in a frenzy of joy, 'Story-man! Story-man!' they cried. Men and boys clapped him on the shoulders or hugged him fiercely. Girls giggled and smiled. They saw the astonished joy on his face for a moment longer, then he was swept away.

❧

Kep and Ash stood silently before the chieftain of the Aurum. Nalina's cheekbones were high and sharp like Sarin's, but her eyes were dark brown, as typical of her clan. Her gaze lingered on Ash the longest, but if she was surprised at the arrival of 'the Grey Boy' she didn't show it.

At last she nodded to the diminutive woman at her side, who drew a small pot from somewhere amongst her garments and unscrewed the lid. Nalina dipped her thumb into the pot, coating it with blue powder. She rubbed it onto Ash's forehead, leaving a bright blue smudge.

'Ash of Mildaresh, you are granted temporary protection. The Aurum will treat you as one of their own, until the dye fades. Then you will leave the clan, on pain of death.' Ash made an uneasy bow.

Nalina then turned her steely attention to Kep. 'Trouble follows in your wake, Kep of Mildaresh, and harbouring you goes against my better judgement. The protection of my own people must ever be paramount in my purpose. We live in evil times, and I'm afraid that you are a liability of the worst kind.'

The tiny sage nodded agreement.

Kep blinked, feeling sick, but she refused to drop her eyes.

'The Calkinon Empire does not take kindly to rebels, especially those who spark mutiny in others. The wisest course would be to abandon you to your fate.'

The advisor nodded her approval again.

Kep clenched her teeth. Her hands formed tight fists at her sides.

Then Nalina lifted an eyebrow. 'Yet ... Fate is a curious thing.' She glanced briefly at Ash's pale face, then at Sarin. 'Only the gods know the part we are required to play.'

A terrible pause followed. Kep felt sure every person there could hear the thumping of her heart.

Then Nalina delivered her verdict: 'I grant my grandson's request ... for now.' She dipped her thumb, ignoring the disapproving eyes of her advisor.

Kep felt pressure upon her forehead. She bowed her head and tried not to tremble.

'Sarin, we will speak further of this,' Nalina declared. 'You will be summoned.'

Sarin nodded. Kep saw that he held his grandmother's gaze right up until the moment she turned away.

❦

The Glade was a huge open space, flanked on all sides by dense forest. A few massive trees stood on the grass like shaggy-headed giants, their feet rooted in pools of shade. The gaily decorated tents of the Aurum were scattered in happy clusters. Smoke from cooking fires rose into the air in fragrant spirals. People were going about their tasks, often singing out to their neighbours. The children skipped and cavorted, excited by the new arrivals and the prospect of a feast. As Sarin led Ash and Kep through the heart of the commotion, there were whispers and murmurs behind hands, but there were also smiles.

Kep was startled when a small hand slipped into her own. She looked down to see not one child, but a whole cluster. The young woman behind them gave Kep an appraising glance, but her real attention was on Sarin. 'The Aurum welcome you, Sarin,' she cooed. She held her palm flat on her heart, then swung it forward in an open-handed salute.

Sarin responded with the same gesture.

'This is Maralin,' he announced coolly.

The girl fluttered her eyelashes before offering Ash the same greeting.

Flustered, Ash forgot what Barnham had taught them and just nodded. 'Er. Hello, I'm Ash.'

Maralin laughed musically. 'Boys! They're all the same!' She moved her hips, making her skirts swing.

'I'm Kep,' said Kep, somewhat sharply.

The girl laughed. 'I know. I'm to be your keeper. And my first task is to rescue you from clumsy boys and scallywag children!' Sarin had already turned away, but she smiled brightly at Ash as if to reassure him that no offence was intended.

Hooking her arm through Kep's elbow, she swept her away before she had time to protest.

❧

Maralin shared a tent with two younger sisters, one a smaller replica of the other. They stared at the stranger from identical pairs of brown eyes. Although the outside of the tent was painted vivaciously in blues and reds, the inside was a plain greyish-brown. Gorgeous tassels and decorative fabrics more than made up for the plain walls. Kep was directed to rest on the embroidered cushions, while Maralin bossed her sisters into action.

'Come now, you two. We've a feast to dress for! Joaquin, fetch some water. Kep must be thirsty. Piabelle, let's start with you.'

Kep watched as Maralin twisted and braided the little girls' hair, weaving in their choice of ribbons and threads and beads. Then the younger girls did their sister's hair, following her instructions closely, and starting again twice when it all went wrong. The effect of the green ribbons against her chestnut curls was charming, and they clapped with pleasure at the result.

'You look beautiful!' they exclaimed. 'You should wear it like that for the Gathering!'

'Perhaps,' Maralin replied, surveying the effect with a critical eye.

Then they all looked expectantly at Kep.

After the encounter with Nellie Karendon, Kep wasn't at all keen to have her hair done, but she had the distinct impression that it would be rude to refuse.

The girls marvelled at the colour of her hair as Maralin brushed out the curls; apparently black hair was rare among the Haelrum.

'But, there is Sarin. His hair's black,' chirped the youngest. 'I wonder who's going to braid his hair tonight?' Her eyes opened wide with a sudden idea. 'You should ask him if you can do it, Maralin!'

Maralin's brush was still for a moment. 'I'm sure Sarin will have lots of offers, as usual.'

Kep guessed she was scowling a warning at her sister, because Piabelle made a face back and began threading beads onto a ribbon.

Her sister, Joaquin, exclaimed suddenly: 'Is Ash your boy, Kep?'

The little one snorted. 'Don't be silly! Kep's a slave. She's not allowed to have a boy.'

'Piabelle!' Maralin dealt her a smart slap on the cheek.

Kep gasped, horrified at the tears that welled in the little girl's eyes. 'No, it's all right. It's true. Slaves can't choose their own partners. But ... I suppose ... Well, I'm not really a slave anymore.' She touched the child's wet face gently. To her surprise Piabelle wrapped her arms about her, burying her face in her stomach. Maralin arched her brows, whether at her sister's behaviour or at what Kep had said, it was hard to tell.

Finally, the outling was ready. 'There! Now you look like one of us,' declared the little girls.

Kep contemplated her reflection. She certainly didn't feel like herself. Joaquin had found the 'perfect' dress in the share store: the bodice fitted snugly with a scooped neckline; the sleeves were slim to the elbows, then flared in soft folds. The colour matched her eyes exactly — and the smudge of blue on her forehead. Maralin had swept Kep's hair into a wave of curls and braids, decorated with a simple row of purple beads. It was decided that the bracelet Kep wore already was sufficient adornment, except it needed fastening properly.

'Look,' murmured Maralin as she undid the band, 'there's a secret. These strands fold back here, like so.'

Kep spun it around on her wrist. 'How ingenious! Thank you.'

Maralin gave a sideways smile. 'It's one of Sarin's. I could tell by the fastener — and the wolvern of course.' She noticed Kep's frown. 'They're a symbol of protection, not danger.'

'Yes, I know. I mean ... I hadn't noticed them,' Kep confessed. She looked at the bracelet and flushed, recalling her accusation of theft.

Maralin raised her eyebrows. 'Really?' She crossed her arms. 'Well, the gift of a bracelet is significant in the clan. It's a mark of friendship,' her mouth hardened, 'at the very least.'

Kep nodded uncomfortably beneath the other girl's suddenly stony gaze. 'Yes, it's beautiful. I shall certainly treasure it.'

'Good.' Maralin's mouth was smiling again, but she hadn't quite banished the disapproval from her eyes. 'Let's see what we can do about those awful boots.'

❧

Ash had the distinct impression that the clan had been warned to steer clear of Rilka's tent. People watched curiously, but no one followed them to the edge of the camp. Pale brown, like the underside of a mushroom, the tent looked odd next to the brightly coloured ones, as if it had sprouted in the wrong spot.

A voice spoke from within as they approached. 'Sarin?'

He smiled. 'Yes, it's me.'

He ducked through the opening, motioning for Ash to follow.

Rilka immediately claimed her brother in a tight embrace. Embarrassed, Ash shuffled his feet and looked around him. The tent was as extraordinary on the inside as it was plain on the outside. Sarin hadn't exaggerated Rilka's love for birds — they were everywhere. Every cover and every cushion featured birds of some sort. They decorated the walls in a riot of colour: it was like being inside an aviary.

Finally, Sarin disentangled himself. 'Rilka, I've brought someone.'

Everything about Sarin's sister seemed fragile; her wrists were thin, and her collarbone stood out like the breastbone of some tiny bird. Her hair was auburn, cropped short and close to her head. She didn't look anything like her brother.

'Um. Hello.' Ash awkwardly performed the gesture of greeting.

Her eyes settled on him, then flitted away again. 'You're the boy from my dreams,' she stated solemnly. Her voice was surprising in its huskiness.

Ash just stood there feeling ridiculous, not knowing what to say.

'I knew you'd find him.'

Although she gave her brother a small, quick smile, her eyes darted about. She dropped her voice to an intense whisper as she squeezed Sarin's arm. 'It's coming, Sarin — the no-name. And it's growing.' The colour seemed to drain from her face, accentuating the shadows about her eyes. 'The people — the people with holes for eyes ...' She seemed reluctant to look at Ash, and instead stole quick sideways glances. 'They are coming.'

Ash swallowed uncomfortably as Sarin took his sister gently by her shoulders. 'Rilka, let's not speak of this now. The evening draws in. Tomorrow when the sun is bright, that's the time for such conversations. Did you know Barnham's returned? You used to like his funny songs and stories. Rest now. I'll bring Barnham later — if I can haul the girls off him.' He attempted a chuckle, but it faded. 'You must sleep; you're exhausted. Here, I'll get you some water.'

Ash suspected Sarin was turning away to hide his own distress. Rilka nodded distractedly as if she wasn't quite following his words. Then, gasping, she suddenly stared at Ash with awful focus. To his horror, her eyes fluttered back and she collapsed. He lurched forward, but only partially broke her fall as she crumpled to the ground.

Sarin reacted swiftly. Sweeping his sister up, he laid her gently on the sleeping mat.

'Sorry. I'm sorry,' stammered Ash. 'Is she hurt?'

Sarin shook his head, as he smoothed Rilka's hair and pulled up the covers. 'I'll stay while she sleeps. It's not your fault.'

Not his fault? Ash forced himself to breathe. The panic was rising in his breast. It certainly felt like his fault. She'd been staring right at him. What terror had she seen?

Ash sat by Sarin's side, even though he wasn't sure whether he was welcome. He hugged his knees, thinking; then, after a long silence, he asked quietly, 'Sarin, what's Rilka scared of? She said the no-name was growing. What did she mean?'

Sarin was silent for a while, but then he rubbed the back of his neck and sighed. 'You've a right to know, Ash — of all people. But remember, the things Rilka sees aren't always what they seem.' His frown deepened. 'It's not as if she sees actual events, like a story unfolding in her mind; she doesn't. Do you understand?' Ash shook his head, so Sarin continued slowly. 'Rilka had a vision once: of a girl holding a dead pup in her arms. She told us that girl would never have children.' He sighed. 'Sadly, later, it came true. The poor woman has had three pregnancies, but in each case the child died in the womb.' He scowled at his feet. 'Unfortunately some in the clan hold Rilka responsible for what she sees, as if she somehow causes bad things to happen.'

'But could she not just keep quiet?'

Sarin nodded. 'She's learning, but she finds it hard.' He turned his face to Ash. 'Her visions are not always bad, you know.'

Ash tried to swallow. *Some were apparently bad enough to make her faint.* 'And the no-name? What's that?'

Sarin grimaced. 'I gave it that name, a long time ago. Rilka's dreams have always been haunted by some dreadful menace. As a child she was so terrified that she wasn't able to describe what scared her, so I called it the "no-name". I hoped she'd grow out of her nightmares, but she didn't. They got worse as she got older.'

'So, what is it? This no-name? Why is it so frightening?'

Sarin studied Ash's face, seemingly reluctant to speak. 'As I said, what Rilka sees may not be real. It might be something else in another guise. And … Well, it doesn't make much sense. It probably won't sound terrifying to you, but she describes a spinning tower of darkness, like a whirly-wind on the plain. Only the tower is made up of snakes, or eels, all glistening and writhing and deathly black. The image strikes absolute terror into her heart. When she wakes, she's inconsolable.'

Ash felt as if a cold hand had suddenly been placed upon his neck. Icy fear spread down his spine.

'It doesn't make sense, does it, Ash? I mean, such a thing can't be real.'

Sarin narrowed his eyes when Ash didn't answer. 'Ash?'

Ash couldn't speak. He wanted to deny all of his instincts, to say that of course such a thing was impossible, but he couldn't. He couldn't repay Sarin's trust by evading the question, or by lying. 'No ... but ...,' he was struggling to find the words. His scalp crawled at the awful memory.

Sarin was watching him closely, eyes glinting.

'Kep and I ...' He hesitated. He couldn't exactly say they had *seen* it. 'There was something: it was just as you describe. It passed us by, under the mountain on the path from Mildaresh.' He shuddered. 'I think what Rilka sees is real.'

Chapter 35

NALINA

The welcome feast was a merry affair. Those who had been ousted were once more in the arms of the clan, quite literally in Barnham's case; every time Kep caught sight of him he was embracing one or another of his kin. The night was clear and still, and the lanterns threw soft light onto laughing faces. Many of the younger folk were trialling new hairstyles before the Gathering; some laughed self-consciously, as if they were rehearsing that, too.

The food was set on swinging tables suspended from the trees, and everyone helped themselves whenever they pleased. There was soft flatbread, succulent roast meats, and all kinds of fresh greens, nuts and fruits. Kep was most surprised by the baked pods, which broke open to reveal rows of plump nuts. She and Ash had seen hundreds of the curious pods dangling from the trees; she had never considered that they might be edible.

As she nibbled at the sweet nutty flesh, laughter rang out from a nearby group. She flinched at the word 'outling', then frowned at herself. Why should it upset her to be called an outling? They would be moving on just as soon as they could. What did it matter? She hugged her arms across her chest and scanned the crowd. Where was Ash?

When Ash finally appeared he was accompanied by Maralin, who had taken it upon herself to locate the missing guests of honour. 'Found him! He was sulking with Sarin. Honestly! Boys!' She gave a tinkling laugh. Sarin had obviously evaded her charms.

Kep watched Ash fill a wooden bowl with food. His half-guilty, half-frightened expression was making her uneasy. She was anxious to hear about his meeting with Rilka, but Maralin was doing her best to educate them about the Aurum and their customs. She obviously considered them unbelievably ignorant as she patiently explained how the clan created food forests, planting and cultivating as they travelled. The season had been excellent; they had plenty of food and goods to share and trade at the Gathering. They were to journey to Pendle Ring in two days' time, but there were whispers. Maralin dropped her voice to repeat the rumour: 'Boys have already been sent to retrieve the herd.'

'The herd?' Kep was suddenly focused. 'You have animals?'

'Yes, of course. How else would we travel with all this?' Maralin waved her hand at the camp.

Kep was delighted to learn that the Aurum kept pallgoats, one or two to each family. They weren't just beasts of burden; they provided milk, meat, fleeces, skins and bone for carving. Their wool was fine and soft, their leather strong yet pliable. Maralin was explaining how they stretched the tent leathers when her sisters came running up, shining with news.

'Deltari's going to play! Come quickly! You have to come and dance!'

'But we don't know how to dance.'

The little girls stared at Kep with shocked eyes, then decided she could just watch them. So, while Ash managed to excuse himself by pointing at his food, Kep was dragged off towards the music.

As soon as the musicians had finished one jig, they launched into another that sounded identical, only faster. Everyone roared approval and clapped their hands in time. Kep was trying to catch sight of Piabelle amongst the capering dancers, when two sour-faced men pushed by. The taller of the two glared at her as he passed.

Maralin caught her mystified expression. 'Defenders,' she murmured.

'They don't look too happy.'

'No, the watch has been doubled since your arrival, and those who have returned are not welcome to all. Bet you can't guess who the tall one is.' Kep shook her head. *How could she possibly guess such a thing?* 'That's Tarbol — he's Sarin's father.'

Kep was taken aback. The man scowling at the musicians looked nothing like Sarin. He was thickset, with stubborn shoulders and a jaw to match. Perhaps Sarin was more like his mother.

'Sarin's mother died when he was young,' continued Maralin, without taking her eyes off the dancers. 'A few days after giving birth to Rilka. That's why Tarbol hates Rilka — that and her bizarre behaviour. But he hates Sarin more.'

Kep blinked. 'Why would he hate his own son?'

'Hmm? Oh, partly on account of Rilka; Sarin's always protected her. But also Sarin had a twin brother, looked the spit of Tarbol. When the infants came down with fever, only Sarin survived. Tarbol never got over losing the son who looked just like him.' Maralin snorted. 'Men. Honestly! Pig-headed fools. Why do we bother with them?'

At that moment Barnham appeared. His hair was brushed and braided, his face flushed from dancing. Kep blushed under his appraising gaze.

'Kep, you look absolutely gorgeous,' he said solemnly. Then his brown eyes twinkled. 'But I must steal *this* lovely lady for the dance!' Maralin laughed merrily and let him whirl her into the circle.

Relieved, Kep seized her moment to slip away and find Ash. He was sitting in the shadows, not far from where she had left him. She settled beside him, tucking her legs beneath the long gown. They wouldn't have long until Maralin remembered her duties as 'keeper of the outling', so they spoke quickly, sharing news.

Kep felt a cold, hard dread settle in her stomach when Ash described Rilka's vision. All of a sudden the lantern light seemed less cheerful, the shadows more menacing. They had barely spoken about that encounter in the dark under the mountain: she had tried to put it down to fear and imagination. Now she held her hands over her mouth in dismay. Neither of them moved. They both just sat there in silence, numb with dread.

When Sarin materialised suddenly beside them, they jumped. He gave them a quizzical look, before speaking: 'We've been summoned.'

⁂

Nothing signalled that Nalina's tent belonged to the chieftain. If anything, it was shabbier than the others, and the inside was equally unassuming. The faded furnishings were deep red, comfortable, but not lavish. A clear-lamp hung from the centre, providing adequate light. Nalina remained seated at her table, but Henna stood when they entered.

'Ah, thank you, Henna, that will be all. Go and partake of the festivities.'

The little woman looked quite affronted, she obviously didn't consider herself in a festive mood. She shot Sarin an indignant look, who gave her a charming smile in return, then, muttering something under her breath, she shuffled out with a sniff.

Nalina gestured for them to sit and got straight to the point.

'Sarin tells me you are seeking T'al Jazure.'

Ash bobbed his head. 'Yes.' He wondered how to address her. She looked so stern. He wished he had thought to ask Sarin.

'And you think you can find the lost city.'

Sarin's face was impassive, as if the topic had nothing whatsoever to do with him. Ash swallowed. 'We have to try. And … Sarin thought you might know something that could help.'

Nalina raised an eyebrow. 'No doubt Sarin thinks he's finally found a way of raising the subject without breaking his promise to his grandmother.'

She shot Sarin a look from under her brows, but he didn't react. Ash had to admire his nerve. Nalina held her grandson's gaze for a moment, then she sighed deeply. 'You have kept your promise, Sarin.' Her expression softened. 'And, though my heart wishes it were otherwise, it is time to speak of matters about which I have long kept silent.'

Sarin couldn't hide the excitement that leapt in his eyes. As Sarin bowed his head in gratitude, Ash wondered at the fleeting expression of pain that crossed his grandmother's face.

Nalina folded her hands in front of her. 'When coincidence piles upon coincidence it is a sure sign that destiny is at hand. Sarin's heart was captured by the lure of the Azuri long ago. And now, here you are,' she motioned at Ash, 'the boy in Rilka's dreams. Some might think it a strange chance that brings you here at this hour, to this place. But perhaps your arrival is the inevitable consequence of events set into motion many, many years ago.' She shook her head. 'None of us can escape the fate-lines of the past. When they reach out to ensnare us, all we can hope for is to play our part with honour and accept our future with courage.'

Ash felt his throat tightening. Her words were so serious, her tone so grave.

'In my own heart, I fear the city of T'al Jazure is lost forever, yet I will tell you what I know, and perhaps from that you will draw hope.' Nalina's next words made their hearts leap. 'If it still exists, T'al Jazure lies but three days' journey from Pendle Ring.' She held up a hand. 'Nay, do not look so confounded. It is no accident that the clans gather at the Ring at Mooncross. It has been thus since ancient times. The chieftains would meet to discuss which of their people, if any, would be permitted to study at T'al Jazure. If the Haelrum's blessing was granted, the Seekers would set out from there to find the Stone.'

'The Stone?' Sarin leaned forward in his chair.

Nalina answered him by chanting softly:

Under the light of crossing moons, Seekers pledge your faith,
There at the Stone, by solemn troth, Azuri yet shall wait.

'It's a fragment of an ancient oath-song. It tells of the promise sworn by the Azuri to all peoples. If those seeking T'al Jazure waited at the Stone during Mooncross, they would be met by one of the Azuri.'

'And this Stone, is it hard to find?' Ash hardly dared to believe the end of their journey might be within reach. Kep's eyes were shining, too.

'The Stone lies at the heart of the Enigmata.'

Sarin let out a groan. His shoulders slumped, and the excitement drained from his face.

'What's the matter?' asked Kep. 'What's the Enigmata?'

Sarin shook his head. 'It's a forest, but like no other. It has a strange magic which fuddles the wits. Within minutes of entering, a person becomes disoriented, lost in a maze of bewilderment. Even our kin do not venture there.' He grimaced and ran his hands back over his hair. 'If the Stone truly lies in the Enigmata, it will be impossible to find.'

Nalina clicked her tongue. 'Not impossible, Sarin. The Enigmata is indeed a treacherous place, and I would certainly never advise you to set foot there, were it not for this.' She opened her hand to reveal an object, swinging from a fine silver chain. She let the token fall into Sarin's palm, then closed her trembling hands over his. 'It will guide you to the Stone.'

Ash wondered at the grief in her eyes as she rose swiftly and turned away.

Sarin held out his hand so they could all see the object, a silver triangle overlaid with the design of two moons. 'The sign of the Azuri,' he breathed.

Kep's brow was creased in confusion. 'But, I don't understand how this helps. Even if we find the Stone, who would be there to meet us? I mean, weren't the Azuri destroyed nearly a thousand years ago?'

'Not all.' Nalina's back was still turned. The three of them exchanged startled looks. She turned stiffly to face them. 'The Azuri were destroyed, as you say. But one survived. His name is Nirias. He is the last Azuri, and only his death would prevent him from being at the Stone at Mooncross.'

She smiled a bitter smile, and nodded at the comprehension dawning on her grandson's face. 'Yes, it's the same man. Nirias was granted the protection of the Haelrum some years ago. He came to us in great need, a broken man in body and soul. The token you hold in your hand belonged to him.'

Ash turned the idea over in his mind. A surviving Azuri? How could that be? That would make him ... How old would that make him? Surely she was mistaken?

Nalina arched her brows at their obvious disbelief. 'Not everything that seems impossible is so. Nirias survived because he wasn't just Azuri,' she dropped her voice, 'he was also one of the Malshorne.'

At that moment a girl arrived bearing a flask of warmed wine and a tray of food. Nalina waved her away, choosing to pour the wine herself, one glass for each of them.

Ash tasted the wine politely, but barely noticed its spicy sweetness. His mind was reeling.

Setting down the flask, Nalina seemed lost in her own thoughts until Sarin broke the silence.

'What did you mean? One of the Malshorne?'

Ash held his breath.

'Of the Malshorne little now is known. Even the name is misused. Nowadays any witch, hermit or healer might be referred to as a malshorne, but legend has it that the true Malshorne number only three, never fewer, never more. They are blessed with long lives and special abilities, although one might wonder whether either of those is truly a blessing.' As Nalina toyed with the stem of her glass, Ash had the distinct feeling there was something she wasn't saying.

'But I still don't understand.' Kep frowned. 'How did Nirias survive when all the other Azuri were destroyed?'

Nalina smiled wryly. 'He survived because he was able to change his shape. The Malshorne are shape-shifters. They can manipulate their features, their build, the colour of their hair, even their eyes. Nirias avoided detection for one simple reason: because he could hide the mark of the Azuri etched upon his palms.' Her eyes fell on her grandson. 'He wasn't much older than Sarin is now when T'al Jazure was lost.'

Ash was thinking of Credé's strange eyes and his awful passing. 'What of the others? The other two Malshorne. What happened to them?'

Nalina traced a finger around the base of her glass. 'I know nothing of the others. Nirias never spoke willingly of his past. If I hadn't nursed him through his illness, I would probably have thought him an ordinary man like everyone else. But his shape became unstable during his fevers. I saw the shifts in his features and the moons that appeared on his hands. His mind took even longer to mend than his body.' She winced. 'When he seemed well enough to bear the question, I asked what could drive a person to such despair. He refused to answer.'

Her gaze lingered on Sarin. 'There is an awful darkness in Nirias's history of which he would not, or could not, speak.' Her mouth quivered. 'There is little I can say to deter you from your path, but know this: Nirias is a brave man, perhaps a good man, but he has a terrible destiny. I cannot say if finding him will lead you to T'al Jazure, but one thing is certain: finding Nirias will undoubtedly bring you closer to evil.'

Chapter 36

SCOUTS AND DOUBTS

*A*sh was running. Running from something he couldn't place. Rilka was running beside him in her bare feet; then she became Tarlyn and he lost her. The streets were confusing. Some things were familiar, some strange and warped. He heard strains of the Song and pushed it away. Every turn, he feared he would arrive at the fountain. Suddenly Braig was there, pointing, and he understood: he had been carrying the Malshorne with him all along. He opened his knapsack to see Credé's gaunt, accusing face staring out.

Ash woke with a strangled cry and looked straight into a pair of eyes. For a dreadful moment the dream had become reality.

'Sorry.' Sarin moved back to give him some space.

Ash pulled himself upright, his heart racing.

'Sorry, Ash.' Sarin frowned. 'But Rilka wants to show you something. She says there isn't much time.'

⁂

The morning was sparkling under fresh-washed skies. The floor of the forest felt springy underfoot. Fallen leaves had gathered in mottled drifts. When they reached the beginnings of a path, Rilka put her hand on Sarin's arm. He murmured something about investigating the waterhole, then vanished. Ash groaned inwardly. The last thing he wanted was to be on his own with Rilka. He should have stayed in bed. *Why hadn't he stayed in bed?* But Rilka was already leading the way up a thin track, so with a sigh, he followed.

The track led to the top of a small hill, which was crowned with a single tree. It was huge and so ancient that its trunk had split open. Rilka perched on a massive gnarly root, with her feet tucked beneath her. Ash looked around awkwardly, scratching his head, then selected a crook in which to sit. He leaned back against the tree's lumpy skin, inhaling the fragrance of

253

fallen leaves. The morning light caught the wings of darting birds, making them shine silver and green. Sarin was right: it would be easier to talk of dark things on such a morning — except neither of them seemed inclined to speak.

At last Ash cleared his throat. 'Rilka, why do you think I'm in your dreams?'

Her eyes met his briefly before flitting away. 'Your fate is connected with the no-name. You are paired.'

This wasn't at all what he wanted to hear. He glanced sideways, and noticed for the first time that her feet were bare. *Weren't they cold?* He wriggled his own toes in his new boots. He had never had such comfortable boots. He hated the silence. He didn't know what to say, but it felt odd just sitting there.

'Is there anything else? In the dreams, I mean?'

Rilka shrugged, as if the question didn't concern her. She seemed more interested in Tarlyn, who was prowling in the foliage above. Ash sighed. *Why were they here?*

Long minutes went by, then there was a sudden thrashing in the bushes below. Ash guessed Sarin must have shot some wild thing. He shivered. He marvelled at Sarin's bush skills, though: he would never have guessed he was down there. He looked sideways at Rilka again. She had plucked a leaf and was rolling the stem between her fingers to make it spin. She seemed so intense, as if it was something to be deciphered. He frowned, looking about and scratching his head. 'Rilka, why did you bring me here? Is there something I'm supposed to see?'

Rilka shrugged. A strange expression crossed her face. Was it anguish? Frustration? He had no idea. 'We can go now.' She got to her feet, brushing tiny twigs from her clothes.

Ash stood up, too. The tree had marked his hands with moss. He rubbed his palms together, but only succeeded in making it worse.

Rilka had turned to leave, but then she paused and looked back with a tilt of her head. 'There are faces in the circle.' Before Ash could respond, she skipped off. He tried to catch up on the downhill path, but she flitted ahead, just out of reach. He was definitely starting to understand why she wasn't too popular with the clan.

The circle? What circle? He scowled. He didn't need more riddles, more things to worry about, and he felt foolish for traipsing after her. It was ridiculous. So she happened to dream of a boy with grey hair. So what? Just a coincidence. And this no-name of hers, that could be anything.

He looked about for Tarlyn, who appeared immediately out of nowhere and leapt softly onto his shoulder.

By the time Ash reached the end of the path, he had almost wholly convinced himself that Rilka was just too strange to take seriously.

❧

'No, Kep! You're doing it all wrong!' The sisters howled with laughter, delighted with their discovery that it was true: the outling couldn't dance at all! Kep clasped her hands behind her head and sighed irritably. She had barely slept. It wasn't just the unsettling news of Rilka's vision; Sarin was well and truly part of the quest now. Nalina had given him the token, along with her strangely reluctant blessing, and Kep wasn't at all happy about it — there was something about him that she just couldn't fathom.

She certainly wasn't in the mood for dancing, but the little girls had taken over as 'keepers of the outling', and were insisting that she learn the steps of The Wheel. Kep would much rather have been helping Maralin and her parents. They were seed-keepers, a highly revered role in the clan, and were busy cataloguing seeds and wrapping them in small pieces of cloth for trading. Kep felt insulted by their polite but firm refusal of her offer to help — surely it wasn't hard to wrap a few seeds.

'Do it again,' commanded Piabelle.

Trying not to grit her teeth, Kep moved into position.

Maralin had explained the function of the dance. The Gathering lasted for only three days, so there wasn't much time for young people to meet prospective partners. The Wheel was designed to gauge a couple's interest and speed up the process. Anyone who wasn't bonded was obliged to dance. The young women formed the inner circle of the wheel and the men the outer, with each revolution bringing a different couple together. They would dance a series of steps, finishing with their palms touching. Then they would either gently push their partner's hands away, to show their disinclination to take things further, or hold their position for a moment. If the couples were very much attracted, they might even lean forward and kiss, just lightly — as a promise. Then the wheel would turn again.

'Don't worry,' the girls had reassured Kep: 'No one will want to kiss an outling!'

Kep was trying her best to follow their confused directions. It didn't help that they kept squabbling about the steps, and, although Joaquin was the obvious choice to be the 'boy', she only came up to Kep's shoulder. Kep counted and watched her feet. 'Now turn about!' Kep turned about. 'No! That's not right: you should be facing each other. Kep, you're all wrong!'

'Well something's amiss, that's certain enough.' They turned to see Sarin leaning against a tree, his bow and a bundle of game lying at his feet. Kep felt herself blush and scowled, annoyed at his obvious amusement. She wondered how long he had been standing there watching.

He sauntered over. 'It's not Kep's fault. It's you, Joaquin. I have to say, you're not a very good boy.'

'That's 'cause I'm not a boy!' she retorted. 'It's all backwards and confusing.'

He grinned and ruffled up her hair. 'Poor thing. Guess you're just not man enough.'

Glowering and smiling at the same time, she ducked beneath his reach and punched her fists into his stomach. With a happy chortle her sister launched herself into the fray as well, but Sarin just picked her up, flipped her upside down and lowered her onto her head. Then when Joaquin leapt up and hung dangling from his neck, he groaned and allowed himself to be wrestled to the ground.

'I surrender! You are man enough! Both of you!' he laughed. 'Except you're missing the honey-cakes.'

'Honey-cakes?' Squealing, the girls abandoned the lesson and hurried in the direction of the treat.

Kep blew out a long sigh of relief as Sarin pulled himself to his feet.

'That bad, eh?' He laughed when she pulled a face. Then he raised an eyebrow in challenge. 'Come on, then. Let's see if you know your steps. Can't have you letting the clan down.'

Kep was protesting, but he already had his back to hers. He counted them in and she found herself skipping to catch up. Sarin was the right height, which certainly made things easier, but it felt so strange; she'd never danced with a boy before. She concentrated on her feet and keeping her forearms upright.

As they turned, first one way, then the next, she tried not to think about how close he was, or how warm the backs of his hands felt when they brushed against hers. They circled again, fingertips just touching. He smelled of the forest, fresh and grassy. She blushed and counted, turned and counted, until at last the steps brought them together, palm-to-palm. She could feel the energy coursing between them as she studied the backs of her hands, waiting for Sarin to push away. He didn't.

She raised her eyes. His expression made her heart skip. The sounds of the forest didn't cease and time didn't stop; it was just that all sensation seemed to melt into a single heart-pounding moment. Then it happened. The light on the leaves; the birdsong; and the brush of lips, unexpectedly soft, unexpectedly warm. And the moment hung there, suspended, softly burning.

Neither was aware of anyone approaching until they heard a cough. They sprang back as if stung. The messenger grinned. 'Nalina requires your presence,' she announced with a chuckle.

⚶

Ash was already waiting outside Nalina's tent. He saw immediately how Kep and Sarin were avoiding each other's eyes, and suppressed a sigh at their awkwardness. *Things would be so much easier if they could just get along.* Inside, Nalina was seated at the table with three others: Henna, Barnham and a worn-faced defender they hadn't met. They were all poring over a map.

'There, at the delta,' the defender was saying, 'and here above Zondra.' Waved to the seating area, they listened intently, trying to work out what was happening.

'Send scouts to double-check that position,' Nalina frowned. 'But we go ahead as planned. Are we agreed?'

'Agreed.' Her companions rose swiftly.

'And, Barnham, if anyone resists, send them to me.'

Barnham gave a quick nod. He shrugged apologetically at the others' puzzled expressions and left with the defender.

Nalina rose, her face grave. 'There has been disturbing news of your enemies. Calkinon airships have been sighted in Jerra-bal. Guardians have been asking after a blue elpha-bird and two runaway slaves. They have set up blockades in the villages, and are checking wrists.' Her eyes flashed. 'The audacity!' Her mouth was a straight, hard line.

Sarin nodded. 'What was that about Zondra?'

'We think there's a troop presence in the valley. Perhaps they suspect Haelrum involvement in harbouring the fugitives. Perhaps not.'

'Surely they wouldn't dare move against the clans?' However, Sarin's tone suggested he wasn't so sure.

Nalina narrowed her eyes. 'It's not unthinkable. The spirit of the rebellion increases with every day Kep remains free — and Calkinon does *not* abide dissent.'

Kep's hands formed tight fists at her sides. 'But, I only did what was right. Nobody should have to be a slave for eternity, not Braig — not anyone!' The mention of Braig's name made her blush. She could still feel Sarin's kiss warm upon her lips — if she had been going to kiss anyone, it should have been Braig, shouldn't it? Not this boy she hardly knew.

Nalina snorted. 'It was well done. You have nothing to be ashamed of in that regard.'

Ash's eyes were worried. 'Do you think they know Kep's here?'

'If the snout is with them, then yes. And that would normally be the case: the snouts have right of passage on all Calkinon birds.' She frowned. 'Kep's snout does have an odd preference for travelling alone,' she mused, 'but Calkinon has other spies.' Her eyes rested on Kep for a moment, then she lifted her chin. 'So we must leave, and swiftly. I've given orders for a night stride.'

'A night stride?' Sarin looked surprised.

Nalina nodded, returning to the map. 'All is in place. Barnham's transporting those who can't manage the terrain in his elpha-bird. He will head in the opposite direction, then double-back to Pendle Ring.'

Kep's heart sank. 'But if they're looking for his bird, won't that be dangerous?'

Nalina shook her head. 'They'll stop and search. And all they'll find is several cranky old folk, two heavily pregnant women and a bevy of bawling babies.'

'And Barnham, grinning at them with a feather in his cap,' Sarin added.

'Yes,' Nalina admitted with a twist of her mouth. 'Barnham did rather seem to relish the idea. With luck, his decoy will draw off the airships so we can pass unnoticed to the ford of Elan.' She tapped the map. 'But I'm afraid there's further need for haste; heavy rain is coming: we'll need to cross the river here, before dawn, before its banks swell. Then, all being well,' she traced her finger across the map to rest on a circular symbol, 'the Gathering at Pendle Ring will provide refuge, at least until we can get you to the Enigmata. Calkinon will be unable to track you in the forest, and with luck it may confound your snout as well.'

Kep was absolutely astounded. Nalina clearly took great pleasure in thwarting Calkinon authority, but it seemed extraordinary that she would put her own people in the way of danger to help a couple of lowly slaves. 'Thank you,' she stammered. 'I don't know how we can ever repay your kindness.'

Nalina sniffed. 'There's no need for gratitude. You are as kin to us; the smudge on your forehead bears witness to that. Besides, the Haelrum can't abide slavery. We'll waste no more time on words. There is much to be done.' And with that she waved them out.

The Aurum packed down their camp remarkably swiftly. Tents disappeared in no time; the braces were converted into carrier frames, and tent leathers were tucked about each load to make everything secure and watertight. It was ingenious. The pallgoats seemed unbothered by their burdens; they kept grazing, stopping only occasionally to stare at proceedings from their long-lashed eyes.

By dusk, the whole clan had been served a hot meal, the latrines had been filled in, and the Glade looked as if they had never even been there, except for a few tilled patches which sprouted new seedlings. Kep watched as the first of the Aurum moved out. Shrouded in their hooded cloaks, they seemed to vanish into the forest before her very eyes.

Chapter 37

THE NIGHT STRIDE

She was close. He could feel it. His nostrils flared. He could smell others on the wind. They travelled lightly, these Aurum, barely touching the ground. But he could still perceive them. Discern the shapes they carved from the darkness. Feet fell softly in his mind. Some firm, some light. Some bare whispers: children. Gooel sent out his mind. The children were radiating tendrils of fear that drifted toward him like ribbons. He sniffed. Not long now. She was close. Long chase soon over. Last hunt soon done. He heard the night hoot. A few moments later, an answer. He smiled his strange smile, appreciating the ruse.

Kep stopped when she heard the signal. The first calls had caught her out: they had sounded so precisely like haunt-owls that she had ignored them and had crashed into the people in front. The answer echoed back, acknowledging the need for a halt. Even the children were showing complete discipline, obeying the strict protocols of the night stride. They waited, silent, breathing in the dark. It was the stifled type of silence that made you want to shout out loud.

Up until now the ground had been washed with moonlight, but the grey clouds were thickening, shrouding the moons, smothering the stars. She could hear murmurs behind as one child was lowered to walk for a spell, and another hoisted into a harness to sleep.

The mournful signal went up, and the night stride resumed. A few steps were all it took to re-establish the stealthy motion of the host. *Night stride? Night glide would be more accurate.* The Aurum moved like a whisper, a rumour in the night. All around, the padded feet of the pallgoats rose and fell with hypnotic certainty. It would be hours before the rhythm was broken again.

❧

Kep was blinking away the first cold drops of rain when she realised that ahead someone was breaking formation. A dark figure infiltrated the lines, holding up a mist-lamp on a chain; it cast weak light about his feet, and the people parting to let him through. The defender whispered hoarsely, turning his head this way and that. 'Sarin?'

'Here.'

Kep jumped. She had had no idea he was so close.

'Come forward, we need your sharp eyes.'

When she glimpsed the profile of Sarin's face and the sharp edge of his cheekbone, her stomach did a peculiar flip, before he became anonymous once more – one grey figure among all the others.

As she raised her hood against the rain, someone touched her elbow. She stepped aside to make room for Ash. Something tense in the way he was moving worried her, and his breathing was coming quick and shallow. She risked a whisper since the host had not yet settled. 'Are you all right?'

He didn't answer. Perhaps he hadn't heard.

❧

They strode on, hugging the brink of the woodlands. When at last they came to a stop, Kep dropped her hood. The trees offered reasonable protection, but occasionally the leaves tipped down heavy drops that seeped icily into her scalp. The featureless form beside her has turned out to be Maralin's father. He was explaining quietly how the plain before them sweeps down towards Jerra-bal. They would avoid the scattering of villages along the Elan, and ford the river higher up at the old bridge. Kep could sense his anxiety; the grasslands would give scant cover until they reach the river shore.

'This land has a black history,' he muttered. 'The Elan plains have seen as much blood as they have rain.'

Ash was huddled on a damp rock. Kep could see Tarlyn's eyes glint momentarily from beneath his hood. Someone has passed them rolled-up flatbread, and Kep was now biting hungrily into hers, savouring the taste of salted meat and sharp herbs. Ash was ignoring his. She could sense the strain in his body. He was listening.

'What is it, Ash?'

'He's here.'

She stiffened at the strange quality in his voice. 'Who? Who's here?'

She was about to repeat the question when Sarin returned and crouched before them like a creature about to spring. 'Bad news. We've got company. It's Gooel.' Kep's chest tightened. 'He's keeping his distance, though. You'll be safe in the midst of the host. The defenders have sent a couple of arrows his way to keep him wary. We can't hit him in this light, but at least we know where he is.'

Kep tried to breathe. She imagined Gooel circling, snuffling, waiting for his moment.

'Here.' Sarin pushed something at her, and she recognised the shape of Ash's knife.

'No, it's yours now.' It was hard to keep her voice low. 'That was the deal.'

'Maybe, but you need it more. Anyway, it doesn't work for me. There's some sort of knack to it.' The rest came out in a rush: 'And Ash and I would be much happier if you were armed. Isn't that right, Ash?' He flicked Ash's leg with the back of his hand to gain his attention. 'Ash?'

Ash looked around then, his eyes wide with fear. 'Can you hear that? Can you hear the drums?'

Exchanging glances, Kep and Sarin shook their heads. All that could be heard was the soft pattering of rain on the covered loads.

'I thought ...' Ash retreated into his hood, hugging his knees. 'No, it's nothing. Just rain maybe.'

Kep forced down the fear in her throat. They couldn't afford another episode like the one at Senna.

'We'll be moving soon,' said Sarin, rising suddenly. 'Stay here. I'm going to find Rilka.'

Kep frowned and put her hand on Ash's shoulder. 'Ash, what did you mean when you said, "He's here"? Could you hear him? Could you hear Gooel?' She shivered. Even saying the name was terrifying.

'No, not Gooel. I just thought ...'

'What? What did you think?' She waited, then shook her head. 'Come on, Ash. I'm too tired to force it out of you. What is it?'

'I heard Credé. It was his voice singing among the others. That's all.'

As the host crept onto the plain Ash knew he had to fight the Song. He tried. But it was stronger now. Its strains reached into his mind like tentacles. He tried to fend off the rhythms by thinking of something else, anything else. But then there *was* nothing else: just the Song, and his feet marching, and the drums, the drums...

... with drums they march, to war, to war. 'Victory or death!' they chant. The rain pelts his amour, pinging sharply. His comrades' eyes shine through the slits in their battle masks, and the Song surges, strident as a war cry. They number so many. Countless warriors. Brave beyond bounds. The trumpets shout. The banners stream red and gold.

When the melody soars and shifts, he rides with it, and wheels above the battlefield on silver wings. Below, the masses surge, slapping into each other like converging rivers. The armies reel. His captain screams and plummets, struck from the sky.

The tenor shifts again and he's running, charging the front line. His blade sings. Men scream their hatred with gaping mouths in the battle clash. Fear and fury both. The spell of wrath is upon him.

Then a single note pierces his mind. He knows the voice at once. It rises in a thin and terrible lament. All melody shatters into discord. A great cacophony rises and now he sees their eyes. Shining holes of black. Inhuman. Agents of terror. They are revelling in the battle fury. The devastation fueling their lust.

Artus! What have we done?

Anguish, blood and joy. They kill. They scream. Then fall. Human again, bewildered and pitiful in their dying moments. Their lives empty onto the shingle, and he is screaming. I didn't know! I didn't know.

His mind splinters. The world wheels and turns. Images spin like shields cast upon water. The fragments whirl out of time and place. He is lost ... lost ... lost ...

Until a whisper. It drifts into his mind like a falling leaf. Remember? Remember? The word twirls on its end, but he catches it and holds fast. He sees the path. Her bare ankles. Then the tree. The tree. Braig's creased brow. Starting with that stupid tree? Starting with that stupid tree. The tree. At the beginning and at the end.

'Is he back?'

'He's so pale.'

'Let him take his time. He's coming around.'

Ash's eyes flickered. Where was he? It was dark, but the kind of darkness that was yielding to the power of dawn. Three forms were hovering against the glimmering sky.

Kep made the sign of the triangle. 'Thank you, Argess.' She grasped his hand and smiled.

Sarin and Rilka were kneeling there, too. Squinting, he could make out other groups of people crouching in quiet huddles beneath the trees. The humpy shapes turned out to be pallgoats, resting with their legs folded beneath them.

Sarin gave Ash's shoulder a quick squeeze, then rose. 'I'll let them know you're all right ... and see if there's news.'

Rilka threw an odd little smile in Ash's direction, then followed her brother.

'News?' He looked around. 'Where are we?'

'In the woods near the ford. We're waiting for the all-clear signal from the other side of the river. So far they have flashed warnings for us to wait ...' Kep was trying to smile but failing.

'What happened?'

'Don't you know?'

He rubbed his neck. 'The Song overwhelmed me. I couldn't fight it any longer. There was a battle. No. Many battles. It was awful. Something terrible happened at this place.' He rubbed his face, hoping to clear his mind. 'Credé was part of it. I heard his voice singing. Then I saw ... I saw ... horrible things, and everything started spinning . ...'

Kep slipped a hand under his arm. 'You were in some sort of trance, Ash. A walking trance ...' She faltered. It had been so bizarre: everyone else had tripped and stumbled during the blind trek across the plain, but Ash had marched along as if it was plain daylight. 'You were doing really well, then you just collapsed. We couldn't stop out there on the plain, so we carried you over the back of a pallgoat.' She has decided not to mention how weirdly Rilka had behaved, trailing along, holding his hand.

Then, after a moment he asked uncertainly: 'Was Rilka there?'

Kep took a deep breath before answering. 'Yes. She seemed to think it might help if she walked beside you.'

'It did,' he replied quietly.

When Sarin returned, he was accompanied by Nalina herself. She squatted down and held Ash's face in her hands, turning his head from side to side as if it was a pot she was considering buying.

'You look better,' she said with a sniff. 'Not good, mind, but better.' She pulled several stalks from a pocket set upon her sleeve. 'Chew these. They'll help.' Then she addressed Kep. 'Sarin has told me a little of what ails him. Nirias will help if he can. So long as—' She didn't get to finish, as the pallgoats were suddenly skittish, quivering with fright, and several clambering to their feet.

Then they all heard it: a howl that rose and hung in the air.

'Wolvern!' The word repeated around the host, like an echo.

Kep moved instinctively to calm the nearest pallgoat, but Sarin was ahead of her. He didn't speak, just held out his hands as if to embrace the terrified creature, and almost instantly the animal bowed its head. It bleated and sank back to the ground, and to Kep's amazement the others followed suit. Even when another howl rose, the herd remained calm.

Sarin cocked his head, listening, then grinned at Nalina. 'It's all right. I know that call: it's Kia-tan.'

Nalina scowled, shaking her head. 'He's kin. Of the Natora clan,' she explained disdainfully. 'Sarin, go and meet the young fool — and stop him bringing those wolvern near the herd.'

⁊

Gooel sniffed the air. New scent on dawn air. Wolfish? Yes. He parted branches. He watched. Focused eyes and mind. A defender turned his head. The light was better now. Too dangerous to move. Wolvern howled and defender moved away. Gooel snuffled. Discerned fur stink from man fear, goat fear. He hid and waited. Patient. Weary. Bones aching. Long task. Last task. He watched and waited. She was close. Soon over. Soon long sleep. Gooel hid and watched and waited.

⁊

Kia-tan swept off his cap. 'I bear greetings to Nalina from Tai, chieftain of

Natora. His message is dire and to be related without delay.'

Nalina returned the gesture of welcome. 'The Aurum welcome Kia-tan,' she replied, but her sour expression did not match her words.

When the young man continued with breathless excitement, Kep was sharply reminded of Pan.

'Tai sends warning. Calkinon troops occupy the eastern bank. They barred the bridge last evening.' His eyes slid towards Ash and Kep. 'They're checking every wrist.'

'Are they indeed.' Nalina stamped her staff. 'Calkinon's reach stretches far beyond her worth.'

Kep and Ash looked at each other, dismayed. 'Is there nowhere else we can cross?' asked Kep.

Nalina shook her head. 'There is a place downstream, but it is treacherous. The water flows quickly and the leap from one stone to the next is wide.' She looked disparagingly at Ash, 'You'd never manage it, not with the waters rising.'

At that Kia-tan let out an excited hoot. 'No … but …' He grinned conspiratorially at Sarin, who had re-appeared behind him.

'Young man,' Nalina glowered, 'we are hungry, and weary, and much aggrieved. If you wish to evade the ire of my defenders, or indeed the bite of my own staff, which I am sorely tempted to visit upon your skull, I suggest you stop smirking at my grandson and reveal whatever foolish notion is filling that empty head.'

❧

The captain of the Calkinon Thirty-third had almost finished dressing when his underling arrived.

'Captain. There are more Farlings wanting to cross the bridge, sir.'

'And?' The captain flapped his hand. 'You know the procedure, Wald. Check them all.' He inspected his whiskers again in the mirror. Perhaps those tough grey bits did need plucking after all.

'Yes, Captain. But, Captain …'

As he fastened his collar, the captain found himself wondering whether his lieutenant had always had such large, pink ears. They really were quite prominent and seemed to waggle as he shuffled from foot to foot. Strange. Wald was usually a steady sort of chap. 'Stand still, man!'

'Yes. Sorry, Captain. It's just … Well, there's a woman, sir. She won't budge, sir. She's demanding to see you personally, sir.' The young man licked his lips. 'She's quite formidable …'

'Won't budge? A woman, you say? Humph!'

The captain fixed his helmet upon his head and checked the effect. As he suspected, he looked magnificent; a true captain of Calkinon in the prime of his career. He felt a little thrill of satisfaction.

'Formidable, eh? We'll see about that.'

❦

Nalina of the Aurum turned out to be more than formidable. She stood midway along the bridge; not quite as tall as the man before her, but immovable and utterly livid. The captain's shining buttons and polished boots were no match for the scorn in her eyes. Here was a woman who had walked all night, who had propelled her people through darkness and peril, and whose heart was aching with grief. No one would stand in her way, least of all some petty captain with a curled moustache. She sliced through his salutation as if she cared nothing for the grandeur of Calkinon. 'By what authority do you block this bridge?'

The captain's moustache quivered with surprise. 'I am captain—'

'I don't care who you are. I simply asked by what authority you obstruct the passing of my people. We are Haelrum.' She banged her staff making the timbers bounce at her feet. 'Calkinon has no jurisdiction over this bridge, nor over my people. Let us pass at once.' She ran a dismissive eye over the buttons of his rank. 'I'm sure you are aware that an incident with the clans would not bode well for your career, *Captain*.' She spat the word as if it tasted foul.

The captain stiffened. He was perfectly aware that this woman did not stand alone; the Gathering at Pendle Ring numbered many hundreds and was swelling by the hour. Blinking several times, he thrust out his jaw. 'Madam, I can assure you Calkinon has no quarrel with the Haelrum. I have merely been charged with the task of apprehending a dangerous pair of rebel slaves.'

'Slaves? You will find no slaves here,' Nalina rapped. 'We are Aurum.' Her eyes glittered.

'Yes. Your people are welcome to pass, of course.' He bowed stiffly. 'We merely ask to check all wrists. I think you'll find that is within the bounds of the Calkinon Peace.' His moustache had suddenly started to twitch with a life of its own — it was most disconcerting. But to his relief, the woman seemed to acquiesce.

'Very well. But *you* ... you will personally bear witness to the truth that Aurum are not slaves, and you may begin with me.' She held up her left hand in a fist, her bare wrist towards him. Her next words were articulated loudly for all to hear: 'I am no slave to Calkinon.'

And so, as the rain began again, the Aurum passed over the ford of Elan, each presenting a fist to the captain in the same manner as their chieftain. The captain soon grew heartily sick of the phrase 'I am no slave to Calkinon.' Even the children held up their little fists and declared the words. Despite their compliance, he couldn't help the sneaking suspicion there was something rather defiant about the whole affair. Of course he held his ground, but it was most unpleasant and, in the end, totally unnecessary. Although every man, woman and child was checked, and every load uncovered, no slaves were discovered. The information must have been false.

The captain cleared his throat as the Aurum disappeared into the rain. 'See, Wald? No need for concern. You just need to know how to deal with these people. Let them know who's in charge.'

Wald blinked. 'Yes, Captain. Shall we search the woods, sir?'

'No need, no need. The river is too swollen. There's no getting across that current. If they're still in these parts, they'll have no choice but to cross here at the bridge. And we'll be waiting, Wald. Oh yes, we'll be waiting.' The captain of Calkinon couldn't help noticing how Wald's ears waggled as he saluted. He frowned and made a mental note. He really must appoint a less ridiculous lieutenant.

Chapter 38

WOLVERN

Kep's heart froze at the sight of the Natora wolvern. They were even bigger than Karendon's beast. They eyed her with yellow, watchful eyes. Soulless. Killers. Every instinct told her so.

'This is Petara. She's gentle, really,' said Kai-tan. He showed her the girth-belt. 'Look. It's even got footholds.' Petara was staring at her with predatory interest; it was as if the huge beast could see into her chest and was watching her heart beating.

'She won't let you fall,' urged Sarin. 'Not now she's decided to bear you.'

Decided? What if she decides she'd rather eat me? Kep bit her tongue. Everything told her to resist the plan, to run from those dread creatures as humans should. But there was no choice. The blue mark on her forehead, blurred and faint from the rain, was no defence against Calkinon rule. And Calkinon was here, blocking the bridge. The Aurum could protect them no longer. It was simple. Ride or die. No choice.

❧

Rain, wet fur, and fear. It all began with the river crossing, and it very nearly ended there, too. Kep could barely hear Sarin shouting above the din of thundering water. She couldn't respond. The river's headlong charge into the valley had induced a sort of frozen panic. Rocks jutted wet and angry between rising shoulders of water. It was madness. Narsis was in a foul mood — they would surely be swept to their deaths.

Sarin started shouting and gesticulating, pointing back towards the trees, but she still couldn't move. Then he gave a command. At once Petara lunged forward. Kep gasped and clung on. She hadn't yet learned to trust the wolvern's strength and judgement. She wasn't used to the split-second calculations, nor the mighty thrust of shoulders and haunches that lifted them clear into the air, and, worst of all, she didn't know to shut her eyes. When she saw the gash of water racing beneath them she let out a scream of pure terror. Petara snarled, but didn't falter. One impossible leap, a miraculous foothold, then another — a slip, a slither — another leap and they were across.

Kep released her hold and tumbled. She landed face-down, clutching at mud and mosses, but she didn't care. This was insane! She would rather walk! She tried to rise, but the wolvern rounded on her at once, growling and snarling. Kep froze to see the expression in its eyes. The creature's snout was wrinkled and black. The lips were curled back, revealing glistening fangs.

'Get up, you idiot!' Sarin had dismounted swiftly beside her. She saw his elbow lift as he fitted an arrow. 'Hurry!' The arrow whined. Then he sent another across the river to follow it. In a swift sheet of horror she understood. Gooel's bent form was recognisable just for a moment before he dived for cover. He had evaded the defenders!

'Ride! Ride!'

And there was no choice. Ride or die.

Kep tried to remember Kai-tan's instructions: 'Lie low. Mould yourself to her back. Don't show fear.' She closed her eyes to shut out the racing ground, and pressed her cheek into wet fur. It was terrifying to think of Gooel running behind them bent on all fours. How long would it take him to double back to the bridge? Or could he cross the river at the same point they had? She couldn't shake off the image of his strange flat face, no more than she could shake off the tracker himself. He would never give in, Kep knew that. No matter how swiftly the wolvern could run, Gooel would inevitably catch up.

And so they rode for hour upon hour, plunging through dripping woodlands thick with ferns. They chased along shingle beds, then abandoned the lowlands, winding their way higher and higher above the valley floor. When the path left the cover of the trees and faltered up into the ranges, they had no choice but to follow. They picked their way precariously, until at long last they were forced to a halt.

Sarin held up a hand of warning. Up ahead where a rocky spur jutted out, the path bent and disappeared. Sarin slid from his mount and crept forward. Ignoring his warning gesture, Kep dismounted, too. Ash stayed slumped where he was, tucked in against the cliff face. Kep's legs wobbled from riding so long, but she followed Sarin and worked her way out onto the spur. The outcrop gave a view into the next valley and excellent cover, except the footing was loose; any false move might send a shower of rocks careering down. She shuffled forward on her stomach until she could see over the edge.

The rain had eased slightly, but it was still hard to see. Kep could only just make out the tiny figures below. 'Who are they?' she whispered.

Sarin acknowledged her presence with a frown. Sweeping a lock of wet, black hair from his eyes he replied, 'Most likely Calibraen. That's closest. But they could be Zondran raiders. Hard to tell.'

Kep swallowed, her throat tight. She knew they couldn't afford to run into either. Barnham had described the legendary strife between Calibrae and Zondra. They had disputed the fertile valley for centuries and loathed each other, but they distrusted strangers even more. 'They'll sell you out to Calkinon without blinking,' Barnham had warned. 'That's if they don't kill you on sight.' The group seemed to number around thirty or so.

She glanced at Sarin's profile. His cheekbones shone with rain.

'Looks like they're making camp.' He grimaced, backing away from the edge.

Kep studied the path. It was sketchy in places, and, even worse, there was no cover, just tussock and tough grasses — nowhere to hide.

Sarin read her face and nodded. 'The path's too exposed. We can't risk them spotting us. We need to go back.'

'Back? We can't!' Kep bit her lip.

'Yes, we can — just as far as that cleft we passed earlier. We'll rest there until nightfall.' He studied the figures below. 'Maybe they'll move on, but if they don't we can slip past in the dark.'

'No!' she retorted. 'We can't make it along there in the dark! It's impossible!'

He smiled. 'Not for us. Wolvern prefer hunting by night. Trust me.'

She wanted to argue further, but he had already turned back towards Ash and the weary wolvern. She had no choice but to follow.

❧

The cleft was further back than they had remembered, but it did open wide enough to give shelter from the incessant rain.

'We'll be safe here for a bit,' announced Sarin.

Kep held her tongue with difficulty. *Safe? The place was a trap. A stinking trap.* The wolvern lay at the entrance, huge muzzles resting on huge paws. Every now and then one would shake its head or flick an ear. Otherwise they were intently still. Steam rose from their flanks. The place reeked of wet wolf. They all reeked of wet wolf. When she nibbled a biscuit, that tasted of wet wolf, too, but she forced it down.

Ash had curled himself up on the dirt, his head resting on his pack, and Tarlyn nestled in the crook of an arm. Kep wondered fleetingly why the wolvern completely ignored the creature, it was as if she was completely invisible to them, but she was too tired to think. She was even too tired to worry about Ash. She scowled at Sarin's back. He was sitting with the wolvern, staring into the rain. She rubbed her eyes. Sleep was out of the question.

❧

Ash was hauled sweating and trembling from the dream. Sarin gave his shoulder another shake.

'You all right? Ash?'

'Fine. I'm fine,' Ash croaked. He sat up and tucked his hands under his armpits in an effort to stop them shaking. His whole body was running cold with sweat.

Sarin watched him closely for a moment. 'Right. Sorry. Probably the moaning that confused me.' He backed away. 'It's time we moved. If we ride hard, we should make the Enigmata within a few hours.'

Ash grasped at reality, which threatened to swing out of reach at any moment. Time? Where were they? What time? It was late, he realised. Late enough to be deathly dark.

As Sarin roused Kep, Ash willed himself to stay in the present. The drums were still beating, beating in his mind; it took all his strength to keep them back. When Tarlyn nudged his hand, he stroked her silken fur gratefully. Then he experimented with his legs, flexing calves and feet. Every muscle ached, but he rose stiffly.

Kep snapped at Sarin, then staggered to her feet, too.

Brushing off her concern, he concentrated on gathering his things, trying desperately to shut out the rhythm of drums.

❧

Outside, the rain was falling from a pitch sky. Kep strained her eyes behind to where the path must lie. She shivered. How far behind was Gooel? Sarin whispered terse instructions, and the wolvern picked their way forward once more.

Sarin was right. The men in the valley had set up camp. The lights of several fires seemed to float below like islands in the dark. Kep held her breath as they edged along the path, reminding herself that no one else could hear her thumping heart. It seemed unreasonably loud — louder than any sound the wolvern were making. They slunk forward with stealthy ease, assimilated by the darkness. The fires passed slowly to their left. Then, in response to some unheard command from Sarin, the wolvern suddenly began to run.

Swiftly, impossibly swiftly, the race began anew. They traversed the ridge, then wound down through grasslands. The wolvern had to zigzag then, negotiating boulders and rocks that blocked their way. At last the stands of trees grew larger and merged, until they were once more chasing up through dripping woodlands. Still they ran on; climbing, climbing, up into the forest, until finally, almost unbelievably, they stopped.

'What is it? Are we lost?'

'No. This is it.'

Kep stared at the expanse of trees. 'Are you sure?'

'This is it,' repeated Sarin. He slid to the ground, eased his pack from his shoulders and let it fall. 'There. See the markers? They warn travellers not to venture past that point.'

Kep dismounted slowly, not trusting her legs. She stretched her shoulders, frowning. The stones stuck out in a wiggling line like broken teeth sunk into the muddy ground. It would be easy to miss them and walk unwittingly into the Enigmata.

She gritted her teeth. 'Well, are we going in?'

Sarin shook his head. 'Not until dawn. We don't know how the token works yet.'

Kep screwed up her face. She was fed up with his arrogance. It wasn't his decision to make. She turned to Ash. 'What do you think, Ash?'

Ash didn't respond. He was staring at his hands as if he had never seen them before. Then, as they watched, he groaned and sank to the ground.

Not again! Kep moved to his side, followed quickly by Sarin with the lamp.

They shook him, called his name, even slapped his face, but nothing could divert Ash from his fascination with his shaking hands. Tarlyn pushed herself into his lap, but he ignored her, too. Then, without warning, he let out an awful bestial wail. His face contorted. '*Lemar anun!* I didn't know. I didn't know.' He kept groaning the words in a horrible singsong voice. His body shook and rocked.

The trees seemed to lean in, amplifying the sound. The wolvern bristled and raised their hackles. Then the rain began again in earnest.

'That settles it,' said Sarin. 'We need to get him inside the star-shield. Set it up. I'll bring the others in closer.'

'The others?' Kep's voice shook. 'You mean them?'

'Of course.'

'No!' The word exploded, fuelled by a potent mix of exhaustion and fear. 'No! I won't lie down with wolves! Not inside the shield! I don't trust them!' She knew they weren't wolves. She knew her words were ungrateful and insulting. The wolvern had probably saved her life. But sleeping inside the shield with them? It was too much to ask. Far too much.

Sarin had to raise his voice above the pelting rain and Ash's moans. 'Fine,' he answered. 'We'll sleep outside the shield. It's nothing to me. After all, I'm not the one being hunted.'

The way he shrugged riled Kep so much she wanted to punch him. It was so typical! He was so calculating, so … stubborn. So selfish! She snapped back, hoarse with anger. 'Fine! Good idea! You sleep outside! Or leave! In fact, do that! Why don't you just leave? Why are you even here? It's not your quest! We don't … even … We just …' Her words tumbled and tripped senselessly over her tongue. 'I don't care! Sleep out here in the rain, with your kin!'

Chapter 39

ENIGMATA

When Kep opened her eyes, everything ached. Everything: from her eyeballs to her elbows, from the muscles in her shoulders to the joints in her toes. There was a root poking into her back, but she couldn't muster the energy to shift sideways. Her throat was sore and her nose was running. She wondered how long she had slept. Not long enough.

At least the rain had been blown away. It was dark, yet not dark. The moons gleamed as if freshly scrubbed. They were close enough to kiss now, and both shone more radiantly as if their proximity doubled their light. She shivered. Mooncross had begun. It wasn't that she believed the old tales; well, not many of them anyway. She just didn't like the prospect of entering the Enigmata at all, let alone at Mooncross

She craned her neck to look at Ash. The Taelstone was held fast to his chest, and he was frowning in his sleep. She sighed. He was getting worse. She closed her eyes, sending another silent prayer to Telion that Nalina was right and Nirias would be able to help. If he was Azuri, at least he would know what to do with the Taelstone. She knew one thing for sure: the sooner Ash was rid of it the better. Kep stared at the moons for a few more minutes, putting off the moment when she would have to face Sarin. Then she sat up. *Might as well get it over with.*

Outside the shield a small fire was burning in a dugout. Goodness knows how Sarin had managed to light it; everything looked sodden. He was leaning against the black flank of the wolvern he had been riding. She couldn't remember its name. Mirka? Or Mika? One knee was bent, the other leg stretched towards the fire. The firelight flickered on his face. Had he slept? What was he thinking about? It was strange watching him, knowing she was invisible to his eyes. This is what he looked like when no one was looking, when all pretences were dropped. Just a young man staring into a fire. She flushed, suddenly embarrassed, then took a breath and de-activated the shield. Instantly, four pairs of golden eyes snapped her way.

The wolvern pricked up their ears. The black one growled deeply as they all snuffled the air, checking her scent. Then they sank their heads back onto their paws. Sarin returned his attention to the fire.

Kep stowed the dopple-star in her pack, then stood and stretched. She chose a spot at the fire, as close to the wolvern as she dared. They ignored her. Sarin gave her an unreadable look, then tossed a parcel in her direction. 'Parch-cake,' he stated needlessly.

She unwrapped it slowly, looking around. 'Don't you think it's risky having a fire?'

He arched an eyebrow. 'Of course. But these three will give us plenty of warning if anyone comes near. They have the most acute senses of any creature. That's one of the advantages of travelling with wolvern.'

'Well ... That's good then.' She winced inwardly. It wasn't a good start. 'Sarin?' Was that the first time she'd called him by his name? It felt like it. She faltered at the intimacy it created. 'I'm sorry. I didn't mean what I said ... about this not being your quest, and ... Well, you know.' She glanced at the wolvern. 'Anyway. I'm sorry.'

He didn't answer, but she detected a faint nod.

She took a bite of cake to cover her discomfort. It sucked the moisture from her mouth, making it impossible to chew. When she tried to swallow, the crumbs stuck in her throat, making her eyes stream. She grimaced, reaching for her water-pouch, but it held only a few drops.

Sarin laughed. 'Here.'

She accepted the mug of warm liquid and sniffed it.

'Don't worry: if I was going to poison you, I would have done it by now.' She thought she heard him murmur something like 'the gods know I've been tempted', as he filled another cup for himself. 'It's made from lilpen flowers.'

He certainly knew a lot about plants and their properties. She had never even heard of a lilpen flower. She sipped and relaxed a little. The tea was sour but pleasantly fresh. It soothed her throat and assisted enormously in her battle with the parch-cake.

As they stared silently at the fire, Kep found herself thinking again of that disastrous kiss. She blushed at the memory. Fortunately, nothing in Sarin's behaviour suggested he was about to mention the encounter, and if he was happy to act as if it had never happened, then that was fine by her.

She felt the warmth creeping back into her limbs, but when something stirred in the bushes her heart jumped and skittered. Petara flicked an ear, but Sarin didn't so much as blink. Just an ordinary night noise; nothing to worry about.

Kep exhaled the breath she had been holding and took a mouthful of tea, running her eyes over the brooding shapes of trees. She wouldn't normally feel afraid in the forest at night, but this place filled her with uncertainty.

Stealing a look at Sarin's face, she wondered what he was thinking. *Pointless.* She sighed inwardly. How had this strange boy worked his way into their lives? Why was he even here? He didn't need to be — not like her and Ash. They had never really had any choice. They had just fled from one danger to the next. But Sarin? He could have stayed with the clan, with his kin.

What was it about T'al Jazure that drew him, regardless of the danger? She wondered again about his pledge to his grandmother, and her odd attitude to the whole affair. Nalina knew more than she was saying, that was certain. But what? And why T'al Jazure? Was it something to do with Rilka? Maybe Sarin believed T'al Jazure still existed and that his crazy sister would be welcomed there. Kep frowned, remembering the peculiar way Rilka had held Ash's hand. Nothing seemed simple any more, and Sarin was a complete puzzle. She hated that she never knew what he was thinking. She turned her eyes to the dark blanket of the Enigmata and sighed.

It was Ash who broke the long silence by crying out in his sleep. They tensed, ready to leap up. When he settled again, their eyes met in relief.

'He seems worse,' murmured Kep.

'Maybe. What worries me is how he's going to cope in there.' Sarin gestured at the forest.

She scanned the trees. 'Is it really such a bad place?'

'Depends which stories you believe. Most are crazy tales designed to frighten children: two-headed monsters that can gobble you up whole, that sort of thing. Barnham used to tell one story that kept the children up all night. Nalina had to have a word with him.' Sarin grinned for a moment, then his expression became serious again. 'But there are worse things than monsters.' He picked up a small branch and began stripping its bark. 'Some claim the Enigmata runs on different time to the rest of the world, so a day in there might last only minutes out here — or vice versa. Others think it has no time at all, that the whole place is outside

Telion's command.'

Kep frowned. 'Is that even possible?'

'Who knows?' He snapped a piece of twig. 'But it's a strange place all right. Plays funny tricks on your mind until you don't know what's true and what isn't. An easy place to lose yourself.'

'You've been in, haven't you?' When Sarin met her eyes, she caught her breath at his intensity, almost certain of her guess.

He nodded. 'I was wintering with the Natora. Some of us younger ones were hunting, but with no luck. Someone suggested sending a couple of us in, tied together at the end of a rope, just to see what it was like and shoot some game.'

Kep pursed her lips. She thought she could guess who the 'someone' might have been.

'We thought it would be perfectly safe and we would come back with our sacks full.'

'Well, what was it like?' Kep breathed.

'Hard to describe. Confusing. It was like being in a dream, or a memory. Or a vision of the future maybe.' His eyes rested momentarily on Ash. 'Or all of those things at once.'

'What happened?'

'I thought I saw— It doesn't matter, my thoughts were drifting, that's all. Then I heard shouting. It was Fenner, my companion. He was screaming. Crying. His voice snapped me out my thoughts, made me remember where I was. Then I realised he was trying to undo the knots that bound us together. He was struggling and shouting that he could see his little brother. He tore free, but I grabbed his jerkin and tugged the rope to signal to the others to haul us out.'

'But what about his brother?' Kep asked, horrified. 'You didn't just leave him there?'

Sarin shook his head slowly. 'His brother had been dead for more than three turns of Eldar.' He tossed the last piece of twig into the fire. It flared in the embers.

'You can't trust anything in the Enigmata. Some things are as real as anything, and some things ... they just aren't.' He seemed about to say more, then he shrugged. 'That's what worries me about Ash. He's not doing so well recognising reality as it is.'

'Well,' said Kep slowly, 'it certainly sounds like a good place to hide something.'

'Like a secret city?' Sarin nodded. 'Yes, but it's a good place to lose things, too.'

He pulled the token from inside his tunic and lifted it over his head. They watched it spinning at the end of its chain until he stopped it with a finger.

'Do you think it will work?'

'Nalina does. So, yes, I think so.'

Kep nodded. Sarin's grandmother's opinion certainly held weight. She hadn't exactly been clear, though. All she had said was 'concentrate on the vision of the Stone and it will lead you'. That was apparently all Nirias had told her.

'Can I hold it?'

He nodded and dropped it into her palm. It felt warm from where it had lain against his skin, and unexpectedly heavy. The metal was dark, as if it needed a good clean.

'Strange design,' she murmured. The moons were overlapped, one full and the other a crescent. '

He nodded. 'And see the two layers? It almost looks as if the top one is designed to move. But they don't budge. I've cleaned it up and oiled it ... I can't work it out.'

Kep tried not to smile; it was the first time she had heard him admit defeat. She handed it back. 'Perhaps it won't work until we're inside the Enigmata.'

'Perhaps. We can test it out as soon as it's light. I have a rope in my pack. You could stay here and hold the end while I go in.'

She nodded, but couldn't help thinking that his rope initiatives hadn't gone so well in the past. What if the token simply didn't work? It didn't bear thinking about. She lifted her chin. 'The gods will help us. We've made it this far, and they'll guide us through — somehow.'

Sarin didn't reply. There was a new intensity in the silence all of a sudden. Kep reached for her water-pouch, not remembering it was empty. She shook out the last drop and replaced the bung.

She saw Sarin watching her from the corner of his eye. 'There's a good spring where you can fill up. Here, take this.' He tossed her the billycan.

She caught it in surprise. 'What for?'

He shrugged. 'Might make some more tea. The spring's over there, through those ferns and around to the left, past the white trunks.' He pointed. 'Don't go past the stones.'

She sighed, wanting to point out that she wasn't entirely stupid, but she was too tired to bother.

The little clearing was easy to find in the moonlight, and the spring gurgled gently, betraying its location. But there was something else there, too. Kep's heart leapt. She nearly laughed aloud with the joy of it. An altar to Narsis, in the shape of a cupped hand! She knelt and stroked the stone, not believing the miracle. She shook her head wonderingly. He had known. He had even cleared the mouldy leaves away. There was a pile to one side; only a few muddy smears remained. Why hadn't he said? She would never work him out.

Using the billycan, she swilled the remaining debris away and filled the bowl, smiling at the way the water danced. The gentle actions of the ritual soothed her mind. Then, when all was ready, she retrieved the offerings she had kept next to her heart for so long, safe inside her tunic. The flowers were dried but warmly fragrant. A white feather she had kept since the Tanglewood, an offering for Braig's soul-flight, was flattened but not broken. She brought her fingertips together to form the sacred triangle and closed her eyes.

❧

Kep knew something was wrong as soon as she returned to the fire. The sweet feeling of peace evaporated instantly. Sarin was on his feet. The wolvern were tense and bristling. Tarlyn had abandoned Ash and was perched on a boulder, the ruff on her neck quivering. They were all staring in the same direction, smelling the air.

Sarin turned swiftly. 'We need to move. Now.' He started pushing in the walls of the fire pit with his feet.

Kep grabbed her pack. 'Why? What is it?'

'Company. We have time, but not much.'

'Gooel?'

'Maybe.' He glanced at the wolvern. 'My guess is a larger group.' He began sweeping leaves over the ground with a branch. 'It won't hurt to create a bit of confusion just in case they *are* tracking us.'

Kep began rolling up items that had been hung over bushes to dry, and tried not to panic. They had lost their opportunity to check whether the token worked or not. 'We head into the forest, then?'

Sarin nodded. 'They probably won't follow us in there. Dawn isn't far off anyway.'

Kep shook Ash roughly. 'Ash!' He groaned and began to stir.

Up until then the wolvern had virtually ignored their movements. Now they whined gently. Suddenly they wheeled about and surrounded Sarin. Kep watched as they dipped their heads towards him. He fondled their ears and ran his hands over their chests, murmuring words she couldn't hear.

Ash staggered to his feet, confused. 'What is it? What's happening?'

'Someone's coming. We have to move.' As she spoke, the wolvern bounded off; with Mika leading, they headed north through the trees and in moments were out of sight.

'Where are they going?' she asked Sarin.

'To find the Natora and join their families,' he answered tersely. 'They'd have borne us willingly into the Enigmata, but it was too great a risk.' His face was stony, as if daring her to disagree. 'With any luck our pursuers might be misled and follow their tracks.'

She didn't answer. Gooel wouldn't be misled. The only question was whether he could track them in the Enigmata.

Minutes later they stood ready, at the edge of the markers. Kep tightened the knot at her wrist with her teeth. They had decided to rope themselves together so at least they wouldn't lose each other. Ash was bound in the middle. Kep wasn't at all sure Ash had understood their hurried explanation. His eyes had that distant quality, and he was swaying as if he was having trouble with his balance. Kep noticed that he gripped the Taelstone in his free hand, but she held her tongue.

The plan was to head straight for exactly one hundred strides; by then they would be well inside the cover of the forest and perhaps it would be more obvious how the token was supposed to work.

'Ready to find the lost city of T'al Jazure, then?' Sarin twisted his mouth ironically. 'Reckless,' he muttered as he stepped past the markers.

They had walked only a few paces before Kep started feeling dizzy. There was a difference in the air pressure, as if she had cupped her hands over her ears. The further they went, the more she had the feeling the forest itself was moving, shifting around them. If she fixed her gaze on one spot she felt better — except that everything at the edge of her vision seemed to shimmer. If she looked away and then back again, everything looked different, only she couldn't tell what had changed. Maybe it was just a trick of the light. The moonlight was cutting through the trees in long, bright shafts, making everything seem strange.

Then, well before the hundred paces were up, she heard Sarin laugh. He turned. 'Look!' He grinned, holding out his palm. The token was glowing brightly: one moon shone silver, the other an iridescent blue. And there was another change. While the silver crescent remained fixed on the base plate, the full moon had lifted away and was hovering. When Sarin moved, it swung about, as if tethered by an invisible thread. Experimenting, he kept his arm straight and turned his body. The blue moon curved, tracing an arc about the centre of the token. Sarin kept turning until the two moons were perfectly overlapped. They gasped. 'Mooncross!'

Before their eyes, a silver arrow appeared, etched upon the face of the full moon.

'It's a wayfinder! We just have to keep them lined up!'

As Kep laughed delightedly, she realised Ash was laughing, too. It was so unexpected; she hadn't heard him laugh for so long. He looked her straight in the eye for the first time in ages and smiled. She smiled back. Perhaps it was going to be all right.

⁂

Ash had felt the change as soon as he passed the markers. The beating drums and blaring trumpets were suddenly subdued. With every step, the clash of the battle song faded, until all he could hear was the wind in the trees and the crunch of their footsteps. He stumbled forward, tears of relief springing in his eyes. Tarlyn made low chirruping noises near his ear. Did she feel it, too? All of a sudden he didn't have to fight to keep the visions away — they were fading on their own.

The further they went into the forest, the quieter it became, until at last he could hear himself think. He had always thought that was a dumb expression: 'hearing yourself think'. Now he knew exactly what it meant.

It was wonderful to find that the token worked, but he suddenly understood: it didn't matter. As they made their way deeper into the Enigmata he started to listen. He knew it would take time to focus his exhausted mind, but he had time. They walked, and they rested and they walked again. And all the time, Ash listened. He knew what he was listening for now, and after a while he found it: the melody that ran beneath all the others. It had been there all along, he just hadn't understood.

Kep was starting to think the forest was trying to suffocate her. The further they went, the harder it became to breathe. She tried to focus her thoughts on the Stone, but that only worked for a while. Her mind kept drifting. So instead she forced herself to think of happy memories: milk splashing into a bucket; the smell of a warm udder; dipping cheeses into melted wax; or picking berries with Pan. It was astonishing how clear the images were.

When she first noticed the figure walking beside her, the observation came to her mind only vaguely, as if it was part of her daydream. Then her mind snapped sharply to attention. *Someone was there!* She turned to look. Nothing. She swallowed hard and kept walking. *Nothing there. There's nobody there.* She repeated the words as she watched Tarlyn's tail swishing across Ash's shoulders. But before long she felt it again — the definite sensation that someone was there, striding along beside her. She turned her head sharply. This time she caught a glimpse and a whirl of blue cloth. It was a young woman with dark hair, she was sure of it ... and there was something familiar ... Then the figure was gone. Just her mind playing tricks.

Sarin was setting a quick pace, as agreed, and they walked on until the sun dazzled through the trees, casting light onto the forest floor in golden splashes. As Kep followed its dance over the foliage, her eyes discovered a thin track. They had passed many such paths, probably made by animals. Her eyes were drawn irresistibly down this one — and there he was. Just standing there! Waiting for her. His arms were folded across his chest, his shoulders at that familiar angle. He seemed older somehow, but his grin was exactly the same. *Braig!* She only just stopped herself from crying out his name. *Not real.* He's not real, she told herself. But then he laughed delightedly and held out his hand. The urge to run to him was too strong. She took the first step.

Immediately the image dissolved and he was gone. Grief struck hard, tipping the world. The trees spun. She was falling. A young woman ran; the blue skirt of her tunic flaring out behind her. She was weeping as she ran, her dark curls tossing about her face. With a stab of realization, Kep understood. Her heart banged with panic. She stared into her own fierce eyes and saw them flood with black. The world whirled and writhed, then shattered. Then there was nothing.

⁂

'Kep.'

She gazed at the hands covering her own, but it took several moments to connect the image with the pressure of his fingers.

'It's all right, Kep. Whatever you saw, it's gone. It's not real. Just a bad dream. It's not real.'

She gasped. A tear splashed from somewhere onto the hands which held hers so gently.

'You're safe. Safe with us. With your friends. Look at me.'

She lifted her head and found herself looking into a pair of worried grey eyes.

Ash?

⁂

The three of them sat in a tight circle. It was Ash's idea: it was easier to ignore the shifting trees that way.

'Are you all right?' asked Sarin. Kep caught Ash's eye and pulled a face, but she nodded.

'Good.' He hesitated before adding: 'You don't have to tell us what you saw. It probably wasn't real.'

Probably? When Kep looked at him, wide-eyed, Sarin added quickly, 'I mean, it's a weird place.' He smoothed his hands over his black hair, then looked at Ash. 'It seems to agree with you, though, Ash.'

Ash nodded slowly. 'It's easier to cope with the Song now. I don't know why, it was getting hard to shut out the visions before,' he admitted. He gave Kep what he hoped was a reassuring smile. 'But it's quieter here.'

Sarin shrugged. 'Maybe there's less history.' Ash had the feeling the Song was more complicated than that, but it did make a strange sort of sense. 'In fact,' added Sarin, 'if there's no time here, maybe there isn't any history at all.'

Ash caught Kep's dismayed expression and shook his head. 'I don't think this place is outside of time, otherwise how could we be talking?' He gestured at the sky. 'The sun is moving, just as it always does.' He wanted to take her hand again, to reassure her, but it would have been awkward. 'Don't worry, Kep, it's not far now.'

'Not far? How could you know?' Her bottom lip was trembling and her eyes shone blue with tears.

He flinched. He had spoken without thinking. 'I don't know. Just a guess, I suppose.' He couldn't explain how he knew. He just did. What was he supposed to say? That Rilka had shown him something after all? That as soon as he had remembered the Tree he had known? It had been so difficult to hold onto that knowledge, so hard to remember, with all the shouting and fighting and blood. But now it seemed obvious. The Tree was at the heart of the Song: it was the beginning and the end, an anchor in the chaos. Everything swung around that point.

And he had been right, too, months ago, when he had tried to teach Braig the verses. 'Think of it like a map' he had said, and he had been right! But what sense would that make to anyone else? What was he supposed to say? 'Oh, by the way, I've worked out that the Song's a map. Well, more like a wayfinder really, with intricate patterns and layers. It could lead us to T'al Jazure, if only I knew how to read it.'

Knowing the Song worked like a map didn't mean he understood it, didn't mean he could control it, didn't mean it didn't scare him witless ... He was just slightly less terrified than before.

He realised they were both still staring at him and shrugged. 'I don't know how I know. I just do. It's not far.'

— END OF PART 2 —

— PART 3 —
SEEKERS

Chapter 40

SEEKERS

'This is it.'

'Are you sure? It's so small.' Kep released her wrist from its bonds, let the rope fall to the ground, and joined the others on the dais. The Stone was nothing like what she had been picturing. She had expected an obelisk, like the ones in Mildaresh, or something more impressive anyway. This was just a large ball held by three claws upon a simple pedestal. The enormous circular platform it stood on was far more remarkable, though. It was deeply inscribed in complex sections, like a massive stone dial.

Ash nodded, his eyes shining. 'This is it.' As he placed both hands on the Stone, Tarlyn leapt from his shoulder and wove herself about his legs.

Kep frowned at Sarin. 'What do you think?'

Sarin examined the token again. 'I suppose it must be,' he said looking about.

Kep didn't like the place. It felt peculiar. There was something odd about the light, and the way their voices seemed to ring. She scanned the cliffs beyond the dais. They were craggy and pock-marked, dotted with patches of vegetation. 'There's no one here.'

Sarin's eyes were flitting constantly across the cliff face, too. A bird somewhere above made a harsh croaking sound, which echoed weirdly. 'This place is too open,' he frowned. 'We should take cover.'

Kep nodded her swift agreement.

Ash hadn't moved. All his attention was on the Stone, almost as if he was listening for something.

'I'll get him,' said Sarin quietly.

As Kep jumped down from the platform she was struck by the sweet fragrance of herbs and saw that the ground was completely covered by a rambling plant with tiny leaves and puffy blue flowers. She bent to pluck a piece. It released a strong herbal scent when bruised between her fingers, making her even hungrier. It would be parch-cakes again. Still, at least they could gather berries. She could see some bushes from where she stood — it wasn't far.

Sarin was still urging Ash to move away from the Stone. It wouldn't hurt to start collecting a few. She counted the steps from the edge of the dais. Sixteen. Sixteen long strides in the direction of the sun, and easily within shouting distance of the others. Nothing stirred when she listened carefully, so she stepped towards a shining cluster and, avoiding the thorns, grasped a berry with her fingertips. It came away easily. Plump and soft, it burst in her mouth releasing a flood of sweet juice. She began picking in earnest then, folding her shirt into a sling to hold the fruit. The best ones would be tucked beneath the foliage, out of the reach of birds. She worked her way methodically around the bushes, stripping the fruit as she went.

When she heard them coming she tilted her head. That wasn't Sarin — the footfalls were far too noisy for him. Ash, then? She frowned, suddenly uncertain. Some instinct made her reach for her knife. *Please. Let it be Ash.* Somehow she already knew it wasn't.

When a man broke through the trees her eyes flew wide open. He was dressed in the black and red uniform of Calkinon, but that wasn't what made her heart freeze. A wave of dread surged through her and the berries bounced unheeded to the ground. His eyes were black. Pure black, just gaping holes of nothing.

She tried to raise the knife. It fell from her hand. The soldier made no gesture, only his lips moved. His voice resonated strangely, like many voices spliced into a single thread.

Join us. Black snakes writhed in her mind. *Kep of Mildaresh, join us!*

⁂

Kep's scream reverberated in the clearing. In a single bound, Sarin was at the edge of the dais, Ash close behind.

'Where did she go?'

'Kep!'

Tarlyn hissed and raised her spines. They turned. Two figures were pushing through the trees. Calkinon soldiers. Their faces were blank, and there were dark pits where their eyes should be. *Men with holes for eyes. Oh, Rilka.*

Ash reeled with icy fear. He felt again the sensation from that awful encounter under the mountain.

The soldiers didn't move. They didn't speak. They just stood there, blocking the way.

Kep screamed again, a desperate drawn-out sound.

Sarin drew his knife, cursing that his bow was unstrung.

Then came a horrible, dragging cry, like an animal being tortured. The soldiers suddenly turned and moved toward the sound, in fearful unison.

Sarin's knife flew and lodged itself in the thigh of the closest soldier — he just pulled it out, let it drop and continued on.

Ash lunged in a desperate tackle, grappling at the waist of the other. The man staggered momentarily, then simply peeled Ash off and hurled him against the rim of the stone circle.

'Hey! Hey!' Sarin flicked his wrist and sent a rock flying. It connected with the back of a head, but with no effect. The soldiers marched on.

Launching himself, Sarin rolled and caught up his knife. Then, at the sound of a sudden familiar whine, he ducked instinctively. An arrow whizzed over his head, followed by a second.

The leader toppled and fell. As his companion turned, a third arrow plunged into his neck, then another hit his chest. Unbelievably, both soldiers lay dead, blue-shafted arrows buried deep in their flesh.

Sarin whirled and looked up. The cliffs were still and silent.

He raced to Ash's side, keeping low. Ash groaned, dazed, but his eyes were open. *Didn't look too bad.* 'Stay here. I'll find Kep.'

Sarin ran with his head down, expecting to be hit at any moment. 'Kep! Kep! Where are you?'

'Here! I'm here.'

The answer was faint, but close, much closer than he had thought. He covered the ground in a blur, then stopped dead, taking in the scene.

Kep was kneeling in the undergrowth, and he had to circle the body of a third soldier to reach her. The vegetation had been smashed and flattened all about. Kep's arms were covered in blood.

'Sarin! Help! We have to help him.'

There, sprawled on the ground, was Gooel, his chest soaked in blood.

The knife Kep held in her hand was shaking as wildly as her voice. 'I pulled it out, but I don't think I should have. There's so much blood! Help, Sarin. We have to do something. He's going to die.'

Sarin knelt and put his hand on her trembling shoulder. 'Kep ... This is

Gooel. We're not going to save him. That'd be stupid. He's been tracking you for one reason: to kill you. He brought these soldiers. He must have done — it's the only explanation. We let him die. If we don't, he'll just keep hunting you.'

The snout moaned.

'No, Sarin!' Kep's eyes were wide and frightened. 'He saved me from ... from that.' She cast a terrified look at the body, as if she thought it might rise up again at any moment. 'Gooel shot it with darts, one stuck in its neck, but they didn't work quickly enough. It just kept coming. It had no eyes, just black pits ... black pits ...' Her voice wavered. She was shaking uncontrollably.

'Gooel shot it? Are you sure? He wasn't aiming at you?' As Sarin studied the tracker's ugly face, Gooel moved his lips slightly.

'No! I know it sounds crazy, but he protected me. He tried to fight it off. But the soldier — it stabbed him.' She shuddered. 'Sarin, please! Please help him!'

Her eyes were desperate.

Sarin hesitated, calculating. He shook his head slowly. 'I'll do what I can. But you go back: Ash needs you, he's hurt.' He paused. 'Get him to cover. I'll do what I can here.' She was moving already. 'Kep ... leave that.' He relieved her of the knife and watched her go.

Sarin hesitated for a moment, staring at the grotesque face of the tracker. He turned the knife slowly in his hand. A quick twist was all it would take. That would be the clever thing to do. Put an end to the hunt. She would understand that, once she had recovered from the shock.

The snout groaned. His body gave another spasm. Sarin frowned deeply, thinking. Then he made his decision. He pulled his tunic over his head and stripped off his undershirt. Ignoring the cold breeze against his bare skin, he ripped the material and used it to staunch the blood. Applying pressure directly to the wound with one hand, he used the other to locate his phial of candrel essence. He pulled the stopper out with his teeth, then dripped a couple of drops into the tracker's mouth. He had no idea whether it even worked on snouts. With any luck it might kill him.

The effect was extraordinary and immediate. Gooel spluttered, then gurgled, then opened his eyes.

Sarin put a hand on his chest. 'Don't speak. Lie still. Save your energy.'

Gooel paid absolutely no attention to the advice. 'No kill.' His voice croaked: amphibian, inhuman.

Sarin pushed more firmly on the wound, trying to stem the bleeding. 'If it was up to me, you'd be dead already. But no, I'm not going to kill you. Just be still.'

Gooel winced, his brow creasing into deep folds. His lips moved again. 'Tell girl. Gooel no kill.'

His eyelids closed halfway, like shutters over the strange lenses of his huge eyes. 'Gooel no kill girl,' he gasped. 'No kill. Message. Boy ... tell her ...' The tracker's hand went to his chest. His long, pale fingers pawed at his clothes. Fluid gurgled horribly in his throat, and he choked.

Sarin frowned, wiping the blood away. 'Be still. You're just making it worse.'

But Gooel was insistent. 'Mess ... Message.'

Sarin followed the movement of the searching fingers. 'What? Here?' He spied the corner of something yellow and drew out a small, creased envelope. It was sealed with green wax. He frowned. 'Who's it from?'

'Message. Mata ... pharni.'

As Sarin studied the seal, Gooel let out another ghastly gurgle. Blood and saliva bubbled in a stream from the corner of his mouth. Yet still he struggled to speak. His fingers raked at Sarin's clothes. Fighting his repugnance, Sarin leaned closer to catch the creature's final words.

'Message. Girl's boy ... lives. Not dead. Boy lives.'

Sarin rocked back on his heels, staring at the lifeless tracker. His eyes narrowed. *Which boy?*

There wasn't time to puzzle it out. He pulled his tunic back over his head, paused for a long moment, then slid the envelope into the secret lining near his heart.

❧

It seemed to take Kep a long time to get back to the dais; it felt as if she was racing down a tunnel of trees that extended before her just as fast as she could run. When she reached Ash, he was already struggling to sit up. Blood streamed from his knee. She rushed forward to help. 'How bad is it?'

Ash didn't answer; he was gaping at the body of the nearest soldier. When Kep saw the protruding arrows, she put her hand to her mouth. 'Did Sarin ... ?'

'No, it wasn't Sarin. Archers. Up there.'

Wide-eyed, she scanned the trees. 'We should take cover.'

He shook his head. 'They weren't aiming at us. They could have hit me easily. They were targeting the soldiers — if that's what they were.'

He was shaking as much as she was, and his injured knee was bleeding freely. Kep stared at the hanging flap of skin. 'That needs binding.'

Turning his head, he noticed she was covered in blood. 'Kep! What happened? And where's Sarin?'

She started to answer, but the words dried in her mouth. A loud crashing sound was coming from the base of the cliffs. Someone, or something, was breaking through the undergrowth.

As they scrambled to their feet, two figures burst from the bushes and charged across the dais. Dark cloaks swung out behind them like inky sails. Both wore masks. One wielded a long sword; the other brandished a pair of curved daggers, a longbow bumping wildly over his shoulder. 'The third! The third soldier!' he shouted. 'Where is he?'

The one with the sword leapt down to inspect the bodies.

Their interrogator's eyes glinted through holes in his mask. 'Quickly! Where is he?'

'Dead. He's dead,' Kep stammered. She pointed at the bushes.

'Make sure of it!' The man's partner ran to obey. 'How? How did he die?' The words came in an urgent rasp. The straggly grey beard that flowed beneath his mouth accentuated the movement of his lips. 'Speak, girl!'

Kep answered shakily. 'My tracker killed him. He shot him with a dart.' She sensed Ash's astonished reaction beside her, but now wasn't the time to explain, even if she could have.

Moments later the other warrior returned, escorting Sarin at swordpoint. His arms were bare and he was wiping his hands on a bloodied cloth. When Kep caught his eye, he shook his head. Then, to her surprise, he stepped forward and embraced Ash with sudden emotion. 'Thank the gods you're all right!' He held on tightly, slapping Ash on the back several times before releasing him.

Ash looked startled. 'You, too,' he answered.

Their captors ignored the exchange. 'Definitely dead, Jaibari?' demanded the one with the beard.

'Utterly and definitely.' Kep blinked. She hadn't expected a female voice. 'There's a dead snout, too.'

The woman pulled off her mask. Her skin was smooth and dark, her eyes swept up at the corners, and her hair fell about her shoulders in a curtain of glistening braids. She wore a thin, silver band across her brow. Kep only just stopped herself gasping. She had never seen such a fierce-looking young woman. She dropped her eyes when the girl glared back.

The man undid his mask too, revealing a face worn by the care of many winters. Like his partner, he wore a thin silver band across his brow. Kep glanced at Ash. *Could this be Nirias?*

The man ran his eyes over Sarin. 'Is he armed?'

'Not any more.'

'Good. Search the others, Jaibari.'

There was no point resisting, or even thinking of making a run for it. Where would they go anyway? The woman was thorough in her search. She relieved Kep of her knife, pausing only momentarily to wonder at its strange design, then she turned to Ash. Kep held her breath while she emptied his pockets. After several moments she held up her hands. 'Nothing.' Kep noticed that Ash slipped his hand into a side pocket. His look of sheer panic made her heartbeat skip. *Where was the Taelstone?*

The old man thrust his daggers into sheaths on his belt. Then, to their surprise, he made a formal bow. 'Do not be alarmed. We mean you no harm — in fact, quite the opposite. We've been watching for you.' His face became a map of creases when he smiled. 'Please accept my apology for our rudeness. Dark times do not admit courtesy, I'm afraid, even in the case of Seekers. But now perhaps introductions are in order.' He waited expectantly.

Sarin replied for all of them. 'I am Sarin of the Aurum. My friends are Ash and Kep.' Kep noticed he didn't mention where they were from. The man's lips parted, but he didn't speak. When the pause lengthened, Sarin folded his arms and raised an eyebrow. 'We seek a man by the name of Nirias.'

To their discomfort, the young woman laughed scornfully. 'Look at their faces! They think it's you! They think you're Nirias!' When the man frowned a warning, her laughter subsided, but her smirk lingered.

'I am not Nirias, but it is a frequent mistake, to the great amusement of my young friend here.' He shook his head. 'I am Daska, and this irreverent young woman is Jaibari. But do not despair, we will bear you to the man you seek. It's a long climb, though,' he glanced at Ash's bleeding knee, 'and you are injured. You must rest first.' He cast his eyes over the fallen men, then gave Kep a quizzical look. 'Besides,' he added, 'there are questions to be answered before we proceed.'

Was it true? Would these people really take them to Nirias? It seemed too much to hope for. Kep took Ash by the elbow and guided him to the edge of the circle. His face was pinched and drawn. Sarin took his other arm — rather unnecessarily, she thought. They settled him on the ground against the stonework.

If she hadn't turned her head at precisely the right time, Kep would have missed Sarin's wink and how Ash's face relaxed into an expression of pure relief. In a split second she understood. She had thought there was something odd about that fumbling embrace! It had been so unlike Sarin. Of course! He had guessed they would be searched, because the woman had already searched him. The Taelstone was safe, wrapped in that bloodied rag somewhere in one of his many pockets. She had to marvel at the smoothness of his deception. By Telion, he was a sly one!

Daska made a quick inspection of the gash on Ash's knee, then motioned to his companion. 'Jaibari, I believe you need some practice dressing wounds.' He smiled at Ash. 'Don't worry, she's gentler than she looks. You can call your pet back, too, if you like. We won't harm it.'

Jaibari seemed less than impressed at the request, but she dealt with the wound methodically enough. Ash noticed that she kept one eye on Daska as she worked. When she was nearly finished the binding, she spoke in a low voice. 'I suppose you're looking for T'al Jazure.' She looked full into his face, her dark eyes flashing. 'Well, it's not here. It's lost. So forget it. Only thing here is the League, and you sure don't look like warriors to me.' She yanked the ends of the bandage into a tight knot. 'You're done.'

'Thanks,' Ash answered weakly. She had already turned her back.

Daska reclaimed his blue-shafted arrows with respectful care. When he had finished, he laid the dead men gently on their backs and folded their arms onto their chests. As he smoothed their hair and closed their eyes they heard him murmuring words of prayer. His face was grim when he stood, the bloodied arrows in his hands.

'Are they yours?' asked Kep quietly.

'Yes.' He sighed, wiping them clean. 'I killed these men.'

Sarin frowned. 'They are men then?'

'Yes. Men with families, with people who loved them. Their bodies will be taken to the edge of the Enigmata so they can be claimed.' Daska shook his head. 'But when I shot them they were far from human. Nulls, we call them. Agents of the Melk.'

Ash caught Sarin's eye. It seemed the no-name had a name at last. 'What is the Melk?' he asked hesitantly.

Daska held up a hand. 'I must see to the other body first — and the tracker. Then we will speak further.'

❧

Jaibari dumped a parcel of dried meat and a broken hunk of dark bread before them. Then she turned her back and began pacing to and fro on the stone dais, her hand restless on the hilt of her sword. Kep stared at the bread. It looked wholesome enough, but, despite scrubbing her hands and arms with water and sweet herbs, she couldn't remove the stench of blood. The others didn't touch the food either. They sat in silence, waiting.

After a murmured conversation with his companion, Daska joined them at last. Jaibari went off to sulk at the base of the cliff as the old man lowered himself to sit on a flattish rock. His boots were caked with mud and cracked by long wear. The lines on his face told a story of long journeys fraught with hardship. His cloak wasn't black after all, but a very dark blue. He surveyed them in silence for a long time, his expression grave, until at last he gave a weary sigh.

'I will tell you a little of what you ask, you are entitled to that much. But you must learn the rest from Nirias. The Melk has been his life's study. Nirias is our leader — the head of the League.'

Sarin tilted his head. 'The League? What's that?'

'The League has one terrible purpose: to find and eliminate the Melk.' Daska stared hard at Kep. 'Perhaps you already know of what I speak?' She blinked, not knowing how to reply.

'We know nothing of this thing,' Sarin interjected smoothly. 'We're hoping you will tell us.'

It was hard to tell whether Daska was convinced by Sarin's earnest expression, but he gave a slow nod.

'Much of what we know about the Melk is uncertain. We do know that it is a single consciousness made up of many parts. It has no bodily mass, but is able to inhabit human hosts.'

He shook his head, making his beard waggle. The effect might have been comical if his expression hadn't been so serious. 'It creates colonies, if you will, all linked by a shared energy, and it grows by feeding on negative feelings like hate, jealousy or fear. The stronger those feelings, the stronger the Melk's hold. Finally, it becomes powerful enough to take complete control of its human hosts. At that point it can't help but reveal itself: the host's eyes turn black, utterly black. Any residue of humanity is nullified. That's why we call them nulls.'

The long, dismayed silence was broken by Ash, asking quietly whether the Melk could move of its own accord. Daska gave him a sharp look, as if the question was wholly unexpected. 'Yes,' he frowned. 'It can move independently of its human hosts, but it does so very rarely. When it does swarm, it has the ability to move very swiftly. The few people who have witnessed this event describe it as a spinning tower of darkness.' Daska took in their exchanged glances and paused. His eyes narrowed. 'That is all I can tell you for now. But one question must be answered before we go any further.' He leaned forward and fixed his eyes upon Kep. 'What makes you so special, Kep?'

'Special?' Kep hugged her knees to her chest. 'What do you mean?'

'The soldiers were completely in the thrall of the Melk. We could tell that, even from a distance. The way they moved betrayed them. Their eyes were black pits, weren't they?' When they all nodded, he continued: 'In such a case the Melk usually attacks. It delights in causing pain. Don't forget, it's sustained by negative energy. But occasionally the Melk has another purpose.' Kep squirmed beneath his searching gaze. 'The nulls ignored your friends, because the Melk was focused on one thing. It wanted you, Kep. It wanted you to join it. What I'd like to know is: why?'

'It's true,' she told the others miserably. 'It knew my name. It spoke to me.' When Daska repeated the question, she lowered her lashes. 'I don't know.'

Finally Sarin let out an impatient sigh. 'Because she's Kep, of course.' He gave Daska a long stare. 'She's Kep. Kep the Valiant.'

Chapter 41

THE TAELSTAUN

Daska's thoughts were black indeed as he strode alone into the labyrinth. The Seekers would be safe at the north mouth where he had left them under Jaibari's watch. For now, at least. This place was the safest of the League's refuges, a defensive anthill of secret ways, sculpted by water, slow time and ancient toil. His feet knew the path well; he no longer needed to watch for hidden markings, no longer counted the turns in fear of becoming lost.

He passed a line of spyholes, then three more set in a cluster followed by a sharp turn. Ducking into a simple niche, he felt for the ledge and hauled himself up. Painfully, bones aching, he edged upwards, until the chimney-tunnel opened onto the uppermost maze. He followed the hidden path that chased along inside the north face until he reached the little alcove. As a young man he had scorned the need for the bench set there. Now he eased himself down, grateful to whomever had taken the care and time to chisel it from the stone. A deep fissure blessed the place with light, and a draught that disturbed his beard with its sweet breath. He sat there for a while: his head bowed, hands on knees, willing the searing pain in his chest to lessen, waiting for his wheezing breath to quieten — and wondering how best to deliver the news.

At last Daska sighed and continued his journey, up a narrow stairway and on through a curved passageway. Like the rooms beyond, it was lit entirely by dazzle tubes that spilled light onto the walls in dappled patterns. Daska still thought of them by the name he had invented as a youngster; somehow there had never been an opportunity to ask Nirias their real name, or how they worked. He paused again when he reached the door. It was perfectly round and ingeniously fitted: another secret within a maze of secrets. He knew from experience not to waste time and the skin on his knuckles by knocking. He banged its dense surface several times with the hilt of his knife, then pushed. The door pivoted to admit him.

The room beyond looked as if it had been ransacked. Every book, every map, every chart had been disturbed; they lay in great untidy piles on the tables and on the floor. The shelves were devastated. Only a few volumes remained, like the last leaves on an autumn tree.

The agent of all this ruin stood under the light of a clear-lamp, poring over a black notebook. Daska knew what it contained: endless pages of tiny script, detailed maps and intricate diagrams; he had peeked into one once out of curiosity. He glanced at the tray of food and frowned: it was untouched.

Nirias lifted his head with the air of a man emerging from deep thought. His expression was haggard, his eyes sunken from lack of sleep. Acknowledging Daska's presence, he tossed the journal onto a pile to join the others, then held out a thin ribbon of parchment. 'There's news, my old friend. A swift came from Mildaresh. It is as we thought.'

Daska read the simple message. *Swarm located. Nexus confirmed, presence strong.* Nirias leaned wearily over the huge table, then stabbed his finger at the map. 'Why, Daska? Why would the Melk be drawn there? Of all places, why Mildaresh?'

Daska cleared his throat and swallowed. Before answering, he collected the food tray. Pushing the maps to one side, he placed it deliberately on the table. Nirias frowned sideways at it, but he stood upright and stretched, easing his shoulders. 'Yes, my old friend.' He attempted a smile. 'You are right of course.' He took a swig from the mug and wiped his mouth. Only as he tore a piece from the loaf did his shrewd mind catch up. 'You're back early,' he observed. He froze with sudden realisation. 'Seekers?'

The expression in his eyes made Daska's heart ache. 'Yes. Three.'

'Three!' Nirias discarded the bread and stepped forward eagerly. 'Tell me.'

Daska sighed. 'They're young. Too young. A girl and two boys. One is promising. He's from the Aurum, one of the Haelrum clans.' He was surprised by the fleeting expression on his leader's face and the manner of his reply.

'I know the Aurum.'

'He bore this token. Claims it was given to him by his chieftain.'

Nirias received the pendant and held it on the flat of his fingers, gazing as if recalling some lost memory. Daska shuffled his feet. *This was going to be impossible.* 'The second boy isn't much to look at. Frail-looking — in body and mind, I fear. He'd be a burden, that's my bet.' He shrugged when Nirias held up a firm hand. 'He doesn't look much like a League warrior, that's all I'm saying.'

'Nor did you, my friend.' The reproof was gentle but pointed. 'And the girl?'

'The girl ...' Daska blew out a long sigh. It was his duty to make the point, even though it would make no difference. 'Nirias ... The girl is something we simply can't afford. She is hunted — and not just by Calkinon.'

Nirias didn't bother trying to mask his impatience. 'Tell me, Daska!'

'She's the slave girl. The one at the heart of the uprising, the one who has exasperated Calkinon by remaining free. "Kep the Valiant" the people call her.' Daska groaned inwardly at the expression dawning on his leader's face. 'Nirias, we can't protect her. It's too dangerous. She brought the Melk to our very doorstep. They were here, in the Enigmata. Three nulls. They must have tracked her snout: this was tucked into his clothing.'

Nirias scowled at the object and turned it over. 'A Calkinon drawstone?'

'Yes. The nulls were Calkinon soldiers. They died swiftly.'

Nirias's shoulders sagged, betraying his exhaustion. 'So our worst fears are confirmed: Calkinon is compromised.'

'I only wish I could have brought better news.'

'Ah, but you did.' Nirias's smile hurt them both. The weight of his hand on Daska's shoulder was heavy, too heavy. 'Seekers, Daska. That always brings fresh hope. And if the League does not protect this girl, then who will? Tell me more. Where is she from?'

Daska winced. He had known he would never convince Nirias to abandon any Seeker, but he doubted the League could feed three more mouths, let alone protect them. The warriors had been pushed to the very edge of endurance. Mooncross couldn't have come at a worse time.

'Daska. Answer me. Where is she from?'

He heaved a sigh. 'That's the strange coincidence. She and the thin boy, they're both from Mildaresh.'

Nirias froze; his face a mask. 'I don't believe in coincidences Daska — as well you know.'

⁂

Ash sank his head onto his knees and tried not to think about vomiting. The hike up to the refuge had sapped his strength more than he had thought possible. His head banged with a dull, thudding ache. After a brisk whispered conversation, Daska had disappeared into the maze of tunnels. They were waiting for his return in a small cave, its open mouth pouting above crests of anonymous trees that flowed untidily into the empty valley.

The glare of the sky made his eyes hurt. He contemplated the lump of black-bread, then took a cautious sip of water instead. They weren't prisoners, or at least Ash didn't think they were, but Jaibari hadn't taken her eyes off them for a moment. She stood there, seemingly as solid as the thick wooden door behind her: silent, immobile and definitely hostile. It wasn't exactly the greeting Ash had imagined when he had placed his hands upon the Stone. When Tarlyn shifted her weight inside his hood, he was grateful for her invisible presence. She was keeping herself small and still; she obviously didn't trust these people either.

Ash glanced at Kep, who was hunched at the other end of the rough-sawn bench. Her hands were clenched tightly in her lap. She rubbed at her nails every now and then, scratching at some last vestige of blood. He frowned. He wanted to ask her to retell the story of Gooel's death. It made no sense. Gooel had termination orders: why had he acted so bizarrely?

Sarin was sitting on the floor, his back flat against the wall. He had taken off one boot, which he shook out, then laced back on again, coolly deliberate. Any stranger would have assumed he was completely relaxed. Ash knew better. He was pretty sure Sarin could lead them back out through the confusing labyrinth of tunnels if needed. He was probably formulating an escape plan, too. Ash just hoped they wouldn't need one.

He held his head in his hands and pressed his thumbs into his temples. It didn't feel like the end of their journey at all. It felt as if they had landed themselves in fresh trouble. What was it Nalina had said? 'Finding Nirias will undoubtedly bring you closer to evil.' He had the horrible feeling she had been right. He closed his eyes until the pounding in his head was matched by the sound of footsteps.

The man who emerged from the tunnels was dressed in the same dark clothing as his colleagues. There was nothing to designate his leadership, unless there was some significance in the tattoo that graced one cheekbone and flirted with the edge of his eye. He wasn't tall, and he wasn't particularly broad. His hair was brown and threaded with traces of silver. None of his features were noteworthy, yet there was something oddly asymmetrical about his face. Some indefinable quality reminded Ash of Credé. Perhaps it was the way his smile didn't seem to touch his eyes. He remembered

Credé's final transformation with a shudder. Did Nirias really have control over the way he appeared? It was a most unsettling thought. Still, his manner was gracious enough. His voice was mellow, yet authoritative. 'I'm so sorry you've been kept waiting. And I apologise for not meeting you at the Stone myself. I am Nirias.'

As he stood and bowed with the others, Ash detected a sudden movement deep inside his hood. Tarlyn was stirring. Nirias regarded each of them in turn, but his eyes rested longest on Sarin.

'Sarin of Aurum, I welcome you.' His rendition of the Aurum gesture was impeccable. Sarin returned the greeting, unreadable as ever. 'I believe this belongs to you.'

Sarin bowed his head slightly as he received the token. 'My grandmother, Nalina, sends her regards.'

An odd expression crossed Nirias's face. He seemed about to say more, but he was suddenly distracted by Ash's quick gasp of surprise. Ash couldn't help it: Tarlyn had startled him completely by scrambling up onto his shoulder, and chirruping happily, right in his ear.

Nirias's reaction was immediate. He froze in shock before letting out a great shout of joy. 'Tarlyn!' In a split second Tarlyn had bridged the gap from Ash's shoulder to his. 'Can it be?' Nirias grasped her in his arms. She didn't struggle. She just stared at him with her huge eyes.

They all watched in amazement as the man's eyes filled with tears. Delighted laughter burst from his lips. 'How can this be? How can this be?' he repeated wildly.

The others stared at each other, astonished. How indeed?

When at last Nirias managed to regain his composure, Ash watched him carefully. Something subtle had changed in his disposition. It was as if something tense had been relaxed. It seemed a change for the better. 'There is a mystery to unravel here, that much is certain,' he declared.

As Tarlyn returned to Ash's shoulder in a fluid leap, Nirias turned suddenly. 'Jaibari, you may leave us.' The girl scowled; she was obviously as fascinated by the peculiar creature and her leader's reaction as anyone else.

When the door had banged shut, Nirias explained. 'That you have a compelling story to tell is obvious, and I suspect it may touch upon secrets that are not widely known.' He bowed his head slightly at Daska, who had positioned himself by the door. 'But let us resume our introductions.'

He held out his hands. 'You must be Kep and Ash. Welcome. You have arrived under the strangest of circumstances, but you are welcome indeed. Please. Sit.'

Nirias dragged up a stool. Then he placed a bundle on the low table. He unrolled it to reveal three items: the dopple-star, the knife from Credé's hut, and the lamp. 'These were found among your things.' He observed their faces carefully. 'I apologise, but such precautions are necessary — especially when our guests carry such unusual items.' He leaned forward and picked up the dopple-star. 'In all my years I have never seen such an object. Yet I know enough to tell that it is not of this world. The knife, too, is most uncommon, both in design and in substance ...' Ash felt his piercing gaze and had a sudden horrible feeling that the man was able to read his mind. 'But this ... This I do recognise.' Nirias spoke wistfully as he cradled the lamp in his hand. 'This is a dymiril lamp. I have seen these before ... but never outside of T'al Jazure.' He gave a nod, acknowledging their wide-eyed awe. 'It is of Azuran make.'

Nirias returned the lamp to the table and brought his hands together. 'I was already more than eager to hear your tale, but I confess I was confounded in the extreme when Daska showed me these items. And now,' his eyes fell again on Tarlyn, 'now I barely know which questions to ask first.' He gave them a cryptic smile, reminding Ash once more of Credé. 'And of course you have questions for me. You are Seekers, and I am the last of the Azuri. I am bound by code and honour to protect you, and I will do so — to the best of my ability.' Daska moved slightly. The old man's face was impassive, but Ash thought his stance seemed somewhat rigid. His fists were curled by his sides. 'So,' said Nirias. 'Where do we begin?'

He stared at them so intensely that they couldn't help feeling it was some kind of test. Everyone in the room seemed suddenly isolated, bound in their own thoughts. The silence hung for several minutes like an enchantment. It was awful.

Kep took a deep breath, then let it out again. This was their chance. They had so many questions and at last the man with the answers was sitting in front of them. She glanced at Ash. He looked pale and upset. He certainly didn't seem about to break the spell. Sarin was contemplating his bootlaces. No help there either. She pressed her lips together. Well, someone would have to speak. How could Ash just sit there, stroking Tarlyn's fur like that? The creature was ignoring Nirias completely now; she sat on Ash's lap as if nothing at all had happened. How was it even possible for them to know each other? It was completely impossible. Wasn't it?

Kep lifted her chin, looked Nirias in the eye, and voiced the immediate question in her mind. 'How old is Tarlyn?'

The others seemed startled from their thoughts. Nirias smiled. 'That's a very good question. But I'm afraid I don't know the answer. Tarlyn was companion to Leynore, one of the Council of Three, when I was very young. That in itself makes her ancient by this world's standards. I'm not sure even Leynore knew much about Tarlyn's origins. She is utterly unique. Have you witnessed her ability to heal?' They nodded. 'That's not to say that she can't be killed. Indeed, until today I believed she had perished with her mistress.' Tarlyn made a mournful muttering noise, and Nirias' brows knitted together. His mouth curved into a thin, painful smile. 'You can't imagine my joy at discovering that this was not the case.' Then he pressed his fingertips together and leaned forward. 'But let us speak of the present. I can read from your faces that your story is difficult, and no doubt there is much you do not understand. Most people would claim it's best to start a story at the beginning, but,' he sighed, 'that can be a complication in itself. Tarlyn trusts you, Ash. That much I can tell. Perhaps the story begins with how you came to be companions?'

Ash swallowed. He didn't have a clue how to start. He certainly couldn't bear telling the whole story from the beginning. He decided to just plunge in. 'Tarlyn was with the Malshorne.' He faltered. 'With Credé.' He read astonishment on Nirias's face, but forced himself to keep speaking. 'Credé is dead,' he stammered. 'I'm sorry if that grieves you.'

Nirias's eyes flickered. 'No, your news does not grieve me. It surprises me, though.' His mouth twisted. 'I had long thought him dead.'

If anything, the news seemed to have sparked anger rather than sorrow. Ash didn't know whether to be relieved or not. 'Before Credé died, he sent us on a quest. Sort of ...' He looked desperately at Kep. It was all so horribly complicated. 'I don't think he ever actually intended for us to seek T'al Jazure. In fact, quite the opposite ... and ... he certainly meant for me to die. But we brought it to you anyway. We brought the Taelstone.' There! It was said. There was a long pause. Too long. Their host seemed utterly baffled.

'The Taelstone?'

'Yes.' Ash felt panic rising in his throat. 'That was our task. To bring it to

T'al Jazure. But … well …' He gulped. 'Everyone seems to think T'al Jazure is lost.'

Nirias's softly articulated response hit them with brutal force. 'It's true. T'al Jazure is lost, even to me.'

Kep closed her eyes. Sarin dropped his head. Ash blinked. It couldn't be true. Nirias stood and walked to the edge of the cave mouth. He gazed into the valley for a long time before continuing.

'T'al Jazure was lost, many centuries ago. It is the truth that every Seeker must face. It was an age of terrible strife, and the Azuran Council took desperate measures to stem the evil.'

'The evil?' Kep almost whispered the question.

'The Melk. It had entered this world from another dimension.' Nirias shook his head, as if the story wearied him. 'It should never have happened, but it did. It took a long time to recognise the threat, such is the nature of the Melk. But the resistance was mobilised at last: the Azuran League was formed. I was one of the youngest recruits. Our world had become full of fear and hatred. The Melk had spread like a dark flood across the lands; its lust for destruction was voracious. The Council must have realised that ultimately they could not hold it back. It had grown strong beyond belief. They acted swiftly, desperately — they emptied the city and hid it in the space between the worlds so none could enter. None but the Council of Three.'

Sarin had been listening intently. Now he spoke for the first time. 'You speak as if you are unsure of their motives.'

Nirias held him with his eyes for a long time before replying. 'It was a time of darkness and confusion. Those of us in the field were barely aware of what happened. But we do know they performed a miracle.' He closed his eyes, then shrugged. 'Yes, it was quite simply a miracle. Suddenly, inexplicably, the Melk swarmed, leaving chaos and madness in its wake. The battlefields were thrown into confusion.' His face was bitter with memory. 'I confess, I do not know why the Council sacrificed the city, but whatever terrible decision was made, it worked. Somehow, the Melk was vanquished.'

'But the Melk, it's still here,' Kep pointed out.

Nirias nodded. 'There was a residue. For long centuries the League has been watchful, hunting down the enemy wherever we hear rumours of darkness that go beyond the human capacity for evil.' His eyes narrowed.

'Unfortunately, it's often difficult to tell the difference.'

They sat in stunned silence, trying to digest his tale. At last their host seemed to register their shocked faces. 'I'm sorry,' he said returning to his seat. 'It's the terrible truth every Seeker must endure.' He sought Daska's eyes, but the old warrior's head was bowed. 'T'al Jazure is lost. It is not within my power to take you there. I only wish it were. The Azuri abandoned the city they loved and fled, trusting in their friends and the loyalty of the people. But they were betrayed. The people had turned against them, and they couldn't survive their enemies for long. One by one they were discovered ...' The sentence faded into silence.

'Except Credé.' Ash immediately regretted the words. Nirias directed such a penetrating gaze towards him that it made his heart pound.

'I never saw or heard of Credé again. Finally I drew the conclusion that he must have died in one of the terrible battles. Until now.' His eyes glittered. 'Now it appears Credé was alive, all these long years ... in hiding.' Nirias fell silent. He seemed absorbed by some thought he wouldn't share. Then he sighed and brought his hands together. 'But what is this object you speak of, Ash? This Taelstone? Its name is unfamiliar to me, yet it must have some bearing on this mystery.'

Ash paused, counting several heartbeats before giving Sarin a slow nod. Daska blinked in disbelief when Sarin produced the bundle and handed it over. Ash unwrapped it slowly, keenly aware of their fascinated eyes. The Taelstone was warm. It glowed deeply red as he held it up.

Nirias raised his eyebrows. 'Well, well. A Taelstone? No, that is not its name. It's a lore-stone.' As he reached out his hand, Ash felt a sudden surge of energy. The stone swirled like a firestorm in his palm. Nirias withdrew his hand at once. 'It won't suffer me to touch it. It's bonded to you, Ash.'

Kep was horrified. She didn't like the sound of that at all. 'What do you mean?'

'Don't be alarmed, Kep. It's not dangerous in itself, although it might prove unstable to an untrained mind. Lore-stones are tools. The Azuri used them to store memories or focus the mind. They were vessels of knowledge. There were thousands in the knowledge stores of T'al Jazure.' He gave Ash a strange look. 'And this one? This one belonged to Credé, I assume?'

Ash shivered, remembering that awful moment when he had wrenched it from the Malshorne's dead fingers. 'Yes. We went back for it, to his hut.

After he tried to kill me. We believed that was the quest: to take it to T'al Jazure.' He stared miserably at the orb. 'We thought it might be a weapon or something. Credé told Braig that T'al Jazure had the power to free the slaves, but we didn't even know it was a city — we were looking for a man.'

'Braig?'

'Our friend. He died.' Ash felt Sarin shift on the bench beside him. 'He was supposed to be the Chosen One. But that must have been a trick, too. Credé lied to us.'

Nirias narrowed his eyes. 'Perhaps. But perhaps not. Credé was a subtle manipulator of the truth. It's more likely that he merely encouraged you to believe what you wanted to believe.'

Ash stared at him, trying to remember where they had got the idea in the first place. He frowned when Kep distracted him from his thoughts.

'But what about Tarlyn? That's what she says: the Taelstone must go to T'al Jazure. I've heard her. We both have.'

Tarlyn sat up, stretched, and looked at Kep with sudden interest. Her eyes shone like black mirrors. Nirias's eyebrows became perplexed arches.

Ash pulled at his hair, as if intending to pull it out from the roots. 'That's it! It was Tarlyn! The first time we heard her speak, that's what she said. And the Malshorne, Credé, he was angry. He threw a glass at her.' His face cleared with sudden understanding. 'Braig guessed that this was the Taelstone. And Credé didn't correct him. He let us believe it, but ... but ... it was all nonsense. Right from the beginning. Just a trick.' His face crumpled.

'Hmm.' Nirias was rubbing his chin. 'So it seems. But the question is: why? What could Credé hope to gain?'

Kep shook her head. 'Perhaps it was a trick, but it still doesn't explain Tarlyn's words.' She turned to Nirias. 'I mean, if that's a lore-stone, then what's a Taelstaun?'

'*Taelstaun?* Is that what Tarlyn said? *Taelstaun?*

Everyone regarded the creature, who thrashed her tail as if in response to the conversation.

Nirias pursed his lips. 'Tarlyn doesn't have words of her own. She only repeats the words of others. It's beyond me why she might have said that, of all things. There were three Taelstaun, one representing each of the empires. They were highly revered in ancient times. Then amidst the turmoil, they simply vanished — all three. If it was known how they met their fate, the story never came to my ears.' He shook his head sadly. 'Their disappearance was a great blow to peace; they might have helped quell the storm, for they were the Keepers of the Song.'

Kep and Sarin turned their heads towards Ash in unison.

'The Song?' Kep's voice wavered.

'Yes, the Song.' Nirias spread his hands. 'The Song was perhaps the Azuri's greatest gift to the people of T'al Agria. It was an extraordinary instrument of peace. The Song encompassed all of the histories of all the peoples of the three empires, and so bound them together in one great united story. It was powerfully moving and incredibly influential in swaying minds. The three Taelstaun travelled throughout the lands, gathering stories, sharing histories, weaving their threads into the Song, and—'

Finally Kep couldn't contain herself any longer. 'It's *you*, Ash! You're the Taelstaun! All that time, Tarlyn was talking about *you!*

⁂

'Impossible.'

Nirias stalked backwards and forwards, muttering so quickly that they missed much of what he said. Kep couldn't help wondering if his feet were somehow linked to his brain. He seemed to have forgotten there was anyone else in the room as he paced ever more agitatedly. 'Impossible ... Well, perhaps not wholly impossible. Credé would have had to impersonate the apprentice ... It's the only way it could have been done. Still ... With time? With patience ... for a Malshorne of his learning ...'

He muttered and paced some more, then suddenly paused mid-stride. He turned and tilted his head at Ash. He folded his arms, his eyes narrowed almost to slits as he deliberated. Then he shook his head. 'It's absurd. Even if Credé had become one of the Taelstaun, even if that were possible, he had no way of passing the Song to you, Ash. That would involve a highly complex ritual — not even Credé could have managed such a feat.'

'Well, he did!' Nirias lifted his eyebrows at Kep's tone and the flash of her eyes. 'So there's no point saying it's impossible or absurd. Because somehow Credé managed it. Listen! Ash sees visions of the past.' Kep was trying not to raise her voice, but it wasn't working. 'He hears the Song in his dreams. All the time! So don't go telling us it's impossible!'

'But how?'

Ash couldn't help shrinking under that interrogative gaze. He realised he had messed up the story. He had told everything out of order. 'Sorry, I don't know how. We each stood at one tip of the darkstone. Then Credé placed the Tael—, the lore-stone at the other, and we sang.'

Nirias stared. 'The darkstone,' he repeated in a murmur.

'Yes. The darkstone. I ... I had to polish it first.'

Nirias groaned. 'The darkstone of Eeroktan!' He whirled and threw out his arms. 'Daska! That's the answer!' He gave a maniacal laugh as he clapped him on the shoulders. 'This is the answer to the question that has puzzled us all! Why Mildaresh? Because the darkstone of Eeroktan was never destroyed. Credé reactivated the darkstone. That's why the Melk swarmed! That's what drew it!'

Daska clearly had as little idea of what Nirias was talking about as anyone else.

Nirias let out another howl of laughter at his old friend's confusion, but it died almost instantly on his lips. He was suddenly still. He turned slowly to Ash, as if seeing him for the very first time.

'You, Ash — *you* are the Taelstaun,' he said weakly.

They had the horrible feeling that Nirias was about to burst into tears. He wore the most curious expression on his face, as if some emotion threatened to overwhelm him completely. He held out his hands, spreading them flat. They gasped to see inky lines appearing. They seemed to glow through his skin, forming the shape of two intricate moons, one on each palm. With a weird smile he turned and strode to the cave's mouth. Raising his outstretched hands he reached up, then outwards, as if tracing an archway in the air. Where his hands passed, the air seemed to shimmer. There was a quick breath, then suddenly before their eyes was a doorway.

The Seekers leapt to their feet. Daska stepped forward, too. 'Is that ... ? That's not ... ?' He searched his leader's face.

Nirias nodded. 'It is the doorway. It leads to the place we all dream of — to T'al Jazure.'

'But where did it come from?' Daska rubbed his eyes, then put out his hand to touch the frame.

'It has always been here,' Nirias answered softly.

'Always? And you never thought to show me?' Daska's eyes were hurt.

'No. What was the good in showing you a door through which you could never pass? My dear friend, it has been the most painful truth of my life. I am the last Azuri. I can summon the door anywhere within the Stone's power, but I cannot open it.' He pointed to the inscription that flowed around the top of the arch. 'Only the Council of Three can open the door — that is what it says. That is why I lost hope. All hope.' His eyes locked onto Ash's. There was an odd quietness between them, soaked in anticipation. 'I never dared to dream that the Song might have survived ... I never dreamed that, after all these long centuries, the Taelstaun might return and claim admittance, as was ever the sacred right of the Keepers of the Song.'

Ash could feel the others' startled eyes on him. He didn't look at them. He still felt dizzy, but it was his heart pounding, not his head. When Tarlyn leapt to his shoulder, he could feel her quivering. He took a deep breath to settle himself, but he knew what to do. As soon as he had seen the archway all doubt had vanished.

He stepped forward and put out his hands, letting the melody come. The energy coursed through him. He found the note and began to sing. Tendrils of light radiated from his fingertips. They curled and spiralled, creating a fine, golden tracery, filling the archway with light. As the tenor of the Song rose and resonated, the patterns swirled and spread until nothing could be seen of the hills and trees beyond. Then the harmonies swelled, and Ash felt a surge of ecstasy as the patterns responded. Shimmering, they dissolved, falling in a curtain of golden rain. He let his arms fall, too.

And there it was: shining like a raindrop caught in the folds of the hills. The lost city of T'al Jazure.

— END OF PART 3 —

EPILOGUE

Kep was waiting — taking deep breaths of the cool autumn air and waiting. She would follow the others shortly, just not yet. When she stepped aside to let one of the warriors pass, he returned her smile with a brief dazed one of his own, before following Nirias and the others down towards the city.

The League warriors were all reacting to the miracle in their own way: some, like Kep, were just standing there trying to take in the astonishing view, believing yet not believing. Many were weeping; others whooped and wrestled; several were praying after the manner of their kind; but more than a few had simply cast themselves upon the hillside, totally overwhelmed by the wonder of it all.

What a contrast to the weary men and women who had straggled back to the refuge over the past few days! Gone were those hard eyes and set jaws. Nirias's speech had transformed them all. 'The Azuri will rise again!' he had shouted and, in sight of that incredible vision, it was perfectly possible to believe him.

Yet, at the same time, T'al Jazure just seemed so utterly *impossible*. Its silver arches appeared to leap across crystalline sheets of shining light; there were spires wrought from what seemed to be glass; shining turrets and steeples and pearl-coloured towers; and mirrored orbs; and sails which threw the colour of the sky back in glittering blues.

Kep knew she would never see it this way again. She knew as soon as she went down into the city she would appreciate it differently — as a sanctuary, perhaps even as a home. And she knew her life was about to change forever. She felt a sharp thrill at the idea of becoming a League warrior: perhaps that was what Narsis had intended all along!

She took another deep breath, then, as she let it out slowly, she noticed Ash was looking back again. He was walking slowly at Nirias's side, at the very front of the ragged procession. From that distance Tarlyn looked like an inky silhouette on his shoulder. He waved again, beckoning for her to join them. This time she waved back and nodded to herself: it was time.

Kep allowed herself one backwards glance, casting her eyes to where the door had been. Nothing remained now, not even the faintest shimmer of the doorway to her past life. She smiled, closing her eyes for a long moment, breathing the sweet air, letting her heart sing with possibilities. As she took her first purposeful step towards the city she realised that Sarin had held back, too: he was lingering close by, concealed amongst the deep green shadows of the trees. He moved quickly to her side with that curiously animal grace of his. She couldn't quite think which animal he reminded her of, a wolvern she supposed, but maybe that was just because of his eyes. They looked so golden and intense as he drew closer. He'd tied his hair back, but one piece hung down across his brow. When she saw his grave expression she couldn't help laughing aloud — trust Sarin to look so troubled on such an occasion!

'You don't look like someone who's found what they have been searching for all their lives,' she teased. He frowned even more deeply, seeming confused. She laughed again, shaking her head, then her eyes came to rest on the smooth hollow of his neck. It moved softly when he spoke.

'Kep. There's something I need to tell you.'

She vaguely caught a sense of his anxiety, but it didn't really register, she was so distracted with the wonder of it all. Then, when her eyes strayed to his mouth, she couldn't help remembering that kiss. She had thought it such a mistake — something she would regret forever. Now she realised she didn't regret it at all. She hid the secret for a moment longer, in the corner of her smile, then she leaned across and kissed him on the cheek.

Sarin's expression shifted immediately — she had never seen him look so dazed. The colour was rising in her own cheeks, too, but she grasped his hand anyway and pressed it between hers.

'What were you about to say?'

Sarin paused for what seemed like a very long time. Then he smiled uncertainly.

'Nothing ... It's nothing ... It can wait.'

'Good. Let's follow Ash, then.' She squeezed his hand and pulled him towards the future.

Far away, in another dimension, in another world, something had clicked. Softly but insistently, it began to whirr.

Thank you for purchasing Taelstone. If you enjoyed the book, I hope you'll consider spending a few minutes posting a review. Your feedback and support is greatly appreciated. You can leave a review on Goodreads, or follow this link to Amazon: bit.ly/taelstone

ACKNOWLEDGEMENTS

There are a number of people who deserve my gratitude, and without whom Taelstone would never have made its way into the world. Firstly, thank you to my beta readers - especially those of you who waded through that first monstrous draft! Your encouragement did such a lot to mitigate my terror at sharing the story with an audience.

Special thanks go to Lynette Evans for her generosity, early suggestions and words of wisdom. Thanks also to my editor, Kate Stone: it was wonderful to have such an experienced and talented professional on board for my debut novel. I raise a glass to my dear friend Jenny Vollmer — thank you so much for listening to those early ravings, Jen; the dance between Kep and Sarin will always be yours.

And finally thank you to my incredible, creative family. To Lara, for filling our lives with song, and feeding my desire to write about the power of music. To Nikki, not only for her beautiful formatting, but also for her unfailing belief in my writing — not to mention those timely reminders that I should stop mucking about and just get on with it. Nikki and her talented partner Nopera are also responsible for my gorgeous website — I can't thank them enough for designing me such a brilliant creative space — as well as the brilliant cover design. Special appreciation and thanks also goes to Katie, who heard every idea first and gave insightful and creative feedback, despite my complex muddle of characters and backstories. A writer couldn't ask for a better sounding board. And, last but not least, thank you to my lovely husband, Keith, for his attention to detail when proofreading, and his incredible patience with a partner who so often spends her time 'off in another world.'

You can find more information about the inspiration and early iterations of Taelstone on my website:

ROBYNPROKOP.COM